ACCLAIM FOR *MAD DOGS* AND JAMES GRADY

"*Mad Dogs* is the literary equivalent of a supercharged Hemi, a rock-and-roll road novel that roars out of the gate and never slows pace. James Grady, the king of the modern espionage thriller, is back with a vengeance."

—George Pelecanos

"Grady is a master of intrigue."   —John Grisham

"A brilliantly conceived premise ripped from the secrets behind the headlines. *Mad Dogs* shines with satire and spies, shocks to the mind, and triumphs of the soul. A bullet-paced book you can't put down and won't forget. James Grady is a pro, and he never disappoints. This is a winner."

—Nelson DeMille

"In a world of fast-food thrillers written by committee, James Grady has given us a three-star feast. It's Ambler on acid, a Ken Kesey *Crouching Tiger, Hidden Dragon*. *Mad Dogs* is an instant classic—Grady's blackest, grittiest, scariest work since *Six Days of the Condor*."

—John Weisman, *New York Times* bestselling author of *Direct Action*

"Oh, what a ride! Terrific characters, hell-for-leather pacing, and an astounding amount of tradecraft. *Mad Dogs* echoes both Grady's own *Condor* and Heller's *Catch-22*. Grady's one of the acknowledged masters, and *Mad Dogs* delivers!"

—S. J. Rozan

"Grady grips you immediately with phantasmagoric writing at a breakneck pace."

—*Library Journal* (starred review)

"Not to be missed!"   —*Rocky Mountain News*

"James Grady writes it straight, pure, and hot as lava."

—Stephen Coonts

MAD DOGS

James Grady

A TOM DOHERTY ASSOCIATES BOOK
NEW YORK

This is a work of fiction. All of the characters, organizations, and events portrayed in this novel are either products of the author's imagination or are used fictitiously.

MAD DOGS

Copyright © 2006 by James Grady

Grateful acknowledgment for permission to use their work to:

"To Elsie," by William Carlos Williams, copyright © 2006 New Directions publishers.

"Jungleland," by Bruce Springsteen, copyright © 1975 Bruce Springsteen, renewed copyright © 2003 Bruce Springsteen (ASCAP). Reprinted by permission. International copyright secured. All rights reserved.

"Feel So Good," by Richard Thompson, copyright © 2006 Richard Thompson. International copyright secured. All rights reserved.

A Forge Book
Published by Tom Doherty Associates, LLC
175 Fifth Avenue
New York, NY 10010

www.tor-forge.com

Forge® is a registered trademark of Tom Doherty Associates, LLC.

ISBN-13: 978-0-7653-5561-4
ISBN-10: 0-7653-5561-2

First Edition: September 2006
First Mass Market Edition: July 2007

Printed in the United States of America

0 9 8 7 6 5 4 3 2 1

This one's for:
>Bob Dylan
>>Billie Holiday
>>>Bruce Springsteen
>>>>Richard Thompson
>>>>>Brian Wilson

howling on the highway.

The pure products of America go crazy—

WILLIAM CARLOS WILLIAMS
"To Elsie"

Outside the street's on fire
in a real death waltz
between what's flesh and what's fantasy.
And the poets down here
don't write nothing at all,
they just stand back and let it all be.
In the quick of a knife,
they reach for their moment,
try to make an honest stand.

BRUCE SPRINGSTEEN
"Jungleland"

MAD
DOGS

1

WE SHOULD HAVE realized that something was dangerously wrong during our Tuesday Morning Group while Russell lied about garroting the Serb colonel.

"Get this," said Russell as sunshine streamed past the jail bars over our windows and drew parallel shadows on the Day Room's lemon wood floor. "That whole scene was like a flipped coin spinning in the air, one side ordinary, one side surreal."

Like us then: five men and one woman perched on circled metal folding chairs.

"There I was," said Russell, "walking another patrol in the Balkan slaughterhouse. Main Street buildings were smeared smoke black. Busted windows. Rubble littered the road. We tramped past a fire-bombed Toyota. Every step, something crunched under your boot. A laptop computer. A woman's purse. Three ropes dangled from a street lamp, but they were cut empty, so the rumors about a cleanup were probably true."

"What isn't true?" said Dr. Friedman.

Dr. Leon Friedman had brown hair. Emerald eyes inside gold metal glasses. As he had for each of the fourteen days he'd spent with us, he wore a tweed sports jacket. That last day, he had on a blue shirt, no tie.

"Place like that," said Russell, "everything is true, nothing is true."

"I see," said Dr. Friedman.

"No you don't," I said. "Not if you're lucky."

"'Xactly," said Zane, who looked like an albino Jesus.

"We're listening to Russell now," said Dr. Friedman.

Russell was fronting his rock star look: midnight lens aviator shades, a black leather sports jacket over an indigo T-shirt emblazoned WILCO for the band, not the military response he'd been taught. He wore blue jeans, retro black-and-white sneakers.

"Make it late May 1992," said Russell. "We were jazzed to get somewhere safe."

Hailey picked scabs into her ebony-skinned arm, mumbled: "No such place."

Russell ignored her. "That once-was-Yugoslavia town smelled like gunpowder and burned wood. Rotten garbage and rats, man, I can still see badass rats with red eyes.

"The restaurant had cardboard over two windows but a sign that read OPEN. When the Colonel swung the door in, a bell tinkled. He turns to us nine guys, says: *'We take turns.'* Then he beckons me and his two favorite goons, a couple of thrill-kill boys Milosovic sprang from prison and made 'militia.' We go in. The place has a handful of customers, all true Serbs like us, and fuck everybody else."

The white Styrofoam cup trembled as Russell raised it to his lips. "Where was I?"

Dr. Friedman said: "You just said, *'Fuck everybody else.'*"

Russell swallowed more coffee. "I mean, where was I in my story?"

"Ahh," said the therapist: "Your story. Of your spy mission."

"Got it," said Russell. "The maître d' glides through the restaurant like he's skating on ice. He's hairless. Pale as a bone. Milky eyes. Stone cold. Four werewolves in army fatigues with AK-47s walk in and ding his bell but he doesn't blink. He's wearing a black bow tie, a white shirt, blue jeans, a black tuxedo tails coat like Dracula. Plus, one hand ballerina waitress style, he's balancing an empty tray."

"Sounds like an LSD trip," said Dr. Friedman.

"Doc!" Russell grinned. "Who knew you're such a rebel!"

"I have an interesting father. What about you?"

"Nah," said Russell, "Dad never did nothing that could

get him in trouble. He never had to. And he isn't in the story—in the restaurant, that was just me, all me."

"And who else?" asked Dr. Friedman.

"I told you: Colonel Herzgl, the fat fuck. Smelled like garlic and vodka. They claim vodka doesn't smell, that's another lie. Believe me, it smells, and I . . . I . . ."

"You're in the restaurant," said Dr. F. "With Colonel Herzgl, his men."

"And the maître d'. Who glides up to us through the tables holding his empty tray, Nazi pin on his lapel, *man,* he lets us fall into his milk eyes.

"Colonel Herzgl glares at him, says: *'You got crap on for music.'*

"Tunes are coming from a boom box on the bar, and the Colonel is dead-on right: it's crap. Some accordion flute zither ethnic bullshit. Colonel Herzgl is an Elvis freak. He's carrying a torch for a bloated icon who bought it in a . . . ah . . . in a bathroom—"

Dr. Friedman blinked. And I caught him.

"—who bought it in a bathroom while Herzgl was still a Commie punk in Belgrade. Now he's got this one lousy tape, the soundtrack from *Viva Las Vegas*! Not the worst Elvis movie, not even his worst bunch of songs, but *man:* after the first forty times you hear it and get ordered to translate it and teach the Colonel to sing along . . . !

"Colonel Herzgl gives the Elvis tape to the maître d', who leads us to a table and on it is a bottle of that plum brandy. *Rakija.* No glasses. We sit, pass around the bottle."

"Please say you didn't put your lips where theirs were!" said Hailey.

"Shit, yes! You think I'd bust cover by playing the snob?" said Russell. "So the maître d' says: *'Potato soup,'* which is all this war zone café has, except for *rakija.* Off he goes. A few swigs later, and boom box Elvis blasts out 'Viva Las Vegas'!"

The Ward Room door swung open, pushed inward by a rolling mirror metal box.

The meds cart rolled across the sun-swept floor. I checked out the nurse driving it who, like Dr. F, had rotated in while the regular staff were on furlough.

The substitute nurse was a pretty woman who'd walked miles of hospital corridors. She wore the uniform white slacks and top with a black cardigan sweater. Wore her brown hair pinned in a bun. She unlocked the meds cart, stacked tiny paper cups on the metal top, checked her clipboard.

Dr. Friedman said: "What did it smell like?"

"Why do you want to know that?" said Russell.

"We know what outside the café smelled like—gunpowder, burned wood, smoke, rubble. What did it smell like at that table?"

"What difference . . . There's that *rakija* plum brandy. Plus us four unshowered army fatigue guys. And kind of a salty smell. Potato soup from the kitchen, the—"

"What kind of salty smell?" asked Dr. Friedman. "Like . . . tears?"

"*'Like tears,'* what the hell difference does that make, it's all about what I do. And now, with Elvis blasting 'Viva Las Vegas,' I finally got my chance *to* do."

The nurse shook pills into a paper cup.

Dr. Friedman said: "You finally got your chance to do *what?*"

"To kill Colonel Herzgl."

"But that wasn't your mission. You weren't an assassin."

"Don't you tell me who I wasn't!" yelled Russell. "I was who I was and I did it!"

Dr. Friedman stared at the trained warrior. "Tell us about your official mission."

"My official mission was, like, *over,* man! None of the factions—not the Moslems, not the Croats, for sure not those damn Serbs, none of them got squat from the caches Uncle Sam's bad boys had snuck into Yugoslavia during the Cold War. None of them had the missing suitcase nukes. Don't you think they'd have used them? They all wanted total annihilation, and there's no better way to go total than nuclear."

"So why were you still there?" said Dr. Friedman.

"How could I leave?" Russell shrank on his chair. "That place went from skirmishes to slaughterhouse in a blink. What was going on outside that restaurant, what I'd had to see and play along with as the rock 'n' roll Serbian-

American kid come back to find his roots and help his heroes . . . Over there, being crazy was the rule. If you weren't when it started . . . How do you think I ended up here?"

"You tell us."

"I killed the Colonel."

"Why?"

"Because I could. I couldn't stop anything big, but if I iced that one fat fuck monster who I'd latched onto when I still had a sane mission . . . Before I bugged out, I could put him down for . . . for all the horror he did. Was going to keep doing.

"When Elvis kicked in with 'Viva Las Vegas,' Herzgl said, *'I not wait.'* He tells me, *'You next,'* and walks through the dining room to the bathroom."

"Did he go alone?"

"What do you mean, *'Did he go alone'*? Of course he went alone! What do you think, that we were a bunch of Kansas schoolgirls on prom night?"

Russell shook his head. "They wouldn't listen to me. Didn't believe me. Phones worked. Not everywhere, but . . . I'd reported to my case officer in Prague. Hell, I called Langley direct! They insisted I was 'off mission.' Or 'overloaded.' I was to ex-filtrate stat. Good job. Mission over. Come home and . . . They wouldn't believe me."

"That was only at first," said Dr. F. "Then satellite photos, other sources—"

" 'At first' is where you start. You gotta get to 'at last.' ' "

"So you stayed."

"I went into that bathroom." Russell blinked. "That was my chance.

"I told the two goons *fuck the Colonel,* I had to go now. They laughed.

"Nobody looked at me as I walked through the dining room. The bathroom was through a set of swinging doors, down a hall. The bulb in that hall was burned out, so it was a long dark tunnel. Stank. Urine, rats, *rakija*—I know you want to know how it smells, Doc, no need to thank me."

But Friedman said nothing to interrupt. He sensed the roll. Knew it was coming.

"I put my right hand in my fatigue jacket pocket," said Russell. "My knife and AK-47 were back at the table, but two days before, the day they burned up the schoolhouse full of kids, I found a steel wire about a yard long, stuck it in my pocket. Figured I could rig a grenade trip to get the Colonel and his whole squad. But that was me being optimistic, not practical. Walking to the bathroom, I was the zen of practical.

"I had one end of the wire cinched around my right grip before I hit the swinging doors. Ten steps down that long dark tunnel to the closed men's room door, *Viva Las Vegas,* and by the time I get there, the other end is cinched around my left grip.

"Two ways to go in for a whack," Russell told us. "Blitz or sly—sly ninja or sly bold like Skorzeny, march in banners flying.

"I've always been a Skorzeny man. I burst into the bathroom singing Elvis over the tape of Elvis, and Herzgl, why he loved it. He was at the mirror. The stall with . . . The stall with, *um* . . . He was boogying with his back to me as I sang and then *wham!*"

Russell twisted in his seat as he pantomimed flipping the wire loop around the Colonel's neck from behind and garroting the trashing Colonel.

"He was tough and it was hard. For you, Doc, I could smell his garlic and sweat. The flesh on his neck burned like acid on my hands."

Whoa! I thought: *"The flesh . . . burned like acid."* That was a new detail. A key sensory memory. Bravo Dr. Friedman! In two weeks, you'd moved Russell off the same-old-same-old to the reveal of a touch of flesh.

"Of course I left the wire," said Russell. "Walked out to find out I'd fucked up."

"How?" said Dr. Friedman.

"The fire exit was locked! Nowhere to go but back to those two Serb militia pricks—who, luckily for me, had pulled the big joke and eaten my bowl of potato soup."

Nurse coughed: "Time for their meds."

Fuck her, I thought. *Maybe Russell is on the edge of a breakthrough.*

Dr. F's negative wave to the nurse agreed with me.

So I asked: "Did anybody say anything when you came out of the bathroom?"

Giving Russell a chance to bust the lie himself. To see it himself.

"Yeah. They all laughed at me 'cause I wasn't going to eat."

White-haired Zane picked up on my riff: "What did they say about you?"

But Russell just shrugged. "They said, *'Tough luck, American!'* Them eating my soup gave me an excuse to get pissed off, grab my gear, and storm out of the restaurant. I got outside, marched right through the other six guys, turned the corner—and ran like hell for three days. Rode a black ops Navy carrier chopper out. Told the Agency what I did, and now here I am."

Zane looked at me. We could have busted Russell. But that was Friedman's job. Besides, if you don't bust somebody else's lies, maybe nobody will bust yours.

Russell said: "The funny thing is, I don't feel anything about killing him. Just . . . nothing. Of course, I won't listen to Elvis anymore. I guess that's why I'm here."

"I don't think so," said Dr. Friedman.

Russell arched his eyebrows above the black lenses of his sunglasses. Grinned. "Doesn't really matter what you think, now does it, Doc? You're leaving us."

Nurse said: "Dr. Friedman? Our schedule."

He nodded. She passed out water cups and our meds like candy for the movie: uppers, downers, smoother-outers, sugar pills in Hailey's cup, a rainbow of pebbles geared to Post-Traumatic Stress Syndrome with icings of schizophrenic disorders.

"We've got one last Group this afternoon," said Dr. Friedman. "I'll see some of you individually before then, but I'm leaving here before dinner."

Eric raised his hand to blurt out that it was meatloaf night, but didn't get the nod.

"There's something we need to talk about this afternoon," continued Dr. Friedman, "and we should all look forward to that. Have a nice lunch."

He smiled as he left the Ward. The nurse collected our empty pill cups. I watched her thick brown hair in its pinned bun, watched her round hips in white slacks as she pushed the cart out of our Ward. Russell and Zane, even Hailey and Eric watched her: the substitute nurse was new and thus interesting, though she'd kept a professional distance from us. Then the Ward door closed. Locked. We drifted to our private rooms not knowing that we had less than five hours of safe time left *before*.

We should have known.

The *tell* was there for us to see.

We had the training. The experience. But we missed it, each and every one of us.

What the hell. We were crazy.

2

CRAZY IS WHY we were locked up at RAVENS castle.

Actually, the whole truth includes Our Special Circumstances.

"Our" being "us": Russell, Zane, Eric, Hailey, and me.

"Special Circumstances" includes that we're Code Word Access/TOP SECRET.

RAVENS is one of America's first and most secret "black sites," an acronym that appears in no directory of Federal programs and decodes as *R*esearch *A*nd *V*erification *E*pidemiology *N*etwork *S*ystems.

Sounds like Horrible Scary Infectious Death Disease. Which is what it's supposed to sound like. Nobody likes to linger around a door with that plaque. Of course, that door is itself almost impossible to find, because it's for a phantom facility in a nowhere place called Waterburg, Maine.

Waterburg is a rural crossroads. A gas station, one motel, a few houses—and a big square redbrick hulk set back from the road, with the RAVENS plaque screwed next to the double-locked front door. The "medical facilities" reputation of RAVENS accounts for the nurses and doctors who live in normal Maine towns and commute there. The doctors and nurses park their cars behind the RAVENS brick building, ride a blue bus through the woods to work in the Castle.

The Castle is a looming complex built by a timber baron who went bankrupt. Our home hides in woods where the aspens and birch trees grow thick around a chain-link fence topped with razor wire. The Castle is a hospital. An asylum protecting us from the world and the world from us.

Our Ward held only the five of us in that spring of America's *empire daze*. We each had a private bedroom with bath, a sitting room with a TV and bookshelves. Paintings had to be approved. Knick-knacks and art that were transformable into a weapon were taboo, but truthfully, all art is a weapon.

Like Harvard, the Castle is hard to get into.

Bottom line, you must be one of Uncle Sam's Intelligence or Security Officers, Executives, Analysts, Administrators, Operatives, or Agents.

A spy.

Then you need to go crazy.

Where else can Uncle Sam put us? Some cut-rate maniac barn with a revolving door where anybody can get in and snatch Globe Changing Secrets from a drooling mouth, then cycle back out to Go Over to the Other Side? Some "normal" insane asylum where if we told *actual reality* they'd call us crazy, but if we told *cover stories* we'd be set free to run wild in the streets?

America needs RAVENS Castle.

Where on that April Tuesday after our Morning Group when Russell lied about garroting the Serb colonel, Dr. Leon Friedman came to my private rooms for my last Individual Session before the big *oh-oh* changed everything.

3

FIRST HE KNOCKED on my open door.

Said: "Hey, Victor, may I come in?"

I shrugged. "I'm just a guy who can't say no."

"If only that were true," he said as he entered my quarters. "You're not Eric."

But I didn't take the bait. Didn't turn my back on him as I sat in my comfy red leather chair and let him take the lumpy faded blue sofa.

From down the hall came the rolling scream of Russell singing Warren Zevon's "Lawyers, Guns and Money."

Dr. Friedman said: "Do you like that song, too?"

"Let's say I *identify* with it. We all do, not just Russell."

"Speaking of Russell," said Dr. F, "what did you think of his story in Group?"

"Good story. He lied."

"How do you know?"

"Come on, Doc, we all know. Knew the first time he told that story years ago."

"How do *you* know?"

"The wire. We knew he lied because of the wire."

"Because . . ."

"Because if you use a wire to garrote an oaf like that fucking Colonel Herzgl, the least that'll happen is that the wire will cut your bare hands. As you strangle the guy, the wire cuts into his neck, slices his jugular, so *whoa*, we're talking a waterfall of blood spraying the walls, the bathroom mirror, on him, on you. Russell would have been all bloody and cut when he came out of that bathroom. He said he walked back to the table where the Colonel's two goons were waiting, and that they didn't say boo. They might have been stupid. They might have been drunk. They might have hated the Colonel. But they'd have noticed blood on the American who supposedly just went to the bathroom. Self-preservation would have made them ask *What's-up-with-that?* But Russell says they didn't. So his story is a lie."

"All of it?"

"We know he won't do Elvis. Know that his cover was lead guitar and singer in an Oregon bar band touring Europe, playing third-rate dives. Belgrade was where he activated his cover, his 'Serbian roots' quest. Infiltrated the slaughterhouse team."

"What's the true heart of his story?" asked our shrink.

So I thought about it. Said: "The bathroom."

"Why?"

"Because in the story it was the kill zone. The hot spot. The powerful place."

"Like Malaysia was for you?"

Should have seen that one coming. I said: "If you want to talk about Asia, walk down to Zane's room. He got the secret Congressional Medal of Honor for service there. His war was long gone before I showed up. Now all he's got is that hunk of metal in his dresser drawer plus what turned his hair white and scares him awake at night."

"What scares you awake at night, Vic?"

"Look, this is our last time together. Doesn't make sense to get into all that now."

"It makes perfect sense. This being our last time makes it safer for you to get into it with me than with Dr. Jacobsen when he comes back."

"Like you won't pass notes on to him? Passing notes gets you detention."

"You're the one who's detained, Vic."

"The Castle is a pretty good place to be trapped."

"But Vic, isn't life about freedom? Choosing?" He watched me say nothing. The second hand swept a circle around his watch. "How do you feel about the others?"

"Very carefully. None of them like to be touched."

"I don't think you're a joke. But if you treat me like I am . . ." He shrugged. "So again: How do you feel about the other four people on this Ward?"

"They're fried, each and every one. On a good day, they're frazzled. On a bad day, they're batshit. They can piss me off or make me laugh. But we get each other better than any of you doctors or nurses, maybe because we've been there *and* off the edge. You haven't. We're locked up. You're not. There's us. Then there's all of you. The five of us, the four of them . . . They're who I've got left."

"Sounds like family." He waited for me to say something. Filled my silence with another question. "What's your role in this family? Father?"

"Don't lay that on me. Uncle Sam is our father."

"So you're all his kids." Dr. F shrugged. "Are any of you going to grow up?"

"And suddenly get 'not crazy'? Hey, you tell me, you're the doctor."

"Are you still thinking about suicide?"

"Who doesn't? Who hasn't?"

"But you've tried it. Twice."

"What, are you saying . . . You don't think I am—I was *sincere*?"

"No. I think you were—excuse the expression—dead serious about suicide."

"So the CIA must be right and I am incompetent."

"Bullshit. You're the most competent crazy I know."

"Then why couldn't I kill myself?"

"You're a hard man to kill—even for you. But the more important question is *why* have you stopped attempting suicide."

"Maybe I'm waiting for the right moment."

"Or for the reason not to."

Our eyes pointed at each other through a waterfall of silence.

Until Dr. F glanced at his watch: "Now I have to go listen to Hailey run down symptoms that aren't there."

"She picks her own scabs to prove she's right about being sick," I said.

"If you know that about her . . ."

"Other people are easy."

"Of course. Why do you think so many screwed up people become shrinks?"

"Hey, Dr. F: Are you screwed up?"

"Not anymore."

When he left, he closed the door behind him.

Our Ward is on the Castle's Third Floor. After Dr. F left, I stared through my shatterproof window, looked out over the naked trees, watched white clouds drift across a blue spring sky, and felt a lone tear trickle down my cheek.

4

"SO HERE WE are again. Final session. Our last chance."

Call the speaker *prophet*. Call him the man with the right questions for wrong answers. Call him Dr. F, like we had since the first morning we pulled our folding chairs into a circle in the sun-drenched Day Room for Group, like we did that Tuesday afternoon when we all gathered together for the last time.

"This afternoon," he told us, "I want to talk about *all* of you."

"Clinical practice isn't my specialty," said Dr. F. "I apply psychiatry to crisis management and international analysis for the CIA. Soon as I get back to D.C., I will start as a watchdog and profiler for the National Security Council. I won't even have time to go home to New York. I had two weeks between postings, but when I heard about the staff training furloughs here, rather than go sit on the beach at Hawaii—"

"You'd sunburn, Doc."

"Good, Russell, looking for the bright side of a closed-out option."

Russell pushed his sunglasses up his nose. "I'm so bright I gotta wear shades."

"Too bad being smart isn't enough," said Dr. F. "Anyway, the chance to sharpen my clinical skills, the chance to get to know—"

I interrupted: "To get to know us broken tips of the 'national security' spear."

"Always the poet, Victor. But now I want to talk about all of you through the prism of my organizational analysis, not my—"

"Not your *psycho*-analysis," said Zane. "Us being psychos."

"Don't limit yourselves," said the real doctor. "You're

more than psychos. Right now, you're the inmates who have taken over the asylum."

The substitute nurse unlocked the Ward door and entered. She carried a batch of files. Took a chair outside of our circle. A quick glance showed me her reflection trapped in the dark screen of the Day Room's turned-off TV.

"We haven't run things for a long time," said Zane. "Especially around here."

"You got the keys, Doc," said Russell.

"And you all like it that way. *No,* don't interrupt."

Dr. F's gold metal glasses reflected five inmates coiled on metal chairs.

"My field is *gestalt dynamics,* how groups function, with a specialty of the aberrant individual in a high-stress environment. But," smiled Dr. F, "the description in my CIA file is better. In our shadow world, they call me a *spotter.*"

"Like for a sniper?" said ex-soldier Zane.

"More like a shepherd, but this isn't about me, so let's get through this so Nurse and I can get to the Route 1 motel and pack before we go back to . . ." Dr. F smiled. "Back to the real world."

"*Whoa,* you found it?" exclaimed Russell.

"Hey," I said. "Call Dr. F the peerless spotter."

"Peerless spotter!" obeyed Eric.

"Call me a taxi and I'm out of here," said Russell.

"You're a taxi!" chorused Zane with Eric.

Hailey said: "Go where you gotta go."

Clap! Dr. F's hands slapped together. He yelled: *"Shut up!"*

Dr. F's face burned red: "I bust you on being inmates who've taken over the asylum, and to avoid dealing with that, you try to riff away the time we've got left!"

The visiting shrink shook his head. "Crazy people see with powerful clarity. Distorted vision, sure, but clear. And you're the most insightful and yet the blindest patients I've ever had. Look at the five of you."

Eric swiveled his head to comply.

Russell pushed his sunglasses on tighter: "We already looked at me today."

"Oh really?" said the shrink. "Was that you we saw? Or your story?"

"Stories are what we got," I said.

"What you've all got," said Dr. F, "is your lives made into stories instead of your lives full of stories. Okay, Russell, we did you today, so we'll skip you now. Hailey?"

The Black woman gave our substitute therapist her poker face.

He said: "Do you know why you keep muttering, *'Gotta be worth it'*?"

"Because that's true."

"Truth is irrelevant if you use it to drown out meaning or if you inven—" Dr. F shifted to a softer word: "If you *use* drama to hide what you don't want to face. I know the horror that happened to you in Nigeria and I know the horror you did, but you've got to face it. Face it without . . . the protection of judgment."

"Doesn't matter what you think I have to do: I'm dying."

"How convenient. But you look fine."

"Appearances are deceiving," she snapped.

The therapist said: "So who are you fooling?"

Her ebony skin glowed with anger.

I said: "In the land of the blind, the one-eyed person is crazy."

"All our eyes work, Victor," said Dr. F, "but good diversion. I was done with Hailey anyway—unless she's got something new to say to us."

She glared at him.

Dr. F swung his gaze to Eric. That bespectacled, pudgy engineer stiffened to attention in his chair. Waiting. Ready. The therapist opened his mouth—found no words, closed it. Knew he had to say something about everyone or no one would listen.

"Eric, two days ago, Victor said he agreed with Mark Twain that history doesn't repeat itself, but it rhymes, and then pointed out that *Eric* rhymes with *Iraq*."

Dr. Leon Friedman's shaking head broke free his smile.

"If I were a poet like Victor," said Dr. F, "maybe I'd have

more than a notion of the connected sense of all that. But notions are key now—for you.

"You beat Saddam Hussein's Iraq way back before our first war there, but they turned you into a robot. Yet I have to believe that somewhere in you, there's a notion of Eric as a free human being."

Dr. Leon Friedman told the pudgy hero in thick glasses: "This is not an order, but try to imagine a notion of space between commands of *do* or *don't*."

"'Xactly what the hell does that mean?" said white-haired Zane.

"*Exactly* is what you've got, right, soldier?" replied our therapist.

As Eric frowned. Took Dr. F's suggestion as an order. Eric's hands cut a square frame in our circle's air like a mime building the notion of space.

While Eric mimed his work, Dr. F. worked on Zane.

"All you've been through," Dr. F told that white-haired soldier. "Bombs. Heroin. Slaughter beneath your boots. Jungle heat that now makes you melt down. You fought since Vietnam so you can carry that weight and never cry. That's *exactly* who you are."

"What's your point?" snapped Zane.

"Congratulations. You won. Look what you got. *Exactly.*"

Zane angled his head toward Eric: "I'm not him. You can't tell me what to do."

"I wish I could," said Dr. F. "We'd drive out of here together."

"But now it's time for you to scoot back to the real world," I said.

"Before I get to you, huh, Victor?"

I became ice. He was only an image in my eyes. A sack of red water.

As he said: "Zane, you and Vic here rhyme."

Zane argued: "He ain't my generation. Plus, I never tried to kill myself uselessly. And I don't zone out."

"But you're both crazy from responsibility," answered the therapist. "Though you cling to your weight and Victor uses his to dig his own grave."

"I did what I did," I said.

"And if you did anything differently," Dr. F asked me, "in Malaysia, with 9/11, would anything be different now?"

"The names of the dead."

"Maybe. Maybe not. But you did what you *could.*"

"So that's not enough to justify me going crazy?"

"That's more than enough. But you've got to move off of paying for what was possible *then* to buying what's possible *now.* You've got to look for that."

"Or get shocked into seeing it? Like this little 'blitz therapy' session, Doc? Shock therapy—sorry, Eric—call it whatever you want, didn't work. For any of us."

We stared at the doctor who'd spent two weeks doing his best.

Russell said: "We're here."

"And we'll be here after you're gone," said Hailey.

"'Xactly."

Sunlight streamed through Eric's invisible notion of space.

"Is that what you want?" asked our shrink. "Don't you see? You're set in your situation and thus resist challenging your troubles. You resist working on getting out."

"I shouldn't leave," said Hailey. "I'm dying."

"We're all dying," said Dr. F. "How and when . . . Who knows?

"None of you is close to 'cured.' I don't know if you can ever reach that point. But I want you to open your eyes. Who knows what you'll see—with therapeutic help."

"Plus getting stoned," said Russell. "Everybody here must get stoned."

"Meds are tools," said Dr. F. "The work is up to you."

"Bottom line us, Doc," I said.

"No, that's your job. Always has been, always will be. No matter how out of control the world is, you've got some ability to draw your own bottom line."

"You're supposed to be a shrink," argued Russell, "not a philosopher."

"Sometimes the only difference between those jobs is that I write prescriptions."

"And orders to lock people up," I said.

"Do any of you want me to write an order for your release?" None of us said a word.

"What I am writing is a strong recommendation that your treatment shift from maintenance to management designed to get you out of our custody."

"So you'll get credit for lowering the budget," said Hailey.

"Do you think I give a shit about the budget? My job is to spot when the emperor is naked and say so. To take risks. And here, that seems appropriate."

"So what will happen to us?" asked Russell.

"Nothing bad, nothing dangerous, nothing soon," lied Dr. F. "And nothing that I won't monitor with your regular staff. Even with my new duties at the NSC, I want you all to feel free to reach out and get in touch with me whenever—"

Eric leaned forward in his chair, his arm stretched toward Dr. F.

Who said: "I mean later, Eric. Via e-mail."

"Oh, *sure*," said Russell. "In between Israeli-Palestinian clashes, war in Iraq, the atomic bomb in North Korea and who knows where next, narco wars in South America and Burma, evildoer hunting in the hills of Afghanistan, terrorist attacks in Des Moines, genocide in Sudan, Russia rattling empire dreams, resurgent Nazis in Europe, the clear-cut Amazon causing snowstorms in L.A., Pentagon budget battles, congressional inquiries, press scandals, and White House state dinners with boob job Hollywood blondes, *sure*, you'll find time to check in with us Maine maniacs."

Dr. F shrugged. "Who wants to talk about this new program?"

Our circle of chairs now had two sides: us, and Dr. F. He felt that, too, had known the risk and taken it rather than coasting out easy. Got to give him credit.

"Well," he said after three minutes of silence, "if I'm the only one who's got anything to say, we might as well not waste the group's time."

The five of us stood as Dr. F said: "The nurse has paperwork for me. I'll sit here in the Day Room in case any of you want to come back, talk more."

Without a word, we turned and walked away. Write-offs and walk-aways came easy to us. We were trained and experienced.

Still, I looked back. Saw him sitting there, alone in the Day Room as the nurse walked toward the Ward door. Saw a pile of files on one chair beside Dr. F. Saw him take a fountain pen from inside that tweed sports jacket. Saw him push his gold framed glasses up his nose and turn his emerald eyes toward the file open on his lap.

Inside my room, I shut the door. A moment later, I heard Russell's stereo in his room blasting the Barenaked Ladies' concert cut of "Brain Wilson." Blasting it loud so that no one would mistake his playing a ballad about a genius's artistic crack-up for *passive* aggression.

Then I zoned out. Dr. Jacobsen called it disassociation. Laymen might mistake it for a nap, sitting in a chair, eyes draped, oh so completely gone.

Until abruptly I blasted back.

Was sitting there. My chair. My room. My books. My . . .

Eric. Standing in front of me, shifting back and forth from foot to foot like an anxious third grader locked out of the bathroom.

My door was open. Eric opened my door! Came in without being told to! Never before, never *imaginable* before, and now . . .

Now he stood in front of me. Shifting from shoe to shoe. His face twisted, pale.

"*Uh-uh,*" said Eric. "*Oh-oh!*"

5

DR. FRIEDMAN SAT on a metal folding chair in our sunlit Day Room.

Dead.

My guts told me that the moment Eric led me into the Day Room, though I wasn't certain until I pressed my fingers into the rubbery flesh of Dr. F's neck, found no pulse.

Down in his lair, Russell had moved on to the Beatles' *White Album*. The sound of "Everybody's Got Something to Hide Except Me and My Monkey" poured into the Day Room where Eric and I stood beside the sitting corpse.

Then I spotted the smudge of blood in Dr. F's right ear.

"Eric: go get all the others! Now! And only them!"

Two minutes later, five of us stood staring at the slumped body of our therapist.

"Gone before he thought," said Russell.

"Look at this," I said, pointing to the blood smudge in Dr. F's right ear.

Zane held his long white hair back, leaned over and looked. "There it is."

"Somebody went to school," said Russell. "Sorry, Dr. F."

Hailey said: "What is it?

"DAST," said Russell.

DAST—Defense Against Subtle Termination. A secret training program run jointly by the Pentagon and the Agency. Trouble Boys like Russell, Zane, and I cycle through for training. Like the military's DAME program—Defense Against Mechanical Entry—DAST obscures what it teaches. DAME may teach how to defend against mechanical entry, or as you might call it, *burglary,* but it for sure turns out lock pickers and safe crackers. DAST teaches "defense" against "subtle termination." Learning tricks the opposition might use to kill you in Bangkok gives you a better chance of getting in and out of such a town alive. Of course, knowledge you pick up along that educational path . . . Assassination is illegal for U.S. spies.

"Not a perfect job," said Russell. "Whatever was rammed through Doc's right ear up to his brain pan kept its path open long enough to let blood trickle out. Maybe in the boonies this could be passed off as a stroke, but here, the coroner will know the score."

" 'Xactly," muttered Zane.

"He's not the one who's supposed to die," said Hailey.

"Logic says one of us killed him," I said.

"Means, motive, and opportunity," said Russell.

"He wanted to change everything," said Zane. "He told us so."

"Him sitting down here," I said. "Alone. We all had the chance."

"None of us wanted what he did," said Hailey

"Well Dr. F," said Russell. "Looks like you won. Everything's changed."

The pat Russell gave the dead man's shoulder was meant to be congratulatory.

Dr. Friedman tumbled out of his chair to sprawl on the floor.

"Sorry!" Russell gave us his *shit-happens* shrug.

"What a brilliant murder," I said. "We're trapped here as the perfect fall guys. We're certified dangerous and crazy. Nobody will believe we're innocent.

"So did we kill him?" I asked.

I stared at their faces—Russell, Zane, Hailey, Eric. They stared at mine.

Together we said: *"Nah!"*

"So," said Hailey, "if we didn't do it, who did?"

"Here's the more urgent question," said Zane. "Are we targeted, too?"

"Absolutely," I said. "If the CIA buys the killer's frame and calls us guilty, they'll bury us. If we miraculously convince the Agency that we're not guilty, then someone else is—and we're witnesses, extreme liabilities to the killer or to a cover-up."

"Oh boy," said Eric. "Oh boy."

We whirled to look at the Ward door. Locked shut.

Zane said: "One hour to dinner."

"Meatloaf," said Eric.

From Russell's room came: "While My Guitar Gently Weeps."

"We are," said Zane, "in trouble."

"Exposed," said Hailey. "Endangered."

"You know what else?" I said. "Pissed-off. Some hitter wrecked our Ward, set it up so Admin will blunder around like a herd of elephants. Chain us up. Transfer us. Dope us more. Sure, a killer here means some spy has penetrated America's top secrets. That's a huge security risk, but what pisses me off is that a mechanic nailed our Doc."

Hailey asked: "Was it something we said?"

"If it was," said Zane, "even worse. Then they're truly after us."

"Ghosts." I shook my head. "They always get you."

Russell said: "The inmates won't run this asylum anymore."

"Whatever happens will be terrible," said Hailey. "Won't respect who we are. What happened to us. What's going on with us. Our fate."

"Whatever the big bad is, it's coming for us," said Zane.

"They promised safe here," said Eric.

"Big surprise," said Russell. "They lied."

In physics, critical mass is obtained when the minimum number of individual elements needed to create a transforming process coalesce in one time-space continuum.

Consider us. Five maniacs. Spies. Trained, experienced professional paranoids who'd been programmed to Do Something. Scarred beyond repair, but still, once upon a time We'd Been Somebody. Forces with which to reckon. Now locked in a castle. With the corpse of a guy who'd earned our respect. Whose murder we were set up to take the fall for. With Keepers scheduled to catch Our Whole Situation in less than an hour. We had nothing to gain but all that we had left was on the line to lose.

Physicists, psychiatrists, and snipers talk about the trigger. The event that starts the chain reaction. When I think about our trigger, I hear the sudden wave of silence rushing into the Day Room that April Tuesday afternoon as Russell's CD player shut off.

There we stood.

Five maniacs staring down at a corpse.

With no theme music.

"Two choices," I said. "We either stay here and suffer what gets done to us . . ."

"Or?" said Russell.

"We bust out of this place."

6

"WILD," SAID RUSSELL. "But we gotta take the Doc with us."

"He's dead!" I yelled.

Zane said: "Nobody gets left behind."

"Are you nuts?"

"Well," said Hailey, "technically . . . *yeah.*"

"Think of it as poetry," argued Russell. "A great lyric. You can't just walk away from a killer line because it's inconvenient."

"Think of it as strategy," said Zane. "We take him with us, we fuck with the Bad Boys' setup. What could be smarter than that?"

"Or more fun," said Russell.

Hailey sighed. "Victor: If it was you lying there, what would you want?"

In a blink, I saw it.

"Doesn't matter," I said. "You're right. We've got to take Dr. F. We need him to get past security."

And I told them how. Said: "Get your GODS, link up back here in fifteen minutes."

"Wait," said Russell.

"Now what?"

"You forgot." Zane's eyes pointed up through the ceiling.

Eric nodded as Hailey told me: "Good people say good-bye."

7

RAVENS CASTLE HAS five floors.

First Floor is Administration, doors with electronic locks, the Keepers' lounge, the Computerized Monitoring System installed before the secret black money that creates the Castle's budget started being siphoned off to fuel the war in Iraq.

Second Floor is the Medical Unit with an operating room where you can get a face switch, a fingerprint graft, a bullet removed. You can stay on Second Floor and never know about your upstairs neighbors.

Third Floor belongs to Wards A*ble,* B*ravo,* and C*razyville.*

Able is for short timers. The temporary hysterics. Spy Plane/Jungle Crash *crispy critters* adjusting to burn scars they can never tell the truth about. Pentagon Apocalypse *Bluesboyz* haunted by mushroom cloud/plague dreams. Able Ward houses the *just passing throughs* who the doctors will be *able* to recycle.

Bravo is for the broken but bandageable. Battleground Beirut Bravehearts who went batshit but who can get by after six months or so of Castle therapy. Bravo veterans take their bandaged act home and lead "a productive life" sitting in their living room clothed in cover lies, waiting for their cried-out wife to finally walk out for good and leave them watching flickers of the TV or their NSA-monitored computer, leave them waiting for the mailman to deliver their secret pension check.

Crazyville is our country. All the Wards have locked doors, but to get out of Crazyville takes knowing extra keypunch security codes. Took the five of us days to spy out those codes. Pros like us should have busted the codes sooner. But don't forget, we were crazy. Functional but so far gone nobody figured we were ever coming back.

Fourth Floor is Main Street. The dining room with its serving line. Main Street has a "cyberroom" to let you surf the Internet—our Keepers track every wave. Russell had "a thing" in 2003 with a Security Monitor who got so intrigued by the list of songs he snagged through file-sharing programs that she finessed a security review to meet him, fell into the darkness of his sunglasses. She cried when Admin caught her, swore the sex was consensual, that she'd never known the slamming surge of being bent over her desk by anyone except Russell, but still they shipped her out to sanitizing duty at an Alaskan NSA listening post. Next to the cyber room is a gym with weights, Eric's treadmill, and

Hailey's mirrored ballet studio that Russell, Zane, and I use for *gung fu*.

Fifth Floor of our Castle is a long corridor of locked doors.

My black shoes stepped with nary a sound on the Fifth Floor's sunlit green tile. I eased my way down the corridor from the stairwell exit. Scents of ammonia and tears floated around me as I pressed against Door Number Six and oh so softly, tapped it with our secret knock, slid open the observation slot. He's one of those people who even his lovers call by his last name, so I whispered: "Malcolm!"

Wait for it. Wait. No time, gotta evac or they'll—*Wait*.

Finally, unseen, he said: "You're Victor."

"Right."

"Last visitor was the woman. Hailey. Two breakfasts ago. I had a lemon poppy-seed muffin went purple smoke."

"We meant to visit more often."

"Life gets busy. Visits are hard."

"No excuse."

"But true. You were the first. Snuck up here. Took me, *oh,* a while to figure you were real—*did not eat yours!* Before you, all I had was decades of secret lonely. And the whisperers. Thanks."

"Yeah, well it was good for us, too." Locked alone in that padded room, he couldn't see me smile. "Sneaking up here kept us sharp. Kept us *us*. Plus, we could have been you. Always gotta remember that. We could be you."

"Does that work the other way around?"

"Sure," I lied. Switched back to true. "Besides, we like you."

"I'm such a charmer."

"Malcolm, we've got to go."

Silence of a dozen heartbeats. I leaned on the locked steel door.

Then he said: "Who?"

"The five of us. Hailey. Zane. Russell won't be able to sneak his Walkman up here to play you more songs. Eric, I wish we could have let him come up here alone so you could have gotten to know him better, but we didn't dare because, *ah,* because . . ."

"Because in a freak I might have triggered him."

"Yeah. Listen, we got dropped into a hit—or it got dropped onto us."

"How many down?"

"One—so far."

"Seven bodies fell on me. The first time. Do you remember 1974? Nixon?"

"I was still wearing diapers. Sorry about this, but we gotta run."

"You mean a mission, not flee. *He's talking to me! Put your tits away!* When?"

"We're all but on the road."

"I did seven runs. Really six, because that first one wasn't supposed to exist but— *Was too my fault! And the airport bathroom!* Victor?"

"Yeah?"

"Run hard."

"Hang in there, Condor."

"They took my belt away when they locked me up."

"You know what I mean."

"*Yes we do worms and Sten gun!* Can I help?"

In forty minutes, the understaffed Keepers were scheduled to head toward Ward C so they could escort us to the elevators for the ride up to Main Street's meatloaf.

"Can you count three-thousand beats, then scream? Start everyone up here screaming?"

"Sure."

As I raced toward the stairwell door, his count echoed behind me: "Three-thousand. Sixty-four. Two thousand, nine hundred, ninety-nine. Two thousand, nine hundred, ninety-three. Forty-seven . . ."

8

When I got back to the third floor, everybody had their GODS in the Day Room.

GODS: Get Out of Dodge Soonest. The gear you grab when you gotta go. IDs. Cash. Credit cards invisible to hunters' computers. Clothes for cover, camouflage, and comfort. Protein pills and vitamins. Weapons are a hard call. You're a spy, not a cop or a soldier. You must protect your cover and weapons get you noticed. Plus weapons wipe out wits. When you strap on a gun or slide a shiv in your sock, you think you're twice as tough as you've ever been. You load your brains into the gun, so your first thought becomes: *squeeze the trigger.*

Took me three minutes to grab my GODS. Paranoia propels preparation. We kept all our gear ready to go in plain sight of the Keepers. If they realized we were maintaining op alert status in the safety of our homeland insane asylum, that awareness became simply more proof that we were crazy and right where we belonged.

What I stuffed into my black nylon computer case bag:
One set of underwear and socks, a polypropelene skiing shirt.
One toiletries kit—soap, toothpaste, toothbrush, deodorant. Like airport security guards, our Keepers rationed our razors, fingernail clippers, or scissors.
One notebook and two of the permitted felt-tip pens.
One leather flight jacket that held my wallet with $84 and my expired California driver's license.
One first edition of William Carlos Williams's *greatest hits* that hid a snapshot of shy Derya on a roof, her cinnamon hair floating in the breeze of Kuala Lumpur.
One hand-size souvenir of New York City that I didn't get there.

What I didn't stuff into my black nylon computer case bag:
Weapons we didn't have.
A Palm Pilot or address book of people who cared and would help.
Maps of the zero safe places I could go.

Five of us, geared up to go, met in the Day Room by Dr. F's body.

Zane kicked two support planks out of the couch and Russell helped me lug Dr. F.

Hailey bypassed our Ward's locks, stepped into the Third Floor hall.

"Clear!" Hailey dashed toward the two elevators and pushed the Down button, her brown eyes flicking from one end of the corridor to the other, from one closed door to the next. Russell and I lugged Dr. F's body toward her and the elevator. Eric followed us, strapped to our GODS bags and swiped first-aid kits. Zane came last, carrying a metal folding chair and the two eight-foot support slats he'd kicked off the couch.

Russell and I propped Dr. F face-out against the elevator cage's back wall as the others scrambled on board.

An engine whined and cables clunked for the elevator next to us.

Hailey jabbed the First Floor button.

The other elevator clunked to a stop one floor up. Its unseen doors jerked open.

"Push the button again!" said Zane.

The other elevator whined *coming down*. Toward us.

Hailey's finger pecked our First Floor button like a starving woodpecker.

"I can fake Dr. F's voice," said Russell. "Vic, hold him. I'll say we're going—"

"Nowhere," I said. "This fucking elevator—"

Clunk. The elevator next door stopped. On our floor. Those doors whirred open.

As ours slid shut.

We dropped like a stone down the shaft through the heart of the Castle.

On the first floor, Hailey stepped off the elevator. Looked both ways.

Like we hoped, she saw an empty hall stretching toward the corridor crossroads.

The first-aid kits let us tape Dr. F's eyes open, then bind him into the metal chair. We taped his head level on his shoulders. Strapped our GODS on his lap. Russell dropped to his hands and knees behind a similarly posed Zane. Hailey and Eric taped a plank on their spines.

Hailey balanced Dr. F's throne on that plank while Eric and I scurried into position beside the other two kneeling guys. She taped the plank to us.

Four of us knelt strapped into a corpse-carrying caravan. Hailey crouched ahead of us. Fifty feet away from her dark eyes waited the corridor corner: around it was the door to freedom or the moment when we'd be caught.

"This is a sad and risky plan," said Russell.

"Crawl in time." Zane pictured the team-building/body bustin' drills in Special Warfare school where he and his squad jogged with a telephone pole on their shoulders.

"Wait!" said Russell. "Did anybody grab our meds?"

"Uh-oh," said Eric. "Uh-oh."

Meds at the Castle are locked up in a guarded pharmacy. The medicine cart for the five of us carried a vast rainbow of pills dispensed four times a day.

"Guess we just said *no,*" whispered Zane.

"We gotta go!" I said. "Need to go now! On zero!"

"We can't hear Malcolm counting!" argued Zane.

"Not Malcolm! On me! When I say! Three, two, one—"

Crawl. By the third 'slide,' we were crawling together. Sweat dripped off my forehead. Tapped on the ammonia mopped green floor tiles between my sliding hands.

"Aaaahhh!"

Like a scream it ripped through the Castle, but this wail was a cacophony of voices.

Malcolm.

Our caravan scrambled around the corner—

Where the budget cuts saved us and no guard stood behind the hall counter.

A blue stripe painted on the green tiles from the counter to the wall marked the Castle's secured border. As our sedan chair moved Dr. F's face across that blue stripe, motion sensors activated an electronic hum. A blue band of light flowed over Dr. F's lifeless face. Found his taped-open eyes. Matched his irises to stored data.

The metal cover over the exit door latch whirred and clicked, then slid up to reveal a touch screen beside the door release handle. The touch screen glowed to life.

We shuffled our burden as close to the door as we could. Hailey pressed Dr. F's dead left hand to the glowing screen.

The door lock buzzed.

And we were out.

9

A BLUE BUS idled in the night mist of a Maine parking lot. From the bowels of the castle beyond the parking lot came a wail. The bus driver's posture behind the steering wheel claimed he didn't hear that. But he heard the *Bam-clang! Bam-clang!* on the bus's folding door. The driver popped open the doors.

Standing out there in the night was a woman wearing a trench coat darker than her cocoa skin. She said: "Are you ready to go?"

An albino Jesus charged into the bus, dropped a grip of steel on the driver's shoulder, said: "Do you know the way out?"

"Ah, just past the gate guards, down the road ten minutes an— Who are . . . ?"

"Do your job," commanded white-maned Zane. Eric obeyed Hailey and got on the bus. Russell and I staggered toward the steps, our burden draped between us.

"Doing your job," Zane told the bus driver. "Isn't that what life's about?"

"That guy those two are carry—*Hey*, you supposed to bring him on here?"

"We all gotta go sometime," said Russell.

He and I dumped Dr. F in the seat *right behind* the driver's chair.

"What's wrong with him?" asked the driver.

"Bad luck." Russell slid into the seat behind that slumped-over passenger.

Zane said: "How's your luck?"

"G-g-good." The bus driver's voice said he knew he was in trouble.

Curled on the floor by the Dr. F's shoes, I said: "Do you know who you are?"

"The . . . the bus driver?"

" '*Xactly!*" Zane plucked the twenty-four-inch black steel Mag flashlight from its dashboard clamp. He flipped the black metal flashlight end over end, then chopped it through the night air as if to smack somebody in the head. "And we are *so* on the bus.

"Drive." Zane flicked a flashlight beam toward the grimy metal floor of the front seat across the aisle from the driver's perch. "I'll be right there."

The blue bus rumbled out of the lot, down the long and winding road, through the trees to the Security Gate where the two guards packed nine-millimeter Glocks. Looking at the bus windows, the guards saw one passenger slumped behind the driver: the visiting shrink.

A guard held up his hand and stepped into the glow of the bus headlights.

From the bus floor, I told the driver: "Slide open your window."

Footsteps crunched gravel outside in the night. The guard's words flowed into the bus: "Going back early."

The driver said: "Just doing what they tell me."

The guard said: "*Ay-yuh.* How you doing in there, Sir?"

I grabbed Dr. F's elbow, raised his limp arm above the window sill . . . waved his hand in a floppy salute.

"Good for you. See you later."

The chain-link gate clanked open.

I let the dead man's hand plop in an encouraging tap on the driver's shoulder.

The blue bus chugged forward and the chain-link gate slid shut behind it.

We bounced through the night in that blue bus. Trees danced alongside us like Mardi Gras ghosts. Exhaust, oiled metal, and something sour perfumed our every inhale.

Ten minutes later, the bus drove alongside the brick building with the RAVENS plaque. Two dozen cars napped behind the building in its parking lot's shadows.

"Shut it down," I told the driver.

The blue bus engine died.

"Clear!" whispered Zane.

We took the driver's wallet with its forty-one dollars. Taped
his mouth shut and his hands to the bus's steering wheel.

"Here," Hailey told him, "this will keep you warm."

A wool blanket from the winter survival kit parachuted
over the driver like a tent.

All he saw was scratchy darkness. He heard the accordion
door pop open. Felt the blast of night air. Something
dragged over the bus's metal floor. Clumped down the stairs.
Shoes crunched on the gritty parking lot.

Then the door closed, and he couldn't see anything, hear
anything, scream anything in that Maine night parking lot, in
a blue bus, under a blanket.

10

STANDING BESIDE THE blue bus, I pointed Dr. F's keys at
the herd of empty cars, thumbed a black plastic button.

Bweep-boop!

Headlights flashed on a four-door silver Ford.

"Wild!" said Russell.

"Saw that in a TV commercial," I confessed.

Vision hit me. An epiphany so pure and clear I was
breathless.

Dr. F stuck to Zane like a drunk sophomore being held up
by his prom date.

"They know," said Zane. "By now, for sure, the Keepers
know."

"How much?" said Hailey.

"That we're missing," I said. "They might still think we're
hiding or trapped on the grounds. That's logical. That's
where they're looking."

"But not for long," she said.

"And Dr. F is getting heavy," said Zane. "But if the Keepers don't know *proof certain* that he's dead, they'll have to deal with more contingencies."

"Dibs on driving!" said Russell.

"That's mine!" Zane's outburst shook the corpse he held. "It's been thirty years!"

Their argument brought panic to Eric's face.

Hailey held out a calming hand: "It's okay, Eric. Don't worry. I'm driving."

She glared at Zane.

Who frowned at her, flicked his eyes to Russell.

Who watched them both with the intensity of a base stealer dancing on second.

Zane blinked.

Hailey ran toward the silver Ford, her dark trench coat flapping.

Russell blasted off after her, his black leather coat billowing like a cape.

Zane swung Dr. F's body toward Eric: "Hold him!"

Eric caught our therapist on his right shoulder like a linebacker slamming into a pass receiver. Eric stumbled with the crash of the corpse on his shoulder, staggered, stood straight so he hefted Dr. F like a rolled rug.

Zane chased Russell and Hailey, his white Jesus hair flowing in the night.

The parked silver car seemed to zoom toward their charging mob. Russell and Hailey ran neck and neck, with Zane only three, now two lunging strides behind their flapping coats. Their hands clawed for a handle in the night air.

Bweep-boop!

Headlights flashed on the silver Ford and the racers heard door locks *thunk.*

Walking to the silver Ford, I jiggled the keys. Ignored their glares, just as they ignored Eric as he staggered behind me with a corpse thrown over his shoulder.

"Besides," I said: "I know who killed Dr. Friedman."

11

THE NURSE.

Who wore her hair pinned in a bun.

Pinned. As in "pin." No medical staffer—even one on temporary rotation—no one in her right mind would take a sharp object into an insane asylum. Dr. F didn't even wear a tie for a freak to grab. That was smart and policy.

So if she wore a hairpin into Crazyville, she did so for a reason.

Unfold the right kind of hairpin and you've got a nifty toy for playing Puncture the Brain Pan.

Dr. F, sitting in the soft light of the Day Room. Waiting for us to come back. The nurse who rotated in on temporary duty with him hands him files. Stands behind him. While he's reading a file, she unpins her hair. Maybe other nurses had done that. He was an okay-looking guy, smart. If he realized anything, maybe it was a sensation that told him: *She's letting down her hair; we're all alone; I'm going to get lucky!* She clapped her left hand over his left ear, put her hairpin in his right ear—shoved it straight up hard, fast and far and he jerked rigid, brain burst. She'd feel that. Pull out her pin. Fix her bun. Then leave him sitting there for us to find and be framed.

We should have realized something was dangerously wrong during Tuesday Morning Group while Russell lied about garroting the Serb colonel and the nurse came in pushing the metal medicine cart, her hair *pinned* in a bun.

Dr. Friedman had been right. We'd been in the Castle too long. We'd gotten too sane to recognize what we were seeing.

Now we were out. Seeing the night highway illuminated by our headlights as the road rushed toward the windshield of our stolen car. I drove, Zane beside me in the passenger seat, navigating from a rental car map, from memories of what Dr. F had told us. The rearview mirror showed me Russell in the backseat by one door. Hailey sat on his lap, not Eric's—Eric knew enough about torture. Dr. F rode in the middle of the backseat. He was the only one wearing a seat belt.

Zane said: "Any second now. Should be . . . There!"

A clapboard roadside motel with a red neon sign flowed toward us. The full moon glistened on the tall chain-link fence surrounding the motel's empty swimming pool. Our silver machine skidded to a stop on the motel's asphalt parking lot. Car doors flew open. Zane, Russell and I fanned out in a skirmish line marching toward the only cabin where lights glowed. This was the town's lone motel, the place Castle short-time staffers like Dr. F called their home away from home. Hailey ran to the bungalow where a sign read OFFICE. Eric and Dr. F stayed with our vehicle.

"Take it smart!" said Zane as Russell surged ahead of us. "Smooth!"

Russell kicked in the motel room door.

She wore a white bra and panties. Looked lovely and lost. Stood in the doorway of the bathroom, backlit by its flickering light. Brown hair hung past her pale shoulders.

Russell was three steps from grabbing her when he froze.

Crowding in the motel room after him, Zane and I saw Russell freeze. Stare at her, through her, past her. Our advantage of surprise vaporized. She blinked—dove past Russell to grab her purse off the bed, rolled behind the bed out of sight.

She popped up on the far side of the bed and blasted a bullet from a black pistol.

Zane slammed to the floor.

I leapt for the open bathroom—knocked Russell out of the way.

The gun roared. Splinters exploded off the bathroom doorjamb beside me.

Zane pulled the bed over on top of her. Crashed beside her bare heels as she struggled under the crushing bed. Zane caught her ankles—and pulled.

Nurse Death slid from under the rubble of her bed, bare arms trailing behind her like a joy rider reaching for the sky on a rushing roller coaster. The bed scraped the white bra off her breasts. Zane sprawled flat on his back, clinging to her ankles by his ears, her white-pantied hips pressing on his loins as her hands cleared the bedding heap. She jackknifed to a sitting position and stabbed the pistol at the man beneath her.

I dove toward them from the bathroom.

Saw Zane's head rise off the floor between her ankles he trapped in his fists.

Saw the black automatic pistol stab toward Zane's white-maned face.

Saw her finger curl as Zane kicked her forearm, knocked her hand back. The pistol muzzle clunked her forehead as the gun roared and an explosion of blood splattered the tossed bed mountain.

My dive crashed me facedown on the two of them.

"Wow!" Russell's voice floated as I stared at the cheap carpet. "That was so weird! I've never done that before."

"Damn it!" said Zane. "Now we can't get any answers from her!"

"Hey, I'm a door kicker, rock 'n' roll guy," said Russell. "But this . . . Now . . ."

"Climb off, Victor."

I crawled off the dead woman. Off Zane. Turned to see Hailey appear in the kicked-open door and say: "Office sign reads GONE FOR DINNER, and it's true."

Russell sighed: "Gotta say I'm sorry, guys. Especially to you, Victor."

"Vic," said Zane, "look at this."

Zane sat on the motel room floor, the dead woman's legs splayed open and out to his sides, her hips cradled across his thighs like one of the *Kama Sutra* techniques I've never gotten to try. I focused where Zane pointed, toward the white cotton crescent of her pubis; blinked then saw what he wanted me to, a rash like dozens of pin pricks high on the inside of her left thigh.

"There's an answer," said Zane. "Mice."

Russell said: "I'm sorry, Vic. For what I did. *Spacing out.*"

"She was a '*C*' girl," said Zane.

"Spacing out is your thing, Vic," continued Russell. "Hailey's our mumbler . . ."

*MICE: M*oney. *I*deology. *C*ompromise. *E*go. The Four Horsemen of Espionage. The four categories of motivation that create spies or traitors.

"Zane here melts down in heat . . . ."

"She's probably a real nurse," said Zane. "A stressed-out medico who got hooked on dispensary stock and salesmen samples. She probably ran out of other skin to shoot. Somebody found out, somebody owned her. Somebody stocked her and schooled her, sent her on her way. Straight to us. To Dr. F."

"Eric is Mister Robot. . . ."

I shook my head: "She killed him, but she was a puppet on a string."

Nurse Death sprawled against the heap of bed. Zane got to his feet, picked up her pistol—a .380 Walther PPK like James Bond carried. She stared at me with five eyes.

The pushed-up bra revealed her brown nipples and they stared at me.

Her mascaraed lids drooped down over glassy green orbs and they stared at me.

A singed red star dotted the meditative center of her forehead and it stared at me.

"But me," continued Russell, "I'm Mr. Kick-ass Guy. Yet I froze. Kicked the door in cool, plenty of Op Time . . . Froze. When I saw her standing there. In the bathroom. What's up with that? What the hell do you think that means?"

"Things happen." I dumped a dresser drawer of Nurse Death's clothes, checked the drawer's bottom and back where nothing was taped.

"'Xactly," said Zane. "But don't screw up again. I wasn't born to die dumb."

"We're running hot." I dumped the next drawer. Hailey filled a bag from the closet with Nurse Death's cell phone, purse, all the paper. I threw Russell the motel room key from a different corpse. "Dr. F's room. Four minutes. Toss, Grab, and Go."

We met in the parking lot.

Hailey threw the bag with Nurse Death's litter in the car.

Russell tossed Zane a tan Burberry topcoat from Dr. F's room: "Your long arms will geek out of the sleeves, but a guy running around the last days of winter in only a shirt, pants, and sneakers billboards: *Call the cops on me!*"

He put a suitcase in the silver car's trunk. "Doc's laptop, address book, disks. He had under a hundred in cash stashed in a James Dalton novel about Watergate."

"Thanks for the coat," said Zane. "Smart thinking."

"Yeah, well, I'm still sorry about that weird freeze-up." Russell sidled closer to the white-maned Jesus. "So, *ah*, smart thinking says I should carry her gun."

"You froze."

"But that was back there and this is out here."

"No."

"Why not? *Victor!* Not fair. You won't let me drive, but okay, you were the last one locked up, you got the most recent road muscles, so I'm cool with that. But everybody knows I'm better with a pistol than any of you. Zane won't let me have it!"

Hailey rolled her eyes. "We gotta go."

Eric bobbed his head in agreement, his eyes full of her and the road.

I said: "Not yet."

Ten minutes later, the red neon MOTEL sign trembled in the rearview mirror of our road rumbling silver car. With the steering wheel vibrating in my grip, I watched that crimson sign disappear as we swooped around a night-black highway curve. The rearview mirror was full of dark. So far.

But by now, our Keepers had found our empty ward. The blue bus. The blanketed driver. Data confirming Dr. F was missing and implying that he was dead. They'd hit the red neon motel parking lot. Maybe they'd get there only after red-light spinning, siren-screaming State Troopers called by a hysterical retiree who thought running a motel in the great Maine Nowhere was his cushy ride to the big gone. Our hunters would find a kicked-in door. Nurse Death with her five eyes.

And Dr. F. Not lying on the floor. *Fuck that.* We left him on his feet in the red neon night. His belt cinched his waist to a t-pole of the motel's chain-link swimming pool fence. White tape from the Castle lashed his wrists to the chain links. Taped his arms out high and wide away from his body as if he were crucified. Crazy, *sure,* just like us, but we all told ourselves that it was also a perfect Psy War freakout to rattle our hunters as we roared away down the dark highway.

12

"LUCKY YOU GUYS got here in time," said the smiling salt-and-pepper–haired woman holding the steaming coffeepot and standing beside our table in the bright yellow light.

"We're lousy with luck," I told her.

We walked into the Hideout Diner after the dinner rush. Our stolen silver car hid out back of that lone shack along a two-lane highway. Wood paneling and sconce lights filled the diner with a homey feel. Only we five sat at the metal tables. A display case held cherry pie. The diner smelled like coffee and beef gravy.

Our waitress gave us menus. "Hate to rush you, but we need to start cleaning."

"We're in a hurry, too," I told her.

"So many choices," whispered Zane. The glow from the laminated menu pages reflected in his wide eyes. "Not just a line you stand in for the one thing they give you."

Our waitress smiled at Hailey: "You ought to take these guys out more, Hon."

"Don't I know it," answered Hailey.

We ordered five different dinners. With pie.

"It's okay," said Russell. "We got enough money."

"Nobody ever has enough money," I said. "Not when you're on the run."

"Money's not the only thing we don't have enough of," said Hailey.

"We've got a Walther PPK with one bullet in the pipe, two in the mag," I said. "We got eight hundred and forty-seven dollars, minus pie. A stolen rental car with half a tank of gas. Our GODS. Raw intel we scooped up from Nurse Death and Dr. F."

"And hellhounds on our trail," said Russell.

"One thing's for sure," said Zane. "I'm not going back."

Hailey said: "Somehow I don't think that's an option."

"Feels good, doesn't it?" said Russell. "To finally just go." Even Eric grinned.

"Yes," said Hailey. "But where?"

"And how?" said Russell.

"No alone." Eric trembled. "No alone."

"'Xactly. Nobody's leaving anybody. We already did that back at the Castle."

"I'll be with you as long as the plague lets me," said Hailey. Eric trembled. She forsook her honor and caution to gently touch his arm and his eyes misted.

"Hey, it's okay," Russell assured him. "We'll all be gunned down long before any sickness gets you. The Oppos are playing for keeps."

"Who are they?" asked Hailey. "Who is the opposition?"

"The Keepers who'll be freaked by losing us," I said. "Whoever contracted Dr. F's hit and framed us for the fall. Lawmen who got two murder corpses. The Agency whose number one rule is no mess gets stuck on them. *They* is whoever is out to get us."

Russell said: "You gotta be practical to make it as a paranoid."

"Who's Dr. F's ultimate killer?" asked Hailey.

"We're everyone else's answer to that question," I said. "We're on the run. That's enough to make us prey."

"So what are we going to do?" said Hailey.

"Fuck 'em," said Russell.

"We already did that," I said. "It's not enough. And it's not enough to just survive. We need to take back what got lost. What got done to us. And more."

Hailey said: "And get what?"

"A chance."

Zane said: "A chance for what?"

"Beats me. But I'm not going to go down like a chump just because they can play it that way. Besides, I'm still pissed about Dr. F."

"So let's get them," said Zane.

"If we do it right," I said, "we can nail the Doc's real killer. Find out who's the traitor spy in Team USA. Clear up Nurse Death. Buy ourselves a pass from Uncle Sam."

"Oh sure," said Russell. "That'll work."

Everybody laughed.

I asked: "What's our better choice?"

Zane nodded. "You need to do something more than save your own ass to justify running free in this world."

"Right," I said. "Nothing's worth much if all we are is drifters."

"What the hell," said Russell. "I'm hungry."

He held his right fist over our table.

Zane and I put our fists to his.

Hailey let her clenched hand touch ours, nodded to Eric whose fist made us five.

"Time is our one certain enemy," I said. "We're all off our meds. How long do we have until we just plain go off?"

Hailey shrugged. "Five patients, five different drug regimens. Hard to say. We won't go over the edge all at once, and we each have a different ticking clock."

"But the big clock," I said. "The countdown ticking toward when we decompensate so far we're worse off than a bum drooling on a park bench. How long do we have before we go down?"

Eric whispered: "Already missed dinner dose. Bedtime, too."

"I've seen guys like us skip their meds," said Zane, who'd been locked up longer than any of us. "Best guess is that we've got a week before we crack up."

"Seven days." Russell made his rock star face, sang: *"Time has come today!"*

That diner gave us our first taste of freedom. Real mashed potatoes and gravy and beef and dark meat turkey and fresh broccoli, hot coffee in tan mugs. Clear clean water. Zane ordered cold milk that was as white as his hair and beard.

Inspiration jelled between the main courses and pie. Hailey made the trip to our car with Zane covering her. She brought back a cell phone.

"You sure it's hers and not Doc's?" Russell held up his hands, backed off from Hailey's glare, alibied his insult with: "You only live once, so check twice."

She clicked the pen, moved plates aside to set a notebook on the table, and thumbed on the cell phone, hit Redial. Watched the LCD screen and wrote the *had-to-be-another-cell-phone-area-code* number it showed on the notebook: 772-555-4554.

The phone clicked in her ear.

"It's me," said Hailey.

"Why are you calling again?" said the man in the phone. "You reported success."

"We're broken," said Hailey to the man. "We need to meet."

"Don't panic! Do not come to D.C. Don't . . . My mother's house is blue."

Hailey licked her lips. Waited.

She'd bluffed him past the Recognition Code Sequence, and when he realized that, truly heard her voice, he fired the RCS at her, got nothing back . . .

Hung up.

Zane said: "Go!"

Hailey pushed 0.

"How can I help you?" said the woman operator,

"Remember when you were a teenager?" said Hailey.

"Excuse me, Ma'am, this is the Operator."

"This is the mother who let her fifteen-year-old daughter use her cell phone and now can't find her but knows that guy at the Mall Friday night looked more twenty-three than seventeen when I picked up Jenny and her friends, and now she's not downstairs doing her biology like she's supposed to and I'm scared to death that she's in trouble because all I've got is the number she called on my cell phone and it's answering 'Not in service.' "

"I can try that number for you if—"

"Won't help. I tried it five seconds ago. I need you to tell me this creep's name and everything else about him so I can . . ."

"I'm sorry, Ma'am, that's against company policy."

"So Jenny getting her whole life run over *is* company policy?"

"I could lose my job."

"Were you ever fifteen and knew everything?"

We waited. Waited. Russell's fork hovered with a bite of cherry pie.

Hailey's brow wrinkled as she strained to hear a whispered: *"Kyle Russo."*

"Please be right!" said Hailey. "Jenny told her friend he lived on a street called—"

"Thank you for using Tower Cell Service," said the Operator.

For the second time that night, Hailey got hung up on.

"There is no Kyle Russo," guessed Zane as Hailey turned off the phone.

"Yeah," I said, "but there is a D.C. like our Killer mentioned, Washington, D.C."

"How long until we get there?" asked Hailey.

I shrugged. "On paper, we could make it in twelve, fourteen hours."

"We ain't on that paper," said Russell.

"Seven days to get somewhere and do whatever it is we've got to do," said Zane.

"More swell news," said Russell. "Whoever's hunting us knows we're too street smart to run north, hit the Canadian border that's been beefed-up with Homeland Security."

"We could bust that," said Zane.

"Yeah," said Russell, "but we're too smart to work that hard when we've got to keep running. And way up here, the best direction to run is south, toward D.C. Even if they don't know where we want to be, they know which way we're going."

"So let's get gone," I said, car keys in my hand.

Twenty minutes from the diner, our stolen car rumbled over a two-lane highway's low wooden bridge spanning an ice-skimmed river, rounded a curve—

Red lights spun in the night a mile beyond our windshield: *Cops.*

13

"ROADBLOCK!" I YELLED, killing our headlights, steering the car by moonlight, shifting to neutral and pulling on the emergency parking brake so our taillights wouldn't flash. Gravel crunched under our tires. We sat lightless on the side of the road. The silver car smelled of burned brake pads and fear.

Spinning red cop lights stayed on our night horizon.

"Could be an accident," said Zane, but even he didn't believe that.

"Can't be for us!" said Hailey. "No matter how much the Agency wants to catch us, the CIA's mantra is Never Say Nothing. They wouldn't tell the cops!"

"The Firm wouldn't tell the cops the truth," I said. "Not the whole truth. But they probably haven't had time to nail a full lid on us. That roadblock—Hailey's right, those cops aren't after us. They're looking for this stolen car tied to two murders."

"License plate was probably on file at the motel," said Hailey. "I should have . . ."

"Can't go back," whispered Eric.

"We can bullshit our way through," said Russell.

"We're in a stolen car with its original plates and no driver's licenses," I said. "Those are the first things roadblock cops will check, hard facts no bullshit can hide."

"We can ditch the car, hike around the roadblock," said Zane.

"Wandering won't work," said Eric. "Forest. Swamps. Cold."

"Cold works for me," said Zane.

"We need a dead man's car," said Russell. "No stolen car report."

"We've got what we got," I said.

Zane said: "Anybody got an idea?"

We sat on the side of the road in the dark car, knowing that each second we did nothing increased the odds of us losing everything.

Then I said: "James Dean."

"Fuck you!" said Russell. "Don't make us part of your suicide!"

"It'll work."

"In theory!" argued Russell. "Hell, they don't let trainees play James Dean now! Too risky to learn outside of 'in theory.' "

"I practiced it once."

"And?" said Russell.

"Now I'll do better."

"James Dean is—"

"All we've got."

14

HEADLIGHTS OFF, THE stolen silver Ford idled on the road to the bridge. My hands gripped the steering wheel. I was alone. Frigid air flowed in the open windows. The night outside smelled of pines and river ice and highway.

Half an hour since we first spotted the spinning red lights of the police roadblock.

Now or never.

Headlights on. I shifted into forward gear. Let the gray road's yellow stripes reel the car ever closer, ever faster. The car tires rumbled over the wooden bridge. Guardrail planks flowed past my windows. Shapes on the side of the road flicked past in my headlights as I tried to memorize, calculate, gauge. The car slid into the curve that came before we'd seen the roadblock's flashing red light.

I stomped on the gas pedal. Sped out of the curve. Red lights spun ever closer in my windshield. I flicked my head-lights to the high and hopefully blinding beam an instant be-fore a spotlight winked on from the three cop cars blocking the road. I stomped on the brake pedal. Tires cried. Metal shuddered. Red lights loomed closer, coming closer. The spotlight grew bright.

Crank the steering wheel! Jerk on the emergency brake! The silver car skidded—

Stayed on the road as it whipped into a 180 bootlegger turn, slid backward as I shoved off the emergency brake, stomped on the gas and raced back the way I'd come, hoping that the triggered cops couldn't tell it was *just me* in the flee-ing silver machine.

Sirens cut the night. Wind rushed in the open windows as the road sped under my tires. My eyes flicked to the rearview mirror: spinning red lights chased my wake.

Forget about them! Concentrate. Calculate. Wait . . . Wait . . .

The road curved. My foot jumped off the gas pedal. My hand pulled on the emergency brake so the cops couldn't see I was de-accelerating. Brakes howled. Cops wouldn't hear that over their own sirens. Rushing toward me came the nar-row slot of the guardrailed bridge as my car shuddered down from seventy to sixty-five, sixty . . . fifty-five . . .

Too fast! Going too fast!

Bumpty-bump went the bridge under my wheels. *Can't wait!*

My left hand jerked the door handle door beside me. Wind pressure from my race pushed against that steel slab. The silver car's warning buzzers kicked on to join the wail of nearing sirens, the woosh of night air, tires bumping over the bridge.

And I whipped the wheel to the right. My windshield filled with the headlight vision of the bridge's wooden guardrails hurtling toward me.

My left shoulder rammed the unlatched door.

But I didn't have enough force to knock the door open, let

me roll out free and safe like James Dean had in the chicken game of *Rebel Without a Cause.*

The silver car blasted through wooden plank guardrails and flew through the air above the ice skimmed river. Boards splintered out from the impact. The rental Ford's airbag mushroomed out of the steering wheel. I was already pressing against the unlatched door: the exploding white air bag shoved me out of the car.

Time stopped. Sound stopped. My life became something I watched in a movie. *Oh, look:* there I am, floating through the night above a river silvered with a sheen of ice. My arms and legs flail like useless wings. Plummeting ahead of me is a dented silver car. Busted boards flutter near me like confetti. Up there, in front of my face, falling farther and farther away stretches a bridge with a gap blasted in its guardrails. Tendrils of red lights flick across the dark sky.

A crashing ton of metal car shattered the river's sheen. I gulped a frantic breath as a wall of liquid swallowed me into a brutal dark swirl.

Every inch of my skin screamed in pain from the burn of the cold river. I forced my eyes open. Saw blackness. I tumbled in dark water and felt it soak my clothes to pull me down, keep me down.

Easy, so easy to just let air out and suck in death.

But something in the deep fought me to the surface. I popped up under the bridge. A white-haired, white-bearded giant pulled me to the shore through the frigid water. Sirens screamed closer. Cop cars skidded to a halt on the bridge, their headlights revealing the hole punched in the ice by the fugitive car that sped out of control. Car doors opened and slammed. Cops rushed to the busted guardrail and shone flashlights to the river below. Zane muscled me through the brush, through trees to the family Jeep that minutes before, we'd hot-wired away from a country house where everyone seemed asleep and thus for hours wouldn't report their vehicle as missing, presumed stolen.

My crew stripped me naked. Wiped me down with our spare clothes as fast as they could, Zane stripping and drying off, too. They stretched me out in the Jeep's folded-down-rear-seat cargo bay. Naked Zane piled in beside me. Eric and Hailey surrounded us with their clad bodies, pulled a scavenged canvas dropcloth over our prone huddle and the scent of old paint told me I was still truly alive.

Russell drove the Jeep onto the bridge where cops shone flashlights on the icy water below. He slowed the Jeep to a crawl. A quick glance showed a flashlight-waving cop only one man in the vehicle as Russell leaned out the driver's window and yelled: "Hey, officer! What's going on? You need help?"

"Keep moving!" answered the state trooper, who like his partners had broken their roadblock to chase the suspicious silver car that had veered out of control and smashed through the bridge railings. As our classic Decoy and Divert tactic planned, the black hole in the river's ice claimed all the troopers' attention. "Clear the area!"

Russell obeyed. Sped the Jeep gone into darkness.

Naked under the paint-stained canvas, I couldn't stop shivering.

"You'll be okay," said Hailey as she held me. "I don't have any open sores."

Eric said: "Zane, you okay?"

Zane told us: "Sure. Cold works for me."

15

ZANE FELL FROM sanity through the cold stars of Halloween, 1968.

Trick or treat, he thought before his fall as he rode in the B-52 bomber refitted from its globe-busting role in the *Dr. Strangelove* movie that Zane had sneaked out of the orphanage to see. Now only stadium-busting "conventional" bombs hung in racks below the vibrating ledge he sat on as the warplane flew over North Vietnam.

He turned his fishbowl helmet to see the five pressure-suited men on his team.

Intercom static crackled as Jodrey's voice said: "You and your crazy ideas."

Zane crackled back: "Better a crazy idea than no idea."

Like he always did, Jodrey said: " 'Xactly."

Zane was a Wyoming orphan raised by penguin nuns to fear the fires of Hell, carry the weight of his sins, and never, no never, cry. He turned twenty-one while getting shelled at Da Nang. Inspiration seized him from the blue sky outside a Studies and Observations Group/spy unit Quonset hut in Da Nang, but he barely got the commanders with ice eyes and Hawaiian shirts to listen because: "He's just a kid."

Then Sergeant Major Jodrey said: "Out of the mouths of babes."

"It's a great idea!" Zane had argued to officers who shared his Army Green Beret as men in Hawaiian shirts watched.

"Washington sent us to Vietnam to fight the good fight," said Zane. "Right?"

No one answered the young man.

So Zane figured they were on the same page as him. Enthusiasm bubbled through his logic. "So let's fight it smart. The North Vietnamese have miles of phone lines through the trees along the Ho Chi Minh trail in Laos. What if instead of bombing or cutting those phone lines, we tap into them?"

Zane's spy idea infected the Quonset hut. Compounded itself when the pocket protector whiz from NSA told them about new toys. Spread its wings after Sergeant Major Jodrey told the bosses that if the plan was a *go,* so was he.

If.

"That's the life word," Sergeant Major Jodrey told Zane during a stroll inside the barbed-wire/claymore mined perimeter of Da Nang where they couldn't be heard by the brass and spooks who would say Go or No.

"But it's your word to call, isn't it Sergeant Major?" said the younger soldier.

" 'Xactly," said Jodrey. "That's my word: *Exactly.* What a thing is down to its bones, Troop. That's what I need to know about you."

Helicopters chopped the muggy sunset air above them and made it bleed.

"I do what has to be done," said Zane. "And I'm tough enough to take it."

Marines jogged past them. Zane felt himself fall into Sergeant Major Jodrey's gaze.

"'Xactly right," said Jodrey. "But not completely true."

"Sergeant Major, I would never lie to you."

"You didn't lie, young'n. You just don't know the whole truth."

"What whole truth?"

"The whole truth is everything you shovel into this hole called your life. And one thing you better shovel is that a man needs to be more than what he has to do."

Jodrey walked away.

Zane ran after him. Didn't ask and didn't care *where*.

Four weeks of training in Okinawa later, Zane, Jodrey and four Hmong volunteers stood waiting to be strapped in amid coffin-size bombs in the belly of a B-52.

"Last thing I gotta know," Jodrey told Zane: "How come you're still a virgin?"

"Wha-what?"

"You heard me. A virgin."

"I was raised strict Catholic."

"Yeah, but you got over it. We're talking now. How come you ain't got laid?"

A fighter plane took off to air cover Marines out of the shit in a jungle firefight.

As that jet whine faded, Zane said: "If we're more than animals, sex can be special. That's what I got to be. Want it to be."

Before he pulled on the two Halloween thermal stocking-cap–like hoods and the visored helmet fitted with a breathing apparatus, Jodrey shook his head at Zane:

"Special is what gets done special. When we get back, you need to talk with a nurse who reminds me of my second ex-wife. But here and now, you being a virgin is your *mojo*. And your *mojo* is 'xactly what's going to bring you home alive and true."

Now here I sit, thought Zane as B-52 engines droned. With somebody who sees 'xactly who I am. And with four stone soldiers who'd follow us into Hell.

Being this heavily dressed on the ground would make him feel as hot as Hell. Two layers of thermal underwear and socks under Russian army paratrooper boots. Triple gloves. Double hoods and jungle fatigues under a winter jump suit that's zipped to the fishbowl helmet. Canvas bags strapped on Zane's team held an NSA tap/transmit system. Strapped to each man's chest was a brand-new thing called a Global Positioning Scanner programmed to guide them to where the CIA predicted jungle phone lines. Canvas bags held five days' rations, one canteen, water purification tablets, two antipersonnel grenades, a purple smoke grenade, a folding stock Russian AK 47 assault rifle, and three mags of ammo.

Only Jodrey and Zane carried special fourteen-shot nine-millimeter automatics with silencers.

Only they carried the paperback book–size Flash Code Transponders that were the new delight of the CIA. Pushing keys on the FCTs created a text message the FCT "remembered" with something called a chip. When you pushed Transmit, your message zapped up to a satellite, then back down to CIA headquarters and Da Nang.

Steel groaned and whined. Wind rushed in through the bomb bay doors swinging open beneath the racks of coffin-size cylinders below Zane's dangling feet.

Zane's stomach fell as the B-52 jumped starward with its release of explosive tonnage. By the time the plane stabilized and Zane looked down at the black sky flowing below his boots, the bombs were halfway to explosions ten miles behind the plane.

We'll never even see them flash. Hear the boom. Trick or treat.

Bomb bay doors clunked shut.

Intercom crackle filled Zane's ears: "This is the pilot. Be advised turbulence and wind shifts require altering course. We factor a twenty-minute delay."

Ride it out. Something always goes wrong. We're lucky it's only time. *Mojo.*

Blue lights snapped on.

Zane's team switched from the plane's air to their own oxygen tanks.

Yellow lights snapped on.

The team unbuckled themselves from the bomb bay shelf. Huddled as close together as they could in a line on top of the juncture for the swing-open bomb bay doors.

Red lights flashed like a sprinter's heartbeat.

Zane, Jodrey, and the four Hmongs all closed their eyes.

Bomb bay doors swung open. Six men plummeted from the belly of a B-52 in Zane's inspiration: history's first bombing run/HALO intel combat insertion.

HALO: *H*igh *A*ltitude, *L*ow *O*pening.

Eight miles high and gliding like eagles. Zane and his team spotted their helmet beacons flashing in the dark sky and surfed their bodies closer together. Followed their pop-up GPS screens toward the drop zone, gliding down, covering twenty horizontal miles in their long starry-night descent that weather made thirty minutes late so they popped their parachutes in the mist of near-dawn.

An emerald sea of jungle canopy rushed up toward Zane's pressed-together boots. Leaves, branches, vines slammed him as he crashed through them. Birds screamed. Tree branches grabbed his parachute canopy. He bounced like a yo-yo until his boots dangled fifty feet off the ground that he could see through a dappled netting of leaves.

Hung up! I'm hanging in a tree!

Through the leaves that screened him, Zane saw the ground, saw another parachutist who'd landed in a clearing, saw him bundling his black chute.

Zane pushed off his fishbowl helmet, tore off the two hoods that helped keep him from freezing to death during the freefall through minus forty degrees high altitude night sky. His teeth and fingers ripped off his outer right glove as the steam heat in the jungle treetops grew cooler than the heat trapped inside his jumpsuit. *Hot like Hell.*

Zane licked his lips to call to the Hmong paratrooper on the ground.

Machine-gun fire ripped the Hmong's black costume to red shreds and he fell.

A second machine gun chattered somewhere far off in the jungle below. Screams.

Zane dangled fifty feet above the ground. Made himself go still, silent. He swayed like a pendulum. The soles of his boots brushed a lacework of leaves.

A tiny figure wearing black pajamas and a conical peasant straw hat glided over the jungle floor to prod the dead Hmong with the barrel of a machine gun.

Still! Zane ordered himself. *Stay absolutely still.* His boots brushed the screen of leaves. Sweat rivulets trickling down his cheek obeyed gravity. Fell off him like kamikaze drops. Hit the black pajamaed machine-gunner.

A monkey screamed.

Black Pajama whirled, machine gun scanning the walls of jungle.

Wild orchids opened to scent the dawn.

An NVA Captain joined Black Pajamas. The NVA Captain barked orders and Black Pajamas passed him gear stripped off the dead Hmong.

Zane swayed in the trees above that jungle's execution ground.

Three Hmongs stumbled into the clearing, hands clasped behind their necks. Five new NVA soldiers and two guerrilla warriors kept guns trained on their prisoners, dropped the Hmong's gear in a heap at the Captain's boots.

Black Pajamas removed the conical peasant hat.

Pathet Lao guerrilla, thought Zane, *under NVA command.*

Woman, he realized as he saw black hair tumble to her shoulders.

Pretty, was the truth.

Hot, so damn hot baking in this flight suit and dangling from a tree . . .

Can't risk unzipping the belly bag. Not just the noise. If my gear has shifted, if something falls out before I can swing out the AK-47, chamber it, and start firing, they'll look up—*shoot* up, even if they don't have a clear view of me through the leaves. But—

Snake slipped down a silky tangle of vines to land *plop!* on Zane's head.

Don't scream!

Don't move.

Don't blink.

Don't breathe, but sweat's pumping out in gallons, *hot so hot,* as a rope uncoils on Zane's head, as it slides down his face, as that three-foot-long jungle strand arcs out in front of Zane's *Don't blink* eyes and meet Zane's gaze with its own beady black orbs.

Don't. Move.

Viper. Maybe it's a *Ten-step,* for how many you can take after it bites you. Maybe it's an *Eyelash,* because it likes to hang head-down from the trees at just that level, bites you *dead* right there, right where the snake now flicked its black tongue.

The serpent spiraled down the peculiar monkey hanging in a tree. The snake looped its tail around a left boot while stretching its head straight out, seeking—

Zane kicked his boot and flicked the snake off him.

Mojo, keep your *mojo* working.

In the clearing below where he swayed, soldiers were tying the Hmongs' hands.

Time! Got no time! Can't get to my AK-47 but shoulder holster, fourteen silenced shots and at the first dropped guard, the Hmongs will—

Jodrey flew into the clearing and crashed, stripped naked, at the captain's boots.

The dozen NVA soldiers who threw him there laughed.

The captain booted Jodrey to a kneeling position and—in English—yelled the question that changed the universe: "Why were you late?"

Jodrey told the captain: "I had to fuck your mother."

The captain slapped the kneeling naked prisoner.

"Where's the other one of you? Other American?" the captain yelled at Jodrey.

Who said: "You got a sister?"

Zane froze as the captain's boot arced toward Jodrey's face: *Change plan. Escape now not the priority.*

Zane's hand slid to the pouch around his neck carrying his FCT communicator.

Jodrey caught the captain's boot midkick, upended the officer, dove on top of him, and swung a skull-smashing rock high above the captain's head.

Miss Black Pajamas shot the foolish American.

Hanging in a tree, Zane watched Jodrey die.

Don't give a damn now, thought Zane. *It's only me dangling in Hell's tree. Hmongs won't make it out of this clearing. They're worth nothing to the enemy.*

Slowly, painstakingly, Zane pushed the FCT keys to build a one word/eight letters message in that thing called a chip.

The captain barked orders and sent his patrol of had-to-be-forty soldiers out in a wide search pattern for the missing American spy from the sky.

Zane was on letter seven of his first FCT message when his parachute ripped.

Not a loud rip. Not a long one. *Hot, so hot. Baking in the jumpsuit.* Zane knew it was only a matter of time before his chute ripped all the way and he crashed to the jungle floor. He finished the eighth letter of the key message and pushed Transmit.

Rrrr-rip . . .

Easy! Don't jerk. Ten more letters. Two words.

Smell cigarette smoke. Zane flicked his eyes down as he one-handed keyed buttons. The captain was smoking. Miss Black Pajamas watched with disdain.

Letter nine—done. Letter ten—

Rrr-rip . . .

—done. Thumb's on the Transmit button . . .

The chute tore with a loud rip as Zane pushed the Transmit button. He dropped straight down until the chute cords caught and swung him like a pendulum smack into the tree. Inertia flung the FCT transponder from Zane's sweat-slick hand.

Every inch of Zane hurt from being slammed into the tree. He burned in fire.

Ignore that. Time. Need time. Did the messages go through?

Miss Black Pajamas machine-gunned the tangle of parachute cords above Zane's head until they parted and he crashed/slid the last twenty feet to the jungle floor.

But he had some *mojo* left: they cut off all his clothes,

freed him from the most suffocating heat. They poured water over his head. Gave him one drink. Yelled questions. Slapped him. Gave him another drink. The clearing floated into focus. Three Hmongs, hands bound behind them. The oldest sent him a smile.

The captain leaned close, and in English said: "Why are you in our jungle?"

Zane said: "Tourist."

Soldiers jerked him to his feet. Chopped a shovel into the dirt beside his bare toes.

"Dig a deep hole for your friends," ordered the captain.

Already have, thought Zane.

"One question you will answer," said the captain as naked Zane shoveled jungle muck out of the pit that was now as deep as his knees and longer than he was tall. "Will you stay in this pit for the rest of forever?"

Yes, he knew, but said nothing.

Guerrilla-dressed Miss Black Pajamas had an oval face with butterfly lips. A woman had cut him down from Hell's tree to put him in his grave. Zane froze as she used her machine-gun muzzle to push his naked penis first to the left, than to the right. She withdrew her gun. Yawned.

"Dig," said the captain.

When the pit was hip deep, they dragged over Jodrey's body.

"Do you want to join him?" asked the captain.

Then he put his pistol to the head of the nearest Hmong and blasted crimson gore on the emerald jungle.

Urine rolled uncontrollably out of Zane's virgin penis.

"So much for those who are useless," said the captain.

"Can I bargain for their lives?" said Zane. *Make time!*

Zane knew the captain lied when he said yes. The captain asked about the radio frequencies for Special Forces A-camps. Truth was, Zane didn't know. He would have lied if he had. The truth was what he told the captain. Who shot another Hmong.

"Now you must dig deeper."

So he did.

"Only one left. Who do your counterintelligence people suspect in Hue?"

Know that, can't tell them, don't say anything, time buy— *Bang!*

"Now there's just you," said the captain standing by the heap of dead bodies.

Now it's all just drama, Zane believed as he dug. Honest, I'm too valuable to kill.

Birds rocketed out of the trees.

Because he knew, Zane had a heartbeat to dive in the grave.

God's fist hit the jungle floor. That impact bounced Zane in his hole. Bomb blasts tore apart trees and birds and monkeys and snakes and people and hurricaned a greenish-red mush. Threw logs over the ditch, a roof that absorbed a hail of skin-ripping debris. Only six bombs fell, one stick horded from an already planned run diverted to answer Zane's second, two-word FCT message, but they were 1,000-pound bombs and one stick was enough to grant his plea:

ARCLIGHT ME

Arclight: 'Nam speak for a B-52 strike. Called in by a soldier on top of himself and his FCT homing signal. A last stand tactic to wipe out the enemy's gain—in this case, one that included captured Top Secret spy gear. The times in Vietnam that a soldier dove on a grenade to save his buddies or called in lethal ordnance on top of himself in a defiant last stand merited the awarding of the Congressional Medal of Honor.

This time that medal had to stay secret because of Zane's first message:

BETRAYED

How else would the captain have known that the insertion team was *late?*

Four days after Zane's Arclight, thirty Shan State mercenaries picked their way through a shredded soccer stadium of Laotian jungle. Mist floated in the snapped-off trees. They found a white orchid blooming in a patch of squishy cloth.

Back in the mountains of Burma, they grew poppies. But their American friends had a briefcase full of greenbacks to trade for a hand-size box they said was still beeping to their satellite. So the mercenaries took the tracking device the Hawaiian-shirted man gave them, slid through this jungle. They found the stubborn transistor radio–thing between two rocks. Ants swarmed over it. They congratulated each other, turned to walk home.

Almost shot him when he popped up in a trench like a naked jack-in-the-box toy.

And screamed in American: *"Mojo!"*

He was covered with leeches, sunburned and blistered. His lips were cracked and had barely been able to slurp pools of groundwater filled with parasites. But what was the most startling about the zombie who leapt from the grave was how his growing-out hair and beard had turned absolutely stark white.

They dragged the zombie out of the pit. Poured water on his face and in his mouth. Bomb blasts had scrambled his electronic insides. He babbled. When he took a step with his left foot, his right hand flipped up like a broken wing.

So they hung him from a pole. The mercenaries carried samples of their cash crop product. They sprinkled their white powder in his wounds to stop his gibberish by stopping the pain. The zombie swung from that coolie pole for five jungle-tramping days. The Hawaiian-shirted man gave the mercenaries a $50,000 bonus for him.

Eight years later, in the psych ward at Bethesda (Maryland) Naval Hospital, Zane's bomb- and trauma- and heroin-shocked neural pathways had rewired enough so that when he looked out from his wheelchair at the night sky's purple-and-red starbursts of fireworks exploding over Washington, D.C.'s Mall for America's Bicenntenial bash, a nurse heard him mumble a coherent thought: "Pretty."

Two years later, he could walk and talk, feed and bathe himself. But he rocketed awake every night. By his thirty-second birthday, he'd regained enough willpower to refuse to cut his snow white hair, saying: "I earned it."

When Zane was thirty-three and President Jimmy Carter

halted U.S. grain sales to the Soviet Union because they'd invaded Afghanistan and ex-Beatle John Lennon was assassinated by a creep obsessed with *Catcher in the Rye,* military doctors ruled Zane functional but fucked-up, physically fine but oh-so-crazy. Plus his white hair and beard spooked the staff and other patients. The staff strapped him on a stretcher, lashed on an Army paratrooper briefcase full of his medical records and his Congressional Medal of Honor, rolled the stretcher into an Army hearse, and transported Zane to a new Top Secret facility in Maine.

Zane pioneered Ward C. Lost to nightmares most nights. Went violently batshit when he got overheated and the temperature reminded him of hanging in a tree in Hell. But he carried the weight of all that had happened to him and he never, no never, cried.

Oh, and he couldn't have sex.

Couldn't sneak advantages when he was forty from a harshly divorced nurse who wore musk perfume, kept *innocently* touching him.

Couldn't follow up on what he inevitably initially felt for Hailey after she showed up. Not that she'd have let him . . . follow up, but if she could have in good conscience bestowed that mercy, she would have.

Couldn't even masturbate.

Everything Zane or the shrinks tried . . . failed to function.

Russell claimed it was madman's *mojo.*

And Zane said: " 'Xactly."

16

THE WRECK ON the highway caught us thirty-nine minutes after we James Dean–ed the roadblock at the Reiss river bridge.

Russell piloted our stolen Jeep. Hailey sat beside him, Zane and Eric shared the backseat. I huddled in the rear cargo compartment, clutched the painter's tarp around me. I wore my GODS's ski underwear top, boxer shorts, and socks. Chills shook me even though I was perched in the path of the warm breeze streaming from the heater.

"You look like an old gypsy lady in a shawl," Russell said as his eyes met mine in the rearview mirror.

He shifted his gaze to the backseat Buddha reflection of Zane, who wore only a faded Army shirt and dry underpants. Cold worked for him. The river had tangled his long white hair and beard. Russell told him: "You look like some kind of pervert."

"Keep your eyes on the road," said Zane.

"Chill," said Russell. "We're doing great."

We'd avoided interstate toll thoroughfares, fled south on back roads like this two-lane late night deserted state highway through rolling hills and scruffy woods.

Russell checked his watch: "The troopers on the bridge are thirty-seven minutes behind us. They're still trying to figure out what happened."

Yellow light lanced our Jeep's back window.

"Duck down!" yelled Russell and I did, knew Zane and (of course) Eric did, too.

The yellow light dialed up ever brighter until the Jeep's passenger compartment glowed with a surreal intensity.

"Shit!" I heard Russell yell to a rumble racing toward our rear bumper. "Back off, man! Slow the fuck—"

A blast of wind hit our Jeep. Our vehicle buffeted to the right from that impact, then got sucked to the left by the slipstream of the eighteen-wheeler semitruck rocketing past us. My stomach churned. Russell fought to keep our fishtailing Jeep between the white lines. Through our windshield, I saw the truck's trailer box whipping from side to side like a furious dragon as its teamster steered from *passing* back into the right lane he claimed as his sole property. Taillights on the truck disappeared over a hill.

"Somebody else needs meds," said Zane.

Russell sped up. "Fuck him! Nobody gets away with almost killing us!"

"Let it go!" I said. "We can't afford more trouble!"

We surged over the hill—

"Look out!" Hailey braced herself against the dashboard. Russell stomped on the brakes.

Our Jeep wheels locked. We skidded, fishtailing again, but again Russell kept us between the white lines and our Jeep—

Slid to a stop in the middle of the highway.

Our high beams filtered an eerie blue glow over that night scene. The wreckage of a family minivan blocked the road ahead of us. The minivan lay on its driver's side. Steam hissed from the van's mangled hood and as we watched, one tire spun to a stop.

"Oh my God," whispered Hailey.

Zane and I pulled on shoes. Neither of us slipped into our soaked pants. We all jumped out to the road. Beads of glass crunched under our feet.

"He blew them off the road," whispered Russell.

Can't stop! Killers are chasing us! I thought. I said. "Gotta do it!"

We ran to the wreck.

"Gas!" yelled Hailey. "I smell gas!"

Safety glass in the van's windshield had splintered into an opaque mosaic.

Eric yelled: "Fuel tank rupture!"

Russell and I climbed onto the upturned side of the van. The glass in that front door's window was gone. A deflated air bag filled the empty front passenger seat.

A woman slumped against the driver's door that was now the bottom of her van. The air bag from the steering wheel draped her lap. Blood flowed from her nose. She moaned. Her right hand twitched, so that seemed to rule out spinal cord injury, her left arm lay in an unnatural zigzag.

I jerked on the passenger door: frozen shut. Russell and I stood on the passenger door, muscled the sliding side door: it refused to budge.

"Frame's bent!" said Russell. "Lost control and flipped it. Tumbled and rolled."

"I'm going in!"

Russell helped ease me through the punched-out passenger door window.

Eric yelled: "Yes, Zane! Use that chunk of bumper to dig

your canal for the gas! Hailey, grab those pieces of metal, dam it that way!"

Russell lowered me into the cramped and topsy-turvy passenger compartment. My feet brushed the driver's head. My shoes found a hard surface. I bent my whole body into the car, my head dropping below the window I'd come through, my bare legs tingling from a myriad of cuts. As I wedged myself lower to reach the moaning driver, the bluish glow cast by our Jeep's headlights revealed them:

The baby boy snug in his car seat behind his mother, a pacifier still somehow sucked tight in his mouth, his wide-open eyes the size of his tiny fists.

The toddler girl, call her six years old, proud to ride in the backseat where she wore the seat belt and the shoulder strap that in the wondrous ways of childhood and car wrecks was now cinched tight around her neck.

"Knife!" I yelled.

The girl's face turning blue in that cramped topsy-turvy car told me that even if one of us would have had a knife, I had no time to get it and cut the strap.

I pulled on the shoulder strap to loosen it: locked at that extension, tight so the girl wouldn't fly out of her seat, so tight I couldn't get the clasp to release, so tight that she was dying from gradual strangulation.

Unless.

If I was wrong, at least she'd die quick.

Like a killer, I pulled the strap tighter around her neck.

She thrashed, gurgled, her arms—

The safety rollers released their lock on the strap and it slid loose with my reversed pull, just like it was designed to do.

The girl gasped, wheezed. She fell into my arms like a heavy rag doll. I passed her up through the window to Russell.

An intercom voice filled the van: *"This is Janet with On-Board Wireless Services System. Our indicators show that your air bags have deployed. Is everything all right?"*

Twisting my head down and to the right let me see a red bulb glowing on the box built into the van roof by the rearview mirror.

"Is anyone in the vehicle?"

"Come on!" I frantically battled the release on the baby's car seat.

The baby boy waved his arms with my efforts and never dropped his pacifier.

"Hello? Is everything OK?"

The car seat release popped open.

"Our protocols assume your vehicle has been in an accident. If you can, please try to push the Transmit button. Please!"

Hailey yelled: "I can't stop gas trickling under the car toward the hot engine!"

Pacifier and all, I passed the baby up to Russell.

"Please remain calm. Your Global Positioning System has given us your location. The state police are on their way."

Russell yelled: "We gotta get out of here!"

Hailey yelled: "The gas is gonna hit the hot engine!"

"One more to go!" I yelled.

But no matter how I twisted like a contortionist in that cramped jumble of van seats and dashboard, I couldn't reach the mother's seat belt clasp and lift her free.

"State police say they are approximately three minutes away. You're almost safe."

Hailey yelled: "Hurry!"

Exhaling let me brace my hands against the van seats and ram my underwear-clad butt against the safety glass mosaic windshield. Once, twice, third time cracking it free from the frame, fourth time knocking it out, gaining space to bend over, free the mother and pull her out of the van, drag her far away and lay her beside her kids.

The little girl stared up at me and with a hoarse voice said: "Are you angels?"

"No."

And I ran away. Left the family laying on the side of the road. Russell used our Jeep's four-wheel drive to navigate around the wreck, race us down the dark highway.

A candle burst of orange flame flashed in our rearview mirrors.

Red emergency lights flickered over the horizon beyond our windshield.

Russell killed our headlights as he whipped the Jeep off the highway. Rough terrain bounced us like dice shaking in a cup, but we managed a stop in the trees that was neither a collision nor a quagmire.

Red lights whirled on two police cars that rushed past our improvised exit.

Russell waited until they were red dots by the distant flickering candle, kept our lights out as he gingerly navigated our way back to the highway. We drove away using the not-yet-full moon to light the road until our mirrors held no spinning red lights or burning candles, then on came our headlights and our Jeep roared forward.

"Least we know there can't be many cops left in front of us," said Eric.

"What about that damn trucker?" said Russell.

I shook my head. "Some people get away with murder."

"Don't tell us that," said Hailey. "Not that. Not now."

We rode through a cluster of roadside houses too small to be a town. Saw no one in the homes' dark windows, were certain that no one saw us.

"That kid back there," Zane told me. "She thought you were an angel. Thought you were already dead."

All I could say was: "Out of the mouths of babes."

17

CALL MY FIRST suicide an homage to James Vincent Forrestal.

The unforgettable Forrestal.

Dartmouth. Princeton. Wall Street bonds whiz. One of FDR's White House West Wing bright boys. Undersecretary of the Navy. Made history after World War II as America's first Secretary of Defense. President Truman pinned America's highest official civilian honor, the Distinguished Service Medal, on Forrestal's business suit.

Forrestal went crazy on the job. Got paranoid about what "they" were scheming. The Soviets who'd stolen our atom bomb secrets and were terrorizing our American way of life. Pentagon power players who kept knifing his plans for battling the Red Menace. The "high-placed congressional sources" who kept whispering: *Forrestal cares more about oil and Arabs than he does about the fate of the Jews and Israel."*

In 1949, he checked into Bethesda Naval Hospital—the medical factory that decades later housed Zane. At 2 A.M., on a Sunday in May, pajama-clad Forrestal stopped hand-copying a Sophocles poem praising death after writing the fragment "night" from "nightingale," tiptoed from his secured-window room to an unguarded kitchen, took a screen off a window . . . and jumped outside, sky diving thirteen stories into the great darkness.

America bestowed his name on a government building and an aircraft carrier.

Not all big shots who melt down are famous. Few people can name the cabinet official from the Ford administration who hit the fence. President Gerry Ford, who loved cottage cheese with ketchup, took over the presidency after oh-so-sane Dick Nixon skipped town ahead of the law in a Marine helicopter. A Ford cabinet prince lost it one Friday afternoon when a newspaper shark caught scent of blood the prince had shed sheltering a friend from America's Watergate posse. While Zane was locked in Bethesda Naval Hospital and car radios played Bruce Springsteen's "Born to Run," the cabinet prince drifted to the White House black pole iron fence, begged perplexed Secret Service guards to let him in so he could get the hell out of Dodge. His resignation was accepted.

No building or aircraft carrier bears his name.

Then, years before my first suicide, along came Vincent W. Foster.

July 20, 1993. Vincent Foster ate lunch at his White House desk. He had a cheeseburger, French fries, a Coke, and M&M candies. Told staff members: "I'll be back." He drove his car to Fort Marcy Park in nearby Virginia, turned off his pager, sat on the grass near a Civil War memorial cannon, and shot himself in the head.

Officially (after $30 million dollars' worth of investigations), Foster killed himself because of despondency over his failures to protect his friends President William Clinton and future Senator Mrs. Hillary Clinton from the sharks of Washington, D.C., where, Foster said, "ruining people is considered sport."

No building or aircraft carrier bears his name.

Conspiracy theories cast him as a key player in covert wars for power in America.

James *Vincent* Forrestal.

Vincent Foster.

Victor is my name.

Tell me three *V*'s are coincidence. I like cheeseburgers and Coke, not Pepsi. Eat M&Ms. I write poetry. Have been a player in covert wars for America. Worried about how "they" were scheming to terrorize us.

Making connections is a condition of sanity.

My first suicide took place on a sunny day at CIA headquarters. I wore a black linen suit tailor-made for me in Hong Kong. My tie was a soft silver striped with black lines given to me by an ex-lover. Not Derya. My shirt was Oxford blue.

The Director of Central Intelligence, the head of the CIA who back in those pre-9/11 days was also nominally in charge of the rebellious, multifiefdom republic known as America's intelligence community, had just shown me my medal. Unlike Truman and Forrestal, the DCI didn't pin the medal on my suit. Unlike Zane, they didn't give it to me to keep, though like Zane's honor, my boxed medal is secret. We dozen people present shook hands and smiled. No one took photographs. We were all some level of spy.

My boss's boss looked at me, said: "We think you should take some time off."

"Okay," I said.

"Don't worry," said my boss. "You'll be back."

Like Vince Foster, I said: "I'll be back."

Aides ushered us from the DCI's seventh-floor office.

A cool rush of outside air swept over me as I stood in the DCI's outer office while my boss and his boss and other Agency hotshots lingered behind to grab a few heartbeats of precious face time with the man who ruled their careers. I glanced to my left.

Tarps covered the secretaries' empty desks in the outer office.

Tarps like shrouds.

Waves of cool outside air came from the huge windows in the outside wall—windows without any glass. The curtains were wide open. The sky was bright blue.

Without a word I sprinted toward that wall of sky. Leapt on a tarped-desk and sprang straight out to the big blue seven stories above the earth.

Fell twelve feet. Hit the motorized scaffold rising up from below with the replacement pane of bulletproof, anti-eavesdropping glass. Slammed on to that wooden platform so hard two workers holding the new pane dropped it. The pane bounced when it hit the concrete six stories down. My crash flipped one worker over the scaffold rail.

Stunned, gasping, I saw him go and instinctively grabbed his shirt.

His tumble pulled me off the wildly swinging scaffold and we fell together.

He grabbed me.

And he, of course, wore a safety harness. His safety line jerked tight as his legs scissored around me. His arms hugged me to his chest. We bounced up and down like a yo-yo on the side of the CIA's glass walls.

The only thought my jarred brain could form was: *Caught.*

18

OUR MEDS SLACKED off at dawn as we neared Bath.

Zane drove our stolen Jeep. The radio played the "Good Morning Maine" show. Vents blasted hot air to where I huddled on the front passenger seat inside the topcoat Russell'd scrounged. My flight jacket in the cargo bay filled the vehicle with the scent of wet leather. My pants were drying on the dashboard. Zane wore only his boxer shorts and his decades-old khaki Army shirt. Running the heater full blast to heal me was risky: *Don't let Zane get hot!*

The highway swooped on to a half-mile-long bridge spanning the valley where the Kennebec river empties into a bay. When my dad came home from fighting in Korea, Bath was one of America's smokestack cities. Progress poisoned that culture, though on this twenty-first-century April morning, the bay still boasted seagoing shipping. From those docks rose a beastly steel T, a wondrous fifteen-story-tall industrial crane.

Hanging from the crane's long steel arm were our five bodies.

Ropes around our necks. Arms dangling. Swaying high above water in the chilly morning light. The eyes of my corpse flicked open. The lynched faces of Zane and Eric, Russell and Hailey popped their eyes open. They watched us drive past on the bridge.

"Listen!" said Zane, as he spun up the volume dial on the radio.

. . . a traffic mess for the folks up north! First, there's the clean-up of an accident where a mom and two kids were pulled from their wrecked car by a good Samaritan who then vanished. Plus, state police have blocked off Route 703 while they work to recover a stolen car that crashed into the Reiss river last night. No word on any occupants of that car. In sports—

Zane spun the volume down.

"Cover story," I said, then thought: *Don't tell the others about our hanging corpses. They'll see what they'll see soon enough.* "The Firm's nailed some kind of lid on us."

"Cover-up," said Russell. "But now the Agency is stuck with it. The CIA's cover story will work like blinders on all regular cops. The Agency can't make their lies to the press too different from their lies to non-CIA badges because local cops leak."

"But not to us," said Zane. "We need more intel. Or at least coffee."

The Jeep swooped down a long exit ramp, caught a green light and carried us through a zone of warehouses and factories. The arrow on a traffic sign told us CITY CENTER was straight ahead, so Zane wisely turned left.

A motorcycle cop loomed standing in the road a block ahead. A blue light spun on his Harley parked crossways on the median stripe. The cop wore a white helmet, shiny black nylon jacket, mirror sunglasses that reflected our coming-toward-him Jeep.

"Ambush!" yelled Russell.

"No!" Zane slowed the Jeep. "Not here, not now, not this way. Too random."

The black-gloved gun hand of the motorcycle cop beckoned us.

"Get your pants on," Zane told me, but I was already pulling those damp, clingy trousers over my scratched-up bare legs. He passed me our pistol.

Hailey sent her dark wrap forward for Zane to drape over his bare legs.

The motorcycle cop beckoned us ever closer.

Don't do it! I willed to the cop as I gripped the pistol. *Don't make me do it!*

As our Jeep slowed to a crawl, Zane told me: "Don't let 'em see you're hurtin'."

He braked the Jeep to a full stop. Lowered his window.

The cop swaggered to us. Radio calls crackled from the mobile unit on his belt.

Zane smiled. "How you doing, officer?"

Reflections of Eric and Hailey and Russell slid across the cop's sunglasses. I saw my drowned rat self in those lenses. But when they stopped moving, what filled those mirrors was the image of a white-haired, white-bearded driver wearing an old Army shirt.

The cop pointed to a red curbed bus stop. "Park it over there, sir."

"Sure."

The cop watched our Jeep park, waved another car to drive on past.

Hailey said: " *'Sir'?* "

"Look at the people on the sidewalks," said Russell. "Ordinary Wednesday morning, business, tradesmen, going this way and that. But see those other people all hurrying the same direction? Men, women—there's a lady holding hands with two kids who should be going to school. That guy's got just shined shoes."

"Walking like they're going somewhere," said Eric.

Zane struggled into his still-damp pants. Cold worked for him.

The cop directed a City Works pickup truck full of white sawhorse barriers further down the street we'd been traveling. Turned his mirror glasses toward us.

"Get out of the Jeep," I said. "We gotta go where we're expected."

"Not good," said Russell as we stood on the sidewalk. "Broad daylight. Middle of town. Out on the street. No backup. No evac route. No idea what's what."

"Nobody's gunning for us," I said. Nodded to the cop. "Least, not him."

We flowed with the strangers headed to the intersection city workers had blocked with white barricades. Stood amid quiet citizens who couldn't all be secret agents.

"It's a parade," said Russell.

"No," said a gray-haired woman in a worn cloth coat.

They were both right.

First came the honor guard. Men my father's age. Even older men, two of them pushing a comrade in a wheelchair. They wore blue blazers and rectangular caps, gold braid; one had pinned up his empty left sleeve. They valiantly failed to march in step with three National Guardsmen who bore the flags for the State of Maine and America. Behind this honor guard tramped a dozen younger men and three women who wore a hodgepodge of military gear—jackets, shirts like Zane's, caps, what was left of uniforms that they could still get into. The dad came next. His blue suit was crumpled. The mom's black dress hung loose. They clung to a rein for a dark horse who clumped along behind them pulling the cart with its red-white-and-blue American flag–draped coffin.

What struck me in that crowded city street was the silence. Silence broken only by a whisper of wind. By the clomping of a horse. By the creak of cart wheels.

Though maybe he was talking about more than spies, Zane whispered to us: "Never forget that what we do matters."

"Gotta be worth it," muttered Hailey.

Shivering, I said: "We gotta go."

The Jeep took us to a trailer park neighborhood on the edge of town. A mom and pop convenience store had a window sign proclaiming: COFFEE! We bought newspapers, go-cups of java, boxes of donuts. Held our War Room picnic in the Jeep parked near a wrecking yard where skeletons of cars were stacked like pancakes.

"Nothing," said Zane after skimming the newspapers. "Nothing in the Bangor or Portland or Bath papers, nothing in the Boston *Globe*. Nothing about us. No 'Psychiatrist Dies of Heart Attack.' No 'Bizarre Drug Murders at Maine Motel.' After the roadblock, the Firm regained control."

"No vibe from that cop suggested an alert out for five freaks," said Russell.

"Could come later," said Hailey. "Even if the Agency has spun the cops, they'll alert Homeland Security or the FBI or whoever's in charge for something like us."

"Never been something like us," I said.

Russell shrugged: "Hell, since the 9/11 Commission caught them not talking to each other, I bet the Agency and Bureau are even more freaky about sharing stuff, but—

He slammed his mouth shut. All of them reddened with embarrassment.

I ignored that, said: "We're a secret the Agency wants to keep."

Zane shook his head. "Who knew we were so important?"

"It ain't about us," said Russell. "Maybe it's about keeping the Castle secret."

"No," said Hailey. "It's about keeping Top Secret that they fucked up, lost control, and two people died."

"Plus they let five maniacs escape into America," said Russell. "Bosses believe that getting caught as responsible for a mess is worse than the mess itself."

"So," he added, "that means we're a problem to hide or disappear, not fix."

"But," I said, "that works for us. Feels like they've tied FBI or Homeland Security desk warriors with hands-off orders, and honest cops with believing lies that won't backfire if they're leaked. If we're still such a secret, then our real hunters are hiding, too. Which means they're limited."

"They'll have maps on a wall," said Zane. "Circles of escape time estimates."

"So we fuck with their strategies," I said. "They know we're running south. So let's go to ground. I'm beat to shit, shaking from the river and cut up from the car wreck. We all need to sleep. Plus . . . What if we detour for a strategic Recon?"

"Six days," said Hailey. "We've only got six days."

"If we don't use our time smart, doesn't matter how much we have," I said.

Russell said: "What do you mean 'detour'?"

"And *'Recon'* what?" said Zane.

So I told them *where.* And *why.*

We found a hospital where *no way* could we black bag the pharmacy, but where there was a multilayered parking lot. We took a ticket from the machine, the crossbar lifted and we drove to an unguarded level. Eric and Russell jacked a gold four-door Toyota. Zane switched the new vehicle's plates with the set from a Mercedes. When we drove out, all the bored parking lot attendant saw was the two dollars charge on her screen.

Hailey looked embarrassed as she stood next to Russell at the vertical motel ten miles out of town. Russell *casually* leaned close to the registration clerk, *casually* asked for two adjoining rooms: "Not on the same floor as the rest of the MWA Symposium." The clerk knew nothing about any symposium. He looked at Russell, looked at Hailey. Took Dr. F's credit card and *casually* agreed that since Russell was paying in cash for both rooms—"expense account issues"—he'd run the card as a security deposit but not charge it. Hailey and Russell took their room keys, rode the elevator to the fourth floor. Russell came down, parked the gold Toyota out back, went up to his room.

Zane, Eric, and I snuck in the side entrance, followed the stairwell to the fourth floor, waited until the cleaning woman's cart stood deserted in the hall. *Presto,* we were in two adjoining motel rooms with four real beds and eight hours until dark.

"You're the walking wounded," Zane told me, assigned the others their guard duty shifts and sent me to bed.

I stared out the motel window to the tops of spring trees. Almost like I was back in my room at the Castle, waiting for the day's lone tear to trickle down my cheek.

Only here, I wasn't alone.

Outside that glass waited a giant beast of a crane.

With our five hanging corpses.

19

THE SOUND OF scissors woke me before I got caught by my nightmares.

My motel room was dark. Light glowed under the closed bathroom door. The bed beside mine was empty. Hailey stood sentry at the window overlooking the parking lot and highway. She turned as I woke, said: "Nothing." Went back to watching the night. A glance into the connected room to my left showed me one empty bed while on the other were a man's legs: Russell.

Snip!

Zane sat naked on the lowered toilet seat, a white towel covering his groin. Even though he was long past fifty, Zane was a rope. His wrinkles were tight from our daily *gung fu* workouts plus weight lifting like a lifer in prison. Instead of tattoos, he had scars.

And when I opened the bathroom door, he had no long white hair, no Jesus beard.

Eric held a pair of scissors as he stood behind Zane, who said: "We got them from a sewing kit left in the Jeep. How do I look?"

"Real," came out of my mouth. "Like an eagle with a cap of white feathers."

"I could shave it all off."

"No," I said. "A cue ball is as memorable as a white-mane Jesus."

"We'll flush all the hair. Hailey and Eric are ready. You can shower after me." Behind me, Russell filled the doorway. His eyes met mine in the mirror above the sink. And the gun. Russell said: "Time."

20

NEW YORK CITY'S night skyline filled our windshield seven highway hours after we left our Maine motel. Black slabs of skyscrapers dappled with window lights rose majestically into the indigo night air, but as we entered the city above Central Park, what filled our eyes were two pillars of empty sky.

Our strategic detour to NYC required us to do our Recon before we went to ground and before the streets filled with morning rush-hour bedlam, but at that moment, we needed to get out of our vehicle, stretch, breathe fresh air.

Dawn painted Manhattan a magic rosy glow as we parked the stolen Toyota on an upper–Central Park street. The sidewalks we walked were deserted. We drifted apart so no random witnesses saw "a group." Strolling with Russell on one side of an avenue, Zane and Eric half a block behind us, I glanced across the empty road to Hailey.

She glided on sunlight past a wall of store windows where mannequins posed in well-clad visions of how we all should live. She stopped in front of a window diorama that put a magazine mother center stage with two perfect children. Hailey hugged her arms over her heart. Her slim black hand floated out but could only touch the glass.

Hailey twitched, jerked. Her hand jumped off the window. She crossed the street to us, her face aglow with a smile.

And proclaimed: "I've got a plan!"

21

THE CIA'S PLAN in June 1998 was definitely *not* for Hailey to be sitting in First Class on a night flight from Paris beside a snoring bald Black man in an Armani suit named Christophe, a deputy cabinet minister of Nigeria's Department of Energy.

Hailey was the junior operative on a CIA Paris-based team targeting loose nukes by posing as a network of black marketers. The team established their bona fides by hooking Christophe with a routine bribe for Nigerian end user certificates to facilitate an arms shipment for another CIA Op. They reeled Christophe in with a commission from a diversion of 100,000 barrels of oil from the renegade truck caravan that every day rolled over the border from U.S.-UN-embargoed Iraq and into Turkey. That scheme papered the illegal oil into Nigerian gasoline that was legally pumped out of service stations along America's highways. To grease that scam, the CIA worked with Milli Istihbarat Teskilati, their Turkish counterparts who—in my time—helped the Agency profile Derya.

Guns and oil smuggles were the setup to get Hailey's team inside a heroin-for-plutonium swap Christophe had concocted with rogue Russians who were more cautious than he was about electronic intercepts. Christophe needed seed cash and a European team to transport sensitive, bulky materials: his newfound network colleagues let themselves be persuaded to sign on for his grand venture.

But the CIA team leader's appendix burst in Paris two days before he was to fly to Lagos with Christophe to make sure the Nigerian didn't run off with the Agency's buy money. The two other out-front male team members were locked-down setting up the Op's Prague connection. The Americans knew Christophe would balk at any stranger dropped into play so close to endgame. Hailey was the only other face Christophe knew.

This is why you joined the Agency, Hailey told herself as the airliner hummed through the dark sky. To win the good fight. Stay in control. Run the mission. Stop heroin, loose nukes plutonium. It's worth it and now it's all up to you.

She was jet lagged when the plane landed in Lagos. Christophe led her through the bright bedlam of the airport. Even with his diplomatic passport and government ID, he needed to bribe a customs inspector.

A toadish Nigerian met them at the curb.

"Who's she?" he demanded of Christophe.

"Asking questions is not your place," said Christophe. "Ken, this is Hailey."

Ken muscled their bags into a blue Ford. Christophe climbed in the front seat, Ken slid behind the wheel. After a moment's hesitation, Hailey climbed in the backseat.

Lagos swallowed them like a giant anthill with its "go-slow" of traffic.

"You must see this thing," Ken told his boss.

Lagos held 11,000,000 jammed-together people. The humid air smelled of car exhaust and rotting waste. Children held out their palms, chanted: "God bless!" Vendors sold radiator caps, water bottles, tomatoes, videos of movies still premiering in New York, toilet paper, T-shirts with portraits of Elvis and NBA stars. Teenagers swung dead rats by their tails as proof that they sold the best poison. A pack of men on the sidewalk stared at the creeping-past Ford with rage in their eyes.

"We call them *area boys,*" Christophe told Hailey.

"*Yan daba,*" muttered Ken. "Sons of evil. No jobs. No plans. No connections."

"But sometimes useful," said his boss.

Traffic stopped for a red light. Cars all around the Ford shut off their engines.

"Saving gas," said Christophe.

"But Nigeria is one of the largest oil producers in the world!" said Hailey.

"Not for them," explained Christophe, with a nod toward the people of this city.

The jerky bob of an ebony man in a white short sleeve shirt on the other side of the street caught Hailey's eye. *Why were other pedestrians mimicking his high step as they shuffled through the sun's fire?* Hailey blinked. Realized the crowd was stepping over a man laying on the sidewalk. Flies buzzed above the prone man's open mouth.

"Over there!" shouted Hailey. "That man laying on the ground: *He's dead!*"

Christophe looked. Yawned.

One mile and twenty minutes later, Christophe squinted through the windshield, told Hailey: "Hold your American passport so it can be seen. Say nothing no matter what. And move very, very slowly, always with your hands in sight."

Three parked Jeeps barricaded the road. Men in mirror sunglasses carrying AK-47s and wearing parts of uniforms stalked from car to car.

"The Mobile Police," said Christophe.

"The *Kill-and-Go's.*" Ken spat on the floor.

A trio of mirror sunglasses *Kill-and-Go's* thrust AK-47s into the blue Ford. Instead of a bribe, Ken flashed his ID picture, told them: "State Security Service."

As the roadblock shrank in the rearview mirrors, Christophe smiled at the American: "Welcome to Tomorrowland."

Ken parked across from a modern office building where a Nigerian in a white shirt directed fifty people picketing below the logo of a multinational oil company. A boom box by the organizer blasted a man singing pidgin reggae–type English Hailey couldn't understand. The pickets carried signs: Fair Wages Now! Pollution Poisons Children! Justice for All!

Christophe said: "Look at Bobo with his bullhorn. He thinks he's a rock star."

Hailey said: "What's that music?"

"Stupid!" snapped Christophe. "Stupid music from stupid Fela Kuti. If he was so smart, why is he dead of white man's disease? Of faggot disease? He was a monkey-fucking whore. General Abacha was right to ban his stupid filth."

"Fela's dead," said Ken. "But Bobo . . . Many of our friends wonder about Bobo. What the Ministry of Energy will do about his complaints to the UN."

"Who gives a shit about the UN," said Christophe as they drove off.

Christophe's house had the greatest of all luxuries: space. Three floors, a courtyard with an alley entrance. Christophe led Hailey inside, where beneath the spinning ceiling fan stood a woman wearing an orange-and-red wrapped dress.

"This is Janna," said Christophe as he walked past the Nigerian woman in the bright dress. "She'll look after you."

Janna stared at Hailey.

"Here," said Christophe, handing Hailey a bottle of water.

Hailey drank the water as she followed Christophe into the living room, while he dodged her questions about delivery schedules and back-up plans and—

Blink.

Hailey blinked again. *Head throbs, full of smog.*

She was on her back, staring up at a whirling ceiling fan. Blinked again and she realized she lay sweating on a bed.

Remember, can't remember . . .

I'm naked. CIA, Christophe, Lagos, I'm . . . naked.

She felt pain *down there.* And knew.

Christophe strode into the sunlit room. He wore an African shirt, slacks, Italian loafers, scooped up a wad of cash from the dresser top. Noticed her open eyes.

"It's about time you woke up."

"What . . . ? You . . ."

"Woman, your people sent you with me. Wasn't just that man's appendix. I know what you wanted, they put it in the deal to help everyone trust everyone. But when you kept telling me no, changing the subject, I knew you would drag out negotiations. Who has time for that? Be thankful we've moved on."

Hailey bolted from the bed and made it to the toilet before she threw up.

Retching until she could retch no more, Hailey stayed curled on the bathroom tiles, her hands around the porcelain toilet as the water swirled before her eyes.

From the doorway, Christophe said: "Be sure to drink plenty of water."

"What . . . ? What did you . . . ?"

"In America, they call them Rufis. Less profit in them than in heroin."

He tossed a hand towel to her. She caught it without thinking.

"Don't act shy or be stupid. The deal is done. You can't

refuse to eat or drink, and anything else . . . You are just a weak woman. Relax. You enjoy it, so do."

"Protection," she whispered. "Did you—"

"I trust you." He stroked his ebony hand over the different shade of black skin on her back and she almost threw up again. "We have no worries about faggot's filth."

He left her alone all day.

She had a cell phone. Emergency numbers. One panic call, rescuers would come.

But the mission would explode.

Nothing would happen to Christophe except that he'd be harder to catch again.

The heroin would hit the streets of America.

The plutonium . . .

Worth it. Make it worth it.

She showered until the cold water made her numb. E-mailed an On Target message to her "network associates" that wouldn't alarm Christophe if he snooped on her laptop. She found food, forced herself to eat, forced herself to drink more bottled water.

Hailey found Janna smoking a joint in the courtyard and listening to a music CD.

The way Janna stared at her, Hailey knew she knew—and didn't care.

Make her care, thought Hailey. *Bond with her.*

"That's Fela Kuti, isn't it?" Hailey asked her. "What is he singing?"

Janna answered: " 'Teacher Don't Teach Me Nonsense.' "

"How long have you worked for Christophe?"

"He married me ten years ago." Janna shrugged. "My family had a little money. Knew the right people at a foreign oil company."

The African wife stared at the new Black woman. Said: "What did you have?"

Two hours and the heat of the day passed. From the bedroom, she saw Ken talking in the sunlit alley with a *Kill-and-Go* and two *area boys.*

Long after dark, Christophe came home, reeking of Scotch. *Worth it,* she told herself over and over again, making it a mantra that beat in time to the bedroom's whirling ceiling fan. *Worth it. Worth it.*

Morning brought a newspaper with a photo of Bobo's machete-hacked corpse. The Mobile Police announced that he'd been killed by robbers.

Sunset brought four men to the house who never took off their dark glasses. The visitors left five foil bags of heroin that looked like packaged coffee beans.

When they were gone, Christophe told her. "E-mail your people. Day after tomorrow we go to Prague. Tell your people they must be ready to transport the plutonium. I will tell our Russians."

He smiled. "And we have two nights."

Worth it, she told herself. *Worth it.*

The ceiling fan whirled.

The phone rang in the darkness before dawn.

Christophe bolted awake—Hailey was not sure she'd ever been asleep. The naked bald Black man slid from the bed to answer the phone. Candles in the night flickered outside the open window at the barrel fires for roadblocks.

"No!" Christophe yelled into the phone. "This changes everything!"

"Was it poison?" he said. "What about the girl? . . . *Two!* No wonder he died! . . . Of course! You will tell me everything as I will tell you! Immediately."

She snapped on the bed lamp.

"Remember last night's date forever," Christophe told her as he hung up.

"June 8, 1998," said Hailey. That day, both the Unabomber madman and right wing terrorist bombers of an Oklahoma City building marched through the America's courts.

"Exactly!" Christophe said. "Last night. Today. Now is when the world changes."

No! Hailey wanted to scream. *That's planned for tomorrow!*

But all she said was: "Why?"

"Nigeria's supreme leader General Sani Abacha had his usual private party last night—this time with two Indian prostitutes. Abacha drops dead! Heart attack! But everyone knows it was the drugs."

"What drugs?"

"Viagra! If the wrong people realize it was me . . . ! I gave him ten Viagras in a silver box from Tiffany's. The idiot! Stupid old man! He probably took one pill for each prostitute, then one more just to be sure! Look what he's done to me! He was my protector. Already the hyenas will be circling. They'll eat him, all he has, and if I'm tied to his corpse or blamed for his death . . ."

"Doesn't matter if Abacha is dead. All we have to do is catch the plane to Prague, carry the heroin as your diplomatic luggage, link up with the Russians and my people."

When they would land in Prague, a CIA Special Operations Group would be on line to track Global Positioning Units in her laptop computer and cell phone. Plus, her team would be at the exchange site. A SOG strike force would swoop in. Grab the heroin and plutonium. The Agency would cut a deal with the Czechs to turn Christophe and the Russians into corpses, convicts, or co-opted assets eternally leashed to the good guys. Then, knew Hailey, *then* everything would be worth it.

As dawn lit the sky she told Christophe: "We've got to follow our plan."

"I've got to stay alive." He dressed, drove away.

Morning heat baked the house.

Noon came.

Noon went.

The thick golden light of afternoon filled the second floor living room. Hailey wore sneakers and carried her passport and cash. She sat on the couch with her cell phone, her laptop, and a kitchen knife hidden in the waistband of her slacks.

Outside, a car door slammed. Hailey jumped to her feet. Shoes pounded up stairs.

Christophe stormed into the room, his shirt soaked with sweat. He staggered to a locked cabinet. His hands shook as he unlocked the door, reached inside—

Whirled around waving a bottle of Scotch and two tall glasses.

"I'm saved!" He thrust a glass into her hands and filled it with Scotch. Winked. "Death played a joke on your plan. So I made another deal. With the British. I now serve their Queen as a valued spy."

"The British? You're . . . I'm . . ."

"You Americans always think you're the only game in town," he said. "I almost went to the Americans, but Abacha's people practically own them ever since his associate gave four hundred thousand dollars to President Clinton's Miami group called Vote Now '96. So now, if anyone blames me for Abacha's death or tries to squeeze me out of power, the Brits will stop them. I got there in time, thanks to people in an oil company who called a man from the British embassy who is letting me make him a hero to his home office."

"You—"

"I gave him the Russians—though the Brits won't get *all* the plutonium, something I arranged but didn't bother to tell them about. Midnight tonight, the Brits's SAS will kick in Prague doors. All thanks to me. I'll have proven myself invaluable to people who can tell even the Americans to fuck off."

A ceiling fan whirled in Hailey's head.

"Don't worry," said Christophe. "Since you and I are not going to Prague, your people will never be in the Brits' gunsights."

Hailey whispered: "The heroin?"

"Gone. I brokered it to New York. Your people will still profit." Christophe refilled their glasses as they stood face to face. "This should be British gin. Imagine, me partnering with the old rulers of my country! Ah well. You colonialists are like cancer, but nobody who's truly clever gets killed."

He raised his glass: "To success. It all comes out in the end."

Clinked his glass against hers.

And she shattered.

Hailey threw Scotch in Christophe's face. He bellowed, pawed his eyes and blindly grabbed for her. She felt the kitchen knife fill her hand. Thrust into his groin. Blood spurted from Christophe's crotch. Sprayed all over her. He thrashed to the floor. She straddled him while the kitchen knife hacked and stabbed his face, into his body, his groin. She felt herself washed by a crimson fountain.

Janna found them two hours later as sunset filled that room.

Christophe lay on his living room floor, a red slab under the spinning ceiling fan.

Blood-smeared Hailey slumped against the far wall. Eyes wide open.

Ken responded to Janna's phone call. They stood in that room with the two human wrecks as darkness poured in through the open window.

Janna told Ken: "He's dead, so his family will come take everything for themselves. Just themselves."

She smiled at the man who clearly knew her smile. "As soon as he's dead."

"Close the window," he told her—gently. "We don't want to attract flies."

"What about her?" he asked when the room was sealed.

"Her partners know she's here. If we dump her at an American oil company, her friends will find her. She can't say anything without cutting her own throat. Besides, look at her. She's a broken doll. What could she say that anyone would believe?"

Hailey mumbled: "Gotta be worth it. Gotta be worth it."

The Agency believed most of what Hailey said when they got her back home.

But she couldn't believe what they told her at Langley or in RAVENS Castle. What she heard through all the doctors' protests was the whirring of ceiling fans that spun her to logical clarity. *Gotta be worth it,* was what she knew. What she'd done/what had been done to her couldn't be worth it if everyone walked away clean and free. Even her. Especially her. Failure her. Whore her. Murderer her. What she'd done/what had been done to her must be worth the ultimate price, so she knew that unlike Fela Kuti, she'd justly earned the historic death sentence meted out to failed spies; she had AIDS.

22

OUR RECON STAGE 1 unfolded in Manhattan as the maturing dawn gave us enough light to see and enough waking-up traffic to not be noticed.

Then we triggered Hailey's on-the-street plan.

The Starbucks Hailey chose for us was a deathtrap. Set in the middle of a block, the coffee shop had one front door, no back exit, and a street wall of glass.

Zane had our lone gun. He slipped ten dollars to a flower vendor across the street to let him hunker inside his booth. Teenagers swarmed outside the private Marat School near the Starbucks, so Zane told the flower vendor that he needed to keep an eye on his crazy daughter.

Eric roamed the corners at the other end of the block. We ordered Eric to defy strangers. Worried: if a piano fell from the sky, he'd refuse to obey a civilian's "Look out!" We put Eric on a four-count surveillance: *One,* check the Starbucks. *Two,* confirm our Toyota was still safely parked. *Three,* scan for hunters—Uncle Sam's Guns, NYPD, Keepers, or Random Trouble Boyz. *Four,* watch out for our team—especially Hailey.

Russell and I timed our arrival at the Starbucks door to look like coincidence. Stranger-to-stranger, I held the door open for him.

He nodded *thank you,* and as he passed me, whispered: "Can she pull this off?"

"Got a better idea?" I replied.

Inside the Starbucks, steam hissed, milk bubbled. The air smelled of coffee.

Russell got in line to order while I strolled to the back room and made sure no ambushers hid behind cardboard boxes of coffee beans. Found no one hiding in either bathroom. Mirrors above the bathroom sinks caught my reflection: I looked like a ghost.

Russell was waiting at the beverage pick-up bar when I walked out front. I saw a green-aproned college grad barista hand him a steaming café mocha with one hand while with the other, she gave him a thumbs-up.

Russell! What have you done? I wanted to scream as he claimed a window seat where he could watch the street, the door, and all of us inside the café.

Suddenly the café's speakers switched from playing a mellow CD for sale at the counter to the operatic sound of Springsteen's "Jungleland" and I knew Russell had charmed the barista into playing one of his CDs. As Bruce sang about *the magic rat,* I got a café au lait, claimed a perfect table, sat with my back to the rear wall of bathrooms and No Exit for retreat.

My watch read 7:37.

Outside in the street, Hailey made her move.

She studied the teenagers jostling on the steps of the Marat School from the corner near the flower stall. The traffic light turned green. She strode across the street.

Sixty-some kids crowded the Marat steps, hanging out before morning classes. The lean, white boy Hailey locked on had beaten pimples, wore his brown hair shaggy but natural, didn't push at her with his blue eyes but didn't look away. What cinched him for Hailey was the paperback he carried: Dashiell Hammett's *The Glass Key.*

Hailey stopped in front of the school. She shot her gaze at the Hammett lover . . . and angled her head for him to join her.

Took him ten seconds to meet her on the sidewalk. Before the catcalls of his gawking schoolmates broke her hold, she said: "Buy an alumnus a cappuccino."

Then she walked toward the Starbucks where he'd feel safe, giving him the choice of being left standing on the concrete like a doofus or stepping into the wake of an exotic *older woman.* When he was by her side, she said: "You got a cell phone?"

"Yeah, but—"

"And so do your buddies whispering and watching us walk away. Call the one you trust." Hailey's diamond eyes wouldn't accept no for an answer. "Now."

He fumbled in his jacket for the phone as they marched past the wall of closed stores between the school steps and the Starbucks. Hailey hammered words at the boy.

"That plaque on the wall as you go up the main stairs? The Literature Award? Run your buddy inside to check out the winner for 1993."

They reached the Starbucks while he was cell phoning her instructions. Hailey stopped at the entrance. Waited. The teenager grabbed the door.

Her thank-you smile was dazzling as she walked through the portal he opened.

Two men in business suits ogled the classy Black woman gliding past them into the Starbucks. They were no threat so Russell didn't blast out of his chair. Their attention shifted to her escort—registered *white teenage geek*. The boy felt a primal surge as those adult lions could only glare at him and walk away.

Then she was inside, he was beside her, his buddy chirping in the phone. Hailey watched his face register the report. Beat him to its delivery by saying: "Clare Marcus."

The boy nodded as Hailey spoke the name of her best friend in high school.

"Tell him to hang tight, you'll call him soon." She ordered two cappuccinos, turned back to him. "So what's your name?"

"Nate—Nathan."

"Well, Nate Nathan, you've got lunch money. Pay the cashier."

She left him fumbling in his pockets, already in the habit of *going-along,* of *obeying,* of *believing.* She sat at the table I just then *coincidentally* vacated.

"Bring the coffees, Nathan," she said as I drifted off. As the boy sat, Hailey told him: "We don't have much time. Who's your buddy?"

"Ah, Brandon."

"Of course his name is Brandon. Can we trust him?"

Nathan nodded.

"Here's the deal, Nathan, and if you're cool enough to not

fuck up, the least that will happen is you'll get your lunch money back. Is your coffee good?"

"You haven't given me a chance to—"

"I'm your chance, Nathan. This is your chance. And you worry about coffee?"

"No, I—"

"Get your balance. Get your head in the game. Are you cool? Can you be cool?"

"Yes!"

Hailey said: "So aren't you going to ask me?"

"Wha-what—?"

"Use my name. We're not strangers, we're friends having coffee."

He blinked.

"Clare," she said. "Ask: *'What do you want, Clare?'"*

She waited. Her eyes never left his as he whispered that question.

"Good job, Nathan. Maybe you are the right man. Let's see if you can get me what I need."

"I'll do—"

"Don't promise. Sincerity without action is bullshit. Don't be a bullshit person."

"No way!"

"We need to score, Nathan. You and me."

He blinked.

"Drugs."

"Why, you came back to our school looking for—?"

"You, Nathan, I came looking for you."

"But you don't know me! And . . . I mean sure, of course, yeah, I've been high and I know guys who got pot and some guys say they have Ex or acid, or even—"

She leaned away from him. Made him flow forward to follow her. "I thought you knew that stuff was shit. Thought you knew that messing with your mind before you've built one is as dumb as smoking corporate shit where the only high you get is cancer."

"But drugs . . . If you don't want—?"

"I need what's in your pocket."

Nathan blinked.

"If it's not in your pocket, it's in Brandon's. Plus the two of you know a hundred kids in our school who are carrying. Hell, at our high school, it's not who's high, it's who isn't. Zoloft, Valium, Ritalin, Risperdal, Zanax—street cools call it *ben-zo*—Prozac, Lithium—you guys pack a whole rainbow of helpers to school every day."

"But that's medicine!"

"High is high. The good news is you got no law to dodge. You and Brandon get two dollars a pill, and we've only got thirty minutes to first bell."

"Why—?"

"Because I don't have time to do this any other way. Because you want to do it. Or do you want to stay a book-smart, street-sucker poseur forever? Are you cool? Somebody who hungers for real adventure, not just a geeky kid video game? Use your balls and live now. Don't just suck on the bullshit promise of some *maybe later*."

He stared past her at a whole new constellation of mirrors.

She reached out and let their fingers touch. "So, who you going to be, Nathan? A boy who sits around drinking coffee, or the man who's cool?"

"How—?"

"Everybody wants to be cool, Nathan. That's what it's all about. Not drugs. Not money. Make them want to be as cool as you are. Promise them two bucks a pill, you'll keep a buck. We've only got twenty-five minutes, so make that your advantage, not your problem. Go so fast they ride your wave. Now hit the road and bring it on home to me."

He watched her for so many heartbeats she thought she'd failed.

Then he hit Redial and dashed toward the door.

Nathan didn't notice me following him. On the way out, I glanced to the window table where Russell sat as his CD now played Nirvana's live "Come As You Are." Russell nodded his head with the savage guitar beat, kept his spy eyes working.

Outside on the sidewalk, I walked to Marat behind a fat

man who cooed to his leashed poodle. Nathan never looked back. He and a buddy scurried from teenager to teenager on the school steps. Kids dropped things into the clean paper cup Nathan had brought from Starbucks. My watch said 8:17. Hailey told us that First Bell rang at 8:30. Kids drifted into the school. Nathan dashed past me.

I walked into the Starbucks just as Nathan plunked down at the table across from Hailey, handed her the rattling paper cup. Drifted past them as he said:

"Seventy-nine, got seventy-nine pills. Antidepressants, sedatives, speed, stuff I don't know! Miranda dumped in her whole prescription bottle, said she could use her mother's. Jenny never takes hers anyway. Alex had two different kinds plus some antibiotics that I made him keep, wanted to know if tomorrow . . . *I did it!*"

"Did it great!" Hailey told him. She peeled bills off our wad. "But you've only got a few minutes to get to class. I owe you—"

"I don't want your money."

"It's not mine or all yours. You've got to pay what you owe. A deal's a deal."

She made him take enough cash. Stood. "Thanks. You really helped me."

"No I didn't."

That stopped her walk-away.

Come on! I telepathed to her. *We gotta get out of this deathtrap!*

"This isn't helping you," said Nathan. "But I will. Help you. Anything. Anything but . . . bullshit like this."

Hailey's gaze collapsed to the floor. Her lips moved in silent mumbles.

Rescue her! I was five steps from them. Two steps . . .

The Black woman willed her eyes up from the floor to capture Nathan.

"Just tell me what you need," he whispered, not noticing me abort my rescue charge to feign sudden interest in a sales display of mugs on the wall.

"What I need," she said, "is for you to get back to school

but never forget it's not about making it to the bell. It's how you do it. *Do good, be happy, stay true.*"

"Will I ever see you again?"

She smiled. "All the time."

Then she led him outside and cut him loose.

As we walked to the Toyota, Hailey and Eric linking up ahead of us, Zane stalking our rear guard, Russell gave me a grin, said: "Everybody must get stoned."

23

OUR NEW YORK hotel was nine stories of nickel-dime grim wedged into a block of million dollar condo buildings on Twenty-third Street, far from where we'd ditched the Toyota. Walking into the hotel lobby put us in a smog of dust and tobacco smoke. Somehow I didn't think we were the first crew of desperate souls to come there looking for a fix.

As we climbed the stairs, Zane whispered: "Risky to go to ground as a group."

"You're right," I said. "But we don't do so well on our own."

We turned one room into our Operations Center. Morning sun fought its way through the shade we pulled over the smudged window.

We rationed our buzz, inventoried our GODS, and built matrices.

Rationing our buzz came first—*had* to come first.

We worked from memory: Zane and Hailey sorted the seventy-nine pills into four categories—antidepressants, stimulants, sedatives, unknown.

"Those three little white ones?" said Russell. "I'm pretty sure they're like Ritalin, some sort of new generic speed to calm kids' brains."

"Teenagers," said Zane: "The cutting edge of American culture."

"The *cut* edge of American culture," I said.

"There's none for my HIV cocktail," said Hailey.

We didn't bust her delusion. That wouldn't work, plus it

didn't matter how much we cared about her. The lies we live are our own business. Or our shrink's, and he was taped to a chain-link fence.

Guesswork gave us each doses akin to what we'd been pumped full of.

"How will this effect our countdown?" asked Hailey.

Zane shrugged. "All this home brew med mixing can do is smooth out our edges. Buy us a grace period where we're gone but don't realize it. Hell, maybe even mask how much we're really falling apart. Or kickstart some craziness we never had before."

"So we still may have only three more days of truly functional madness left," I said. "We have to run this thing as hard and as far as we can."

Russell swallowed his rationed known pills with bottled water. Picked up one of the unknown tiny white pills. Popped the stranger. "Let's get it on."

Inventorying our GODS took five minutes.

"We're down to $434," said Hailey. "That's a lot of not much in Manhattan."

"And you've still got the gun," I told Zane.

"But not a full mag," he answered. "We're a few bullets short."

"No kidding," I said.

Building matrices: the heart of any spy investigation.

Matrices are the webs of data that make up a smart espionage investigation or operation. Intelligence analysts in a modern spy shop use computers to create visual "maps" of known facts and reasonable assumptions, maps that fill computer monitors or are projected onto screens to reveal connections, possible lines of cause and effect, characters who must be more than they seem because they are so interwoven in a matrix's web.

But we weren't in a modern spy shop like CIA headquarters. We were in a bottom of the barrel New York hotel. Dr. F's laptop was our only computer, and it had no software to let us build matrices. We had to do it the old-fashioned way.

Russell passed out pens and colored construction paper

from a drugstore that we scissored into index cards destined to bear the name of one person, place, or thing.

On purple matrix index cards, Russell listed Bosnia, Serbia, Colonel Herzgl, his rock 'n' roll band and its members, even his Case Officer.

Zane used red paper. Listed Sergeant Major Jodrey. He made cards for Vietnam, Laos, Special Forces/special operations, Pathet Lao, Vietcong.

Hailey had yellow. She listed Clare, Christophe, Ken, Janna, the Russians, Nigeria, Paris, and Prague. She made one card for heroin, another for oil, a third for plutonium. We assumed that many of the names we knew were false—cover identities or work names. But the same lie told independently to two different people creates a truth.

Eric used green paper. Listed Iraq, Saddam Hussein, Major Aman, Eric's cover connections, Weapons of Mass Destruction. He had the skinniest pile of index cards.

"Come on, Victor," Zane coached me. "You've got to write her name."

Silver, my color was silver. Russell handed me a pen. They all watched. Waited.

The pen in my hand shook as it inked the letters for *Derya* on a silver card.

"Way to go, Victor," said Hailey.

Eric got out: "Dr. Friedman proud."

My silver index cards filled rapidly with other words: Malaysia. Al Qaeda. 9/11. Counter-Terrorism Center. Two cards for suicide.

We all worked on Dr. Leon Friedman's pink cards. Listed the CIA. His alma maters. National Security Council. The White House. Eric hacked into Dr. F's laptop and called out every noun, every name, every address.

"We need to know more about him," said Hailey.

"That's why we came to Recon the big city," said Russell. "Why we're here."

"Stage 1 complete," said Zane. "Stage 2 . . . Coming up."

Nurse Death got brown cards. Her Maryland driver's license gave her name as Nan Porter. Many of the entries in her Palm Pilot were initials and phone numbers without area codes or addresses. Her wallet had a photo ID that gave her "detached" status at the military's Walter Reed Hospital in Washington.

Our invisible target mastermind killer *Kyle Russo* scarred a white card.

"White is the color of sorrow in China," I said.

"And purity here," said Hailey. "Go figure."

"Figure *Kyle Russo* will explain it all to us," said Zane. "When we get him."

"Wait!" I yelled. "We forgot somebody—somebody for all our colors!"

They all stared at me.

"Malcolm," I said. "If nothing else, him helping us escape won him a card."

We gave Malcolm a gray card, and on it wrote his code-name *Condor*.

Zane and Eric Scotch-taped more than 200 color-clustered index cards on the hotel room's bare ivory wall. The drafty hotel room trembled the window shade and made waves of sunlight undulate on our rainbow chessboard.

"Wow," said Hailey.

Russell shook his head. "Up against the wall, mother-fucker."

"That's us," said Zane. "That's where we are."

"No," I said, "that's where we started. We're way down the road now."

"What are the intersects on that wall?" asked Zane.

"We all got the Castle," answered Russell. "And the CIA, though Hailey, Eric and I have Directorate of Operations, Zane's got it as a detached duty from the Army, and Victor's got it with both DO and the Counter-Terrorism Center."

"Dr. F worked for the Agency," I said, "plus he'd just been upped to the National Security Council. Remember the story he told about getting lost in the White House?"

Hailey said: "The key intersects are Dr. F, Nurse Death, and Kyle Russo."

"Use her real name or we'll forget it," said Zane: "Porter, Nan Porter."

"Outside of Maine," I said, "the intersect zone is Washington."

"So we've been going the right direction," said Russell.

"Understanding geography doesn't mean you know where you are," I said.

"Right now," said Russell, "we're getting high in a shitty New York hotel room and hellhounds are on our trail."

"But why?" asked Hailey.

"Because we're escaped lunatics," I told her.

"Being escaped fugitives is enough reason for the good guys to chase us," she said. "But why are the bad guys after us? That *why* is the same *why* kill Dr. F."

"Murder is not just *who* and *how*," agreed Zane. He nodded to the wall of colored cards. "There's no *why* up there."

"Just *us*," said Russell.

"Realistically," said Zane, "it's—"

I interrupted him: "'*Realistically*'? You sure we're capable of that?"

Zane continued: "Whatever, the hit on Dr. F was either an inside or an outside job. And since Nurse Death worked as a puppet; it's a team job, not a solo gig."

Russell said: "So it's either an internal CIA coup or an external anti-CIA conspiracy."

"Could it be something else?" I asked.

Zane answered: "Call me crazy—"

"You're crazy!" blurted Eric.

"—but I can't see what else it could be," finished Zane.

"Me either," I said. "But I feel like there's something more *or* less up there."

"Makes my head hurt," said Hailey.

"Already got 'nough pain," said Eric.

"Copy that," said Russell. "Anybody feel any better since we popped those pills?"

"No," I said. "But I've stopped feeling worse."

We stared at the wall. Found no more answers or questions that helped. Zane and Eric peeled our index cards off the wall in case someone came into our rooms while we were gone. We stayed in the hotel, waited for the sun to sink lower, waited for afternoon to crowd the streets.

When my watch said 4:37, I told them: "Now."

24

WE STOOD IN the glowing center of a smudged ivory tunnel. Darkness loomed at each end. Our shoes crunched grit on the platform above steel tracks. Stale air trapped down there with us smelled of metal and cement. We were stones in a subterranean river of a thousand flowing strangers. We were *Low Profile*. We were *Not Being Noticed*. We were safe as long as no one realized we were fugitive imposters in the world of the sane.

Came a clatter, a roar, a woosh as a comet raced past us from the tunnel's black hole. Metal brakes squealed as the subway train screeched to a stop. Car doors jumped open and the five o'clock rush swept us on board.

Hailey and Eric scored a seat. Russell, Zane, and I jostled for a place to stand.

New Yorkers crammed themselves everywhere. Construction workers. Computer jockeys. Sales girls with tumbles of curls and tired makeup. Two nuns. Businessmen in tie-loosened suits. A Brooklyn beauty wearing *fuck me* high heels and a *fuck you* glare. A shoe mashed my foot. *"Lo siento,"* said a Puerto Rican woman. A pale punk in a hooded sweatshirt practiced his *gangsta* stare as his earphones vibrated rap music. A transit cop slouched at the rear of our car, but his gaze floated over the crowd and he didn't reach for the radio mike clipped on his shoulder.

Subway car doors slammed shut. The train lunged forward.

Russell whispered in my ear: "Check Zane!"

That soldier who'd dangled in the inferno jungle now white-knuckle clung to a subway strap. Close-cropped snow hair melted above his slick forehead. The bootleg meds he'd taken were either useless or incendiary. Either way . . .

"Hang in there, man!" I whispered to him. "Stay invisible."

"Hot! Victor—hot! Hell!"

"No, just a trip uptown."

Swooping to a stop jostled everyone forward, snapped us back. Doors popped open. Eight million more people crammed into the car. Nobody got off. The doors banged shut. We jerked forward. Body heat swelled inside our rocketing train.

Last time Zane got this hot was when the Castle's boiler wouldn't shut off. He flashbacked to the jungle and trashed the Day Room before a Keeper grabbed a dart gun.

"You're okay," I told him. His eyes glowed like pits of fire. *Lie:* "We're close."

"Close, here, we're here. Can't stand it. Won't."

"*Ah*, Zane," I whispered: "Do you have the gun?"

The hurtling subway car bounced those eyes and gaped his mouth. "'Xactly."

"Oh good," I lied. "That's good. Keep it safe, keep it out of sight, keep it good."

We clattered into a station. Screeched to a stop. More people got off than got on. The press of the crowd eased. Open doors let cool air into our car. For a minute. Doors clunked shut and sealed in the heat as we rocketed down the tunnel.

"Victor," whispered Zane from a bad place.

"It's okay."

"Not gonna take it. Can't take it. Won't make it. Got to do, do something."

Innocent strangers/proximity casualties rode our car. So did a cop.

The train clattered. The train roared. Swayed from side to side as it hurtled forward into the darkness. And the suffocating heat . . . The heat swelled.

A cool human voice knifed through that sweltering air:

"*Ttttr-rump pump pum. Ttttrr-rump pump pum . . .*"

Russell, rock 'n' roll Russell, holding on to the steamy subway car's ceiling pole as he leaned toward where Zane clung to this universe. Russell hummed and buzzed his tongue like a snare drum: *"Ttttr-rump pump pum pum, pum pum pum pum."*

Mister Slick twenty feet further up the aisle nudged his buddy: *"Yo,* what the hell?"

The Puerto Rican woman saw nothing. Being blind was one of a hundred ways the train car of *witnesses* suddenly focused on Zane who clung to his subway pole in the sweltering jungle canopy, on Russell who filled the car with an oldie-goldie song about paratroopers falling from the sky.

Sitting ten feet from me was a gray-haired man who wore a leather jacket and a face that shone with camaraderie as on cue, he gave Russell's aria its bugle: *"Ta dah-dah da."*

Shake, rattle, and roll, the subway train roared through the darkness carrying fill for body bags and one song. Opposite ends of the car, opposite ends of two decades from forty, two strangers to each other and to us all lifted their voices alongside Russell and the bugler went: *"Ta dah-dah da."*

Zane contorted with a soundless scream. Instead of hanging from a jungle tree, he was hanging on to a subway pole in suffocating heat. But he couldn't ignite to berserk without burning all of us. He refused to be such a traitor. He clung to the pole in that hot roaring train like he held on to his lifetime of pain. He held on and trembled as a subway choir sang "The Ballad of the Green Berets," swept him up in sentiment he'd sought when all he'd known was being young. The train hurtled through the dark tunnel and the song. He clung to the pole. Held on until the train blasted out of the dark to the next station stop as the tunnel angels sang of silver wings for America's best and *finally* he let go of his pain in a wash of sobbing tears that he'd never, no never before, cried.

'Xactly.

25

Outside, the sky bled. Taxis jammed the streets. Armies of the evening tramped the sidewalks. As far as we could tell, none of those marchers were on-our-trail hunters.

As far as we could tell.

And as far as we could tell from our Recon Stage 1, no surveillance teams were watching the Upper West Side apartment building we'd detoured from Maine to hit now in Stage 2. The building was twenty floors of units whose windows glowed out to the coming night. Our target was a sixth floor apartment. We rode the elevator summoned for us by the doorman who'd bought Hailey's bold con that we were there for "the" dinner party.

Once we decided that the building was free of surveillance, we'd hoped the apartment would be empty, a burglary waiting our arrival, but when we stepped out of the elevator, at our open target door stood an old man who looked like a mustache-less Albert Einstein in a black suit. He beckoned: "You're just in time."

Eric rushed to obey the old man's summons.

The old man lunged for him.

Russell surged to rescue our guy. Zane's right hand swept under his coat. Hailey pivoted to watch our rear. I crouched with all the closed apartment doors in my vision.

The old man threw himself around Eric in a hug, so Eric hugged him back.

"I'm so glad you came!" The old man leaned away from Eric and beckoned us closer. "I'm Leon's father, Jules Friedman. Thanks for being here."

"Wouldn't have missed it." I peered into the apartment linked to our dead shrink. Bookshelves lined the foyer. People mingled in the dining room.

"I'm sorry, but you'll have to tell me your names," said our psychiatrist's father.

Eric blurted: "Hailey, Russell, Zane, Victor. I'm Eric."

Too late for my lie, I thought.

Jules Friedman said: "And you knew my son . . . How?"

"From work," Russell said, putting himself between always obedient Eric and the father's questions. Hailey diverted Eric into the apartment.

"Ahh," said Jules.

"Yes," said Russell.

"Your two people who showed up at my high school to . . . to tell me about Leon, they never met him." Jules turned his misted bloodshot eyes to me. "Can you imagine having to tell some stranger that his child is dead? How terrible that must be."

"I'm sorry," I said.

Like a falling child, he wrapped me into a hug. Collected himself and leaned away. "After they left, I didn't think anyone from . . . from his work would show up."

Zane said: "He was special to us."

"He was special to everybody," said the mourning father. "Come in."

He led Russell into the apartment logged in his son's laptop under Home and I realized this was not where Dr. F "lived" but where he felt safe. Where he'd come from and no doubt where he told himself he could always return.

Zane and I stood in the hall. He'd walked here holding his coat open to fresh air.

"You sure you're okay?" I asked.

"Yeah," said Zane. "Or no. Now it's all . . . different. I feel . . . light."

"All we have to do is stay calm. Low profile. Keep cover. Be cool."

He smiled. "I'm not *exactly* worried about temperature anymore."

"Should we abort? Is this Recon smart? Is it safe?"

"Beats me." He went into the apartment.

Where Russell yelled: "What a fuckload of food!"

I stepped into the apartment and closed the door.

Found my comrades in a crowded dining room. An abstract print from a museum shop dominated one wall. Opposite it, someone had tacked a white bedsheet above the mantle where a silver-haired woman in a navy Armani suit now positioned a cylindrical glass vase of red roses. Sandwiches, cold broccoli and carrot sticks covered the dining table. Warm smells rose from a beef brisket and a butchered turkey.

Our murdered shrink's mourning father gave me a grateful smile.

I put my hand on his shoulder. "Mr. Friedman—"

"Please: *Jules*."

"Jules. Did . . . What did our people tell you about Leon's death?"

"A dark highway. Like always, him working too hard. Tired. Driving back from seeing patients at that Army base by the border. Black ice. Lost control. A one-car wreck. Fast—they said, promised it was fast, that he had to . . . to be dead before . . . before the fire."

That haunting lie made him look away. Whisper: "What else is there to say?"

"Nothing," I lied. "Except that he was a good man."

Russell swooped over to us, a plastic glass of red wine in one hand while his other waved a turkey drumstick. "Great food!"

"Thank you," said Jules. "The corner deli, they knew Leon since he was a boy. And the sandwiches: the industrial cooking class at the high school where I teach . . ."

Jules curled into a twisted man in a shiny black suit in a room where he'd eaten 10,000 happy meals, curled in on himself and trembled, not daring to shut his eyes.

The silver-haired woman in dark Armani now stood near Zane. She took a white envelope out of her purse and put it with others in a basket on the sideboard.

Russell aimed the turkey leg at the sheet tacked above the mantle: "What's that?"

"I covered all the mirrors," answered Jules.

"Wild." Russell left us for the wine table.

The silver-haired woman flowed into the space made by Russell's departure. The woman embraced Jules: "I'm so sorry!"

"Thanks." Jules gestured toward me. "Victor, right? Forty years teaching high school history, you learn to learn names quick. This is Dr. Clark, she was Leon's mentor at Harvard—don't deny it! And I saw that envelope go in the basket."

"Whatever I can do to help." Her voice purred like a cat.

"Right now, you can help by excusing me." He left the room.

Her bright blue eyes zeroed in on me. "You were a friend of Leon's?"

"Not as much as I would have liked. You teach at Harvard, Dr. Clark?"

"Please, it's Yarrow. After two decades, sentimentality brought me back to this city. I just opened a practice here, though I still lecture and keep my eye on research."

"Practice? You're a . . ."

"Psychiatrist." She laid a paw on my arm. Her claws circled my bones.

"Tell me," she whispered. "How's he doing?"

"Jules?" I licked my lips. "Doing the best he can. That's all any of us can do."

"Yes, I know. And one never knows what to do at times like this."

Make her talk! Don't you talk! "You met Leon at Harvard?"

"I knew the family. We went to school together. Well, Jules and I did. I admit I thought it was absurd—graduating Harvard to teach public high school in Harlem! But that's who he is. If he believes, he does. I never knew how much I admired that until, well, until after he'd met Marisse when I was doing my residence at the psychotic ward in Bellevue. There's no eye-opener like time in a mental hospital!"

"Really."

"Seems like yesterday." Yarrow clung to me. "That asylum brought me to Leon."

Nearby, Eric stood behind two men so deep in their conversation they didn't notice him even when one of them turned to the mantle, slid aside a hammer, a packet of tacks and a wire loop to set his glass of red wine beside a vase of red roses.

As Yarrow told me: "I remember when Jules first had me over to this apartment. For dinner. To meet Marisse. Two old

college friends . . . And I saw her. Saw her pregnant with
Leon. All of a sudden I realized . . . what a great man Jules
is—was—is, I mean. Better watch it. Think I'd know better.
Those tricky Freudian slips."

"Tricky."

"Marisse was the most honest, magic person. You simply
had to love her. Two years she's been gone. Now poor Jules
is truly all alone. Myself, I've been divorced for a year, a nice
man but . . . Enough of me. What was it you said you do?"

"What?"

"What you do," purred Doc Yarrow. She squeezed my
arm. "Who you are."

Martial arts schooled me on how to break a grip on my arm.
Hit her with my free hand: a palm strike to her temple, a
knuckle jab to her windpipe, smash her forearm with my hammer fist. Jerk away through her grip's weak spot, the thumb-
finger contact. Grab/peel her little finger and snap it back.

"Excuse me," I told Yarrow, "my friends . . . need help."

I wriggled between strangers in the crowded room and
made it to Zane.

Jules called out: "Please, everyone! Could we all start into
the living room?"

"We've got to get out of this place!" I whispered to Zane
as the crowd surged.

"We haven't gotten anything here but food," he said,
brisket sandwich in hand.

"Speak for yourself. And watch what you say: that old
lady is a psychiatrist!"

"And you're crazy. You've got a lot in common."

"If she spots us for who we are . . ."

"You worry too much. What's the worst that could happen? Besides," he said, nodding to the subject of his concern, "it's not her or you we should be worried about."

Russell stood at the dining room door downing another
Merlot.

Jules called from the other room: "Everyone! Please! In
here."

Russell headed toward that voice. I hurried after him to
the living room.

Night filled the windows of that room where couches, chairs, and tables had been pushed aside to create an empty space of rug ringed by a circle of metal folding chairs.

Standing between the memorial table and the ring of chairs, Russell listened to Jules say: ". . . should technically pull the drapes, but he loved this view. The vastness of the city. The sense of the whole universe just beyond a thin pane."

Russell stared at the circle of chairs. "Hey! I know how this works!"

"Really?"

"Oh yeah, I do this all the time."

I said: *"Russell!"*

Jules frowned: "All the time?"

"Two, three times a week," said Russell. "Depending on how things are going."

"My God!" said Jules. "Two or three . . . *a week!* You poor man!"

Russell led the way into the circle of chairs as Jules told him: "All that . . . death, and you so young."

"Oh man," said Russell: "Don't get me started. All I see behind me are bodies."

Night turned the wall of windows into a translucent mirror that reflected the circle of metal folding chairs. The silver-haired woman chose a chair, her therapist's license snug in her purse as she zeroed me with her gaze and patted the seat beside her.

Somehow I summoned the strength to hold up my pleading hand: *Wait.*

I pulled Russell close: "That old woman is a shrink!"

He shook off my feeble grasp. "Of course she is."

Gravity pulled me into the seat beside Dr. Yarrow Clark.

"So much easier not to sit alone," she purred. "Or beside a total stranger."

"Who's not a stranger." *Shut up! Don't talk to her!*

She blinked. "What . . . an interesting perspective."

Two teachers sat beside Zane. Two chairs away sat Eric. Jules politely waited in the center of the circle. Beside Jules stood his new buddy Russell.

"Perspective is key," said Yarrow as Jules's colleagues and friends filled the chairs. "I'm observing a clinic that treats immigrants who can't be related to from an American medical perspective. It's common for Hispanics to have *ataque de nervios* that makes them fall on the floor, scream and cry and beat their chest. Malaysians—"

"Won't talk about that."

"I beg your pardon?"

My lips pressed shut. My head shook *no*.

She shrugged. "Anyway, Malaysians have a psychosis called *Latah* that compels them to mimic other people. Chinese patients often fear the wind. They call that *pa-fay*."

"Pa-feng," shot the correction from my lips.

Dr. Yarrow Clark blinked. "Do you speak Chinese?"

"Yes. No. Not here. Not now."

"Everyone!" Jules swept his arms and gaze around the circle. Russell mimicked his stance, his spread-wide arms, his shushing glare.

No *Latah!* I telepathed a plea to Russell.

Who told the group: "Time to start—right, Jules?"

Russell gestured for our host to sit in a chair with his back to the wall of windows. Russell took a seat facing that wall of night with reflections trapped in its panes.

"Thank you all for coming," said Jules. "This isn't how it's normally done—"

Russell interrupted with a wave of his hand. "Sure it is. We here, circle city, a shrink sitting over there by my man Vic—how you doin', Doc—ready to rock."

"Leon . . ." said his father, then he swallowed. Struggled.

"Dr. F was cool," said Russell. "He did Group okay."

Zane loudly, pointedly cleared his throat.

Russell didn't blink.

Our shrink's father sighed: "Leon dying . . . This isn't how it was supposed to be."

"Man," Russell sighed, "what the fuck is ever like it's supposed be?"

The word *fuck* turned the innocent bystanders in the circle to stone.

"Now," said Russell, "where was I?"

"Where are you?" I said. I cupped my hand over my heart and tucked my thumb out of sight. My wiggling fingers semaphored life's four magic words: *Shut the fuck up!*

"I'm here, man," said Russell. "So are you. Everybody's right here."

Hailey tried: "Except for poor Dr. Friedman."

"Yeah," said Russell. "He was good. Though he kept missing what I was saying. The bathroom: Dr. F totally missed the point."

"Young man," said the therapist sitting beside me. "Are you all right?"

"You think anybody anywhere is all right? What kind of shrink are you?"

"I'm sorry if—"

But a wave of Russell's hand interrupted Dr. Yarrow Clark: "No, I'm sorry.

"Oh man, Vic!" said Russell. "I am so sorry for that bathroom. I froze. Her standing there in her bra and panties in the . . . the bathroom and I . . . I couldn't drop her."

Dr. Yarrow frowned but said: "Good for you."

"*No!* What kind of world do you live in? You kick in the door, she's standing there half naked—*Boom!* Drop her hard or die stupid."

"What's going on?" said one of the women teachers.

I said: "Russ, can I see you in the kitchen?"

"You can see me everywhere." He pointed at the wall of windows. "Look!"

Every eye in that living room obeyed. Saw the windows. Our reflections. The glowing skyscrapers. The dark night.

"You can see out there and back in here, both together because it's all trapped in the glass," said Russell. "Like there is no time. Or place. Out there where we're going and where we been, in here where we are, so what we see is . . ."

With that view reflecting in his glasses, Eric said: "Beautiful."

"That's right, man! You got it. You know. Beautiful. Right?"

Of course Eric nodded yes.

"White pills and red wine," whispered Zane about Russell. But I shook my head. "He knows how to be stoned."

The oldest of Jules's high school teacher colleagues said: "This is—"

"You're not the boss of IS!" boomed Russell. *"I'm talking here!"*

Not an inhale. Not a fidget. We sat trapped on a circle of steel.

"You don't interrupt somebody when they're talking in Group! Where you people been? Don't you know anything? I'm trying—I'm apologizing here, so don't interrupt me. I'm sorry, and . . . I'm sorry, Vic, I should have whacked her."

"It's okay, Russ," I said. "It worked out."

Doc Call-Me-Yarrow had the courage of her therapist's scars to say: "It's good that you didn't . . . It's good that she didn't . . . get whacked."

"Oh, Zane dropped her," said Russell. "Dead accurate, she did herself. But the point is not who killed her. She's just another body. Lots of those to go around."

That news brought zero comfort to the faces in our circle.

"The point is," continued Russell, "you can't leave it up to somebody else to do what has to be done. Sorry about that. Things work out, but if you're there, you're responsible. You're part of it. You've got to do something, and I didn't, and I'm sorry."

"Russ," I said, "it's okay. And you're—"

"Bathroom." His stared at the reflections in the window of who was and wasn't there. "It was the bathroom again. That bathroom and I didn't stop her. I couldn't."

A whisper went from him to the window. "I didn't kill that colonel either."

What I saw was Russell's expression of surprise and awe, his face of discovery.

What I saw was *motion* in my peripheral vision.

What I saw was Dr. Yarrow Clark drop her hand to her side, ease it down toward the purse under her chair, the purse that no doubt had a 911 cell phone.

What she felt was my steel hand wrap her wrist in the Tiger's Mouth of my thumb and forefinger so now it was her in the grip of power.

One of the teacher guests at this shivah of mourning whispered: "What colonel?"

"Colonel Herzgl, that fat fuck. I . . . I didn't kill him. Should have whacked his ass before he burned the schoolhouse. You ever hear little kids burning alive? Stand there on a nice day outside the schoolhouse while they pour the gas? The smoke makes you gag. But it's the sound that gets you. Later it's the stench, burned flesh, but the sound . . . Roar of flames, you pray that the screams stop. You're there, can't do anything but fake a damn smile so you won't blow your cover. Get killed. And I didn't kill him, couldn't rig the wire grenade booby trap and the bathroom . . ."

A sobbing rasp tore through Russell. He trembled. His hands contorted in a wide grasp that found nothing to grip.

"We're with you," whispered Hailey.

"We're here," said Zane.

Eric gave Russell the thumbs-up.

Our shrink's father flushed blood red. His guests paled.

Russell saw me nod. We were way past stopping. Or caring about low profile. This moment was true and true is priceless. Russell's moment, years coming. Dr. F would have called it a *breakthrough*.

Russell slumped on his chair. Words fell from him like rain.

"Herzgl took her from that school. She was a teacher. She had long blond hair.

"Herzgl grabbed her. Beat her. Little kids crying, kicked into a group. Tied her hands. Leashed her like a dog to his belt. We went outside, they poured the gas . . .

"He kept her for himself for two days. Two nights. Like a toy. Like she wasn't a person. We came to that town. Rubble crunching under our boots. Cut ropes dangling from the lampposts. The café—

"Victor, I don't know about the café anymore! It was there, I was there, but . . ."

"It's okay," I told him as Dr. Call-Me-Yarrow's wrist twitched in my grip.

"Bathroom," said Russell. "Herzgl takes her in there. Before he goes, he points at me, says: *'Your turn next.'* And he drags that girl on the leash away. Into the bathroom. I know he left his music, Elvis singing that damn 'Viva Las Vegas.'

"Maybe half an hour crawls by. Waiting with those two torture-loving goons. Herzgl comes back. Points to me. Says: '*Amerik, you next. Your turn now.*'"

Our host Jules began to hyperventilate.

"What could I do?" said Russell. "I had to keep cover and be one of them. Walking away, I hear Hergzl choose which guy is next. Herzgl says we're two hours march from a camp. He'll give her to the camp troops until . . . until forever."

A sigh escaped from Jules: "*Oh!*"

"He strung her up from the crossbar of the bathroom stall. There's a mirror. She can see herself. He cut her. His initials. Notches. She's . . . naked. Looks at me. Brown eyes and . . . It's just me and where the hell is God! It's me and I'm responsible and I'm there and she's . . . They . . . There's going to be even more, even worse horror and she'll be . . .

"But it's now. It's then. Rolling down her cheek: one tear. All she's got left is one tear. They're coming in an endless line to rip that from her. I can let it happen and I can't . . . can't rescue her. Can't stop them. And all she says is . . . is . . . '*Please.*'

"I strangled her."

"Oh my God!" whispered a schoolteacher.

"Her blond hair was like lines of fire on my hands. Her skin burned like acid and she shook. Fought to die, not live and I . . . I couldn't get her out of there so I strangled her to save her from more horror. In the bathroom, it was me."

Silence gripped the ordinary living room that had already been transformed into a mourners' ceremony. Shock and confusion painted the faces of the civilians trapped in our circle. We sat there, welded to our chairs.

Until Hailey stood. Walked to where Russell slouched, to where she, the raped murderer, gently cupped the face of the murderer of the raped.

"You did the best you could," she told Russell. "The best she could hope for. You did wrong for the right reason."

"Doesn't help."

"But it's true."

Zane said: "You escaped. That's what matters now. You got away."

"No," whispered Russell. "Not ever gone."

"No," I said. "You're right. Not ever all gone."

Zane pointed to the window of night. "But now it's out there. And you're here."

"*Oh!*" came the plaintive wail from Jules Friedman, schoolteacher, father.

Tears burst from him and flowed down his cheeks.

"*Oh!*" he cried, his ocean eyes swallowing us. "Now I know who you are!"

26

"WHOA! LOOK AT the time!" I told the curve of stunned faces. I released Dr. Yarrow's wrist—sensed she knew enough of *what was what* to keep cool—and bounced to my feet like a happy preacher on Easter Sunday.

Nobody tore their eyes off me to obey my injunction about *time*.

Except Eric, who checked his watch, saw Still Dark.

Jules stared at us. Tears streamed down his cheeks to his smile.

"Looks like now is when we say our good-bye's!" I said.

"I'm staying!" snapped Dr. Yarrow behind where I stood.

"'Xactly," said Zane. "Us, too. We have that thing to do. Of course, if everybody goes, who knows who else they'll see. Or talk to.

"Unless," he continued, as with a signal for me, he put his hand on his shirt-covered waistband, "if we organize some kind of . . . new party here . . ."

If we put all these strangers under our gun, made them stay put so they wouldn't call the cops, they could become proximity casualties or Find Out Too Much. If we tied them up and tied them down, alive they'd have a more urgent story to tell. And *absolutely no way* were we witness silencers.

"Nope!" I gave the sane people in the room a grin. Got no smiles back. "Time to go home, thanks for coming, but it's nearly pumpkin hour."

One teacher whispered: "What is that one talking about?"

"Cinderella," answered the teacher beside her. He looked at our host. "Jules?"

Zane called out: "Everything's okay here, right, Jules?"

"Better," he said, tears streaming past his smile. "Better."

"There you go." I swept my hand toward the door. "And there you go."

None of the innocents moved. To get out the door, they'd have to walk past where Russell slumped on his chair.

"Eric," I said, "show Russell the view while everybody gets their coats."

Everyone moved. Teachers clustered around Jules. He nodded to whispers of concern. Wept and smiled. Eventually is defined by intensity: that night's eventually took no more than three minutes before his rescuers realized he didn't want their help. Five minutes after they stood, they were hustling out the door. Eric and Hailey stood beside Russell as he leaned his forehead on the cool glass of the night window. If the guests worried about Zane bringing up their rear like a cowboy riding drag, they were too smart or scared to complain. The apartment door closed behind their moved-out herd.

Dr. Yarrow Clark said: "I'm not leaving Jules alone."

"You mean: *with us,*" I said, turning to where she clutched her purse.

"I mean whatever." She laid her hand on Jules's arm.

"You two kids stay put." I joined my friends at the window.

"Russell," I said to the man leaning his forehead against the night mirror. Only a pane of glass held him back from the long fall. "Are you okay?"

"I can see my reflection," he muttered.

"How's it look?"

"Wasted."

"We don't have time for that. Pull yourself together."

"Okay," he said. But he didn't lean away from the glass.

Rage blasted from Dr. Yarrow Clark's eyes. "Who are you?"

Jules patted her hand. "Don't worry, Yarrow. I know who they are."

"Sure," I said, ready to lie and support delusions he had that protected our cover.

"You're my son's patients."

"Well, *technically* . . ."

Dr. Clark clung to our smiling host. "If any of these people are Leon's clients—"

"All of us." Russell, swaying on his feet but standing right beside me.

"Great timing," I told him. "I thought you were through confessing."

"Thank you so much for coming!" Jules clasped my hand. Let go of mine to shake Russell's. Let go of Russell, shook with Hailey, Eric. "This means so much to me!"

Yarrow said: "Means we should call somebody."

"No!" I chorused with Russell.

"No," said Jules. "I don't want to share this with anybody."

Even he felt her flinch. Locked in an apartment with babbling maniacs and her first flinch came when Jules's words pushed her away.

"Except you," Jules told her as he took her hand. "You're here. You should stay.

"Don't you see?" he told her. "These people are my gift."

Her face said she'd listen to anything as long as he held her hand.

"When someone dies, you realize how little you had of him. Leon couldn't tell me about his work and work is a huge part of who we are. You get a person from his stories. With us . . . there had to be even more walls than regular fathers and sons build."

Jules smiled at us again as he wept: "You people are pieces of my boy's life. Thank you so much for coming. You've brought me parts of my son I never had."

"Hey," said Russell, "we'd have brought you more, but we left him taped to a chain-link fence."

The apartment door swung open—and with it, Jules's eyes. Yarrow's jaw fell.

Zane walked toward us, saying: "Nobody cell phoning while I watched, but in the taxis or walking home, Jules's guests will calm down, add up the score, and somebody somewhere soon will call the cavalry."

Jules whispered: "What are you saying?"

Zane said: "That we gotta go."

"You taped my son to a fence?"

"We need to leave," urged Hailey.

"No," I said. "We should talk."

"*All* of us?" asked Zane.

He stared, Russell stared, Jules stared, we all stared at Dr. Yarrow Clark.

She clung to Jules. Shot me with her diamond eyes.

As gently as I could, I told her: "Remember how you asked who we are?"

"Believe me, with thirty years of clinical psychiatric experience plus what I learned in kindergarten, I know exactly who you are. You're all the way crazy."

"Finally!" said Russell. "A shrink who gets it!"

"Knowledge is not power," I told her. "Knowledge is responsibility. And peril. Acquiring knowledge is action. All actions have consequences. If chaos science has taught us anything, it's that for each action, there are unintended, unpredictable reactions. In the marble at the CIA, they chiseled words about '*the truth will make you free.*' Wrong: Once you know the truth, you're stuck with it."

"The CIA?" was her response. "How far do your delusions extend?"

"Apparently way beyond this room," I told her. "And you shouldn't be here with us. But here is where you're stuck while we go somewhere else to talk. Afterward, what Jules tells you is on him. And you, if you listen."

Psychiatrist Yarrow said: "You people are in need of serious medication."

"Whoa, Baby!" cried Russell. "You got some?"

Jules grabbed my arm: "You . . . My son taped to a fence! My Leon! Tape!"

Martial arts schooled me on how to break a grip on my arm. Life schooled me on when not to. I've not always been a good student. Right then I split my focus to include *gently* reversing Jules's grip so that I controlled his arm while I faced Yarrow and Eric.

"Eric, stick with Dr. Clark. Don't obey her. Don't say anything. Don't answer any questions. She doesn't get to leave or contact anybody, but be nice. Here in the living room you can keep an eye on her and an eye out the window and let us know *if*."

Of course Eric's head bobbed yes: an order was an order.

"My son . . . !"

"Time for the rest of us to talk," I said as I gently led Jules out of the room with its circle of folding chairs and wall of windows.

Russell, Zane, and Hailey came with us into Jules's cramped study. We closed the door. He trembled behind the desk covered with school work to correct, with dictionaries that defined words and atlases that showed where you were, with history texts of facts and footprints of forces that let you figure out where you'd been and what could be.

We told him The Whole Truth.

"Fuck you!" snarled the schoolteacher. "Why should I believe anything you say?"

Zane said: "Who could make up a story like that?"

"I teach teenagers! You think *The Homework-Eating Dog* is the only crap I get?"

"What could a wild story like this gain us?" I said.

"You think I'm naive? Lots of people don't do what's in their own best interest—even when they know what it is. And most of them aren't sickos!"

"Crazy," corrected Russell.

"Fuck you!"

"That's fair," said Russell.

"You taped my son to a fence!"

Hailey said: "We didn't leave him on the ground."

"On his feet," said Zane. "Saying *'fuck you'* to those who put him down."

"Bottom line," I said, "crazy or not: we make sense."

Zane said: "You have the right to know how your loved one died."

"What good are rights when all the world is wrong. What good is sense when it all adds up to crazy."

Jules paced behind his desk like a panther behind invisible bars. Back and forth until he slumped in his chair. "They said that all they could do was send me his ashes."

"That was true for them," I told him. "And it was a lie for you."

Jules looked at us. "What can we do?"

"Always the question," I said. "Half the answer is you can help us, then let it go."

"I don't like that half of the answer."

"The other half is that we can't tell you our plan."

"In case," said Russell.

"For operational security," said Zane.

"To keep you safe," said Hailey.

"You guys don't have a fucking clue what you're doing," said Jules.

"Maybe you can help us with that," I said. "With the fucking clue thing."

Jules stared through us. Past us.

"Leon was never an ordinary kid. Nothing against the work Yarrow does, but when he chose public service, it made me even prouder. I knew he could be a star on Park Avenue or at Harvard, but to choose to work for our government . . . And he was a star there! He was so excited to be going to work for the NSC! He'd been living out of his suitcase for a year and he'd finally won a dream permanent post. That's all he'd tell me, those damn initials that run everything: NSC, CIA. We shrink the names of things into initials so they're easier to say, but then the things get harder to see."

"What have you seen?" I asked him.

"Anything that felt funny," said Russell. "Not just wrong, but not right either."

"Something he said," Hailey explained. "Something he did. A joke you couldn't understand. A change in his personal life. Anybody new hanging around or—"

Jules said: "Or a phone call."

We froze.

"A phone call," said Jules. "That's all it was. Didn't think anything of it. The day he left to go—go up to you and that place in Maine, I know that now but then . . . Then I got a phone call. At night. A man. From Leon's office—he said. He asked if Leon planned on coming back to New York. I told him Leon didn't have time to stop over on the way to D.C. The man said he'd catch him at work, hung up."

"And that's—"

"Never happened before," said Jules. "Why call to see if Leon was coming here?"

Hailey shrugged. "New York is an easy place to make someone die."

"They had to be sure," I said. "They would have been cool with him coming to New York, but they needed to know whether or not to trigger Nurse Death in Maine."

"So that still doesn't tell us if it was an inside or an outside job," said Russell. "We can build that phone call into either scenario."

Jules stared at us.

"But," I said, "maybe what's most important is that the call tells us Dr. F had to die before he could get to D.C. Maybe he wasn't killed because of what he'd done, he was killed because of what he was going to do."

"Preemptive strike," said Zane. "Always popular."

"Did I . . ." Jules couldn't say what he feared.

"No," I told him. "Nothing you did or didn't do made any difference."

Hailey threw him Nurse Death: "Did he ever mention Nan Porter?"

"No."

Zane gave him the mastermind of his son's death: "Or Kyle Russo?"

"No. Did he—"

"TV!" yelled Zane. "I saw TV commercials . . . Jules, do you have caller ID?"

He did, a white plastic box corded to the phone on his desk.

"But it only stores the previous twenty incoming calls," said Jules as he scrolled backward through the liquid crystal display of people who'd called. "After Leon died . . . All the sympathy calls . . . Call-backs for the shivah . . . No numbers from before yesterday. But I remember that man's number was D.C., a two-zero-two area code."

He leaned back in his chair. Shook his head.

"One day your government tells you your son is accidentally dead and burned up, then strangers show up to say he was murdered before they taped him to a fence.

"Say I believe you," Jules told us. "Say I trust you. Still, you're . . ."

"Crazy," I said for him.

"At least that." Jules shook his head. "What am I supposed to do?"

"Not tell anybody about us," said Zane.

"Help," said Russell.

Hailey lifted a thick paperback book from a shelf. Held it up for Jules to see.

A thick paperback guide to medicines and pills. Jules said: "Take what you need."

"We need everything," I said.

"I'm fresh out of miracles."

"How about money?" His New Yorker face darkened and I said: "Operational funds. Clothes. Rations. Meds. Logistical gear, whatever you've got. We need—"

"Everything," said Jules. "I heard you the first time."

He pulled a wad of bills from his pants. "I maxed out my ATM withdrawal today for the shivah. There should be about two hundred dollars left there. Tomorrow . . ."

"Tomorrow is tomorrow."

"Well . . . Tonight there's the memorial money. Those white envelopes in the basket on the sideboard. I was going to fund a scholarship in honor of him. The kids at my school organized a cash collection in their homerooms, it's in—"

"Stop!" yelled Dr. Yarrow Clark's voice from beyond the closed study door.

Into our midst charged Eric, the silver-haired woman's wrist tight in his hand.

"Don't hurt her!" yelled Jules as he raced around his desk.

Zane restrained him with a gentle palm on his chest. "He won't."

"Eric!" I yelled. "What are you doing?"

Frustration contorted his face. He ran from the room, us hurrying in his wake.

To the dining room. He gave the silver-haired woman to Zane, who put an arm around her shoulders to reassure her that she was fine, to show Eric that he had her.

Eric held his head with both hands. He scanned the food-laden table. Whirled to face the shrouded wall above the mantel. Let his eyes fall on the mantel with the hammer, wire, and tacks Jules had used to cover the mirror and the vase of red roses.

"What did you tell him?" Hailey asked me.

Eric thrust the hammer in his belt, pulled down the sheet tacked over the mirror.

"What are you doing, Eric?" I yelled.

Russell told me: "Don't bug him, man. He's on a roll."

Eric grabbed the cylindrical glass vase off the mantel, swung it so red roses and water flew through the room.

"Wild!" said Russell.

He helped Eric dry the inside of the vase's glass cylinder. Eric checked to see if its bottom was thicker at the sides or in the center, whether its inner curve was convex or concave. Then he put the vase in my hands and ran from the room.

Hailey didn't need the nod of my head to tell her to shadow Eric.

Dr. Yarrow Clark said: "He's like a robot gone mad."

" 'Xactly," said the man with his arm around her shoulders.

We heard rummaging in Jules's study. Feet running our way.

Eric was back, Hailey two steps behind him.

She told us: "He got rubber bands and scissors."

Eric leaned over the table with its vegetable trays, water soaked rolls, its brisket of beef and a turkey carcass under a gasping red rose. His face lit up and he dashed through the swinging kitchen door.

Hailey started after him—had to jump back as the kitchen door swung toward us and Eric ran back into the dining room holding a box of aluminum foil.

Wrapping the length of the glass vase with aluminum foil and using rubber bands to bind the foil to it took Eric less than a minute. He handed me the foil-sheathed vase.

We all watched him do it.

Like some samurai sword master in movie slow-motion, in our eyes and reflected in the glass rectangle mounted over the mantle, Eric plucked the hammer from his belt, cocked it behind his head and with a soundless *'Kia!'* scream, smashed the hammer smack into the center of the naked mirror.

That *boom!* jerked a glass cracking snap through the whole apartment. The mantel wall shuddered. Ceiling plaster rained on us and the food table.

Jagged spider web lines lightninged out from the pulverized center of the mirror. What had been a smooth, coherent reflected image of us now trembled as dozens of fragmented planes with borders and angles. Our image was in pieces.

Yarrow Clark, M.D./PhD./Harvard-Harvard-Harvard whispered: "Holy fuck!"

Zane said: "Neighbors had to hear, feel that."

"Fuck 'em," said Russell. "Jules pays his rent."

Eric frowned at the mosaic of minimirrors clinging to the wall above the mantle.

Smashed the mirror's starred epicenter with his hammer *again!*

Chunks of mirror flew off the wall. Plaster rained. Glass shattered on the floor.

"Okay," said Russell, "that might have pushed a few neighbors over the line."

"Eric," said Zane, "there's no one behind that mirror watching us."

Eric's eyes measured the sections of mirror still clinging to the wall. He pried off a torso-size survivor and ran to the living room, all of us on his heels.

Folding chairs in the living room still stood in a circle like settlers' wagons waiting for the Indians to attack. Eric put the broken section of mirror on one chair, peered out the wall of windows to the night and the street six stories below. He eased sideways along that glass pane—hammer in his hand.

"Ahh . . ."

"Don't worry, Victor!" said Russell. "This is some kind of beautiful."

And my dumb mistake. I'd split my focus between directing him and controlling the mourning father. I double-weighted my intent instead of centering to face one force at a time, no matter how instantaneously "short" of a time I devoted to each thing. In a Taipei tai chi push-hands battle, such double weighting would have gotten me slammed against a stone wall. Here, in this West Side Manhattan sixth-story apartment, it got me watching Eric walk along a wall of night windows with a hammer.

Eric stopped. Stared out the window. Raised the hammer—

Laid it on the floor by the windows, *just so*. Eric held his hand palm down. Slid his hand along his body to establish a certain measure of height.

"Don't touch anything!" said Hailey. "Remember, he's an engineer."

"And not the train driver kind," said Russell.

Eric closed the heavy curtains over the wall of night windows.

"I don't see what we're doing!" said our host Jules.

Eric snapped on a table lamp. He moved one end of the foil wrapped vase to a point on the closed curtains in line with the hammer. He pressed the bottom of the vase against the curtain at the height he'd judged with his hand, circled a felt pen around the vase on curtain—and scissored that drawn hole from the heavy cloth.

"Hey, I need to live here after you're gone!" snapped Jules.

"Don't worry about that." Yarrow Clark jerked her hand to cover her mouth.

Eric penetrated the curtain hole with the bottom of the foiled vase. Had me hold it. Peered down the open cannon end and angled the vase tube up. He steeled me into a locked solid position with an urgent grip.

"Just tell us what you need!" said Hailey.

Eric grabbed his head like it was going to explode. Glared at me.

"Okay!" I said. "Sorry I somehow made you mute! Just . . . Go! Do it!"

He closed the living room door. Turned out the ceiling lights. Picked up the chunk of mantle mirror. Edged through the circle of chairs to snap off the table lamp.

Darkness swallowed us, darkness pierced only by a shaft of light flowing through the vase poked through a hole in the curtain.

The shaft of light hit a mirror thrust in its telescoped path and bounced up to the white ceiling. That light refracted in reflected glory as a flat plane of illumination.

The mirror tilted as Eric stepped closer and farther back, each motion adjusting the swirl of light's focal length bounced to the ceiling until an illuminated patch of ceiling above us took on form and substance, shape and sense.

"Wow," whispered Hailey.

Ghost movie. The city street below projected onto the ceiling like a diorama from heaven. The scene played live with intense crime lights from the Korean grocer across the street, open then at 9:35 P.M., open with a glow fed by a full moon, by a streetlight, by green-yellow-red winks from a traffic signal. Sound, no sound in that movie or in our room. Above us danced waves of the outer night where a parked car sat across the street from Jules's apartment building, where a person in the driver's seat of that car rested his arm on his lowered window and watched Jules's front door. Sound, no movie sound as specters of two men appeared next to that driver's window, as one of them shaped his hands in what we recognized as *making a cell phone call.*

"That's about us," I whispered.

What I'd told Eric: "*Stick with Dr. Clark. Don't say anything. Don't answer any questions. . . . Keep an eye on her and an eye out the window and let us know if.*"

Don't say anything. Don't answer questions. Keep an eye out. Let us know.

Finally, orders accomplished, Eric could use his voice.

"Uh-oh," he said as in the silent movie on the ceiling, the two men outside the car split up and vanished into the darkness. "Uh-oh."

27

THE ROOFTOPS OF New York under a full moon are a glorious sight even when you're running for your life.

We'd grabbed Jules's cash, all the money from Yarrow's purse, envelopes from the basket on the sideboard table, said *fuck it,* threw open the apartment door and found the hall empty. We took an elevator, used Jules's building key to get on the roof.

"What then?" he'd said as we rushed through his apartment gearing up to bolt. "You so crazy you think you can fly?"

I said: "We're sane enough to know we can die."

We gave Jules and Yarrow pillows and made them lay on the living room floor.

Maybe the opposition agents in the car were a surveillance team. Maybe *outside* was where a snatch squad planned to net us. Maybe they'd use a ruse like we did to get *inside,* get Jules to open his door. If they opted for blitz door kicking—stun/flash grenades, charging armor plated SWAT troops with machine guns and shotguns and Extreme Force Authorized—then the best place to be was flat on the floor like a hostage who needed rescue or a conspirator who didn't need another bullet.

"How long do we have to stay like this?" said Jules as he lay pressed to Yarrow.

"Past dawn!" said Zane as he tossed Hailey her coat. "But that's just a guess."

Jules said: "You don't even know if somebody's out there!"

"Somebody is always out there," I said.

"Car pulls up across the street," said Eric. "Front seat woman passenger gets out. Walks both sides of block. Gets back in. Sits and waits. Watches."

"That could mean anything!" argued Yarrow. "They could be anybody!"

"Parked in front of a fire hydrant," said Eric.

Russell said: "Cops. Catchers. Killers."

"Or arrogant fools," said Jules. "You could be wrong."

Yarrow said: "You're running from invisible enemies."

"Welcome to the real world," I told her.

On the roof, we ran like five mice. If we'd been like the pigeons we spooked who cooed and flapped off to safety in the night, we could have made silhouettes against the full moon like Peter Pan, Wendy, and the Lost Boys.

"Vic," said Hailey as we climbed over the firewall between Jules's building and the next residential behemoth: "How long do you think Jules and Yarrow will lay there?"

"Long enough."

Hailey smiled in the moonlight. "That's nice."

Zane said: "I hope you're right about Jules stopping her from calling nine-one-one as soon the door closed behind us."

We huddled in the shadows of a rooftop storage shed that smelled of tar.

Russell said: "If the team down below us are full service janitors . . ."

"Then it won't matter if Jules and the Doc are laying down."

Somewhere in the night streets below, a yellow taxi honked.

"Unintended consequences," I said. "Proximity casualties."

"We had to go there," said Zane. "It was the necessary, the smart move."

"Yeah. Look where it got everybody."

Under that full moon we were part of New York's indigo skyline. We saw the lights of the Chrysler building. The Empire State building. But no King Kong. No World Trade Center towers.

"Don't worry them," said Russell. "*Wet* won't happen. We're who they want."

"Whoever 'they' are," said Zane.

"Doesn't matter," I argued: "The CIA, our Castle Keepers, cops working blind on CIA strings or even just responding to a nine-one-one call, outside conspiracy agents or inside renegades who've hijacked the legitimate hunt, a combo of all that."

"Any way it plays out," said Hailey, "caught is caught, dead is dead."

Eric hammered open a roof door. We rode an elevator down, strolled out the front door like we belonged. We were one street over from Jules's building, gambled that our hunters hadn't yet scrambled enough troops for a full block coverage.

The first parking garage used an electronic key car gate and was too close to Jules's. Second garage had easy in/out, but felt busy. Zane spotted the attendant in the booth at the third garage: "He's some kind of out of it. Sleeping, on the nod, drunk."

Russell and Eric slipped around him without his eyes opening. When they roared past him in a blue Dodge SUV twenty minutes later, the attendant's lids never fluttered.

"Got it all," Russell said as we piled inside. "CD player, no global positioning unit they can turn on to find us, seating for five, dust on the hood so I figure it's not used every day and won't be missed, and if we're lucky, no secret theft-tracking system."

We parked near our Chelsea hotel, left Hailey behind the wheel with Eric riding shotgun while us three hard guys risked the in-and-out, grabbed our GODS and matrices, went out through a fire door Russell short-circuited so the alarm wouldn't ring, made it back to the SUV without getting killed or caught. Or maybe even seen.

Hailey climbed out and held the SUV door for me: "You drive. Big as this whale is, three men in the backseat still makes a crowd."

"Rock us out of town, man," said Russell in the backseat. "Get us gone."

"No!" I said. "We can't just go."

"We sure as shit can't stay!" said Zane.

"Think!" I argued. "They tracked us to that apartment. Doesn't matter if they monitored the police radio traffic sending a cruiser to check out what a mourner called in or if we made some other slip or if they just got smart. They'll get Jules and Yarrow to tell them we're headed to D.C. They'll get that info, doesn't matter *how*."

"Yeah," said Hailey, "but it matters *when*."

"When is now," I said. "We've got to figure the regular

route is blown. They know we're going south to D.C. Toll booths, highway bottlenecks, a rolling box trap—they'll be working on setting that up now, and they're ahead of us."

"We've gotta get out of here," said Russell.

"But not like we planned," I steered the SUV into traffic. "Or like they think."

We drove away under Hot Zone Rules. Flank Man Russell watched the side streets out one rear seat window, Zane took the other. Hailey slid over the backseat to the cargo bay, rode staring through the red glow from our taillights as Rear Guard. Beside me in the front seat, Eric rode Slack, focused on all the cars streaming toward us in the opposite lane in case they'd organized Waterfall Surveillance with our stalkers circling a loop always coming at us and adjusting to the directions we turned by radio. As Wheel Man, I concentrated on keeping us a moving target.

We came into New York high over a bridge.

We gambled, went out low through a tunnel.

Rumbled through that long bright tube, refracted and reflected like the light caught and shot through Eric's improvised telescope. If any hunters set an ambush for us in that tunnel, we'd all end up on the news, and that kind of high incident exposure meant keeping a cover story intact would be impossible. We paid the toll, knew the cameras snapped us going south, just like our hunters would expect.

But thirty seconds after leaving the tunnel, I whipped our SUV onto a curving off-the-route exit ramp.

"The Long Island Expressway," said Zane. "The 'L-I-E.'"

"Ain't that the truth." I hid us in the slipstream of a wooshing semitruck. All we could see through our windshield was his cargo box's back end. With luck, all any cameras or Waterfall Watchers would have time to see would be his headlights.

Ten minutes later, Hailey reported no hungry yellow eyes stroking our trail. I eased off the truck and let that teamster hurtle toward midnight without us.

On the road again. The dark lonely highway. The everywhere night. The hum of tires on blacktop. The smells of some stranger's car seats, a kid's juice box, our sweat.

"What's happening to us?" whispered Russell.

Out of my mouth popped: "Everything."

"No, man," he said. "Seriously. Zane . . . He finally melts down so far he cools out. Me . . . I got it. I did it. All those years in the hospital . . . I feel . . ."

"Hollow," said Zane. "Light."

"Yeah," said Russell. "You think our bootleg meds are working?"

"Dr. F said any meds are just tools," I said. "That we do the real work ourselves."

"Or get it done to us," said Hailey.

"There is that."

Signs our minds couldn't see just then flicked past the windshield.

Russell asked: "You think we're still crazy?"

"Oh yeah," I said. "Some things never change."

"Thought you believed change was the only certain constant in life," said Hailey.

"How crazy is that," I said. "If I'm right, I'm on my way to wrong."

"But where are we going?" said Russell.

Eric answered: "Washington, D.C."

"Ultimately," I said.

"Kyle Russo," said Hailey. "A voice on the phone. Black letters on a white card."

Russell asked her: "How do you feel? You and Eric?"

She sighed: "Feeling won't matter soon for me."

"So you're the same," said Zane. "And Eric . . . How you were at Jules's . . . You're still who you've been. But Victor's starting to be funny."

"I've always been funny!"

"Nah," said Russell. "You just think you have. You've been too haunted, too much of a worrier, but now . . . You're cutting loose."

"Like this?" I flung both hands off the steering wheel.

As we hurtled sixty miles per hour down the night highway.

"Whoa!" yelled Russell.

Zane lunged forward from the backseat.

But my hands beat him back to their grip on the wheel.

"You think that's funny?" I demanded. "Funny *ha-ha* and not funny peculiar?"

In the rearview mirror, Zane frowned. Said: "Eric?"

Even an inferred command must be obeyed. From the passenger's seat beside me, Eric said: "Vic held the steering wheel with his thighs."

"Reminds me." Hailey rummaged in her GODS. Snapped on a flashlight. Pages in the thick book Jules gave her rustled and turned. "Yeah, thought so. Russell, you know those white pills?"

"Yeah, I took one."

"They're birth control pills."

"What?"

I said: "Now you don't need to worry when somebody says 'fuck you.'"

"See!" yelled Zane. "Vic *is* getting funnier!"

"And I'm some kind of fucked!"

"Well . . ." I replied to Russell.

"If you're fucked," said Zane, "think about the teenage girl back at the school near that Starbucks who dumped her contraceptives on us for a few bucks."

"Amateur crazies." I sighed.

"What about us?" said Russell. "We've been pros, but now . . ."

"We still got our standing," said Zane. "Dr. F claimed that no matter what trauma triggers shot us to crazy, we wouldn't have gone down so deep if we hadn't been predisposed to by broken genes or kid stuff."

"So you need to already be insane to go crazy?" I said. "Seems too absurd."

Our tires hummed over the road as the night flew past us.

Russell handed one of his CDs to Eric. Our engineer fed it to our stolen car, and off his *Nebraska* album, Bruce Springsteen rode in his stolen car and begged the state troopers not to stop him.

Everybody's trying to escape, I thought. *Why do we feel so all alone?*

Eric rode in the glow of our dashboard lights.

"Hey," I told him. "Back there in the city. At Jules's. You were terrific."

His blush radiated all the way to my driver's seat.

"Coming up with that telescope."

"Leonardo da Vinci," he said. *"Camera obscura."*

"What?"

"Been done before. Sort of. Him."

"Oh, well, that makes all the difference in the world, and pardon me for thinking that coming up with something brilliant like that under the gun was special!" I felt his grin. "Here I am driving a stolen car carrying a crew of crazies, hellhounds on our trail, and sitting right beside me is Leonardo da Vinci."

I smiled: "Some guys got nothing but luck."

28

UH-OH, THOUGHT Eric on that long ago and faraway day when the wreck of his life began as they slammed him down in a chair and steel bracelets clamped his wrists with an electronic *click!* Bad enough when police goons stepped out of the blowing sand at the construction site and pulled him away from the other foreigners being loaded into a truck. Bad enough when they put him in a black hood. Whisked him away in a car. Rode him for hours. Bad enough when they hustled him black-hooded through a fortress that smelled of gun oil and concrete, rust and urine. Bad enough he stumbled in the black hood, heard shouts. Screams. Pistol shot. Bad enough when they pushed him down those stairs. But *then* they plopped him in a metal chair and clamped him to it with *prepared* high-tech manacles. That, *that* was real bad.

"You are in the White Lion." A man's voice. English. Accent: Iraqi.

The black hood flew off Eric's head. Searing light made him squint.

Glasses! thought Eric. *Does he have my glasses?*

He saw blurs. A prison room. No windows. Clamps trapped him in a metal chair facing a wooden desk that held a snake-necked lamp. Behind the desk perched the blur of a man in an olive uniform.

Eric shouted in Berlin-accented English: "I want to see my German consulate!"

Whamang!

Oh God oh God oh! Eric shuddered from the *fire blast* vibration that he knew had to be shock treatment through the chair, a jolt of electricity.

"August 17, 1990," said the man behind the desk. "Yesterday, our glorious Saddam extended his protection to you guest workers from Kuwait and Britain, France and Germany. He provided your detention for our mutual safety from the crazy warmongering Americans. You were brought here. To Basra. To the White Lion. To me."

"My name is—"

Whamang!

Drooling, Eric knew he was drooling. Didn' get to tell him m' cover name. Engineer, no wife, no kids—*that's* true 'n' truth is the heart of a good lie.

Guards dragged Eric down a corridor to a black steel door they swung open. They put Eric's glasses on him. The walk-in closet he faced was a box of dizzy. Random bricks rose from the box floor that rose and fell like a wave. A man-size metal shelf sloped out from one wall. Giant teardrops of red and blue and green smeared the walls.

"*Checa*," said the desk man in a state security uniform. He had a mustache. "Our *checa*. Named for the Tsar's secret police. The Soviets who advised rebels in Spain loved your modern art. Kandinsky and Klee. Miró. Pavlov. Our glorious leader admires Stalin, so certain research from the West's past has been provided for us."

"I'm Hans Wolfe. I'm a German citizen here on a privileged work visa."

Guards shoved Eric into the *checa* cell. Slammed the door shut with a hollow metal *bong*. Eric heard the *clack* of an electronic lock.

Standing didn't work. He saw nothing plumb. No horizon. Walls, ceiling and floor winged at him as skreeing planes. Eric tripped over a brick, fell onto the iron bed that sloped down from the wall. Eric rolled off it. The bent planes, wavy ground, explosions of color, strobing lights: he was trapped in a surrealist painting.

Later. Guards pulled him from his cell. Beat him with L-shaped police batons from the previous decade's U.S. foreign aid program. They threw him in the *checa*. He soiled himself. They dragged him out. Knifed off his clothes. Fire hosed him. Dragged him naked to that chair.

Mustache Man sat behind the desk. *"What are the three questions?"*

"I don't know!"

Electricity jolted Eric so hard his glasses flew off his face.

Behind the desk, the blurred man waved his hand in the glow of the snake-necked lamp. "Passport. Visa. Streams of computer code. Data means nothing. What matters is what works. A machine must obey. Or, *engineer,* it is a failure. Failure is unacceptable.

"Three questions. First question: *Who are you?*"

A rolling blast of electricity battered Eric into unconsciousness.

He woke writhing. In the *checa*. Guards jabbed eyeglasses on his face and pushed it toward two wooden bowls. The first bowl held gruel Eric fingered into his mouth. He slurped the second bowl of scum water.

Torture shouldn't have started right away, he knew. They should have waited until I argued my cover story so they could tear it—and me—apart.

Do the math, he told himself. Allied forces massing along the border of Kuwait and Iraq. Langley will know I got yanked from the group of Western engineers at the construction site for the enriched uranium plant. They know I'm missing. They'll find out I'm here. Tanks will roll over the Iraqi border to rescue me.

But not soon enough.

The White Lion will chew me to death.

Three choices:

Blow cover—Heck, spill my guts to convince them I'm most valuable alive.

Die without breaking.

Or escape.

Not going to die. Not going to break. Not going to traitor.

A guard yelled in Iraqi. Swung his L-shaped truncheon down on Eric's leg. The guard's buddy slammed the naked prisoner with a wooden bucket. *Grampa Claude back in Ohio liked Hank Williams's song 'bout a hole in his bucket.*

Guards took turns clubbing and kicking the prisoner. He pleaded in German, in English. The guards were careful not to break his glasses. They want me to see, he thought, then realized *no:* they *need* me to see this swirling box of colors and strobes. They want me locked in here, unable to lock *here* out of me.

They didn't notice his eyes searching beyond their clubs and boots. Dangling on wires from the cantilevered ceiling were metal shapes, some smaller than his hand, others bigger than a basketball. Amidst the wires on the ceiling, Eric spotted a metal box.

Camera mount. But no camera. No all-time unblinking eye.

A guard lifted off the prisoner's glasses; the guard's fist rushed closer as a blur.

Waking up. Clamped in that chair. Glasses taped on his swollen face. Tastes like dried blood and broken fillings. Thick cheek stubble. Ribs, legs, bowels—throbbing with fire. Naked. Cold. Trapped in that chair across from the empty desk. Alone.

Focus, thought Eric. Play the White Lion like you're innocent. Hans Wolfe, not Eric Schmidt. Heidelberg University, not Youngstown U. Engineer. Always an engineer.

A door opened. Mustache Man walked in and sat behind the desk.

Said: "What is the first question?"

"Who . . . Who are you?"

Mustache Man nodded. "My name is Major Aman."

Drops of sweat rolled off Eric. Tapped the cement floor.

Major Aman said: "What is the second question?"

Oh God don't know, he's going to zap me, he's going to—

"You don't know?" Major Aman shrugged. *"Huh."*

The secret policeman leaned closer. "The second question brought us here."

Brace don't brace yourself don't . . . when . . .

"But the first question is key." Major Aman scanned a file. "Hans Wolfe. Engineer rented by us from Volksgotten construction. Is that how you pronounce it? I speak no German, so good you speak English, *ya?*" Major Aman permitted himself the curl of a smile. "One engineer among a firm of hundreds of engineers. No children. No wife. No family. No connections. *Who are you?"*

Whamang!

Oh God God please no, oh. Oh. Over, that one's over.

"The answer to *who you are* is *alone,* and that's key to you being here."

Eric blinked: My cover, my lies plus my true life . . . made the key . . . to this?

"The second question is: *What do you do?"*

Everything seared to lightning crimson blackness.

He came to being dragged naked over gray cement. Risked raising one eyelid: Long corridor. Closed doors. No cameras. No desk for a sentry. No sentry.

Guards dropped him. Eric saw a guard tap a keypad mounted outside a black steel door with a tilted *C* handle. *Electric buzz* and the door clicked loose. Out from the *checa* burst a swirl of color. Eric closed his eyes. They dragged him inside and he didn't move. Didn't flinch when the door *bonged* shut and the electronic lock *clicked.*

Count each breath. Keep a fix on time. Figure they'll go pee, have a smoke, wipe the puddles off the floor by that chair, catch a meal. I'm here. Alone.

The beatings, electrocutions and swirling colored cell made him so dizzy he had to crawl to the door. His hands found the lock plate. Found four screw heads.

He smeared himself up the cool metal door. The lock plate shifted under his hand: loose. Life in wartime, 'specially in Iraq. What works, works. What doesn't work is just the way things are.

When guards pushed open the door, he was still leaning against it. Their shove knocked his naked body through the air, crashed it on the jumble of bricks.

They didn't beat him.

Or take him to Major Aman and the chair.

Instead they quick marched him to the hose-down room and a wooden barrel. *Like a rain bucket* was how Eric thought of it because of Grampa Claude. The guards held his head under the barrel's water. They pulled him up to gasp the wet concrete prison air. Ducked him again. Again. Threw him back in the *checa*.

But *heck*, that was *great!*

Now, *finally,* thanks to Grampa Claude, Eric envisioned hope.

Took it with him to the chair in front of Major Aman.

"There are truths," said the torturer. "People are people. They are who they are. Plus, the American poet Bob Dylan is right: Everyone must serve somebody. Or something. Our great Saddam serves the good of Iraq. We all serve who we call God.

"You serve us," Major Aman told the naked man clamped in the chair. "We are the reason you're here. The rest is your ignorance. *What is the second question?*"

Eric jerked and blurted: "What do you do!"

"And what do *you* do?"

Knew it before it happened, but still the electric shock slammed Eric to white.

"What do you do? You obey orders. You work for us. You are alone.

"Yet when that secretary whispered how she and her Republican Guard husband hated their lives in Iraq. . . . Who conspired with her? You, Hans Wolfe."

Oh please God, no! They caught her! Caught them! They'll be locked in a place like this, or in a ditch . . . !

"That's not you," said Aman. "That's not our lonely engineer."

Not my mission! Eric had told himself day after day at the secret construction site as he watched the secretary tremble.

Not here to rescue! Not here to recruit. Here to play the pudgy geek people see when they look at me. Here to spy, get data, steal info.

"We know the man you sent them to. All you foreigners mixing in the bazaar come into contact with scum like that man who smuggles traitorous dogs out of Iraq."

Got Sa'ad too—or will, he always knew they were close. That poor family! If I hadn't disobeyed Agency orders, if I'd stuck to mission and not got involved to save . . .

"Playing rescuer is not in your profile. Which makes you interesting beyond your isolated state. Special among guest workers we had to choose from. Means you're changeable. Luckily, your change was to 'rescue' our counterintelligence team."

"Wha . . . What?"

"Our team wasn't looking for you. They were monitoring our scientists who think too much, get ideas about fleeing to America or Marseilles. You getting hooked by them was the final sum of fate that brought you here. *What do you do?*"

Eric said: "The husband and wife . . . They were secret police? I got trapped by them for . . . for being . . . *just a good guy!* Only *that*? That's why I'm here?"

Whamang!

Waking up on the floor of the *checa*, Eric remembered: I disobeyed. Broke mission. Tried to be a good guy. Got suckered. Got here.

He found a wall. Stood. Saw the iron bed.

Eric put one foot on the bed and leapt, arms above his head. He grabbed . . .

Got it! Steel wire slices hands when it's grasped. Eric blood-slipped down the wire until his hands hit a green metal mobile—that popped free of the ceiling, and he crashed to the bricks like a bespectacled walrus.

Eric bent the book-size sheet of thin metal until it snapped into two pieces. The biggest section had the wire melded to it, the smaller section looked like a putty knife.

Using his shit like putty, Eric adhered the small blade

from the mobile to the underside of a floor brick. Smeared the rest of the cell with his bloody hands. He hid the true intent of those wounds to his hands with cosmetic slashes on his wrist.

Passed out.

Woke up head held underwater in the barrel by guards who shook the broken mobile in his gasping face before they dunked him again. For a bonus round, they beat him with their L-shaped police clubs. Next thing he knew, he was in the chair.

Major Aman wiped Eric's face with a warm towel. "Can I tell you a secret?"

To Eric's slurping lips he held a cup of warm coffee fortified with milk and sugar.

"You can't kill everybody." Major Aman sighed. "You can try, but it's counterproductive. What the world needs now is not dead people. What we need are useful people. Who obey. Then everything works like paradise, right engineer?"

He waited until Eric finished the tin cup of sweet milked coffee, then into his other ear, whispered: "Suicide is choice and choice challenges obedience. You won't try suicide again unless you're obeying an order. *What is the second question?*"

"What do 'o, do," slurred Eric.

"And what does everybody do?"

"Obey orders."

But I didn't! thought Eric. *I disobeyed CIA orders 'n' look what happened!*

"Next time," promised Major Aman, "we get to move on."

Not one shock, thought Eric as guards dragged him back to the *checa.* They fed him. Clubbed him once out of politeness. Closed the door with a *bong* and a *click.*

Every cell in his body begged for unconscious oblivion. Eric crawled until he found the right brick, the shit-stuck metal blade. He slithered to the door. Took him 232 breaths to remove the four screws holding the electronic lock's plate to he steel door.

Good thing they'd taped his glasses on. Good thing the lights kept strobing.

Eric peered into the metal jumble of the electronic lock. Spotted the two wires, but deep in the lock: *Darn,* no way could he use his metal strip to do the final job.

Hope we go to the bucket soon, thought Eric as he screwed the plate back over the lock. Or there won't be enough left of me to escape.

Next time, they took him straight to the chair.

Major Aman said: "There are three questions. First question?"

"Who are you."

"Second question?"

"What do you do."

"You are what you do. And see? You obey. What we have here is a chance to—"

Crackety-zap!

What's wrong? Can't feel that electricity! Can't—

The snake-necked lamp on Major Aman's desk went *crazy.* Blue sparks and smoke swirled as jolts of escaping electricity made the lamp hop and clatter like a robot gone mad. Major Aman jumped away from the desk. A guard charged from behind Eric and hit the gone-crazy lamp with his L-shaped police baton.

Inertia bounced the lamp off the desk, sparks sputtering. The guard swung the police baton like a golf club, smacked the brass lamp clattering across the floor. Unplugged, the lamp said nothing as the guard clubbed it again and again. Panting, sweat soaked, the guard marched past the naked man clamped in the chair and couldn't help but give the prisoner a grin of triumph.

"Sorry about that," said Major Aman as he took his seat behind the desk. "The curse of an imprisoned country. So often our things, especially high tech . . . break. We have to constantly plan and prepare for such inconveniences."

Whamang!

"Oh good, still works. Where were we? Ah, yes. The third question.

"Before that," said Major Aman, "consider: *Who you are* is one person. Everyone serves. Obedience is the heart of service. Some citizens don't realize that they should serve the glorious leader. That ignorance is common among potentially productive citizens. Scientists. Engineers. Inventors. Executives. Lawyers. Teachers. Writers. Our challenge is to wipe out ignorance without lowering productivity."

Major Aman gestured with a slaughtered snake-neck lamp to the room and a naked man clamped in a chair. "This is an experiment to answer that challenge."

"Brainwash."

"What good is a washed clean brain? We need a brain that embraces the logic of obedience without losing its creative potential. We can't risk Iraqi brains with mere experiments. But we have guest workers. We have you. You have the right kind of mind. You showed yourself to be changeable. You're all alone. You're just a rental.

"The third question," said Major Aman, angling his arm to show the poise of his finger while Eric's eyes gravitated to him. "The third question is . . ."

Wait no wait no wait . . .

"The third question is: *How can you make this life of pain worth it?*"

Whamang!

That session became one excrutiating searing shock as he heard Major Aman reveal how *who we are* means service is inevitable. How the heart of service was obedience. How that perfect formula builds usefulness. Usefulness means an end of pain and aloneness. Usefulness was the answer to the third question of how you make this life worth it. The first question meant *who one was* created the question of *what had to be done,* and that brought usefulness to make this thing called life *worth it.*

When he woke up on the floor of the *cheka,* Eric cried.

But not enough, he sobbed. I need a bucket of tears!

Two chair sessions later—or maybe four—guards dragged him to the barrel.

Waking up choking almost foiled him, but the third time guards dunked his head under the water, he remembered.

Swallowed. Drank as he thrashed. Drank all he could. *There's a hole in my bucket, don't let any water run out.* They dunked him until they were all too worn out to do the routine beating, so *fuck it,* they just dragged it back to the swirling colors/blasting lights *checa* and dumped it on the floor.

Bong! went the slammed-shut door.

Click! went the electronic lock.

Now or never. Eric crawled on his water-swollen belly. Found the brick shit-stuck with his secret screwdriver. Found the door. Unscrewed the lock plate.

Standing. I'm me. I'm a man. I'm standing. Naked. Wearing glasses.

Wish I had galoshes. Hell, even sneakers—they'd be *perfect* for *next*!

You got what you got. You are who you are. You have to do—*No!*

What the heck, it's only one more time.

With the best aim of his life, Eric peed a bucket into the electronic lock.

Whamang! He discovered he'd been knocked back to the wall.

Smoke coming out of the electronic lock! Shorted it out! I took the shock. Did it!

Like a giddy drunk, Eric toddled to the smoking door. Hooked his finger in the wet lock hole. *Gone, I'm gone.* He pulled with all his strength.

On the other side of the *checa*'s door, out there in that *imprisoned country* where *often things, especially high tech, break,* where life meant having to *plan and prepare for . . . inconveniences,* out there in the empty hall, guards had slipped an L-shaped police baton through the cell door's steel loop handle like a medieval bar to back up the unreliable twentieth-century electronic lock.

Eric pulled. And pulled. Pulled. Collapsed sobbing into swirling color and light.

The guards and Major Aman were not pleased. Or discouraged.

Everyone worked harder.

Until Eric remembered the guard's ludicrous smile of triumph.

Laying on his back in the *checa,* naked, glasses taped on, Eric's right hand flopped and hit his face. He cupped his mouth to stop from shouting his new secret:

Sometimes triumph is beating a lamp to death.

Obey orders. That's what Aman/Saddam/Iraq wanted him to do.

Obey orders. That's what the CIA wanted him to do.

Questions of who to obey only brought him pain. Good Guy orders versus Bad Guy orders: the equation null sets if all forces are equal. Obeying everyone equals obeying no one. No pain then. *Who I am* is the engineer, *what I do* is obey all orders.

The *checa* swirled. Bent walls and reckless colors calmed themselves into straight lines with proper angles and sane patterns. He faced the sloping iron shelf. Every time he'd tried to lay on that bed, he rolled off.

Eric stretched out on the iron slab. His left hand gripped the edge to let him lie on a sloped iron bed in defiance of mere realities like gravity.

Making it work, making it add up—with a ludicrous grin—to his own triumph.

Three days later, Major Aman yelled: "You're worthless! You obey anybody!"

Eric stood across the room from that chair. Stood naked, on one leg, his finger poked in his nose, his beard and hair smelling burnt.

"Supposed to belong to just us! I'll get in trouble for screwing up your experiment!"

Bare naked Eric stood there on one leg, his finger poked in his nose like a random guard had told him to do. Major Aman *hadn't* asked the naked man if his real name was Hans Wolfe or if he worked for the CIA. After his epiphany in the *checa,* Eric would have *of course* told Major Aman those answers to obey their questions. But the torturer never asked. Even with his finger up his nose, Eric knew that smelled of victory.

"Stand on both legs," ordered Major Aman on their last day. "Take your finger—put your hands down. You are going off the list of my problems. No more *checa*. Bathe. Eat, sleep, get yourself to look good for the TV cameras. Soon, Saddam will send you guest workers home, public relations gesture. Get on the plane to Germany. When you get there, what you do doesn't matter to us, because clearly, you are crazy."

Eric obeyed and obeying proved his thesis: the pain stopped. A CIA recovery team scooped him off the curb while he was waiting for the Don't Walk sign to change at the Bonn airport. The recovery team gave Eric to the Castle.

Where he obeyed every order. Where we developed a flow that let him lead an okay life. After Hailey walked into the ward, Eric began again to think for himself, speak his thoughts, have desires. But he never violated his triumph of absolute slavery.

29

COLD. WET. DARK.

Words about me as I stood on the beach listening to the waves in the black night.

Cold. Wet. Dark.

Words about spies.

Cold. As in Cold War. As in ruthless. As in the world of invisible battles preceding the public's blasting by bombs and bullets. As in, "cold as a grave."

Wet. As in, "wet work." *Wet* as in *blood*. What the spy services of the crumbled Soviet Union called neutralizations, assassinations, murder.

Dark. As in "covert." As in "black." As in "black budget/work/world." As in "black site."

Walking toward me across the packed sand came Hailey. The full moon made her smile glisten and her eyes bright. We stared at the rippling night as waves swept up to wet our feet and whirl salt spray on our faces. A jillion white dots twinkled overhead.

"How many of those stars do you think are already dead?" she said. "And us just standing here waiting for the light to catch up to being gone."

I said nothing.

"Do you know why it's always out there?" she asked. "The ocean?"

I gave her no answer.

After a dozen crashing waves, she said: "If it wasn't out there, we'd drown here."

Waves lapped at the ground beneath our feet.

She said: "I dare you to smile."

"I'm too cold."

"Go back to the SUV." She angled her head to where our stolen ride sat parked on the beach lit by a full moon. "Zane's got first sentry, hiding with the gun back in that pile of boulders. Russell will relieve him in two hours. As eager as Russell is to get the gun in his hands, he won't oversleep. Come back with me. Pretend you like sleeping huddled in a car parked on the beach."

We listened to the waves.

She said: "What are you worried about? We already jumped into the big wrong."

"I just want . . ." Words stopped.

"Come on. Tell the girl in the moonlight what she wants to hear."

"I want it to work. Even though what we've done is crazy. We're crazy."

"And all in it together," she said.

I thrust words at her like daggers: "Of our own *free will?*"

"Whatever," she parried. "That's not your problem."

"Sure it is."

"Whatever," she repeated. "What's your real problem now?"

"What if I've totally fucked up? This whole thing. Busting out. Jumping over to this damn beach on Long Island to wait out any leaving–New-York ambushes. If the meds you scored don't smooth us out, we've only got three days left before we fall apart. We're three days on the road and we're nowhere. What if I'm totally wrong?"

"Is Dr. F still dead?" said Hailey. "Or was that our mass hallucinogenic hysteria?"

"Oh, he's dead. I went to his memorial shivah."

"Quite a party, huh?" She found no smile on my face. "Did he die or was he hit?"

My silence confirmed murder.

"And instead of us taking the fall like it was framed, we busted out. We might still go down, but we aren't just surrendering. And most of that is thanks to you."

"But what if I fuck up? I don't care about me, but the rest of you . . ."

"The whole world is your responsibility, right?" she said. "Maybe. But only with what you can do. What you can't . . ."

"You pay for," I said.

"Everybody pays."

Waves lapped.

"We all know that," she said. "We all signed on."

"Maybe you should all think about signing off."

Waves washed to the shore.

She said: "You know how Russell took a birth control pill by mistake?"

"Yeah."

"Well he won't throw the other two away."

"That's—"

"Crazy?" she said.

We both laughed.

"Russell figures one of them sacrificed itself for him— even if it was born to be a pill. Maybe it was what broke him through. Makes sense that something absurd like that worked after years of appropriate but useless treatment. Whatever, Russell won't just throw out the other two pills and say forget it. Forget them. That would be wrong."

"What's he gonna do?"

We turned to look at each other in the moonlight.

"Russell won't walk away from two strange pills because their buddy might have helped him," said Hailey. "Even if it didn't, even if it hurt, loyalty is a must for Russell. So what makes you think he would ever leave our thing?".

"He's no quitter."

"None of us are."

Waves lapped.

"So don't worry about what you've done wrong. We're all in this together."

We stood there for a long time. My bones felt like ice.

"Were you thinking about her?" asked Hailey.

"Nah," I said, truth with a hollow heart. "Got that *'thinking about her'* down to three times a day. Once when I wake up. Then again when I let go as I fall asleep and *whoa:* here come those memories."

"When's the third time?"

"Once a day. When it's light and I realize I'm still alive. It's like . . . one tear."

We walked toward the Jeep.

I said: "What if you aren't really going to die?"

"Oh, sure. Like that's true."

"No," I said. "Suppose all your *I'm dying right now* thing is crazy?"

"Okay," she said. "Suppose. Then what?"

"Then you got what's left."

"Yeah," she said. "Terrific."

Sand crunched under our shoes.

"Was what you told me about Russell and the white pills true? Or did you just need to make a point?"

Hailey said: "What do you think?"

30

GRAY FOG LIT the beach where I stood on Day Four. Morning tide rolled steel-colored waves to shore. Our stolen Jeep sat on packed sand. I could see about fifty yards up the sloping beach to the scrub grass beside the highway. The chill made me shiver. Every inhale smelled of wet sand and cold ocean, each exhale birthed a dying cloud.

In the fog on the highway, a car door slammed.

Car motor: purring away.

Out of the fog walked a lone figure in a long coat.

Suddenly I forgot I was achy, cold, hungry and tired.

Zane and Russell took my flanks.

I said: "Target one unknown standing on the highway turnoff."

"'Xactly," said Zane.

"So it's real," said Russell.

"'*Real*' equals what we all see."

"Man, I hope you're right," said Russell.

"Victor, with me," said war boss Zane. "Russell, boots and saddles."

Russell ran to the SUV.

Zane and I fanned out so one machine-gun burst couldn't drop us both as we marched toward the highway.

"What the hell you two doing down there?" yelled the specter.

A woman: an *old* woman. She wore a tan raincoat and a plastic rain cap tied over her shellacked black hair. Wrinkles mapped her chalk face with its gash of ruby. Her pale hands curled like bird's claws as she stood on the graveled apron beside the highway.

"Looking at the ocean," said Zane as we reached her.

"Why?" Three shopping bags with loop handles and a combat-size black shoulder purse waited on the gravel behind her. "Never mind. Which bus?"

"Excuse me?"

"Which . . . *bus.*"

Zane frowned. "Our bus is . . . blue?"

"Like that matters," she said. "Especially if you're dilly-dallying down on the beach when it comes. You're either on the bus or in the fog.

"Atlantic City picks up over there." Fog swirled to reveal two women standing further up the road. "The NJ double-M stops right here."

"The NJ—"

Her waving hand shushed me. "Okay, it's got some fancy-schmansy new name, but it's still the North Jersey Mega Mall. You two taking the motel deal for the night?"

Luck is recognizing your chances.

"How far—how long is the bus ride to the Mall?" I asked.

"Ninety minutes, though in this damn fog . . . Can't see nothing for nothing."

"Too bad," said Zane. I caught his frown.

"How does this work?" I said. "The rest of . . . our family, we parked off the highway where we wouldn't get hit until—"

"More of you down there?" The bird woman squinted into the fog.

"Brother," I said, "go have . . . have Uncle Sam drive you all up here."

"If your uncle's coming too, there's a pull-off just up the road. Put ten bucks under your wiper, the county road crew guys let you park there couple days."

As he hurried down the beach to our car, Zane said: "Don't leave without us."

Bird Woman tapped my shoulder. "Stick with Bernice, you'll be fine."

"Counting on it," I said. "Do you work for the bus?"

"Hell no," she said. "Then I'd have to let things happen their way."

Bernice scoffed at our lack of preparedness, gave us shopping bags to fill with the gobs of loot our GODS bags clearly wouldn't hold. Other riders joined us. Retired couples. Mom and Aunt with a chattering twentyish gonna-be a bride; they smelled of hairspray. A Korean woman.

As Russell walked back from ditching the SUV, the Atlantic City bus wheeled out of the fog. Casino posters covered its metal. A dozen gamblers scurried on board. That bus rolled away with them and left us still standing by the side of the road.

Our silver bus lumbered off the highway ten minutes after the gamblers left.

"Don't hand me your money!" shouted Bernice as she shaped our meager crowd into a ragged boarding line.

"We'll do tickets on board. Grab a seat, Honey. Nobody wants to be the one who holds us up."

We five filled the back rows.

"This better be better," grumbled Russell.

"We're safer where we got tickets than in a stolen car," I said. "Hiding in here, in the crowd . . . We break our trail of crimes. We're so low profile we disappear."

Zane sniffed his clothes. "We're awful ripe for public transportation."

"We need to stretch out and get real sleep," said Hailey.

Eric nodded.

Our silver bus hummed through fog as Bernice worked her way down the aisle.

"Edna, you got your walking shoes? Janice, didn't your daughter-in-law like that quilt? Did you tell her about doctors? No complaints, Melvin: you can always sit on a planter in the mall and watch girls. Agnes, you need tickets or you got coupons?

"Oscar!" Bernice yelled to the bus driver. "You want I should collect?

"Course you do," she answered herself. "Get us off quicker on the other end."

By the time she reached us, we'd learned enough for me to say: "We've got no coupons, and we want the full package with motel rooms."

Bernice had left her rain cap and tan coat on her seat. She wore a pink sweat suit. An unlit cigarette tucked over her right ear poked through her shiny black curls.

"You get breakfasts," she said handing us vouchers. "Bus drops off at the motel before the mall opens, so do some damage to the buffet. The bacon goes fast."

Her hard green eyes notched us off. "You're room res' numbers seventeen through twenty-one, you pick who's what where. Give these slips to the front desk."

"Do they want a credit card imprint?" asked Zane.

"Don't matter. Nobody gets on the bus tomorrow if they got room charges." She squinted at Zane's white hair. "You got grandkids?"

"Ah . . . no."

"*Children:* Just when you think they're done breaking your heart, they give you an encore. I might as well not have my little troubles, much as I get to see them."

Her gaze floated over five strangers sitting in the back of her bus: That white-haired guy without grandkids. The Black woman who looked like none of these guys' sister. The pudgy guy with thick glasses perched on the edge of his seat. The shaggy-haired rock 'n' roll outlaw no grandma wanted her precious to bring home. The poet with ghosts in his eyes and a switchblade smile. "You're an odd family."

"Who isn't," I said.

The unlit cigarette from behind her ear rolled back and forth in her bird claw.

"Families," Bernice told us. "Moms are in your face with what they're not saying. Dads are gone even when they're sitting in that damn chair. Brothers and sisters, forget about it. You carry their troubles and they eat your time. Kids won't listen to how it was, so they know zero about how it is."

The white tube snuck between her veteran fingers.

"I thought they banned smoking on buses," said Zane. "Fires and cancer."

"I ain't smoked for years." The killer stick slid back behind her ear.

Our silver steed rolled onto a major highway.

Bernice stared out the bus windows. "When I was a girl, we went from store to store by going outside. Then we got malls so you never had to see the sun, never had to get wet. Now there's computers, if you got smarts and bucks. No need to leave your house, or even meet the deliveryman. Free to stay locked in where you are. Real stores run bus deals to catch us people who need a reason and a place to go."

I sent her words back to her: "You're either on the bus or in the fog."

"Yeah," she said. But she didn't like it.

Two hours later, the five of us were in adjoining motel rooms, breakfast bar stuffed, Russell caffeinated enough to take first watch and wash our clothes in the motel's laundry center while we collapsed into actual beds. In the hall beyond my door, Bernice urged someone to *get a move on* as I sank into dreamless sleep.

Seven hours later, we blew up the police car.

31

SIX HOURS AND nine minutes after Bernice crossed the road to the white stone mall, our crew stood facing its mirror doors. We carried Bernice's donated bags, scavenged gear, matrices, our GODS. Our reflections looked slept, showered, and shaved, and certain they knew what they were doing in the evening sun.

"Check it out," said Russell. "Five maniacs in the heart of reality."

Staring at our reflections, Hailey told him: "I thought you had the breakthrough."

"Yeah, but turns out it's whacky on the other side."

"'Xactly."

I said: "Let's do it."

The electric eye caught us stepping forward and slid open the mirror doors.

Our pupils absorbed the mall's oceanic light even as it absorbed us. Breathing brought that mall smell. Industrial perfume muted a million armpits and tired feet. Shirts and skirts on store shelves exhaled an aroma of cloth. The deeper we walked into the mall, the sweeter came the food court scent of waffle cones and fried grease. Speckled white-and-black tiles ate the sound of shoes and showed no footprints. We heard snatches of conversation, the whoosh of vacuum, the hum of air processors, *faintly everywhere* recorded instruments cheerfully torturing a vaguely familiar song.

"No!" cried Russell. "That's the Beatles! From the *Sgt. Pepper's* album. 'A Day in the Life' is about how they'd love to turn us on, not sell us shit!"

"Nixon was President last time I was in a place like this," said Zane.

Two old women in stylish sweat suits quick-walked past us, their mouths flapping, their arms pumping, their pure white shoes marching in time.

"They're here to exercise their hearts," I told Zane's stare.

"Oh."

"We're here to gear up and get gone," I said.

Eric shuffled closer to Hailey, said: "Don't leave me!"

"Won't happen," she told him.

We wandered to a kiosk with a backlit map and lists of money stops.

"This one mall has five different sneaker stores!" said Russell.

"Everybody's running," I said for the second time in less than a day.

Eric forced out: "Least we got a reason."

But we walked like we'd lost it, drifted along the wall of chain store windows where headless mannequins sported pants and pullovers cut in communist China's clattering factories or ten toxic steps south of Texas. Trademarks, brand names, merchandized spin-offs, and franchises flew at our eyes like machine-gun bullets. One store promised us herbal vitamin formulas to *naturally* fight ills suffered by vibrant people in the ads who knew they were secretly bald, fat, hollow boned, sick skinned, artery clogged, limp dicked, and anxious. The next store offered miles of gold chains, rings, bracelets, designer watches that also kept time. Nearby windows revealed salesclerks showing customers how to program massage options in leather reclining chairs or how to link a patio-mounted video telescope to a laptop computer so you could sit in your living room and scan the stars.

"How did all this happen?" said Zane.

"Right before our eyes," I said.

"Well," said Russell, "not our eyes. We've been locked up."

Hailey said: "Don't think that makes us innocent."

We walked on.

Hollywood posters for movies at the mall's Cineplex hung on a kiosk. *Beautiful actors* beating the odds to find love. A volcanic world where only *magic* in a heartbroken boy could stop evil's triumph. Back-to-back *rebel cops* blazing pistols at the brilliant bad guy no law could touch. A sexy black-leathered blonde and her sextet of cool sidekicks scoring the *heist* of the century. The *so-lost* affluent family of clueless white people saved by the street savvy of a craggy Black guru. A wildly adventurous *animated* sure-to-be-a-classic for the whole family in which absolutely nothing happened over and over again, the end.

"I'd love to see a movie I'd love to see," said Russell.

The five of us stared into the glowing wonderfulness of a bookstore.

Hailey sighed. "I'd love to visit my better self."

"I'd love to visit old friends." Visions of Faulkner, Lewis, Steinbeck, Camus, Hammett, Marquez, Emily, and Williams danced in my heart. "Make new ones."

"They might have maps we could use," said Russell. "Or great CDs."

Zane shook his head: "They'll be looking for us where we want to be."

Eric nodded.

We turned to walk away—

"Freeze!" whispered Russell, quickly correcting himself: "No! Look natural!"

Eric overloaded, trembled.

Hailey took his arm: "Be calm!"

"What is it?" Zane's hands crossed near his waistband that hid our gun.

"Cameras." Russell pointed his eyes toward heaven.

White metal security cameras hung from the ceiling, swiveled slowly from side to side as they constantly swept the mall with Cyclops glass eyes.

"And in the ATM on that wall!" said Hailey.

"Behind the cash register in that sexy underwear store," said Zane.

"Everywhere," said Eric.

"So what," I said. "Cameras here won't see what matters. They're looking for rowdies or shoplifters, not escapees from sanity."

Eric said: "But there'll be a record we were here."

"If and when anybody looks for us on those tapes," I said,

"we'll be long gone. Plus, as long as there's no reason to check the tapes, it's like we were never seen."

"Still don't like it," said Russell. "It's still not good."

Hailey asked: "What happens to America when Homeland Security finally gets real-time surveillance cameras all over the country?"

Zane said: "Shrinks like Dr. F will need to redefine paranoia."

"Too late," I said, casually leading the crew under the leafy canopy of a palm tree rising from a planter. "Everybody who's not crazy is already paranoid."

"The Animals sang it," Russell told us: "We gotta get out of this place."

"We didn't get what we need!" said Zane.

"They don't got it here," I answered. "But now they got us."

"We've only been here half an hour!" said Hailey.

"Time's up," I said, stepping to a booth where a sign read INFORMATION.

"What do you need to know?" said the booth's white-haired woman.

"Everything," I answered. "Or the fastest way to the biggest parking lot."

"Your nearest exit might be through the all night drug store."

"Should have figured that," whispered Russell.

We went the direction she'd pointed until we spotted the drug store next to a place that sold football jerseys, soccer balls, Team Viagra NASCAR jackets—and sneakers.

"Bathrooms are next to the sports store," I said. "Everybody use 'em."

"Stealing a car from a mall is a bad idea," said Russell. "Forget about how you might get filmed. You never know how soon someone will come out and find what they don't have anymore, call nine-one-one and stick your ride in the system. Stealing it while there's still daylight . . ."

"This is the chance we've got," I argued. "And we've got to get out of here."

"Amen," said Eric.

Zane shook his head: "Look at all your shaking hands. First, we've got to fix."

A water bottle from a vending machine. Hailey shook high school pills out of the jar she'd borrowed from Jules. The only one who took more than three pills was Russell, and his Number Four was small and white. Hailey smiled at me as he popped that one. I was too jangled to pay her with a nod or a grin.

"Gotta get outside," I said as we walked from the mall into the syrupy smelling drug store. Aisles of adult diapers and menstrual pads and mosquito repellent and ceiling lights closed in on me. "Grab what we need, I'll scout us a sled."

Russell tried to stop me: "Popping a ride's not your thing."

"Learn and live."

Zane said: "At least let Eric—"

"*Hey!* I gotta be, gotta get out of here *alone!*"

And I blasted outside to the parking lot.

Pink hues softened the afternoon's long sunlight. I fought to keep control. To look ordinary. Like I belonged.

Must be 2,000 cars out here. I drifted up one aisle and down another. I checked all the SUV war wagons and the minivans. *None of the locks look popped up.*

Few people were in the parking lot. It was as if human beings got sucked straight from their cars to *the shopping experience* by some mammoth vacuum inside the mall. Maybe that vacuum was the hum in the canned music that butchered songs of our youth.

Must be some vacuum, I thought. *I still hear it hum behind me. Now* focus:

Which vehicle to steal? The five of us would barely fit in that red Toyota. The minivan with the "Soccer Mom" bumper sticker has low tires, locks clicked down, the polluted whiff of last year's diapers and this year's bubblegum. That gold SUV has its locks clicked down . . . but its driver's window is open a few inches! Maybe—

Behind me, a woman's voice froze me in my tracks, said: "Can I help you, sir?"

She had light short hair. Tan blouse and pants, black shoes. A silver badge rode her left breast and holstered on her hip was a nine-millimeter Glock. Her idling police cruiser hummed behind her. I saw the radio mike clipped to her epaulet, the black patent leather pouch on her belt for handcuffs, but what truly nailed me were her mirrored black sunglasses that reflected the burning red ball of the setting sun. And me.

"Can I help you, sir?" Second warning.

"Absolutely!" I smiled my most innocent smile.

Even though I absolutely knew she knew. Knew she knew I knew she knew. We stood there, each playing our part, each trying to write the ending for this script. Each living the cosmic wisdom that this was a scene to finish, not start. That choice kept us civil and standing right where we were until the other one made a damning move.

"What seems to be the problem?" Her uniform told me she was a local cop.

"Which one?"

"The one that's had you cruising the aisles like you're shopping for a car."

"Call that luck. My car's in the shop so we used my wife's car to come here."

"And this is it?" The sunglasses nodded toward the gold SUV.

"Yup. We usually take my Ford when we go out, so I only ride in her SUV a few times a month. These days, SUVs are all that's out there and they all look alike."

The black glasses swung from side to side as she worked her peripheral vision without looking away from me. "Where is your wife?"

"She's not here."

"And yet you are."

"Well . . . sure."

"Got a driver's license to show me?"

"I'm not driving."

"I'm helping you out. What if you got the wrong vehicle? Like you said, they all look alike. I'll radio check the registration of this vehicle and be sure it matches the address on your license. You do live with your wife, don't you?"

"Who else would."

She didn't laugh.

"I don't have my driver's license. Well, I do, but . . . It's in the car."

"In the car."

"With my wallet," I said. "That's why I'm out here. To get my wallet."

"You went into a shopping mall but left your wallet in the car."

"Call me an optimist," I said. "But my wife . . ."

"Your wife isn't here."

"She's in the mall. Standing in a cashier's line, actually. Waiting for me to come get my wallet so we can use my credit card, not hers."

"That's a good story," said the cop.

"If only it had a happy ending."

"Let's get your wallet, then we can work on happily ever after."

"See, that's the problem."

"Ahh. *That's* the problem."

"*I know!* I mean it's one thing to leave my wallet in her junk compartment with all those random things that live in there, but then to have her send me out here to get it—"

"For the credit card."

"—for the credit card and have both of us forget to give me her keys."

"So everything's locked up tight inside there."

"There you go." I shrugged my shoulders and grinned. Prayed.

Her black mirror eyes held my reflection as she said: "What *are* we going to do?"

Blue-orange flame arced down behind her idling cruiser—*glass shattered.*

The cop turned so she could keep me in her vision as she glanced left and right, saw nothing that looked like shattered glass. Her sunglasses swung back to target me in the same instant that over her shoulder I saw a wisp of black smoke spiral up the far side of her cruiser's hood, smelled rubber and roses *burning.*

Flames from the made-off-drugstore-shelves Molotov cocktail caught the far front tire of her cruiser on fire.

The cruiser's tire exploded with a *whap!* The cop whirled, drew her gun. Black smoke swooped up from her cruiser. The exploding tire propelled the ignited Molotov brew up into the engine compartment. Flames hit a fuel-injecting gas line.

Wham! A burp of flame blew open the cruiser hood.

The cop staggered backward toward me in the canyon between the parked cars.

Ka-boom! Her cruiser's gas tank erupted in a ball of flame.

Heat blast knocked the cop off her feet.

Me too, a wall of angry heat flashing my face.

Flat on my back on the pavement between two cars, I saw a roaring pillar of orange flame and black smoke rocket straight up into the evening sky. The explosion triggered dozens of honking car alarms.

So much for covert operations. How much of our cadre got filmed?

Get up! Fire roared outside my canyon between two SUVs. The dazed cop lay at my feet, her face and hands redder than mine felt. From everywhere came the stench of melting rubber, burning gas, hot metal, and . . . burnt hair. The gun had been blown from her hand. I saw her groping for her lost weapon.

She's trying to fight the good fight.

So I dragged her back from the fireball. She was dazed, struggling to her knees as I ripped the mike out of the radio on her belt, tossed it away, yelled: "I'll get help!"

And ran toward the mall drug store.

Soon as I charged out of the black swirling smoke, Zane—who'd concocted and thrown the Molotov cocktail—slammed a BMW sedan's driver's window with a back kick. The window crackled into a safety-glass spider web. His second kick pushed in the cobwebbed pane. Russell clicked the BMW's locks, hammered the ignition cap off the steering column and used a screwdriver as a car key. The engine roared to life. Russell and Zane raced the stolen BMW through the parking lot where a crowd stared transfixed by the burning cop car. Hailey and Eric ran to meet my feet-pounding escape. The broken-windowed BMW stopped just long enough for us to jump in with our gear, then in a cloud of black smoke and the honking of car alarms and wailing-nearer fire truck sirens, we roared away from the mall's pillar of fire.

32

"LOOK AT ME!" I yelled at Zane from the backseat of our stolen BMW as Russell drove through the first dark of the New Jersey suburbs.

Beside me, Hailey said: "You've got 'bout half of each eyebrow left."

"Plus a healthy pink glow," said Russell.

Zane said nothing from the front passenger's seat.

Wind rushed in from the kicked-out driver's window.

"I was doing swell!" I yelled.

"No you weren't," said Russell as he made a random left turn. "You always think you're doing swell when you're talking to a woman, but you aren't."

"Wasn't a woman!" I yelled.

"See?" said Russell. "You were that confused."

"It was a cop!"

"'Xactly," said Zane. "And she was on her way to locking you up."

Zane shook his head. "Good thing we had Hailey and Eric shadowing you. If Officer Mirror Eyes had put you in her car, we were all gone. Or you'd have had to lunch her when she did her frisk."

"You almost burned me up!"

"Yeah, I kind of misjudged my toss. I meant to hit it in front of the cruiser where a ball of fire would be a zero-damage diversion you could use."

"But blast was classic," said Eric.

"Wild," said Russell.

"Now the law knows—"

"Not as much as if they'd have nabbed you," said Zane. "What they've got is a dazed street cop's description of a citizen who saved her life when hell broke loose."

"And the coming alert on this stolen car."

Lights snapped on in New Jersey. Rush hour was steady, but we kept moving.

"Wish we'd scored a local map," said Russell, peering out at neighborhoods scattered along the maze of city, county, state and federal roads we drove.

"Keep the ocean on your left," said Zane, pointing to an arrow that claimed beaches were one mile thataway.

Evening became night blowing its chill through the kicked-out window of the stolen BMW. Road construction sent our route this way and that. We kept a gut reckoning on the ocean. Sometimes we were certain that its blackness loomed between light-dotted buildings flowing past Russell's broken window, sure that the night sky held the scent of sea air. Sometimes we drove past minimalls and fast-food factories that could have been in Kansas, through neighborhoods that could have been Ohio.

We were forty-five minutes on the road, rolling *sort of* south on a one-way road past high-rise condo buildings and ramshackle houses. Maybe it was the night blowing through the window while Russell drove, maybe it was my better self realizing that *what the hell,* they were only eyebrows, but I'd cooled down, was about to say something funny *and* nice to Zane when Russell glanced across a vacant lot toward the ocean.

"Holy shit!" yelled our driver Russell.

Look left: no red light spinning police cars.

Behind us: nothing but empty night road.

Same through the windshield.

"Right's clear!" yelled Hailey from that side of the back-seat.

Russell surged the BMW forward only to hit the brakes and skid through a left-hand turn at the first corner. We raced along a deserted park, took another tires-crying hard left, shot down an empty one-way street going back the way we'd come—

Russell hit the brakes so hard we all flew forward, snapped back.

We were at a dead stop in the middle of a one-way street going the opposite direction of our plan. The empty park lay off to our left. To our right, a stone-walled building rose up to the stars and ran for a full block past three lonely streetlights. Straight through its mountain should have been the sea.

Russell slammed the BMW into Park, threw open the driver's door and pulled himself half out of the car to gawk at the building's roof.

Seconds later, he dropped back behind the steering wheel, said: "Oh . . . my . . . God!"

Then punched the gas. The BMW shot forward. Russell steered it into the horseshoe driveway of a World War II Navy hospital converted to a grand dame haunted hotel.

"Wait here!" he yelled and dashed into the lobby.

"Oh," I deadpanned as Russell disappeared into the hotel. "Okay."

I got out of our ride. Rolling blackness a block away had to be the Atlantic. To the left of the ocean stretched a wall of crumbling boardwalk pit stops. To the right loomed that huge abandoned arabesque castle. I glanced up toward what Russell might have spotted that flipped him out, saw a huge unlit sign of bulb lights that read:

WELCOME TO—

"Get in!" yelled Russell, running to the BMW.

Not wasting a blink to finish reading, I did: he was the driver.

"Only five blocks away!"

Russell rocketed us out of the driveway and back the direction we'd been going before he'd seen *whatever.* We roared through that night with our driver. With faith.

Our stolen BMW cornered a left, shot down a wide street with cars angle-parked at a median strip. A car pulled out: Russell whipped into that space. He climbed out of the BMW and groaned in seemingly sexual awe. Staggered across the street to a long one-story building with walls of gray pancake-like bricks and a white awning. I was behind him when he dropped to his knees and spread his arms wide in hallelujah to the promised land.

Black letters on the building's white awning: THE STONE PONY.

Glowing white letters on black background sign read: CAFÉ AND BAR.

Wailing rock guitars, throbbing drums and a husky-voiced woman singer bled out to us as Russell knelt in the street.

"No," I said.

"What the hell," said Zane. "We need to eat."

"Okay," I sighed. Knew then that the unlit electric lights on the arabesque building read WELCOME TO ASBURY PARK, N.J. "We need to eat. We'll be fine."

Eric sealed the BMW's kicked-out driver's window with the wheel cover for the BMW's spare tire. We paid a cover charge at the bar's door and stepped into a black-walled dream factory filled with beer fumes, cigarette smoke, and colored lights. A huge white pony adorned the black carpeted wall behind the band grinding it out on the stage for a crowd of two hundred college boys and hair-flipping co-eds, for twenty-somethings from lawyer shops and cement plants, for faces who looked as set in their thirties as Russell, Eric, and me. A Black man older than Zane limped past with a cane. We edged our way to a back bar. The sand-haired woman bartender with a tan, a halter top, and a navel ring held up a finger: *Wait.*

Guitars chorded with a drum flourish to end the song blaring from the stage.

"Thanks a lot!" said the woman bandleader with a slung guitar. A waterfall of black curls tumbled down her ivory face to her black blouse, cut low and straining. She wore black jeans and strap-on shoes with thick black heels. "We appreciate you coming out to hear us tonight, hope you liked that last one I wrote, it's called 'Sex in a Stolen Car.' "

A few people clapped.

"We're gonna take a break now, but we'll be back with covers of your fav's and a few of ours we know you'll love. You better, or you'll break our hearts." Her crimson lips grinned to show she was joking, but the truth slipped out that she was serious. "Remember, like it says on the marquee, we're Terri and the Runawayz."

Our bartender leaned over and said: "What can I get you guys?"

My hand warded off her smile: "No booze!"

Zane told her: "I'll have a beer."

"Me, too!" said Russell.

"Make it four," said Hailey. She nodded to pudgy Eric. "Ours are light."

"Okay," I conceded, "but only one round!"

Zane asked: "Can we get food?"

"Whatever's fast and filling," I said. "Emphasis on fast."

"Hunger, man," said the bartender. "It's a bitch. The cook's got pasta. Tomato, sausage, and peppers sauce. It's fast, but if you slop it on you, it'll look like blood."

She relayed our food order into her microphone headset as she walked toward empty glasses stacked in front of the back wall's American flag.

I whispered to Zane: "What if someone goes into the BMW? Takes it?"

"Steals our stolen car?" He nodded toward singer-songwriter Terri as she walked across the room to collect hugs from three of her day-job girlfriends. "For sex?"

"We're not a joke! Or a song!"

"Sure we are," he said, handing me a beer. "Relax."

Russell wedged between us: "Do you know where we are?"

"Lots of signs," I told him.

"No, man: Do you know where we *are!*

"There are places," he said, "where magic percolates. Where art meets audience and both transcend. Like the Newport festival stage or Harlem's Cotton Club or the Cavern Club in Liverpool where the Beatles fused or the Texas honky-tonks that spun out Hank Williams and Buddy Holly—or hell, the Globe Theater way back in way back."

"Don't stretch a beautiful theory," I argued. "Rips apart when you compare a beer-soaked bar, some colored lights, drunk college kids, bluesy factory hands and a hot rocker like what's-her-name up there to Shakespeare."

"Hey: America's poets put down their pens and picked up guitars."

"What if they can't sing?"

"Like Bob Dylan?"

"William Carlos Williams wrote real poems after the A-bomb, TV—"

"Jersey dude, right?" said Russell. "Loved Sinatra? Rocked out around here?"

"Here, guys!" Steaming plates of red sauce spaghetti plunked on the bar.

"And this place," whispered Russell, "this place . . . The blue-collar sound rebelling against the suits back when I was a baby in the seventies . . . That stage . . . Springsteen."

Russell shook his head. "Maybe if I hadn't cared about the world blowing up. Maybe if I'd believed my words and music would do it instead of figuring I had to put my ass on Uncle Sam's line. I mean, I was a good rocker—*am good,* and that worked out swell for Uncle, my *what-I-can-do* covering his *higher purpose* in dark alleys and . . ."

"But maybe," he said, his eyes full of the stage where instruments waited in front of a huge white pony. "Maybe. If."

Zane coaxed him back from the badlands of *what might have been.* "Eat."

As Russell obeyed, Zane whispered to me: "How much money we got left?"

"Not a lot," I said. "The bus, motel, whatever you guys used at the mall . . ."

"Oh well. Give me a hundred dollars."

His eyes told me *just do it.* He held the bills I slipped him, beckoned the bartender to us, asked: "Where's the manager?"

The bartender pointed to a trim woman with brass hair.

Zane elbowed his way through the crowd until he reached the manager. She let him do the talking, then turned her no-bullshit eyes our way. Told him something.

Hailey whispered to me: "What's he doing?"

Zane worked his way through the crowd, spoke to the singer Terri as she sat with her friends and band. She said something. He said more. She shrugged *yes.*

Zane gave her the $100 of our operational/survival money.

Walked back to us, told Russell: "Okay, it's paid for. Pick an ax. Take your shot."

"What?" said Russell.

Zane said: "The stage at the Stone Pony is now yours."

Russell stared at him. At me.

Words came out of my heart. I had to say: "Go for it. Time's a-wasting."

For a frozen moment of eternity, Russell only stared at us, his eyes wet.

Then he turned and shouldered his way through the crowd toward the stage.

Off to my left, I saw the brass-haired manager speak to the technician who ran the sound booth against the wall opposite the stage. Break over, he strode back to work.

Russell stood below the stage. Hesitated. Took the long high step and was up there with the guitars and drums, the keyboard, and the back wall white pony.

Across the room, Terri and her band watched their costly instruments.

Russell let his fingers glide over one of the sleek, fully electric guitars. A classic wooden box guitar fitted with a mike caught his eye. He picked it up.

"What if he's no good?" I said to Hailey.

"Then he goes down rocking. Better than not trying. Everybody goes down."

But we each drained our beers.

The sound tech turned the white spot on Russell. Set the mike *live*.

"Wooo!" yelled the bartender behind us and she clapped. "Go old guy!"

I told Zane: "That's for you."

Got back: "That's for all of us."

On stage, Russell plucked a jangling, off-key string of notes out of the guitar.

Embarrassment hushed the crowd. People shuffled on the dance floor, hoping the guy on stage would go away if they all kept quiet.

Then, *oh then,* Russell hijacked their dreams.

Heartbeat strumming the guitar, leaning in and giving them something they'd never heard, his acoustic guitar rapid fire slammed a Richard Thompson classic:

'Feel so good I'm gonna break somebody's heart tonight,
'Feel so good I'm gonna take someone apart tonight.

Third line in, he *owned* them as his fingers flew on strings, a crescendo of poetry.

Zane drifted to the brass haired manager. I saw her laugh, hold up her left hand, point to her fourth finger, and shake her head *sorry*.

Zane! I thought with happy awe. *'Xactly!* Ride that breakthrough! Take a shot.

Russell ripped out a last strum. Stepped back from the mike to catch his breath.

The crowd went wild—screaming, clapping, hooting.

Across the crowded room I saw Terri and her band standing and cheering.

Russell plucked a waterfall of notes. Announced the well-known "All for You" by a group named Sister Hazel. But instead of singing it, he kept plucking waterfall notes, repeating and building that chorus into a rhythm he rode as if waiting for something to happen. I wondered why, of all the songs he knew, Russell picked that one to play.

Terri ran from her band, charged across the bar to stuff our cash in Zane's shirt pocket, bound on stage and grab a mike. Russell smiled to the night, didn't look at her, leaned toward his microphone sang the first line of the song, fell silent as Terri chimed in signing the second line. Then he looked at her. And she realized this was a perfect song for a call-response duet, each of them alternating singing lines of love and time lost.

Her band was on stage, a second guitar strumming behind Russell as her keyboard player handed Terri a guitar while the drummer picked up his sticks, marked time—

All of them came in together with joyous song as the crowd roared.

Our bartender behind us yelled: "Rock out!"

Eric jumped into the crowd to obey her order.

Hailey jumped after him, commanding: "Stay with me! Obey only me!"

And they were both rocking, Eric waving his arms in absolute ecstasy as the best woman he could ever love danced with him, laughing in spite of dying.

Two hundred people jammed the dance floor. Opposite the stage was the sound booth, a rear wall platform with a low bank of sound and light boards, dials and switches. The tech jerked his head for me to join him up there for the best view.

On stage, the band frazzled through the ending "All for You."

Russell cut loose with the *dun-dun, dah dah dun* opening electric guitar riff that came to Keith Richards in a dream for the Rolling Stones' "(I Can't Get No) Satisfaction."

Terri glowed at Russell. Her ebony curls cascaded. She arched her hips toward the man in a noir leather jacket as they ground out the song about what they couldn't *get*.

On the club floor, Zane and Hailey and Eric rocked out.

On the sound booth platform, I glanced beyond the crowd to the front door where—just like Derya—a woman I'd never met walked in and rocked my world.

That night was the Stone Pony, not Kuala Lumpur, Malaysia before 9/11.

That woman was Cari, not Derya.

Cari flowed into the Stone Pony. Two men in long coats flanked her. A familiar magic crackled around her from her cropped blond hair to her hunter's face to her dark jacket and black shoes. Then the cosmos brushed open her dark jacket so I saw her holstered gun and I stone certain knew she was Agency. Knew that she and her crew were our perfect assassins.

33

". . . SA-TIS-FACTION!" SANG RUSSELL on stage at the Stone Pony. Terri's black hair swayed as she stroked her electric guitar and her band rocked the song.

Cari and her two gunmen paused just inside the door to let their hunters' eyes adjust to the spotlit blue glow of the bar. Both of her killers wore long coats. The one in brown leather was bald, the hulk in black space-age fiber sported a crew cut.

"Hey hey, hey!" sang Russell.

The crowd on the dance floor surged with the song.

Eric "rocked out," as ordered, a pudgy, bespectacled *white boy* jumping up and down completely offbeat, waving his arms above his head like he was stirring the stars. Dancing with Hailey shot joy into Eric's obedience. Shepherding him justified Hailey being on the dance floor, but her grin said that she was also having a great time.

They made an extraordinary couple: white boy geek, classy ebony woman.

Cari spotted them from clear across the jam-packed club.

I fled the sound booth platform. A busboy stacked empty pasta bowls on a tray. I stuffed dollars in his shirt pocket, slid his heavy tray onto the palm of my right hand.

Holding the tray level with my face let hunters see only a busboy.

Zane stood beside the manager. His gun held three bullets, one for each assassin, though he couldn't see them across the crowded room. He sensed my *intense motion* and turned to see me, tray balanced on my right palm while my left forefinger cut my throat.

On stage Russell and Terri improvised a chorus of alternating "*I tried*'s" leaning back to back, sharing a mike. They only saw their own world.

I flashed Zane three fingers. My forefinger pointed up, then my hand swept out to signify breasts: *one woman.* My fingers V-ed like scissors, pointed down: *two men.*

Zane's nod told me *got it*, his clenched fist said *Go!*

On stage, guitar man Russell dropped to one knee in front of Terri. Her hips kept hunters from seeing him and him from seeing them.

The tech in the sound booth killed the house lights and bathed the guitar couple on stage with blue and red spots. I pushed my way through the mesmerized crowd of civilians. The tray hid my face as I circled for position, praying that no one realized busboys don't wear leather jackets or carry dirty dishes *away* from the kitchen.

Thirty, twenty-five feet away, Cari cupped the ear of her crew cut hulk to shout her command. He fumbled in his trench coat, turned toward the front exit.

Cell phone: too loud in here so he's going outside to call the cavalry!

I bumped a guy who yelled "*Watch it!*" Bee-lined through tables around the display cases with T-shirts, hurried toward the front door.

Crew Cut's trench coat floated behind him as he swooped toward the night. He ignored the busboy bearing in on him from his right.

The bar tech flipped on white strobe lights. We became stuttered images in a movie with a sound track blaring rage and sex. Life revealed itself in strobing white flashes punctuated by blinding blackness.

White flash Crew Cut raises his cell phone from his side.

Black flash blind can't see.

White flash Crew Cut has his cell phone near his face.

"Oops!" I cried, staging a stumble toward Crew Cut.

I dumped the tray from in front of my face. Dirty dishes flipped toward him. He jumped back as bowls and bottles clattered near his shoes.

My knuckles jabbed his throat.

His eyes rolled. My palm smacked his temple. His brain sloshed. I spun his unconscious weight to a chair at an empty table. Chopped his neck to be sure.

On stage, on both knees, Russell leaned back like an opening jackknife.

On the floor: find cell phone! Got it, thumb it off!

Crew Cut slumped in the chair. I unsnapped a holstered

automatic from his belt and clipped it on mine, tucked a pistol from his shoulder holster near my spine. Two ammo mags from the shoulder holster went into my jacket chest pockets, a pouch of mags went from his belt to mine. One trench coat pocket held a grenade, the other a pronged stun gun: they bulged my jacket. His three ID folders, wallet and wad of cash stretched my pants. I felt body armor under his shirt: *Can't get that.*

I crossed his arms on the table, buried his face on them alongside pasta bowls and beer bottles. He looked like a guy having a bad night in a good bar.

Pushing through the crowd, I saw the backs of the bald killer and Cari. Hailey danced with her back to them. Eric's eyes held only joy.

Hailey glanced to the crowd beyond Eric. Saw Zane's gun hand pressed against his thigh. *Realized.* She danced to Eric, shouted in his ear. His face churned.

Closer, I was closer, ten feet behind Bald Killer's back.

The bar tech flicked from strobes to spinning colored lights. Hailey whirled in a solo dance as on the stage, Terri straddled Russell. She ground lower each time they shouted the song's *"Tried!"* The crowd watched only them.

Cari and her partner locked on Hailey.

In the spinning colored lights, Hailey shot the assassins her middle finger.

Ran toward a neon red Fire Exit sign above a corridor door.

Cari and Baldy bolted after her.

Behind them, I struggled through the bouncing, whooping crowd.

Eric rumbled toward the two hellhounds chasing Hailey.

Baldy spun to meet Eric's charge. Zapped Eric with a pronged stun gun and whirled to run after his leader and Target Two.

Zane and I caught Eric. I shoved the pistol from my spine into Zane's hand and left him holding our stunned but *used-to-it* engineer as I charged toward the fire exit.

Through the exit door—bright kitchen, giant freezer, cool night breeze from around that corner . . .

"Satisfaction" blared as I flew into the night. Solid wood

fence walls made a half-block square outdoor arena. A stage rose from the asphalt, a stage with stairs Hailey ran up, Cari on her heels. Behind Cari ran Baldy.

Who sensed danger and whirled to face me.

Inside the bar, on that bandstand, Russell and Terri chorused: *"can't get no!"* She jumped back from straddling him, he flipped to his feet better than in our *gung fu* practice. The roaring crowd pulled his eyes from her—

And Russell saw Eric slumped in a chair.

Terri and her band hit the last chord of "Satisfaction."

Applause thundered out the back door to the starlit auditorium pen where no one in the audience could see Baldy explode toward me with a flying front snap kick.

Back/block it—block his follow-through punch, grab—Missed!

Baldy swooped an ankle kick but my empty foot took his strike like a tetherball and flipped up. My foot came down before his, lined up with his leg and I flowed forward, my shin wedging into his leg. He yelled in pain but whirled away from my crunch before I could do major damage. His hands disappeared inside his coat.

Weapons! I jumped on his back to grab his coat lapels, pull them over his shoulders and down, pinning his arms with his own garment.

Rather than fight the brown leather coat and give me the second I'd need to slam his head, he leapt forward, his arms straightening and sliding free of its sleeves.

He didn't waste a beat to cross-draw pistols from the double shoulder holster harness on his weapons vest. His hands jabbed toward me. I arced hooks at him, more to keep his hands away from the guns than to hit him. He counter—

Zane slammed him from behind with an aluminum garbage can.

Baldy crashed facedown on the concrete. His hands flexed.

Zane canned him again.

As I ran up the stairs of the outside stage.

To an awe-inspiring sight. Black seashore night. A billion white stars overhead. A rolling dark horizon of icy ocean. Condo buildings three blocks inland where lights glowed in windows of retirees. A chilly breeze. Two extraordinary women kicking the shit out of each other on a bare wooden stage.

Hailey's standard Agent Training course in hand-to-hand combat taught her enough to stun Christophe before she hacked him to death with maniacal fury.

But Cari was an artistic warrior. She'd backed Hailey to the edge of a ten-foot drop from that bare wooden stage. Hailey's hands snapped to *guard-up* as she lunged with two straight kicks followed by the textbook punch. Blond Cari simply wasn't there for the kicks to hit. She blocked Hailey's punch and slammed a back-fist into her ebony face. Hailey fell to the boards like a sack of sand.

My ambush palm strike between Cari's shoulder blades would have knocked the wind out of her and snapped her hands out away from her gun like a crucifixion.

If she hadn't spun and blocked and kicked me in the crotch.

Except I twisted her target off line so her foot slammed my right hip.

I struck to her face so she'd block/not draw her gun. She hooked a punch I deflected as I dodged a kick to my kneecap. I feinted, she didn't buy it and rocketed a right jab I stuck to my left palm and flowed back/forward in tai chi's *kao,* my shoulder slamming her centerline. She blasted backward off the stage. I grabbed her hand. We hung suspended in time. Linked hand-to-hand and splayed out like a 1950s jitterbug couple. I jerked her arm and she flew back to me, her feet tripping across the stage as I pulled her to *o-goshi,* judo's hip throw that spun her over my back—again like a jitterbugger—and slammed her back on the bare wood stage. I saw her dazed green eyes, the soft pink of her cheeks. Before she sucked air back into her lungs I flipped her face down on the wood, pushed her hands out and dug my knee into her spine.

Zane pulled Hailey to her feet, offered me a stun gun that had fallen from Cari's pocket: "Put out her lights!"

"No!" I ripped a holstered gun from her hip. "Hostage!"

"You're nuts!" said Hailey.

"Yeah, but that's not it."

I found handcuffs in Cari's left jacket pocket, a set of keys in her right. As I cuffed her wrist and bent her other arm behind her, I briefly worried that she might be a cop, but then I found three ID folders and a silencer for her pistol. Zane helped me jerk Cari to her feet.

Those green eyes flicked from him to me. Gave me nothing but hard.

We three marched down the stage stairs.

Baldy lay sprawled on the ground, the pockets of his pants turned inside out. His ribs moved, but Zane reported: "He's done for now."

Zane scooped Baldy's brown leather coat off the ground, a gesture that gaped open the coat Zane wore. I saw Baldy's weapons vest now on Zane. Zane whirled the brown coat through the air, settled it on Cari's shoulders to hide her cuffed hands. He buttoned the collar to make it her cape. His pistol slid inside that coat to kiss her spine.

"You choose trouble," he told her, "you get a wheelchair."

Death is hard to picture. But a bullet shattering your spine . . .

Zane marched her out in front of us as a shield.

In, through the kitchen, past the walk-in frig, around the corner, back into the sweat-humid club to where Russell helped Eric to his feet. Revelers pounded Russell on the back. On stage, Terri and the Runawayz cheered. Nurse Death's Walther PPK bulged Eric's back pocket. Russell helped Eric fall into our parade to the front door.

On stage, Terri couldn't believe what she was seeing.

Russell: *Walking out.* Turning for one last vision of her. And to shrug.

Zane whispered in Cari's ear: "If there's guns in the street, all you win is mess."

She kept moving, not *yes,* not *no,* not *please.* So cool.

Woosh and we were outside in the night cold streetlight glare.

No shotgun blast. No bullhorns. No bright lights blinding our eyes.

Zane's free hand passed Baldy's car keys to Eric.

Bweep-boop! Lights flashed on a sedan parked near our stolen BMW.

"Can't take their car!" I said. "It might have a built-in GPS tracker."

Russell took Baldy's knife and jogged to our hunters' sedan. *Pwush* wheezed a tire he stabbed. We hurried to our BMW where Zane pushed Cari to me. Zane didn't waste time working the wheel cover off the kicked-in driver's side window. He back-kicked the passenger window of our stolen ride. Safety glass cobwebbed. Zane kicked again, and this time the glass flew into the BMW. He reached inside, popped open the electric door lock. Eric dove in, dismantled the other broken window's cover, fiddled with the steering column, and tricked the engine to life. Zane pushed Cari into the backseat. Hailey climbed in beside her, Eric took her other side. Zane slid in beside Hailey as Russell ran to the shotgun seat. I leapt behind the steering wheel, peeled us out in reverse then roared away into the night.

Blaps of darkness and blurred streetlights rushed over us.

"Where are we?" I yelled.

Eric yelled, *"New Jersey!"* Russell yelled, *"Crazy!"* Zane yelled, *"Targeted!"* Hailey yelled, *"Alive!"*

And she stretched across the captive woman to punch Eric in the shoulder. "What's the matter with you?"

Eric cringed as Hailey leaned over our captive to yell at him.

"Have you gone *sane?"* screamed Hailey. "I gave you an order and you didn't do it! Before I drew off Blondie here, I told you to take care of yourself!"

She punched Eric again.

"And what did you go and do? Did you take care of yourself? No, you disobey and you do it dumb! You charged after them to rescue me, so dumb, don't you dare get yourself killed *white knight* nonsense!"

Eric cringed.

But all she did was yell: "Explain yourself!"

"Followed orders." He recited, proving his own answer.

"Bullshit!"

"I . . . can't . . . trying . . ."

"No, don't *do it,* you already did it with that bullshit answer."

"Order was, you said: *'Take care of yourself.'* Can't be *me* if you're . . . if you . . ."

Zane blurted: "Got it."

So Hailey could skip that, slump in her car seat, go on—softer—to: "Oh, Eric . . ."

In the rearview mirror, I watched her eyes go wet, her head shake.

"Fuck this shit!" Russell reared over the shotgun seat to scream at our hostage.

"Do you know what you've fucking done?" Veins throbbed in Russell's head. *"I was going to get laid!* Everything was perfect! I'm on the pill and she was special! Then you came along and screwed everything up!"

Zane said: "You weren't going to get that roll."

"Was so!"

"Was not!"

"Zane's just jerking your chain." I yelled.

Russell whipped around in his seat to face me. "Victor! He can't fucking do that!"

"Apparently," said Zane: "Can, too."

"Can not!" yelled Russell.

"Everybody!" I said. "Four magic words!"

All the maniacs *shut the fuck up.*

The road whirred under our wheels. Wind roared in on us through two kicked-out front windows. I cranked the heater on but still our ride felt like the North Pole.

Cari spoke her first words: "Guess I found the right car."

34

"How DID YOU find us?" Russell yelled to our captive as we sped away on a tree-lined, divided-lanes county road.

Cari stared at the night flashing toward her through the windshield.

"Our car!" said Russell. "Vic, there's a theft location transmitter in this car!"

"No," said Zane, using Baldy's penlight to read a paper from the weapons vest. "This is a list of nightclubs and bars south of New York. Stone Pony's number nine, and four are pen-checked, have a manager's name and phone number jotted down by hand."

"Standard practice," I said. "The FBI, CIA, we track a fugitive or a target by what he's done in the past, by what he likes. Magazine subscriptions, who he used to call and probably nowadays, who he's e-mailed or where he's logged on to, who he used to hang out with, places where he might get the kind of job he used to have."

"Somebody tracked your dreams," Zane told Russell.

Zane threw Cari's phone battery out of Russell's window, her phone out mine.

"Littering's bad," said Eric. "Against the law."

"Uh-oh, now we got *big* trouble," said Zane. "Vic: headlights in our mirror?"

"Not yet."

Russell glared at Cari trapped in the backseat. "What's your team's search plan? How many crews—"

Cari said: "If we all stay calm, let me help you—"

Our laughter drowned the rest of her pitch.

"Vic?" said Zane. "How good of a frisk?"

"Ahh . . . Take-down and secure only. I'll pull over so I can—"

"Keep us moving."

My rearview mirror showed Hailey muttering to people who weren't there. Zane maneuvered so that she slumped against the rear door and he sat beside Cari.

"I can do this easy," he told our prisoner, "or I can do this rough."

"How about not at all?"

Zane worked the brown coat off her, passed it to the front seat where Russell checked the pockets, squeezed its creaky leather and tossed it out his window.

The coat flew into the night from our speeding car like a whirling bat.

"Didn't feel a transmitter locator," said Russell.

Eric said: "If she's trace wired . . . Best place in her shoes."

One black shoe flew out Russell's window, its mate flew out mine.

The road fought the rearview mirror for my eyes. White lines raced toward the windshield as Zane's hands massaged Cari's right foot, circled her ankle, slid up . . .

Yellow road stripe for a curve and I yelled: "Let Hailey do it!"

"Gotta be worth it. Gotta . . ."

"She's busy," said Zane. His hands circled Cari's thigh, slid up . . .

Yellow eye headlights across the center line whipped past us.

In my mirror, Cari stiffened as Zane's hand cupped her groin, fingers probed, his left hand circling behind to cup the curve of her—

"Whoa!" His left hand slid inside the back waistband of her pants.

Rip! The sound of tape pulling away from flesh.

Zane held a dagger for Russell and me to see in the glow of dashboard lights. "Plastic, cloth sheath. Double-edged, needle point, no metal detector would catch it, and if her hands are tied behind her . . ."

"Missed it," I said. "Sorry."

My eyes hunted Cari's in the mirror, found only shadows.

Headlights burned past us going the other way.

Zane found no shoulder holsters. His hands explored her belly.

"Hailey!" I cried as ahead of us, truck taillights blinked for a right turn.

"She's still gone." Zane's hand was on Cari's back as he said: "Is this—?"

Cari said: "Bra. Snaps."

"Eric?" said Zane.

We blew past the exit the truck had taken into nowhere.

"Possible," said Eric. "Underwires."

"No," said Cari.

"If I don't go all the way," Zane told her. "You won't respect me."

"Sure I will."

Zane held her plastic dagger in front of her eyes. "This is *sure*."

Dagger in his hand that he slid up under her fuchsia blouse.

Dark highway. White strips racing toward me.

Sounds of sawing cloth cut through the night in our stolen car.

A slashed-off black bra flew out Russell's window.

Under her blouse, Zane's hands brushed Cari's bare breasts.

"It's okay to cry," he told her.

"Like you know. Like you care."

Dark highway rushed toward us. Bitter wind howled through busted windows.

35

"THINK ABOUT IT," argued Cari as our car hummed through a dark suburban neighborhood. "I'm your perfect chance! You were so lucky to find me!"

"Is that how it worked?" said Zane. We slowed at an intersection. A pink neon light glowed off to our left. "Not that way."

He could have been answering her or advising me. I drove into a neighborhood built by the World War II GI Bill that gave America its now crumbling middle class.

"We gotta find a new car to steal," said Russell.

Cari argued: "No! I'm your way to stay alive. That's why I'm here, right? We'll call the Panic Line, set up our rescue. No SWATs or wet teams. We can use your people from Maine. You can explain everything."

"Hey guys," said Zane: "Does anybody ever buy your explanation?"

"Eight days a week," quoted Hailey, now back from her mumblings.

"So forget *explanation*," snapped our captive. "Think survival. Before your gig at the Stone Pony, you were down for two quirky deaths, believed to have one gun.

"Want to know my team's sanction?" *Lying maybe, maybe not,* she said: "Locate, neutralize, recover. *No fuss, no muss* was what the Bosses wanted, but what they cared about most was getting everybody safe."

"Which way?" I asked at the next corner. "Nothing but houses."

Cari said: "Now you're escapees on the run, murderers known to be violent, desperate, paranoid. Armed with my crew's five guns and ammo to spare, grenades—"

"Hell of a *no fuss, no muss* gig you were planning for us," said Russell.

"The grenades are flash-bangs," she said. "Nothing compared to what's coming. The tranquilizer pistol and darts in our weapons vest? The next team won't bother to pack those. You dropped two agents. Snatched me. The bosses will write me off as damaged or dead. And now they're hunting you down like mad dogs."

We drove through darkness where America slept.

"Oh well," said Russell. "Isn't like we were the pick of the litter."

"Sure you were," she said.

Lights winked out in a house we drove past.

"That's what makes this all so hard," said Cari. "For all of us. And that's why if you don't let me bring you in, they've got to come after you full out hard."

"My favorite way," whispered Zane.

Does Cari know the harsh irony of Zane's joke? I wondered. Know *hard* is his dream and nightmare? Know the rape fear she'd felt from his frisking hands is a phantom because of his craziness? Know that my insanity did not stop me from—

"Left face!" I hit the brake, risked the flash of red lights. "Russell: that old house with the huge garage, the picket fence. Newspaper on the front porch. Mailbox stuffed."

"Got it!"

"We'll circle left. Deep Recon: go!"

Eric loosened the BMW's dome light. Russell eased out the BMW's front door and closed it with a click like a switchblade. He stayed out of our headlights, melted into the night, gone from my rearview mirror before I turned left at the corner.

On our seventh lap, Russell materialized from the hedges by our target house, waved me to park the BMW across the street, jogged to my window when my lights died.

"Wild!" he whispered. "You gotta see this!"

"Hailey," I said, killing the noisy engine. "Take the wheel. Eric, check her cuffs."

Russell and I sneaked between the old house's attached garage and the neighbor's picket fence. No dog barked. The back storm door creaked as we eased it open, slid past the inner door and crept into the linoleum kitchen.

"Was unlocked," he whispered.

"This is suburbia," I whispered back, "but still . . ."

"I cleared the upstairs," he whispered, edging around the refrigerator. "Three empty bedrooms, bathroom. Down here is a junked-up dining room, a living room, a study with an old rolltop desk, this kitchen. I thought I was alone."

The pistol holstered on my belt suddenly weighed a ton.

He eased open a door in the kitchen hall. A shaft of light knifed into the dark kitchen. Garage smells flooded over me: gasoline, tires, oil, cement floor, dust, metal tools, last summer's grass stuck to a mower blade.

Maybe some other odor.

"Already checked," he said. "No windows."

"What—?"

"Go in."

Calling that place a garage fails to do it justice. Call it a cavern lit by overhead tubes. This was a mechanics' dream room with floor space for four vehicles. Two walls of work-benches. Giant red metal tool chests. A hydraulic car lift. Drop lights. Oil pans. License plates from every state in the Union nailed to one wall.

A white 1959 Cadillac centered the garage like a king on a throne. Four doors. Swooping tail fins. A gaping hood made that glistening car roar like a giant beast.

The dead man slumped on his knees. His forehead rested on stacked oil cases. He had wispy white hair. Wore a gray cardigan sweater over a denim shirt, blue jeans.

"Heart attack," said Russell. "Betchya."

Soft warm air blew over us from an air heater in the far corner.

"I checked," said Russell, "and he's cold."

I looked at Russell.

He looked at me.

Said: "It'll work."

And I gave him the nod.

Russell ran through the kitchen to the night. Wall switches snapped off the lights. Darkness swallowed me and that garage. Smells swam in that black void. Smells of gasoline and cold metal, of oil and concrete, of warm blowing air stir-ring hairs near my leather jacket collar. I heard only my own breaths, the punching inside my ribs. The sounds of that kneeled-over dead man's heart. Dead ahead of me loomed that white beast of a car, maw gaping to swallow me even as this darkness had swallowed us both. The beast was a shape sensed but not seen. I knew it was there. Knew it knew I stood on its concrete. Knew what it wanted. Knew I couldn't say no.

And that's when I realized that even our bootleg meds were flaming out.

If I'm starting to lose it, what about the others?

Four-plus days on the road. Even without our bootleg meds, I'd thought we had two more days *until.* Now . . .

Knocking: on the metal garage door. The code sequence we used on the padded cell's door back at the Castle to let Malcolm know we were his visitors.

I flipped a switch.

An electric motor cranked up the garage door. The BMW idled in the driveway—headlights out. Soon as the BMW crept into the garage, I switched the garage door down with a clunk. Hailey keyed our stolen car off.

On came the garage lights.

All of us stood looking down at the slumped white-haired corpse.

Zane said: "That could be me."

"Yeah," answered Russell. "But it ain't. Looks like Mister Death made the old guy kneel and took him execution style."

"It's always execution style," said Hailey.

Zane said: "Nobody touch him. And be careful what else you do. We don't want to catch the attention of any neighbors or patrolling cops."

"Eric," I said: "Kill the garage heat."

Russell lifted a coil of clothesline off a wall hook. He and Zane led Cari inside. Hailey stood sentry at a darkened living room window. I slipped outside to get the mail and the newspaper off the porch. Checked the house. Turned on necessary lights.

"His name is—was—Harry Martin," I told our Op council in the living room.

Upstairs, Russell guarded Cari in the bedroom farthest from any exit. And I was fine with that. Russell and Cari, alone in a bedroom. Made perfect operational sense. Didn't nag at me.

"He was seventy-one," I said about the man whose chairs we sat in. "Far as I can tell, never married, no kids. Owned a gas station. Used to bowl. I checked his caller ID. Five calls in six days, three of them showing up as Unavailable."

"Telemarketers," said Eric.

"The other two were a few days back. Local pharmacy and a private call."

"Probably just returning his message." Zane shook his head.

"So nobody knows he's dead because nobody cared that he was alive," I said. "Even if somebody besides us noticed that his newspapers and mail hadn't been taken in, they didn't care."

"But what about neighbors?" said Hailey.

"There are three crayon pictures under magnets on his frig," I said. "But I looked at the scrawled names of two kids who signed them, then spotted their high school graduation pictures mounted on his photo wall."

"Neighbor kids," said Russell. "Gone on."

"His other photos are of his parents or grandparents. Friends from back in the sixties and seventies. A golden retriever wearing a party hat in this living room with President Clinton on TV in the background. Nothing more recent than that."

Hailey said: "The calendar on his kitchen wall has a lot of not much written on it. Optometrist, dentist. Nothing for the next few weeks. How long do we stay?"

"At least until tomorrow," I said. "Cari's right—"

"If that's really her name," said Hailey.

"She's right," I continued. "Soon as those guys we clobbered reported in, the whole system went Red Alert, sent posses out after mad dogs."

"How long can we stay here before . . . ?" Hailey nodded toward the garage. "And I'm not just talking about smell."

I shrugged, my heart and mind upstairs.

36

"SORRY ABOUT THIS," I said to Cari.

"Bet you say that to all the girls you kidnap."

She lay on the narrow bed's white sheet, her blond hair on the white pillow. Her blouse was fuchsia, her slacks black, her feet bare. Her hands rested cuffed on her belly. Miles of white clothesline cocooned her to the bed. She looked like a mummy. Her eyes clawed the ceiling.

"Is Cari Rudd your real name?"

"Why?"

"I'll call you anything. But I want to know who you are."

"All I'm required to do is give you my name, rank, and serial number."

"If all you do is what's required, then that's all you are."

"Worked so far."

"Yeah," I told the woman cocooned to the bed. "So I see."

Cari said: "How's crazy working out for you?"

I shrugged. *Don't tell her about the meds wearing off.*

"Are you going to storm around the bed and scream at me like Russell?"

Maybe she'd already figured we were running near the red line. "Russell wouldn't hurt you—well, unless."

"Put *unless* in an equation, and it adds up to *who knows.*"

"We're trying."

"Trying what?"

So I told her about Dr. Friedman. About blood in his ear. About Nurse Death and Russell freezing and Zane's save-his-own-life kick accidentally helping Nurse Death take hers. About matrices. Tricking the cell phone operator. Kyle Russo.

She said: "At least you and Russell have your fantasies straight."

"Was that you outside the apartment in New York?"

Cari said: "Sure."

"I wish I knew when you were lying."

"I wish I knew when you were crazy."

"What's it like working for the Agency now?" I asked.

"What makes you certain I'm CIA?"

"I'm not naive. Silencers and credentials from multiple agencies aren't FBI issue. Plus, if the Agency had let the Bureau or other badges go full-knowledge, hands-on after us, there'd have been a cover story in the news. No, you and your crew are from my old Firm, and you're running covert."

"Hell of a place, the Firm." She offered me a comrade's conspiratorial smile. "Man, we could use you back. Since 9/11, we've hired more executives, more slick suit and tie directors, more PR spin doctors instead of more street dogs. But now, everybody's finally realizing that guys like you are too valuable to waste."

"Nice try."

She shrugged in her bondage cocoon.

"Is this when you try to work answers out of me?" she said.

"The only question I've got, you might not know the answer to, and if you do, you'll lie, so what's the point."

Took three minutes before she bit. "Okay, I give up. What's your all-important lone question?"

"Are you knowingly working for a renegade Op inside the Agency?" I said. "That's the only scenario that makes you our flat-out enemy. If outside forces killed Dr. F, then the whole Agency—and you—are cool. Just ignorant bullets fired off target. But if a renegade Op killed Dr. F, then either you're one of them or you're their puppet. But an innocent puppet."

"You're the ones who've got me all wrapped up in strings."

"I won't untie ours. And don't have the time or . . . stomach to find any other strings on you."

"So do you think I'm a renegade?"

"No."

"Why?"

"You're too good."

"Not so good. You neutralized me."

"I didn't say you were perfect." I shrugged. "I was talking . . . instincts, faith."

She looked away.

Casually, I said: "What do you think of the car in the garage?"

"That white Caddy?"

Yes! It's real!

Cari said: "You're figuring it's so extreme that people will notice it and not who's in it. But that won't work."

"You work with what you've got," I said.

Cari frowned: "What happened to your eyebrows?"

"Don't worry! I'm okay. Just a thing with fire."

"But I shouldn't worry."

"We don't want to hurt you. I won't let you get hurt. Before, when Zane . . ."

"He didn't touch me like I was a woman. Give him credit for that."

"Absolutely!" I said. "He absolutely didn't. Wouldn't. He's a good man."

"What about you?"

"I have my moments."

"Yeah," she told me. "So I see."

That has to mean something! She wouldn't just say something like that!

"Victor? *Victor!*"

"Huh? Oh. Yeah?"

"Why are you doing this? I know you're . . . troubled, but you're right, you're not naive, you got street smarts and pure fucking brain power. Vision. And all this . . ."

"Seemed like the best choice at the time."

"But what about right now?"

Yeah, I thought, *what about right now. Four days on the road and already I'm drifting. And the others . . . We might not hold together a full week before we crashed.*

Cari said: "What are you going to do with me?"

"Umm . . ."

"We can work this out," she said.

"Okay."

"First, you've got to untie me."

"Ahh . . . No. That won't work."

"What will work?"

"I wish you'd believe me if I told you."

"Vic . . . They briefed us on all of you. I know about Malaysia and that woman—"

"Derya," I said.

Cari shook her head: "A door opens and BAM."

"That's how it gets you if it's good."

Cari shrugged. "Guess so."

She stared at me: "What's got you now?"

"Haven't you heard?" I said, knowing that this was not the time or the place to tell her everything: "I'm crazy."

"I know about your two suicides. I understand your pain."

"I hope not," I whispered.

"If we talk about—"

"Go to sleep," I said, and she heard the jailer's edge in my voice. "I'm on first watch. I'll be right here. Keeping you safe."

"Or something."

"Yes," I said. "Yes."

And I turned out the lights as she lay there. I sat in a chair. Folded my angel wings and dropped into the darkness.

37

RAIN MACHINE-GUNNED Bladerunners Internet cafe in
Kuala Lumpur that December 1999 afternoon. Ex-pats inside that Malaysian oasis ignored the storm. Peruvian bal-
ladeer Tania Libertad moaned Spanish from a boom box on
the bar beside smoldering incense. Gunfire splattered ghouls
in a café computer driven by a sunglasses-wearing *Honky*—
a Hong Kong Chinese cybercowboy. Outside it was seventy-
nine degrees, would be hotter when the rain morphed to
smoggy sunlight.

I sat at a table nursing a beer, my face to the door and my
spine to two Australian girls whining about how they should
have gone to Thailand to smoke opium instead of wasting
Christmas vacation by coming to *fockin' borin'* Malaysia. I
hungered to read their Melbourne newspaper with its head-
line about narcissistic teenagers who'd massacred their Col-
orado high school classmates as if life were a computer
game. But the public news wasn't my *Scramble Red* Op.

My watch read 4:17.

Any minute now, I thought.

The bell above the door dinged.

Derya hurried in from the rain, lowering her umbrella,
laughing with her two female colleagues. Derya's cinnamon
hair fanned out as she shook off the rain, and I knew in my
bones that I was lost.

Derya and her women colleagues claimed a table. They
seemed not to notice me, but women are wizards of discretion.

The bell above the door dinged.

In swooped Peter Jones, so soaked no one could tell he'd
only run across the street. A dramatic gesture wiped the wet
from his eyes.

He *obviously* spotted Derya and her two colleagues first.

"Girlfriends!" exclaimed Peter. "You are *so* predictable!
On your way to work, stop for something *long* and *cool* or
hot and *wet* and— *Oh My God!* It's Victor!"

The women at the table where Peter had lighted swiveled
their gaze to me.

"Victor! What are you doing here? No, wait: What are doing over *there* when I'm over *here* and today, today I'm celebrating!

"Sit here." Peter directed me to a chair he wedged between him and Derya.

The English blonde Peter later introduced as Julia said: "Why so happy, Peter?"

"Because," he said, leaning back with a grin: "I am *so* homeward bound!"

Shabana was the oldest woman and spoke Bombay British. "But what about the law back in New York? You are, of course, innocent, would never traffic in Ecstasy."

"Not as *pills!*" interrupted Peter with mock horror.

"But," said Shabana, "how is that after two years, now you can go home?"

"Let's just say," said Peter, gesturing for a beer, "I have it on good authority that the judge has finally seen the light."

"Still," I said, "if you don't watch your step, make every move just so, the light at the end of a tunnel winks out and leaves you worse off than before."

"Absolutely!" Peter sat straight. "Absolutely right. Do we all know each other?"

In a flurry of spoken names and gestures, he made sure we did, ending with: "And Victor, this is Derya Samadi."

Cinnamon hair framed her lean face, her clean jaw. Her skin was sun-tanned Tupelo honey, her eyes were swimming pool blue. She said: "You're American."

"Some things you can't hide."

Derya shrugged. "People try."

Peter sped to my defense. "Not Victor. Totally a stand-up guy. I mean, we only shared a terrible bus ride in the boonies together, but—"

"Relax, Peter," I said.

"—but," he ranted, having probably steeled his guts with *yaa baa* smuggled from Bangkok, "we clicked, even though Victor bums around Asia beating people up."

"How American." Shabana's voice.

"No," I said. "Martial arts is about integrity, transcending violence. I first came out here on a literature fellowship. Spent the last five years in Taiwan. I teach English, embarrass myself in lots of classic schools. Last few years, it's been mostly tai chi."

Drug-speeding Peter blurted: "And I forgot he's a poet!"

Derya said: "Really?"

My shrug mimicked the one she'd given me. "Call me hopeful."

British Julia grinned. "Maybe I should call you for trouble."

My flat but polite expression told her I wasn't interested. She drank her beer.

That let me turn back to Derya. "You're from . . . ?"

"Turkey. We cobbled together a school for women with grants from NGOs—nongovernmental organizations, foundations, no politics, no religion—"

"Oh *no!*" joked Shabana. "If all you're doing is empowering women, why of course you dabble in nobody's religion or politics!"

Derya and Shabana grinned and clinked their teacups.

Peter clapped. "I've got *the* perfect idea! You all 've been after me to help move furniture around your school—it is a sweet little school, Victor, such a good thing they're doing and not so easy in an officially Muslim country—and with my bad back—"

All three women groaned.

"Don't be bitches!" said Peter with a guilty smile. "But Victor, why, he's a bull."

Julia drew her smile like a dagger. "Now there's an idea. Use trained muscle for something besides bullying."

I deflected her thrust. "Exactly. It isn't what you know, it's what's you do with it."

Peter hijacked the conversation, sparred with Julia, joked until everyone laughed.

Derya laughed from her heels.

Monkeys screaming at dawn outside my balcony found me awake. The condo the Agency put me in was on an outer ring of K.L. Litter from my supposed life was scattered through the place to support my cover. My laptop bypassed

the government censored cybernetworks through one of the
hundred pirate satellite dishes on the condo roof. My machine held coded e-mail traffic. From me: *Linked to access
agent. On track.* Reply from Langley: *Proceed full speed.
Full sanction.*

Monkeys screamed in the treetops close enough to my
balcony for them to jump up and bite me. Or throw a snake
up there to do their dirty work for them.

We'd moved furniture until ten the night before—not late
in K.L. where a lot of "daily" life means hiding from the
broiling sun. "We" meant Julia, Shabana, bad-back Peter.
And Derya, me. I was in the condo by midnight. Dawn
should have found me practicing tai chi in the gazebo on the
condo's grounds, covertly mixing other martial forms into
that already *hidden functions* slow motion ballet. Instead, I
stood on the balcony, a cup of coffee in my hand while the
monkeys screamed.

"You talkin' to me?" I movie-whispered in the thick air.

Purple storm clouds rolled across the sky.

The Agency had stashed a battered Toyota for me in the
condo's underground parking garage and a motorcycle inside
a TV repair shop in the ex-pat neighborhood of Bangsar, but I
rode a bus into town over a superhighway that began at K.L.'s
airport, where runways had been built by a construction company tied to a wealthy Saudi Arabian hero of the American-
backed war against invading Soviet occupiers of Afghanistan,
a rail thin bearded messianic named Osama bin Laden.

Rain fell on my trip. The bus wooshed toward the heart of
K.L. Through my window, I saw the drainage ditch running
parallel with the road. Beyond the storm ditch ran a covered
sewer line. Past the sewer line ran a chain-link, barbed wire
wall. Inside that flesh-ripping fence waited squalid shanty
towns where rain pounding on tin roofs made a maddening
roar and all political power flowed from Muslim *madrasa*
schools.

Derya and her colleagues walked into Bladerunners at
4:19. She wore a white blouse and khaki slacks. Shabana
and even Julia waved and didn't exchange looks as Derya

walked to my table. After all, my offered books had to do with the English she taught (plus keyboarding, word processing). Shabana taught programming, handled birth control/women's health issues. Julia specialized in accounting.

No beer today. I drank Coke. Derya ordered tea without the sugar Malaysians crave to the point of sprinkling it on popcorn.

The first book she picked up was an English translation of classic Chinese poetry she could use with her Chinese students. Next, she picked up a paperback book.

"I don't know this William Carlos Williams," she said.

"American poet, died before we were born. Was a doctor by day, a poet by night. Like a comic book hero. One of the master's theses I'll never finish is on him."

Her face glowed when she picked up a volume CIA trick boys had weathered with water and a clothes dryer.

"You have an English edition of Rumi! He changed my whole life! I tell everybody! One day in college, I'm walking in Ankara and from a radio in an apartment above me, I hear this voice, and it's the poetry of Jala al-Din Rumi! Magic! Opened my heart!"

"Lucky."

"In America, do you hear poets on the radio?"

Russell was still in my future, so I said: "No."

"How sad." She dropped her gaze to sip her tea. "Are you really a poet?"

"Not if you count how many people have read me."

"That's not the count that matters." Her lips curled up ever so slyly as she nodded toward my black shoulder bag. "Do you have your poems in there?"

I shrugged.

"*Ahhh*. I see. That's right, *American*. You are supposed to, what: invite me to your pad to see your—what-do-you-call-it—like tattoos."

"You mean *etchings*?"

"Yes! That is it! *Etchings*." Laughter came from her heels. "But I think for that kind of rendezvous what we are talking about is really tattoos."

"I don't have any."

"Can you imagine? Marking yourself with something until death. Who could be so certain about what would forever be important?" She sipped tea. "So is that what you were going to do? Invite me up somewhere to see your poems? Is that your trick?"

"I don't have any tricks for you."

"Prove it."

The journal I gingerly pulled out of my black bag was genuinely well worn, with a torn blue cardboard-like cover: *Northern Review*. Unlike my fellowship to Asia, what it contained hadn't needed to be orchestrated by the CIA.

Derya whispered: "I was only . . . No. I'm glad you didn't have this somewhere else to take me to. That you knew about tattoos. Yet you brought this anyway.

"Show me," she said.

So I turned to the first page with my byline and she read "Home," my twenty-four lines about birds who absurdly built their nests in trees of doom.

"I was young," I told her raised eyes. "Knew everything."

"Then?" she asked.

I turned the page. "Wrote this a couple years later."

And she read my eight-line "Mirror Blues" about how "all the poems you never wrote have great titles, make sense."

"The good news is you're getting over believing you have so much *important* to say," she told me. "But you are too young to have so many regrets."

"You think?"

"For you, *American* . . . I think yes." She closed the journal. Gave it back. Her smile was wide and sweet. "Now I've seen your tattoos."

She stood to go. Put the three books of other people's poems in her shoulder bag with her notebooks, textbooks, and the full body-and-face covering black burka she wore if she needed to visit strict Muslim neighborhoods.

"When can I see you again?"

"So soon you ask?" she asked.

"Not soon enough," blurted truth from me before I could stop it. "And . . . my name is not *American*. It's *Victor*."

"I know," she said, turned to walk away.

Turned back. Said: "Tomorrow. Right here. Same time."

That tomorrow, she came alone.

For twenty minutes we talked about a million nothings until suddenly Bladerunners was too . . . confining. The rain stopped. City air brushed our bare arms with a chill of seventy-six degrees, invigorating enough to inspire us to take one bus, then another, getting off laughing at K.L.'s City Centre gardens in a business district called the Golden Triangle. As we walked amid tropical flowers, the city glistened.

Two black steel and glass towers connected by a triangle-braced tube bridge rose to dizzying heights in the sky above the gardens and the hills of K.L.

"The Petronas Towers."

"True," said Derya. "They made the Japanese and Korean construction firms build them taller than those towers you have in New York."

"The World Trade Center."

"Yes. What a marvelous competition to win. So much more enlightened than seeing which culture can better feed and educate its people, and do so with justice.

"You recognize the design?" After I shook my head, she said: "The floor plan is based on Islam's eight-sided star and the five tiers represent the five pillars of Islam. What is the design of your World Trade Towers based on?"

I shrugged. "Profit per square foot."

"How odd."

We walked in the cool shadows of two towers.

"Why Malaysia?" I asked. "For you."

"If you're going to leave home . . . *Go*.

"Besides," she said, "after being in it for a few years, I realized that government is not about solving problems but administering them. About process, not solutions. Didn't matter that I had a future in politics—Turkey is more progressive than the U.S.: we elected a woman Prime Minister, though not with my vote. But I wanted to . . . to . . ."

"To touch real life."

"Yes! And help people right now not . . ."

"Not down some long road of negotiated *maybe*."

She finger-brushed strands of her cinnamon hair off her tan face to stare at me.

I couldn't bear it, said: "So Malaysia . . ."

"A friend of a friend with a great idea, no money, and not enough hands."

"And way, *way* away from home."

We laughed.

"We don't shuffle things around," she said, "not for the women who come to us. We give them help and don't make them jump through our hoops to get it. If that makes their lives a fraction better . . . then at least we've done something."

"All you can do is all you can do."

"And sometimes you can and must, how you say . . . push it."

My heart sank. The CIA psych evaluators were right and I was right on track.

We walked over a sandy path through the silence of too much to say.

Until she said: "I read your Dr. Williams. He's not my favorite American poet."

Her shoes crunched the sand.

Ten steps and I could stand it no more: "Are you going to make me ask?"

"Of course."

We laughed so hard we staggered. Derya put her cool soft hand on my bare arm to steady us, our first touch. We stopped and she smiled at me.

Said: "Emily Dickinson."

Our laughter cracked the sky.

A trimly bearded man wearing the leisure suit style popular in K.L. for business walked past us. Scowled. He could have been Malaysian, might have been Mexican or Jewish, Arab, Central European. He had a beard, a job, a firm step, and a stone heart.

Memorize him. For the hundredth time, I wished this Op could afford back-up and react teams. I watched the scowling stranger as I asked: "What's his problem?"

"Laughter scares people. Laughing people are free from

control—theirs, yours, the illusion that any of us are in control as this planet hurtles through space. And maybe, just maybe, they're laughing at you."

Derya looked away. "Or maybe it was just us. Westerners. Acting like equals."

She didn't disguise the question. "Are you a Christian?"

"Wasn't me who filled out my birth certificate," I told her. "And the choice I make now won't fit in any label or rate a check mark in some form's box."

"Allah save us all from men with guns and forms with boxes," she said, proving the CIA psych evaluators had been right and thus breaking my heart.

"Are you going to ask me?" she said.

"I don't care—not like that."

She smiled. "But perhaps you need to know.

"Most Americans think all Muslims are one kind," she said. "Can't believe that I'm a woman and doing what I do and still think of myself as . . . A secular Muslim is what I've heard it called. More boxes. If indeed *it is written*, then I am where I should be, and I'll be judged by the honor of my heart and hands."

We quickened our pace as the darkening sky rumbled.

"Victor? I don't know with Christmas coming, your plans . . ."

"The tai chi teacher I came here to study with is taking a break until after New Year's. Whatever feelings Christmas gives me . . . for that I need snow."

We'd reached a covered bus stop. Both of us knew we had to eventually transfer to different lines if we were to get where we were supposed to sleep.

She stared toward me, not at me. "What I'm wondering is . . . Rain leaks into the school, more every day. We don't own it, of course, and the landlord thing is very complicated, very not what's up front. Our official landlord is a *bumiputra*—a 'son of the soil,' native Malaysian. His manager who we deal with is Indian, which is good because he has a soft spot in his heart for Shabana and even brought his daughters in so she could teach them about condoms and pap smears, but we think the real owner is Chinese, shrewd enough to know that if the answer to our pleas for repairs is *no,* we'll make them ourselves and improve his property at our own cost.

As the bus roared toward us, she said: "Can you work a hammer and nails?"

"If not," I said as the bus groaned to a stop, the doors popped open, and thousands of miles away in Langley, CIA strategists gave each other high fives, "I'll fake it."

"We can't pay you," she said, reaching into her pocket for bus fare.

"Forget it," I said climbing the bus steps behind her: "Merry Christmas."

Working on the roof meant I kept a wary eye on the sky. Finding other tasks was easy in that three-story concrete "school" with holes in the walls and dripping pipes. I was supposed to stay out of sight in this all-women institution, but that impossibility let me walk through Derya's word processing class my first day "on the job."

Tension crackled as I tiptoed into that room. Everyone pretended I didn't exist. Her students sat at plank tables that held computers qualified to be dinosaurs.

Half a dozen of Derya's all-women students were Indian, some with red caste dots on their foreheads, some in saris. Four were Chinese who saw their time as *respected elders* fast approaching and hoped learning new skills would stall that inevitability. Other women dressed in slacks or skirts or Malay wear that showed they flowed from *bumiputra* fathers. Six women in full head-to-ankle sack-like black burkas with only slits for their eyes could have been anybody. One wore green shoes.

By Day Five of my Op, the teachers and I were a team. We ate together, went to Bladerunners, watched pirated movies on their VCR. My spot was always beside the warmth of Derya. She'd use her fingers to brush hair off her face and the air filled with her musk.

Confirm progress, e-mailed Op Control.

Progress confirmed, was all I e-mailed back. Fuck it, I knew what I was doing.

Day Seven's schedule held only two morning classes. Shabana came up to the roof after the last class, told me to come down for an early meal.

"But we've got maybe three hours until it rains," I said.

"We've always got maybe three hours until it rains," she told me. "Come on."

Shabana led me to the cluttered office. A card table stood in the room; on it was a sprig of a plastic pine and newspaper-wrapped bundles. Carryout food from a *kedai kopi* café covered the table: kabob sticks of steaming chicken *satay,* the flat fried bread with curry dipping sauce called *roti canai, mee goring* fried noodles. The red rubber bucket used to catch drips from roof leaks sat filled with vendor's ice and bottles of Thai beer.

Derya led Julia into the room.

"Bloody hell," snapped Julia. "What's all this?"

"Happy Christmas!" said Derya.

"Merry," corrected Shabana.

Julia grouched over tears: "Shouldn't have done all this for a couple bloody heathens like the lanky Yank and me. Neither of us are keen on that manger and cross stuff. Shouldn't have, all this trouble, 'n' . . . And is this *all* you could bloody manage?"

Everyone laughed.

"Thank you," I told the two women. To Derya, I said: "Thank you."

She blushed.

"Open presents!" ordered Shabana as she passed out beers. "Two gifts each."

"Julia first," I insisted.

Derya passed her a newspaper bundle that unwrapped as a Gore-Tex rain jacket.

"This . . . this is . . ."

"Most likely completely stolen," said Shabana, "given that it cost us less than one dinner. Now you have no more excuses for being all wet."

Julia's second gift unwrapped as two VHS tapes, pirates labeled 1 and 2.

Derya told her: "We know you've got the fires for that actor Sam Neill, even if he is old and Australian. This a TV show he did when we were kids. About some British spy before the First World War."

"Ah, the good old days," said Julia, toughing out a grin. "Back when Britain ruled out here. And bossed your hometown, too, Shabana, all the way up through Afghanistan and over to all those oil fields in places we made up like Saudi Arabia, Iran and Iraq, Israel to Africa, even over the pond to your place, you bloody Yank."

We clinked beer bottles, a Christmas tinkle that rang only good things.

"*Rule Britannia,*" she said. "The sun sets on the British empire. Us and the Romans, Alexander and Genghis Khan. Gotta say, while I miss the glory and goodies, I'm glad it's gonna be some other blokes' *blood 'n' guts* that pretends to keep this old world spinning. Though if we're lucky, we've seen the last of empires."

"Of either arms or ideas," said Shabana, who'd lectured me about billboards for Coke and Pepsi, for half-naked plastic pop starlets and cigarettes, for Microsoft.

"Now Victor," whispered Derya.

My first newspaper bundle unwrapped as a thin, battered, first edition hardback book: *Selected Poems of William Carlos Williams.*

"In the used books store's bargain bin for two *ringgits,*" said Shabana, protesting my stunned thanks. "Not everyone values American poets out here."

My second gift was a clear plastic globe encapsulating New York city's skyline—the Empire State building, Statue of Liberty, World Trade towers. The globe filled Derya's hand, and when she shook it, a blizzard of white flakes covered the tiny city.

"Merry Christmas," she told me. "Snow."

She turned the globe over in her hand to show me the MADE IN MALAYSIA sticker.

"Did you think all they manufactured out here were high-tech parts for American defense contractors and drugs for your sick people?"

My whisper said: "I don't know what to think."

"What I think," said Shabana, "is that you two should get out of here before the rain. Go see a movie in a real theater like you're always talking about. Let us daughters of the Queen have some privacy to drool over an actor with a funny accent—and don't be shushing me, you wild Turk girl: you watched these already to be sure they worked. And *hammer man:* What do you care about spy stories starring good-looking men?"

They wouldn't let us help clean up. *"Time is running out, and so should you!"* Julia told us the bus to take to get to a cut-rate movie theater in Bangsar, sent us on our way. As we hurried out the door, she smacked my ass.

"Why'd she do that?" I asked Derya as we ran out carrying our shoulder bags.

"She's British."

Which made no sense, but started us laughing so hard we couldn't stop—

—nearly died crossing the intersection with the green light, not paying attention until I heard a clattering roar and saw a swarm of *killer bees*—mopeds and motorcycles—racing through the lanes of cars like they always did, but now on slick streets, tires skidding those bikes toward us, toward Derya . . .

I swooped her off her feet and she worked with me like a ballet partner as I leapt and swung her *safe* to the other sidewalk while killer bees skidded over the pavement where we'd just stood. *Carnage averted* through alert intelligence and decisive action.

Her blue eyes were wide and the pulse pounded in her smooth neck.

Raindrops spit at us as we scampered onto the bus.

We shared a plastic seat amid bus riders who read newspapers and books. Bad music from boom boxes echoed off the metal walls. Her thigh glowed beside mine. Every lurching block thickened our air with diesel fumes and humid smells of strangers. We looked everywhere but at each other. Shoulder bags filled our laps; our bare arms didn't touch. We rode the bus. The rain turned from a patter to a pounding. Traffic crawled. Cars turned on their lights. Thunder rumbled. I rubbed mist off the window, saw we were in K.L.'s Bangsar neighborhood.

Derya's eyes locked to mine: "If we don't get off this bus I'll explode!"

"I . . . I know a place. Not far. Repair store, my friend's, he's gone and pays me a few bucks to check it and . . . It's empty. I know the key code."

She pulled a collapsible umbrella from her shoulder bag. Jerked the signal chord. Bus stopped, rear doors jumped open. We leapt out to a liquid world. Pressed together. The umbrella barely sheltered our heads. Our shoes soaked through in five steps. We had to breathe with our mouths open to keep from drowning in the crashing rain.

Sheer will navigated us through the downpour to a side street. A concrete box of a store showed an unlit neon sign that read FIX TV above a door mounted with a flapped key pad lock. Derya held the metal flap off the lock as with my free hand I tapped in the code. The lock clicked, I pushed the heavy door open and we were *in*.

Later she'd notice that ground floor's tables of gutted television sets, shelves of parts, workboxes of tools. She'd smell oil and solder and rubber, grease, electricity singed dust, and in the depths of that cavern, see a kick-standed motorcycle.

Later she'd wonder how we made it up rickety stairs to the loft with a curtained bathroom. A bed waited beneath the meshed skylight that rumbled with the drumming rain, a skylight now gray with muted sun and at night prismed with the red neon.

Later.

In, the heavy door locking behind us as we lunged together, more a collision than a clutch. The umbrella rolled on the shop floor. My hands crushed cinnamon hair, her mouth worked up my shirt. We pulled apart to see our reflections in the other's eyes. Then, *oh* then we kissed, her mouth burning hungry against mine.

We dance/staggered upstairs. Tossed our shoulder bags toward the rumpled bed.

Trembling, not daring to touch her, scare her away, I floated in time.

Derya dropped her gaze. Unbuttoned her soaked blue blouse. Two buttons from the top she pulled it over her head. A tan bra paled against honey skin. Her right arm disappeared behind her back. The bra obeyed gravity.

Her breasts were angel tears.

And she pressed my hands on her. Filled my grip with her secrets. Arched her back into my grasp on her soft flesh, her nipples swelling. I pushed her against the wall. Covered her with kisses. She shoved her pants down, used one foot to push them off. My hands tore from her breasts, threw away my shirt, my soaked shoes kicked off. Derya shook as she unbuckled my belt, *naked,* I danced with her to the bed.

We were truly there as I kissed her mouth a million times, circled her breast with my lips and sucked her velvet nub. She cried out/her hips bucked against me and she moaned *"Now!"* but I kissed her stomach, her navel that fed her from the last world to this. The room perfumed salty sea and musk. Her skin tasted like its warm honey color. Fingers plowed my hair and she arched her hips for me to peel off her panties. Kissed the inside of her thigh, opened my mouth to her warm sea slickness and set free my tongue.

She cried out, yelled in Turkish, panted my name. Twisted away, pulled me up. Found her bag and condoms Shabana'd given her and we did that, it was part of it, not awkward. Kissing, my hands molding her breasts, cupping her wet half moon as she alligatored her legs, pushed me flat on the bed, straddled me and guided me *in. Back and forth,* my hands on her back, cupping her hips, cinnamon hair covering me like willow branches as she burned my face with kisses *rubbing her hips back-forth.* Her hair flipped through the air as she rose *up/down,* her hips slamming *up/down* on me, couldn't keep my hands off her breasts and she pressed my hand over her heart side squeezed her nipple with my flesh and came before me.

Panting. Coming back from *then* to *there.* She knelt astraddle me, hair across my face, her hot breath against the side of my neck. Rain pattered on the skylight. Her sweat dripped on my skin while she cradled me close, held me *in* as long as we could.

Laying face to face, she stroked my cheek.

Said: "I'm glad nobody was home."

"I'm home."

Her finger pressed against my lips. "Such words need their right moment."

Those blue eyes glistened. "Nothing about us must be wrong."

Her mouth wet the ribs above my heart and sealed my fate. But we snuggled. She said: "Do you like your Christmas presents?"

I lifted the snow globe out of my bag on the floor. Laid back, set the globe on my chest not far from her chin. We watched the shaken snow settle on the tiny, trapped city.

"I love my Christmas presents." *True* and *safe*. "And I love your name: Derya."

"It means *ocean*. The sea."

"Yes."

She pressed her cheek against me and listened to my heartbeat.

"What do your parents think about this?" said Derya. "I mean, not *this* . . . "

We laughed and the room breathed easier.

". . . But you. The martial arts thing: I understand *transcending,* making sometimes more, sometimes less of what other people see. And the poetry. You not being . . . doing what all Americans are supposed to do, get a job, marry some blonde."

"Blondes are overrated."

She poked me. "You better say that! But what do your parents think of—"

"They're dead. Dad's heart attack and cancer for Mom. The American plagues."

"I'm sorry!"

I kissed her head. "Dad first. Year later, I flew back for another coffin sinking into the ground. No sisters, no brother. But my folks got to see . . . what you see."

"So what did they think?"

"That I was crazy."

Laughter echoed through the room's lengthening shadows. Rain on the skylight.

"I've always been . . . different," I told her. "Maybe I've always been crazy."

"Stay that way."

"Okay." I kissed her head again.

"My parents live in Ankara," she said. "Two sisters, a brother, all love me."

"Of course they do."

"But they worry. Not about me, about the world, out here, so far from home . . ."

I switched on the lamp by the bed and she rose up like a lion in its glow.

"This place," she said, looking around. "Your friend . . ."

"He'll be gone for weeks."

"So it's a safe house."

Accident! Just her English making a figure of speech! Not spy craft lingo!

"We're safe here," I said. "It's like . . ."

"Our place."

She kissed me. Held the kiss, opened her mouth to deepen it, her leg brushing up across my loins. I reached down and guided her thigh up, pulled her on me.

Her whisper turned husky as I felt her nipple stiffen. "No."

Yes, we did the condom thing again.

She said: "Cover me!"

And I did. My left arm on the mattress took my weight, my right hand caressed her breasts as I kissed her, whispered her name. Her legs opened to scissor me, her heels curled in above my hips as I thrust myself over and over again deep into the heart of her.

We had five days for our lie.

Five days. Teaching, hammering, squeezing hands when we passed in the hall. Laughing. Surveillance photos taken by the Malaysian police Special Branch showed me standing on a street corner, alone but unable to contain my grin.

Derya urged me to practice on the school roof: *'You can't ignore who you are.'* She abhorred violence, yet made me show her the Yang form of tai chi I had supposedly come to Malaysia to study, plus *gung fu,* differences between Japanese karate and Korean tae kwon do. I showed her how to turn a bad guy's jab into his broken arm, how an open hand slap delivered with no arm muscle could give him a concussion, how one false step dropped him with a foot sweep.

One false step and down you fall.

That roof was where Julia took the picture of Derya, her hair floating in thick air.

One night we spent in the apartment she shared with Shabana and Julia. The romantic novelty of being *oh so quiet* vanished long before dawn.

One night we spent at "my" condo, a bus ride I took every day—officially to "check my host's mail," truly to stall Langley's insistent e-mail demands for *progress.*

The other three nights we lived at our nearer-to-work place. The safe house. No desire to be anywhere but there with each other, with the billion things to talk about, the skylight and the bed. Nights of cinnamon and Tupelo honey.

The sixth day I was working in the shed on the roof when my cell phone buzzed.

Chinese spoke in my ear: *"Wei! Wang hsien sheng yao hong yu chi se ma?"*

"I'm sorry," I said, English signaling WILCO. "Wrong number."

Thumbed my cell phone off. What any snoop overheard didn't matter. *Wang* was a place, not a man, and it wasn't paint he wanted. The color was *hong:* red.

I stored my work, ran downstairs, found Derya and Julia drafting a grant proposal.

"I've got to go," I told them. "Might not be back today."

Derya hurried with me as I headed down the hall to the door.

I told her: "Tonight, go to our place. You know the door code. Wait for me."

"Is everything okay?"

I squeezed her hand.

Two blocks away I found a killer bee driver willing to earn a huge fee from a crazy American tourist who just *had* to get to the giant art deco Central Market near Chinatown, probably to meet some tall American woman. I clung to the back of that rackety bike zipping through traffic and knew I was racing into a nightmare.

That indigo night, clouds covered the stars. Mist floated above the puddles on roads and sidewalks. I stood in the shadows across the street from the TV FIX store. Lights glowed in that safe house. One on the first floor, two in the upstairs floor behind pulled curtains. My whole life waited in there.

Why couldn't I have run away. Why did I walk across that street.

The store's heavy door clicked closed and locked behind me.

Like a child, Derya's head popped around the edge of the rickety stairs. She hurried to me, her blue shirt untucked from her black slacks, her feet bare.

"I was worried about you!" She kissed me.

I let her lead us up to our loft.

"You left and then I realized you'd gone with empty hands," she said. "Didn't take your shoulder bag, your rain jacket, and—I'm sorry, I know I shouldn't have, but . . ."

She gestured to the pile of my gear on the bed.

"But carrying it here, I stuck your jacket in your bag, and when I got here, I pulled it out to hang it up and when I did, this fell out."

Derya held the scrap of paper that I'd salvaged. Most of the lines I'd scrawled were crossed out. We both knew the surviving words by heart.

> PULSE
> *I only think of you*
> *in light from the sun or stars*
> *or whenever I breathe.*

"It's beautiful," she whispered. Blushed and tried to be businesslike: "We have to get you a notebook to write in, to work, you can carry it—"

"I don't write poems anymore."

"I know, it's a haiku, yes? It's so—"

My hand cupped her mouth and at first, her blue eyes showed no fear. *"Shhh."*

Her kiss wet my palm. Still I trapped her words. Stared into her blue eyes so I would never forget how they looked and looked at me *before*.

"We never get to pick our time," I told her. "We only get to pick what we do."

A wrinkle lined her brow. But she didn't back away. *Then*.

"Underneath all of this, two things are stone true:

"I love you."

Derya flowed into my hand, her eyes misted and as sure as tai chi taught me to sense an opponent's center, I felt her open and let go with joy.

"And I'm a spy for the American CIA."

My hand fell away as her smile melted, her brow scarred, her eyes narrowed to make sense of what they couldn't see.

"What?"

"I spy for the CIA. Since I dropped out of grad school. Out here, I wanted to come anyway, knew Mandarin, been doing martial arts since I was seven, so it gave me a reason to be here, drift and mix with locals and . . . And do what I could do. I'm deep cover. Embassies, Chiefs of Station, they only know I'm around. I've been all over Asia. The Agency calls me a NOC—Non-Official Cover. Alley slang calls me a Trouble Boy or a Hotshot. I—"

"You're a spy?" She stepped back.

I was between her and the stairs. Nodded yes.

She whispered: "This isn't a joke."

"None of this is a joke."

Her face flushed, paled, hardened. "Me! Us! Is all this you being a spy?"

"Wasn't supposed to be like this! Loving you wasn't supposed to happen."

"Oh, so good to know you don't fuck people for a living!"

She stormed toward the stairs, the hell with her shoes, she was going, running to where she knew where she was. I flowed ahead of her. Blocked her exit.

Saw fear crowd betrayal from her eyes.

"Derya, I'll tell you whatever you want to know," I said,

again breaking all the rules. "But first let me tell you what you *need* to know."

I moved a chair close to the stairs. Nodded for her to take it. Wary of telling me no, she sat on its hardness. I sat on the bed. The illusion was that she could make it down the stairs and out the door before I reached her. In trust, every illusion matters.

"What I'm going to tell you sounds like a bad movie, but it's true.

"There's an international terrorist organization called al Qaeda. Muslim fundamentalists but they're not about Islam or reflecting its true heart. They're about earthly power. Al Qaeda's headed by a rich Saudi Arabian named Osama bin Laden. Now he's in Afghanistan with the Taliban who have turned that country into a kind of concentration camp. No freedoms. No laws outside of what ambitious clerics proclaim. Women locked up. Forced to wear burkas, treated like . . . water buffalo: good for work and breeding only. Raped and beaten by any man with clerical clout.

"That's what they want for our whole world. They claim a divine right, just like kings and dictators from the Crusades to the Inquisition to Nazis or Communism. Their way or death. In 1998, bin Laden declared war on all Americans, no such thing as noncombatants. Al Qaeda blew up our embassies in Kenya and Tanzania. President Clinton counterattacked with cruise missiles, just missed nailing Bin Laden.

"Al Qaeda is why I'm in Malaysia."

My head fell into my hands. I looked up and hoped she saw the truth in my eyes.

"I love you. I wasn't supposed to, but I have since . . . since I saw you laugh."

"What do you want? I can't help your American CIA—you've got such clean hands! I know about fake Muslims who are terrorists *and* I know about Chile, the Congo, Vietnam and . . . I can't help you.

"Or," she said, groping for a way out. "Did you have to tell me this because you do love me and because if we're not honest with—"

"The Malay Special Branch knows most of what goes on.

When we press them, when we ask the right questions . . . They helped us put together that . . . You're my access."

"To what?"

So I told her.

"No," Derya said twenty minutes later. "I won't let you use me. I won't let you do that to her. I won't turn her over to you."

"What's your other choice? Events have pulled the trigger. I can't back down. I'll have to come at this another way. That means trouble and pain. You said it: sometimes you have to push it. Everybody chooses sides by what they do. Lots of people get away without doing much. Not us. If we don't do this, how many innocent people will die or be enslaved by pious killers with their boxes?"

Took me an hour, but finally she slumped in her chair. Nodded *yes*.

But said: "I won't let you hurt her."

"Nobody gets hurt. Nobody'll even know what happened. That's a successful op."

She closed her eyes. When they opened, I saw tears. That she banished.

"What then?" Her voice jabbed like a sword.

"Then it's over, and I'm over. Done. Quit."

"Why? You'll be a CIA star."

"Only reason I'm here, doing this . . . I want a world with a chance for us."

"So you say."

That last night of the twentieth century left us in the dark with our clothes on.

Morning, January 3, 2000. I hid in the school shed. Sweat trickled down my sides.

Footsteps, coming closer outside on the roof.

Derya led in a woman sacked by a black burka.

I closed the door behind them.

The burka's hands clutched her heart. Eyes widened in the slit of her veil.

"We're trapped," I said.

Derya said: "No, this is just—"

"Forget Miss Samadi," I told her Malaysian student. "She's out of this now."

I rattled off the student's name, her husband, their home address, their tile shop, the name of the *madrasas* their son had transferred to from a public school.

Fear pushed her down in the chair. In a defiant rebellion to keep some individuality, she wore curled toed acceptably Arabic shoes, green shoes.

Derya paced in the shadows. With Derya, the big picture mattered.

For this woman, life had been ripped down to the personal.

"The Special Branch knows you're al Qaeda."

"No!"

"A month ago, you suddenly started wearing a burka. Special Branch watched you, your home, your business selling handmade tiles all over the world. They knew your husband's cousin is al Qaeda. Now al Qaeda's taken you over. Threatened you, yes?"

She looked away.

"Special Branch told us. The American police. They want to arrest you and your husband. They don't care if you're innocent. We can stop them. Save you. *If.*"

"Please!" she said. "Have mercy!"

"Al Qaeda operatives from all over the world are coming here to Kuala Lumpur in the next few days. For a secret meeting."

"I'm just a woman! My husband is like a prisoner! If we say no to them . . ."

"They'll kill your whole family."

She surrendered to the dread crushing her. Sobbed.

"We Americans are your way out. You're stuck between the Special Branch and al Qaeda. One of them will destroy you. Unless we pull you free."

"Only Allah can save us."

"Perhaps Allah sent us."

Derya turned away with disgust.

"You enrolled here to learn about computers. You own a high speed Internet system. Bypass the government monitors. Al Qaeda killers use Internet cafés, but they know that's not secure. Their local thugs have been coming into your shop. Going upstairs. All that's up there is your fast computer. That's where the foreign killers will go. We need to know what they do on your computer."

"I won't know anything!"

My hand opened to reveal three devices each smaller than my thumb.

"After they've used the machine . . . These are data keys. Not like you can buy. Plug one into your machine. They download e-mail, website histories, documents."

I snapped a key in thirds.

"Geographic programming. This tiny rectangular chunk holds data. It's the part that matters. Operating codes are on different sections. After you break the key, without our machine, no one can use it to know what you've done."

"Why are you doing this to me? To my family?"

Derya came to my side. Crouched lower than me.

"Sister, you are trapped by him. But not trapped like you are by al Qaeda. He trapped us both with truth. You will not be alone. I will not let you be alone. We must trust him to help us."

Don't contradict her but keep control! "Only your own hands can pull you free."

That innocent, broken woman pulled off her burka to breathe the shed's stale air.

We had her.

January 5, year 2000: Two dozen al Qaeda operatives from all over the world drifted into K.L. They rendezvoused for days of planning meetings in a suburban condo.

Derya and I marched through fake lives. We spent nights at our safe house. Kept each other close enough to see. Didn't touch.

"You are America." Rain drummed the skylight above the bed where we lay not touching and with our clothes on. "Fancy technologies."

"Forget what Hollywood tells you. We can't hack that computer. Disconnected when not in use. Major firewalls. Local al Qaeda insists on that. Plus their standard procedure is to destroy hard drives when they scatter. Using a key before then is our only chance."

Malay Special Branch followed the al Qaeda crew. Photo surveillance. Street tags tight enough to track them to Internet cafés. Loose enough to let paranoids feel safe. And show up at the tile shop. Across the street, the Special Branch manned a watch post.

January 7. Derya's cell phone rang. She answered. Listened. Hung up.

Told me: *"Tomorrow."*

KISS. Keep It Simple, Stupid. A dead drop blended into our burkaed agent's established routine. Evening class at the heretical school where the mere woman was learning technology of the decadent West that holy warriors could use for jihad.

KISS. She'd ride two buses. First one from the market near the tile shop to a transfer. She could stand at that bus stop until she caught a second bus that let her out near the school. Or she could walk down a side street, past a store with a TV FIX sign, go to a tea stand and buy a warming cup, then retrace her steps and catch her second bus.

KISS. Snapped into secure pieces or not, the data key was an easy fit through the mail slot of TV FIX's door. In the rain forecast to be pouring at that hour, even if she were followed, her watcher wouldn't see her drop something through the door slot, done, free, on her way to the relocation deal being put together by us and the Special Branch.

KISS. Her phone call telling her teacher she'd make it to class signaled that she'd done the dangerous part, plugged and pulled the data key when no al Qaeda eyes were in the tile shop. All she had to do now was ride a couple buses, take a short walk.

Past me.

Rain raged on the city. Blurred the evening light with trillions of streaking gray drops zinging down like jagged diamonds. Vehicles were parked everywhere, pushcarts stood abandoned until the return of quiet skies. Almost no one walked the streets.

I stood in the dripping arch of a shop doorway across the street and up toward the bus stop from FIX TV. A hooded, charcoal Gore-Tex rain shell sheathed me. That blackish jacket blended me into the shadows. Through the rain-blurring vision, neither the burkaed woman I'd hammered into being my spy nor someone following her could easily spot me covering her play.

A blur of light slid to a stop off to my left at the bus stop.

I wiped rain off my face. *Can't see, not yet, not for sure, not—*

Bobbing through the rain across the street.

A black shape: burka. No umbrella. And running. Running past my post.

Don't break cover. Wait. Wait.

A clattering killer bee tore around the corner, skidded onto the side street and crashed into a parked car. The driver flew off, stumbled, staggered, found his balance . . .

Charged after the running woman in the burka. He wore a green rubber slicker.

Close, he was so close and they were only five feet from the FIX TV door when from behind them, through pouring rain, I saw him punch her in the back.

She staggered, whirled to swing something like a rope at her attacker as I leapt from my doorway, grabbed a six-foot twisted steel pipe from the construction rubble.

Green Slicker man caught the rope-thing and pulled: his jerk ripped the rope-thing from her hands and propelled her into his body punch. She stumbled toward the door. He hit her. She sprawled face-first to the sidewalk.

Puddles splashed beneath my running feet as I threw the pipe. It spun through the downpour like a twisted propeller. The pipe bounced off a parked car, careened over Green Slicker's head to hit the wall. He whirled and saw me racing toward them.

And fled down the side street into the twisting neighborhood warren.

I lifted the burka woman from a sidewalk lake. Her veiled hood pulled off:

Derya.

Gasping from the punches, rain washing her pained face, she sputtered: "She froze at market. Cell phoned. Came, she passed key . . . Local al Qaeda, jus' there, market, he . . . he saw, knew her green shoes. She spooked 'n' 'e came after us. I took it, ran caught the bus jus' 'fore doors closed. He banged, wouldn' let 'im on. Knocked rider off killer bee, stole . . . Chased bus."

"Cell phone!" I yelled to her. "Does he have a cell phone?"

"Kill, he'll kill . . . Stop 'im!"

"Get inside!"

As I charged away, I spotted the rope-thing in a puddle. Her shoulder bag, an accessory only a Western woman carried. Add that to our green shoed agent jumping spooked, no wonder the al Qaeda thug targeted them. He'd been smart enough to chase the stranger who'd been given something. Knew he could always kill a local rabbit.

I ran through a sea of rain.

The side street was a curving obstacle course of parked vans and trucks and cars, of killer bees draped in plastic sheaths, of push carts abandoned like roadblocks across the sidewalks while their owners huddled inside tea rooms. Green Slicker could have dived into one of the tea rooms, into any store that hadn't locked its doors for the storm, but I didn't think so. This was Bangsar, lousy with ex-pats. All Westerners were the enemy. He'd want familiar and safe turf to go to ground or to make a stand.

Don't let him have a cell phone, please, no phone!

Hard as the rain fell, what made it hardest to see in front of me was the jumble of solid vehicles and sidewalk obstacles. I knew this street snaked for a mile before it hit a main road. Alleys spiked off it: as far as I knew, all were dead ends.

There! Up ahead—truly *up:* an abandoned skeleton of K.L.'s 1990s boom.

Back when stock markets soared and money flowed like rain, K.L.'s government decreed a facelift for Bangsar to repair roof gutters so that foreigner shoppers wouldn't get their shoes soaked. The scheme bolted scaffolds to buildings on this street. Before any actual gutter repair, the economy crashed and left no *ringgits* to take down scaffolds.

That evening in the first January of the twenty-first century, my black sneakers were soaked through as I grabbed a slick scaffold pipe, pulled myself up to the planking.

Stared down at the sidewalks and street. Only falling rain blurred my vision of the obstacle course below. I jogged over the bouncy-planked path, scanned the street below me like a black jacketed raptor.

Roofs of cars. Trucks. A homeless man held his begging bowl out to the rain. Three rain-drenched backpackers dodged around deserted vehicles. Children jumped in a street puddle. A blue neon nightclub sign winked on. Tops of umbrellas bounced below me: he hadn't had one and no green flashed under them. No—

Half a block ahead: Green Slicker stumbled around a car. He whirled. Saw no human being chasing him. He didn't look up to see what was hunting him from heaven.

His hands were empty: if he had a cell phone, it was in some pocket.

Moments later I was two stories above him. I could see his waterlogged beard.

A coolness flowed through me. I was an angel walking on rain.

The twisted street narrowed. I could see that the path later widened. At street level, Green Slicker thought he was headed toward a dead end.

Green Slicker wiped his face to peer through the rain. He checked back the way he came, saw no hellhound on his trail. He walked down an alley.

Like Batman, I dropped from the scaffold. Followed him *in*.

Rain poured into this narrow canyon of concrete and brick walls. The alley zigzagged, a broken and uneven cobblestone path. Storm drains gurgled whirlpools. A rat slogged toward me, didn't bother to look up or say *hello*.

Ahead, I heard shoes splash in a puddle, a guttural curse.

I flowed around the corner.

Dead end. Canyon walls made by cement and brick buildings. And turning to see me standing smack in the middle of the only way out: Green Slicker.

My left hand swept the black Gore-Tex hood back off my head.

Maybe he thought I wanted him to see who I was. Maybe I did, but I pushed my hood off so that it wouldn't impair turns or vision. Rain drummed my skull. I was here. I was now. I hadn't come into that alley to *transcend.*

He kept his hood up. His right hand slid into his slicker pocket.

Gun no gun! K.L. guns rare, carrying's a lethal risk, if he's got a gun I'm dead!

Green Slicker's fist jumped out of his pocket with a *click* and a silver flash.

Switchblade! He's got a switchblade—should be a Filipino banana knife, this is back alley K.L., not Tijuana, he's al Qaeda not chulo. Should not be a switchblade.

Should didn't matter. Not in that alley.

Maybe Green Slicker trained in one of al Qaeda's Afghanistan terrorist camps. Maybe in the dusty hills between Moscow and Kabul, he'd blasted Soviet soldiers with an AK-47 or an RPG. Maybe he'd planted bombs in Algeria or the Philippines. Maybe he'd spent weeks practicing commandos' hand-to-hand combat.

Those *maybes,* the rain and slick cobblestones, the ticking clocks of al Qaeda and American ambitions, all that went into the alley's equation. Plus my decades in dozens of *dojos, dojangs, kwoons,* classes in the basements of rock 'n' roll CD shops and over fish stores, in garden courtyards and Japanese parking lots, in Nacogdoches, Texas, and Taipei parks and U.S. military combat pits. Plus, this was not my first alley.

Knife fighting is microns and moments. Too little/too much, that way too soon or too slow, your blade stays clean and you get a boot slammed into your groin.

Green Slicker came in fast, his feet spread wide, front to me more like a judo player than a boxer. He stabbed at me but kept enough in reserve so he wasn't overextended, so he could dodge my strike to his eyes, my kick to his knee.

I snapped my left hand toward him; he lunged like a fencer. Without thought, without plan, without Westernized intention, I flowed away from his stabbing blade, slid right—suddenly perpendicular to make his full front "open," my left hand and foot in a straight line to his groin, his heart, his throat, his eyes.

Green Slicker arced a flat roundhouse hook to stab me as I charged.

Only I wasn't *there*. My right fist snapped and I seemed to lunge forward but truly I dropped back with my left side yielding away from his piercing hook.

And *there* was where his hooking knife slash went. Went through.

My left hand whipped behind the elbow of his stabbing arm, merged with his bones and added push that broke his root. My hand on his elbow aligned with his heart.

He rocked back to recover balance, then with inertia flowed up to—

As he floated between balance points, I pushed his center.

Green Slicker flew backward and hit the brick wall.

Bounced off the wall knife in hand, changing his flailing to a desperate lunge.

I stepped outside his lunge, met/grabbed his knife's wrist, pulled—

Slammed my palm into his hyperextended elbow. The switchblade flew from his grip as I heard his elbow snap, his scream. My forearm smashed his throat.

Gurgling/gasping, arm flopping, Green Slicker staggered.

In that moment, I saw his eyes.

I kicked him so hard he bounced off the wall. I grabbed his head, flipped him over my shoulder. Heard/felt his spine break.

Waves sloshed around a human island in an alley puddle. Green Slicker's hood covered his head with its submerged face. No bubbles marred the surface of that water.

Time! How much time do I have? How soon before someone comes back here?

My hands flew through Green Slicker's pockets. Stuffed his things in my jacket.

No cell phone. Thank God, he had no cell phone!

As I ran from the alley, I scooped up the switchblade.

Down came the rain. Somewhere beyond its clouds the sun set. By the time I reached the side street and FIX TV, I was stumbling through wet flowing darkness.

A lump dotted the puddle on the sidewalk by the locked door: her shoulder bag, still there, she'd forgotten it—too stormy for scavengers/thieves. My fingers raked the puddle and found nothing spilled from it. Clutching her bag to my heaving chest, I tapped the lock code and the door clicked and I was in.

Dark, she hadn't turned the lights on. *Good!* I slid to the floor, my back against the door as I fought to catch my breath, as I sent my hand inside her shoulder bag.

Found foil unwrapped from a condom that was gone, four of its fellow still-sealed warriors, an empty water bottle, her cell phone, brush, a scarf and hairpins for cinnamon—

No data key, in whole or in parts.

Upstairs, she's upstairs and it'll be there, said she had it, and it's all okay.

" 's me!" I weakly called out to the darkness.

Heard nothing back.

In darkness, felt along the wall to the stairs, went up them using my hands and feet like a chimpanzee. Rain rolling off me tapped the grimy, sticky wet stairs.

At the top, realized she'd probably be standing in the dark with a baseball bat, ready to swing and fight until she knew it was me, knew she was safe.

My hand felt along the wall at the top of the stairs, flipped on the overhead light.

Derya slumped on the floor, her back against our bed. Her soaked black burka lay in between us. Her shirt was a motley smudge of rust.

All her blouses, shirts, are white or blue.

Her head rolled up from pointing at the floor, cinnamon hair streaking across her pale face as her eyes opened like snowflakes.

"Doesn' hurt so much," came her whisper.

Green Slicker: not hitting her. Not with his fist. With what was *in* his fist.

Not hitting: *stabbing.*

Cradling her, finding the holes oozing on her back, her
stomach.

"She, she—"

"Safe, she's safe, I promise, Derya! And he's—the son
of—*Got him.* He's not gonna, we won't, he can't hurt anybody anymore, can't hurt y—"

"Thought was gonna catch me, on bus, 'im on stolen kill'
bee behind . . . Smarter, gotta be smarter th'n . . . Broke the
key. Threw two parts on bus floor. Core, core's so small, so
big—'d you know th' size somethin' is depends on what time
it is? Condom, Shabana b' so proud, cond'm sealed 'self
tight!

"Swallowed it," she told me. "Water, needed to . . . Yucky
hurt all the way down, bu' if he'd caught me, found nothin',
even though I just a woman, don't belong to him 'n' he'd
have to let me go."

Hair webbed her face. Her hand tried to brush it away; fell
back to her wet lap. I swept matted cinnamon from her eyes
as she stared into me with shimmering blueness and confessed: "I'd be a lousy drug smuggler."

I grabbed my cell phone.

"Don' you want to talk to me?"

Milk washed through her Tupelo honey skin that felt tepid
and wrinkly.

Who could I call.

"I'll talk to you forever and ever!" I held her face so our
eyes could meet.

"Tell me truth?"

"Always! Forever, the whole truth, I love you, I love you,
I—"

"Olacag' varmis." The Turkish proverb she'd taught me
that I'd joked back to her with the American not-quite-on-
target translation of: That's life.

More Turkish babbled from her, so slurred her family
might not have understood.

Deep breath, she was back, fully there, *here,* face in my
hands as she was *oh so still* while I trembled. She let her
hand float up between us, let her fingers brush my forehead,

their stickiness burning a crimson smear on my skin that she saw, whispered: "Tattoo."

Gone, her hand falling as she was gone.

No, not *gone:* she was dead.

My sobs and screams washed away my faith.

But not my rage.

Then it came to me: *Not all this for nothing.*

Not all that I saw unfolding around me like holographic theater where I was on the stage, seeing myself pull my love into the bathroom, seeing me lift her into that tub, lay her on her back like she did when I wasn't in there with her, when soap bubbles and steaming hot water made eternities we called *Italy* because me watching her bathe was like an Italian movie. But in this stage play she just lay there. I envisioned dawn as I motorcycled through K.L.'s empty streets, rain washing me and soaking the bundle lashed to the seat behind me, a bundle the size of a mattress, a bundle wrapped in the curtain from the bathtub where Derya who I'd love forever lay with lifeless eyes open like on that July afternoon when I was nine and my Uncle who wasn't Sam, no he was Jerry, Uncle Sam stood with me near the trout stream, my hands full as he said: *"Go ahead, son, you caught her, you got to finish the job, an' now she won't feel a thing."*

But so much of that was in the future as I bent over the bathtub where my love lay. So much was in a tomorrow where Special Branch experts detected the death of a woman killed by a hit and run driver who exploded her life into a mess that had to be sealed in a steel coffin and flown home to Ankara, a flight that carried her two friends clinging to a haunted American who *lied, lied, lied.* Lied like the Special Branch who for dollars and comradeship with a tall American woman closed the books on another accident on that January 2000 night. In that strange event, a former thief who'd allegedly found Allah stole a killer bee and ended up crashing and breaking his fucking neck. All those in the market who'd seen him steal the motorcycle never understood why he'd done what they truly saw him do.

But now I was here. Not in that future when I'd work my

hands through wet slippery things to fulfill my patriotic quest. Not in the next future when I'd call the Op Panic Number and bust cover and break balls and make things happen and *deliver.* I was here, now, split apart from my feelings bent over the iron edge of the bathtub where my love lay dead.

Plug the drain.

Did it. Envisioned the flight of a Malaysian family to Kuwait; they'd refuse to go to America. Like a foul rapist, I ripped open Derya's stiffening blue shirt.

The switchblade *clicked.* Electric shock zapped up its mirror blade as it pricked Derya's skin at her *tan t'ien,* that wondrous point below our navel that is home to the chi of every living man and woman. I remember insisting that no one was home beneath the tip of my knife. I remember screaming. Trembling. Trying to make my scream the *Kia!* karatekas bellow to break boards, but my scream *transcended* that as I forgot my last sane thought shoved the knife *in.*

38

MY SECOND SUICIDE began with a 9/11 afternoon helicopter ride from the Castle. Two soldiers who'd come to Maine for me made sure I was strapped tight in that 'copter. Maine's pine forests slid beneath our whumping chariot. Looking down, I saw a deer run through the trees. The sky reddened as we landed at an Army base where a camo-face painted grunt paced with a Surface-to-Air Stinger missile like the ones we'd shipped to anti-Soviet warriors in Afghanistan. My escorts boarded us on an Army plane. We flew in a sky empty of everything but smoke, birds, and American warriors. Stars winked into view before we landed at Andrews Air Force base near Washington, D.C. We marched off the plane. Red dots from sniper scopes danced on our chests. The soldiers gave me to two men in suits. They opened the back door of a sedan and I scrunched myself between their weight-lifter arms. A woman who wore no perfume drove us off the base.

We drove into a Maryland neighborhood outside of the D.C.'s Beltway. The White House was a forty-five-minute drive away; you could get to CIA headquarters or the Pentagon in less time because you didn't need to drive city streets. The destruction zone for a tidy nuclear device detonated at any of those three command centers did not extend to this neighborhood. For a tidy device.

The redheaded CIA security guard sitting to my right was left-handed, or so I deduced from the way the gun on that side of his belt dug into my kidney. He shook his head. "I feel like we're driving through a whole new world."

"We are," said the security guard on my other side.

"Is this what it was like when JFK was shot?" said the redhead.

"I wasn't born then," said his partner.

None of us were, I thought. Remembered what Zane who'd been in junior high back then had said while the five of us in the Castle watched the WTC towers burn on TV. I told the car driving through the night: "This is bigger."

We drove toward an obvious fortress of American public education.

"Closed this high school last spring," said the driver. "Busted budget. Now they bus these kids to a school 'bout thirty minutes away where they have trailers for overflow classrooms."

We drove past two men sitting in a parked car pretending they weren't covert guards. Our driver radioed call signs and code words, got okayed to come in. We pulled into a parking lot filled with vans and cars and green trucks with gray duct tape covered insignias on their doors. Flashlights bobbed on the roof as techs rigged satellite dishes and antennae. A metal detector arch loomed inside the glass doors to the gym. I figured the odds were fifty-fifty that the metal detector belonged to the school.

Lights blazed in the girders above the basketball court. Bleachers ringed the game floor. Cables snaked over the blond wood floor. Maybe forty desks on that wood were already in use, men and women dressed in everything from sweat suits to military camo talked into phones, pounded computers and laptops, poured over documents. Carpenters assembled green plastic walls around the desks, turning this chessboard of workstations into a maze of cubicles. TVs broadcast live shots of the pile in New York, the smoking Pentagon, a spotlit field in Pennsylvania. Phones rang. Hammers clanged. People shouted. The gym crackled with electricity.

"This beehive didn't exist at 9 A.M. today," said Redhead.

A man with a clipboard directed us to courtside bleachers. A fat man in a rumpled suit sat five rows up. Two lean men a dozen rows above the fat man kept casual eyes on him, and when Redhead told me to find a seat in the bleachers, the lean men included me in their watchful gaze.

Seemed impolite not to sit beside the fat man. So I did. Wondered if he ever played Santa Claus. 'Course, he'd need a white beard and no bloodshot eyes. Plus breath mints, I thought as he sighed whiskey.

"Look at 'em," he said.

You talking to me? raced through my mind like a psycho Robert De Niro.

"Scurrying around like ants," said the fat man. "Where were they yesterday?

"I'll tell you where," he said before I could answer. "Somewhere that didn't work, that's where. And you know why? I'll tell you why. 'Cause fighting guys armed with box cutters and go-to-heaven plans don't require brand-new fighter jets. Jets the Air Force doesn't even want but that feed tax dollars to the 'military-industrial complex' beast President Eisenhower warned us about. Then those beasts shit campaign dollars all over Washington."

"Sounds reasonable," I said, merely making conversation.

"Fuck reasonable."

"Did," I said before I could stop myself.

We truly looked at each other for the first time.

"Ain't supposed to say who we are," he told me. "I'm Bureau. FBI. And we're better than this."

His sweeping gesture took in the swarm of people on the floor, the hat racks turned into flagpoles for marker-scrawled paper signs: FBI, CIA, Customs, DEA, Secret Service, SAC, DOT, Marshalls, CTC, FAA, DIA, CDC, NSA, Coast Guard, NCIS, a dozen more alphabet jumbles.

"Or we could have been better than this," said the fat man. "Except nobody believed what everybody knew.

"Last year, I had an informer, Yemeni, born in Jersey, all he wanted to do was prove he could be a patriot so his folks would have no trouble with Immigration. He volunteered to go into the camps for me, *for us,* go get the Afghan *what's what* and *who's who.* The desk boys at the Bureau said no. "Not cost effective" to cough up a lousy three grand for expenses. *"Not our priority."* Plus real spying scares bureaucrats because it gets messy, and the scaredy-cat way to stay clean and out of trouble isn't to figure out how to do human intel right, it's to not do it at all."

My bench partner offered a pint from his inside suit to me.

"No thanks."

"You against it or you already self-medicated?"

Missed my after-Group pills. Oh well.

But I told him: "Whiskey's not my thing."

He squinted at me. Nodded at the basketball court full of uniforms, badges and guns. "If you fire up a joint, at least *that* they'd know how to bust."

Had to laugh. Both of us.

"I don't drink to forget or for courage," said the fat man. "I drink so I remember I can't do everything even if they let me."

He whispered: "So it can't be all my fault."

But those words lacked conviction. He took a swig. Put the bottle away.

At 11 P.M., we shared an everything-on-it-but-happiness pizza passed up to us by a Marine. We followed an escort to one of the public bathrooms.

Splashed cold water on my face at the bathroom sink, rose and saw my dripping reflection in the smudged wall mirror.

High school. I'm back in high school. Knowing what I know now.

They led us back to the bleachers to watch the action on the gym floor.

Straight up midnight. Six expensively clothed men and women marched into the gym. Power rippled from them. Spies and cops and techs buzzing on the floor straightened their posture, kept their eyes on what they were doing yet expanded their gaze to watch the new arrivals stride along the basketball court.

"Ladies and gentlemen, the bishops are in the house," said my fat buddy.

As they reached the midcourt line, I recognized one of the bishops, the youngest gray-haired man. He stopped; stared out at the basketball court. His halt braked his five companions. Two nearby soldiers laboriously wheeled a bulletin board refitted as an emergency gear station hung with fire extinguishers and gas masks.

Gray-haired man jerked a fire ax off the bulletin board, swung it over his head as he charged onto the basketball court and in front of the whole astonished gym, chopped the axe through the nearest plastic partition wall.

The plastic wall shattered.

A dozen people shouted as the gray-haired bishop stormed down the aisle of desks on the gym floor. He swung the ax like a baseball bat and shattered a second cubicle wall, whirled to backstroke a green plastic wall taped with a flow chart. The woman in that cubicle dove past him and scurried away, but he ignored her, shattered another of her walls and leapt on top of her desk, golf clubbed the ax to blast a hole in the wall between her and the next cubicle.

He stood on the desk, ax in hands.

Mesmerized a gym full of frozen people. Phones rang unanswered.

"Don't you get it?" he bellowed. "Walls got us here! Blinders! We only cared about what was inside our own fucking cubicles. We didn't look outside them. We didn't like it when people somehow got stuff in to us—especially if it didn't fit with what we believed, what we'd profiled, who we were. We didn't share what we had or what we knew because our turf was all that mattered. We made plastic walls

and the bad guys walked along the tops of them and killed men, women, and children who trusted us to keep them safe and we fucking didn't and they fucking died!"

He threw the ax to the basketball floor.

Yelled: "No more fucking walls!"

Gray Hair jumped off the desk, led his fellow bishops to the locker room.

"Follow that man into Hell," muttered my fat buddy.

"Already there."

They summoned my fat buddy to the locker room thirty minutes later.

Left me alone in the bleacher.

Zoned out.

Shaking my shoulder, someone's—

"You okay?" Redhead, the CIA gun.

"Same as I ever was." The clock on the wall showed 2:10. "Is that A.M. or P.M.?"

"They're ready for you," he said, added: "The time is morning and it's dark."

We marched down the bleachers, joined his partner from earlier plus a third man whose no jacket/no tie image felt medical. Medical's left hand held what I first thought was a holstered Glock automatic, but what my closer look told me was a taser—a pistol that fired two wired electrodes fifteen feet into the flesh of the target with enough electricity to drop a Brahma bull.

We went to the locker rooms now crowded by men and women at makeshift desks. As we walked, I heard a woman say: *"We swore we'd never let Pearl Harbor happen again. But every year, doesn't matter which President, I've heard the CIA Director tell Congress that we're a billion dollars short of a good antiterrorist package, and every year, not enough—"* That conversation flowed out of earshot. Shower stalls had been converted to a map wall, one map of the world, one of the United States. Cell phones chirped. Static crackled from laptops, faxes, and other high-tech wonders. This tiled room still smelled of ankle wraps, football jerseys and sweat soaked pads, liniment and teenage glory.

Redhead knocked on the door of the glass walled coach's

office. Inside it sat the ax-wielding, gray-haired bishop and five other executives, including a man and woman who, like Gray Hair, had been at the medal ceremony that preceded my first suicide.

Gray Hair beckoned, but my escorts and I all couldn't fit inside the coach's office. I ended up in the hard folding chair beside the coach's desk to face the gray-haired bishop. Taser Man leaned in the office doorway. Redhead and my other escort waited beyond the glass. Five bishops of America's cathedrals of secrets stood and slouched and watched me from the coach's inner sanctum walls.

"How are you, Victor?" said the gray-haired ax-wielder sitting in the coach's chair.

"I'm here, Mr. Lang."

"You remember me."

"I'm crazy, not senile. You talent-spotted me at that martial arts seminar way back when I was in college at Georgetown. Didn't know it was you who'd turned me over to Recruitment until they took me to your cabin for my graduation send-off."

He smiled. "You were Non-Official Cover. We couldn't bring you to Langley."

"Oh."

"Now," said Lang. "We need you to focus. We need you to remember. We need you to be truly, sanely, all here. Can you do that, Victor?"

"Maybe."

Lang reached into a file folder. Put a color picture of first one man, then another down on the desk for me to see.

Face shots—not posed and air-brushed out of context.

Two Middle Eastern men, one with a mustache, one clean shaven.

"Maybe," I said. "I've never seen them in person, but—"

"Good work." Lang laid a long shot candid photo of half a dozen men on top of the portraits. Both those men were in the group, and that photo I knew.

"This is a Special Branch surveillance photo from the al Qaeda summit in K.L., January 2000. I saw it in an after-action briefing."

Lang told me the men's names. My shrug told him the names meant zip.

"Various agencies had alerts and watch-listings for them even before that K.L. meeting. Afterward, we'd ID'd both of them as real killers. Had hard data on their papers. One flew into the U.S. right after the K.L. summit, the other came over that July. Even though they were using credit cards with their real names, even though they were tied to the suicide bombing that ripped up our Navy's destroyer *Cole,* no badges scoped them because the Agency didn't inform the Bureau of our full intel."

Lang's silence pulled my eyes to his, then he said: "We didn't want to go to your asset relocated in Kuwait before we talked to you."

"She won't help you. She and her family went down the rabbit hole and nothing will make them come up to help us again."

The woman bishop said: "Don't underestimate our persuasiveness. Not now."

"She never told me anything about anyone that we didn't already know. It took . . . It took everything I had to get her to do the data key."

Lang nodded.

"Who are those two guys?" I asked.

But I knew the core of the answer before Lang said: "They were on the team that hijacked the plane that slammed into the Pentagon."

"What was on the data key I . . . recovered?"

"Looks like it could have been the key of keys," muttered a male bishop as Lang's expression screamed *Keep your mouth shut!* The other bishop was too lost in anger and sorrow to catch Lang's silent message, said: "Al Qaeda guys at your K.L. summit used your asset's computer to surf websites with airline schedules, flight school info, hell, specs on jetliners and the two towers and a virtual tour of—"

"You did a magnificent job," interrupted Lang. "It was us who fucked up. We didn't recognize the significance of that data, and—in part to protect sources and methods—we didn't share that data with the Bureau or any other security teams."

"Nobody—"

"Nobody saw what we all had locked up in our secret boxes."

"God save us from men with boxes," I muttered, but it was Derya's voice.

The youngest bishop said: "Compartmentalization is key to intelligence security!"

"I feel so safe now."

Lang said: "Thank you for all this, Victor. What you did in Malaysia was . . . beyond heroic and valuable. Helping us today, in spite of . . . True pro."

"Gotta be worth it," I muttered like Hailey.

Lang put a comforting hand on my arm. Training snapped my attention to his touch, and martial artist that he was, he sensed my change.

He said: "It's time for you to go home."

My answer echoed in that packed glass walled coach's office: "Yeah."

Taser Guy turned me over to Redhead and his partner. The three of them escorted me out of the locker room, back through the gym with its shattered cubicle walls. Redhead walked on my left, his weak side right arm holding my left elbow like he was helping a shaky senior citizen make it through a minefield. His partner walked close to my right side. Taser Guy—*somewhere behind me?*

The spy in me thought of the perfect thing to say and gave me a conversational voice to say it: "I wonder if I'll ever see that fat guy again."

"Beats me," said Redhead. His grip on my elbow softened.

We neared the exit to the gym. As point man for our troop, it made sense for me to push open the gym door. The glass doors to exit the school for the outside world were thirty, twenty-five feet dead ahead. Five security guards milled there by the metal detector.

With all those armed guards and all that high-tech help, who wouldn't feel safe?

"Elvis has left the building," I joked.

Redhead and his partner laughed. Relaxed into a slower focus.

My left leg swung forward with my left arm—and Redhead's grip on that elbow. As my left shoe hit the school hall tile, I dropped all my weight through that foot, wheeled my waist to my right. That whirl snapped my right hand like a whip into the face of my other CIA escort. A firebomb exploded his nose. I spun my waist back, a change that scooped my right foot under his floating shoe and dropped him to the tiles.

Even before I swept his partner, Redhead was reacting, pulling on my left elbow—a force I rode with my wheeling waist, my left arm turning free from his elbow-grip as my blood-flecked right hand surfed off my spin in a rising palm strike toward his eyes.

Give him this: he was quick. His left hand arced in a cross block—that I let contact my strike, that my right arm merged with as I sank back. His right hand slammed a low punch straight at me that I caught, pulled, felt him pull back. I flowed forward/sent both our energies through my push. He would have flown backward except I held on to him with my left hand. His weight slamming down through his shoes jarred his spine. As he staggered, fought falling, my right hand ripped his pistol from its left-side holster, then my left palm pushed his center so he truly flew away.

Gun, in my right hand, a beautiful Sig Sauer automatic. I thumb-cocked the hammer as my mouth opened and slid around *steel oil tang.* I jammed the gun bore on the roof of my mouth—pulled the trigger.

Click!

Perfect! I thought as I jerked the gun out of my mouth, my left hand flying to grab the pistol's slide and jack a round from the magazine into firing position: *Mister CIA, great gun, no bang in the barrel.*

Last thing I heard that day was the Sig rack a bullet into ready, then the taser knocked me *back-to-whacko-world* with a jillion electric volts of shock and awe.

39

ON DAY FIVE of our flight from the insane asylum, morning found me sitting in a dark New Jersey bedroom that smelled of dust and sweat-caked clothing. I matched my breathing to the rise and fall of a cocooned bed.

Outside, a newspaper *thunked* on the wooden porch.

Zane flipped the switch on the bedroom wall. The light came on.

He grinned. "So far, so good."

Cari'd been feigning sleep. Zane's light meant she couldn't pretend anymore. "Are you always so damn happy when you wake up?"

Zane shrugged. "Hope so."

Her bloodshot green eyes found me: "Have you been there all night?"

"I relieved Hailey early so I could be here when you woke up."

Cari's eyes closed. "Please say that I smell coffee! I promise I won't escape or capture you while I go downstairs to the kitchen and have just one cup of coffee."

"Of course you can have coffee!" I said.

"Don't promise the obvious," Zane told her. "You're better than that."

"Speaking of obvious," said Hailey as she walked into the room, "first thing in the morning, everybody's got to go. As a woman, I say she gets privacy—with me."

Took us fifteen minutes to unwrap Cari's cocoon. We untied the line belting her cuffed wrists to her waist, but kept her ankles tethered: she could walk, go up and down stairs, but running would be a joke, her knee strike would lack power, and the only kick she could deliver was the movie-awesome, street-silly, jump double push.

Hailey passed me her pistol, followed Cari into the bathroom, closed the door.

Zane leaned there.

I leaned on the opposite wall.

We could hear the shape of words inside the closed bathroom. Hear any danger.

Sounds of a zipper, clothing hitting the bathroom floor.

Sounds of liquid.

"So," said Zane.

"Yeah," I said.

"You get any sleep?"

Our sentry plan was two hours at the windows, then two hours in Cari's room. Who cared that I'd jumped cycle.

"Got some," I told Zane. "You?"

"Guess so."

Toilet flushed.

I shrugged. "Weird dreams."

" 'Xactly."

Water rushed into a sink.

Bathroom door clicked open. Cari shuffled into the hall.

Hailey looked at Zane and me: "You guys ready?"

All of us trooped downstairs.

"So what I'm wondering," said Russell twenty minutes later as all six of us sat in the dead man's living room, "is why do we got her?"

"Her" sat on the couch, poker faced, a steaming cup of coffee in her cuffed hands as she calculated turning that boiling liquid into a projectile weapon, leaping to her tethered feet, and hearing the gunshots of her own certain death.

She sipped her coffee that she took with milk. Just like me.

"Can't call her a hostage," said Hailey. "If they catch up to us . . . You don't negotiate with mad dogs."

"Can't call her a prisoner," said Russell. "That's not our mission."

Eric said: "Shouldn't plan front of her."

"No," I said. "We have to do all this in front of her. She's our witness."

"What?" said Russell.

"Our only way free of everything is if the Agency believes us," I said.

Hailey shook her head. "We're *mad dogs.*"

" 'Xactly," said Zane. "So Victor's right. We can't run forever and it won't matter if we nail Kyle Russo or whoever Dr. F's killer is. The good guys will still hunt us down."

"But if we have a witness," I said. "Someone who the Agency believes, then . . ."

Russell's gesture revealed the pistol in his belt. "Then what?"

"We haven't gotten that far yet," said Zane. "But at least 'then' is somewhere."

Cari cleared her throat, said: "Or—"

"You got something to offer we ain't already heard?" said Russell.

Cari shook her head.

"Then," he said, drawing that word out, "you got nothing to say."

Eric told Hailey: "He's still mad about last night."

"I was going to get laid!"

My voice said: "Nothing personal! This is about us and what we've got to do."

" *'About us'?"* said Russell. "Then why don't we vote? Hell, we all pledged our lives to uphold truth, justice, and the American way of democracy."

Hailey shrugged. "Sounds reasonable."

No words came out of my mouth. What could I say that wouldn't shatter us?

Zane shared my predicament. Shrugged. "We're all the boss."

Eric sighed. "Can't . . . vote."

He pressed his hands over his ears, scrunched his eyes shut. "Hear orders both ways from all of you an' me voting . . . Tear me apart."

Hailey patted his arm.

"So," said Russell: "All those in favor of making her our witness."

Zane and I held up our right hands.

"All those opposed."

Russell and Hailey held up their right hands.

Eric pressed both his hands tighter over his ears.

"It's a tie," said Russell. "And that leaves us stuck sitting here."

Cari said: "What about me? Don't I get to vote?"

Her five captors stared at each other.

Hailey shrugged. "A scientific study in the 1970s proved that the mentally ill are as likely to make rational electoral decisions as the average American voter.

"Given everything," she told Cari, a blond warrior hand-cuffed and tethered and holding a cup of steaming coffee on a dead man's couch, "you look sufficiently average."

"Wild," said Russell. "So your vote is whether or not you get to be our witness."

"Excuse me, guys," said Cari. "But . . . what happens if *'not'* wins the election?"

Brows wrinkled. Mouths frowned.

"Well," said Zane, "most likely, *'not'* won't include murder."

"Such certainty is comforting," said Cari.

"That's politics," I said.

"Hell, I was on my way to a promotion, but I'll be your witness if you want."

"Wild," said Russell—but sarcastically, grudgingly, not like he meant *cool*.

"So . . . now we can lose the handcuffs?" Cari gave us an angel smile.

Earned our laughter.

"Witness is one thing," said Zane. "Walking free you have to earn."

"We're crazy," said Russell, "not stupid."

"Oh." Cari shrugged. "Okay. But where are we going? And when?"

"Nowhere until long after dark," I said.

"I've got an idea," said Hailey. "But we can't try it until just before we leave."

Cari looked at us: "So . . . tonight?"

Zane and I shrugged.

Our witness said: "What are we going to do until then?"

40

IMAGINE CARI TAKING a shower.

Upstairs bathroom. Eric nailed the window shut. Cari couldn't break that glass or tear the shower curtain rod out of the wall without making a racket. The top of a toilet tank is great for whacking somebody from behind, but cumbersome for face-to-face combat. We removed all the dead man's aerosol spray cans and caustic bath potions.

I sat with my back against the wall in the upstairs hall, my eyes on the closed bathroom door that was near enough so I could hear running water/yells/breaking glass/tussle, but far enough away so that a charge sprung from inside that closed room couldn't catch me by surprise. Because I cared, I held the tranquilizer dart gun, not the Glock .45 from the holster on my hip or Hailey's nine mic-mic Sig Sauer tucked in my belt.

Imagine Cari taking a shower.

I couldn't stop that movie playing in my head.

I wouldn't have stopped that movie if I could.

Hailey was in there, our added check on Cari's nature. Hailey sat on the vanity by the closed door, out of striking range from anyone standing in the tub shower, someone inside that clear plastic curtain, a pink flesh blur turning and twisting in rising steam.

Cari raised her face into the nozzle's rain. Pounding water darkened her blond hair. Beads of water rolled down her naked spine. Hot rain washed over Cari's face, over her closed eyes, the steam clearing her sinuses, a cleansing mist that slickened the skin of her bare shoulders, her neck, that trickled down to wet—

Rattling like a prairie snake!

Zane: walking up the stairs, shaking a white coffee mug.

My buddy came and stood above me, said: "I thought this was Russell's post."

"Was," I said. Kept my seat. Kept casual. "But with what he's angry about, with what's going on in there . . ."

I nodded toward beyond the bathroom door.

"You don't need to worry," said Zane. "She's not his type."

"Yeah, but it's been a long time, and if you can't be with the one you love . . ."

"You wait."

You poor guy, I thought.

Water pounding in the shower.

"Think she's bought into our program?" I asked.

"No. But she's along for the ride."

Zane shook the mug that he held at my eye level, made it rattle like coins in a cup.

"Hailey sorted these out for you before she went in there," he said, his nod again keying our glance at closed shower room door.

The mug held three colored pills.

"Last dose for all of us," said Zane.

"Then what?"

" 'Xactly."

I downed the pills with a swallow from Zane's water bottle.

The shower shut off with a shuddering clank of pipes.

Water gurgled down a drain.

"You need to see what we found." Zane angled his head toward the stairs.

"Great," I said. "I'll—we'll be right down. You go on ahead."

"That's okay." He leaned on the wall. "I'll hang here. Back you up."

He nodded to the closed steamy door. "Gotta be careful. She's a lot to handle."

I was on my feet when the door clicked, swung open.

Cari wore a blue denim shirt from the dead man's closet, her own black slacks and his two-sizes-too-big white sneakers. She rolled the drooping cuffs up her bare arms.

Said: "I feel like a clown."

Zane said: "Everybody does."

"You look fine," I told her. "You smell great, too. Clean. Fresh."

"Good thing the guy had a spare toothbrush."

Hailey followed her out, stood clear.

I clicked steel bracelets on Cari. Tethered her ankles. Tied the rope dangling from her handcuffs to her tether.

When I was done shackling her, Cari said: "I prefer a natural look."

Simultaneously, Zane said: *"Good for you,"* and I said: *"Me, too."*

Hailey shook her head. "You two got it now. My turn to shower."

We had Cari lead us downstairs, one shuffling step at a time.

As Zane told me: "Putting together our cash, the $123 we found here—"

"Leave a few bucks in his wallet," I said. "When the cops find him, we don't want them to think people have been here, cleaning him out."

"People maybe, us no. With the bankrolls from Cari's crew, we've got $4,100, plus a jar of coins. We found no guns."

"What kind of American was he?" said Cari.

We watched her clump down the stairs, one at a time.

"Eric found enough food to rustle up a few home-cooked meals," said Zane. "Bottled water we can take, granola bars, peanut butter and jelly sandwiches. Vitamins."

"No Valium? No Prozac or Librium or Sonatas or—"

"No."

Echoing Cari, I said: "What kind of American was he?"

Zane pointed for her to go right as we came downstairs. We followed Cari into the house's small study. An ancient rolltop desk stood opposite the door.

Zane picked up a shoebox that rattled as he passed it to me. "He does have lots of headache pills, and the documents I found in his desk match these."

Sunglasses. Dozens of sunglasses. Aviator sunglasses in mirror and flat black lenses. Wraparound sunglasses sporting Beatnik-era solid frames and cybercool metal girder frames. Discount store box lens sunglasses with imitation tortoise shell brown and cheap black frames. Men's granny sunglasses like John Lennon wore. Blind bluesman wraparounds that optometrists put on their patients after an eye exam. Clip-on sunglasses, one pair clipped on regular sunglasses for extra dark vision.

"He had Nonspecific Umbra Logarithmic Loss."

"What?"

Zane nodded past Cari to the rolltop desk and its stacks of paper. "He had a condition called NULL. According to doctors' reports, insurance forms, lab work . . .

"Everything is white or black or a blend from them," said Zane. "Like day and night, or that Chinese yin-yang symbol of two teardrop half circles snaking each other."

"The tai chi *T'u* symbol," I said. "But each extreme contains a dot of the other."

"Not if you have NULL. 'Umbra' is the darkest part of the shadowed area. In your—*in our*—eyes, that means the darkest part of where light comes in—and the coming in of that light. He was losing his umbra."

"He was going blind?"

"Yeah, but not to dark. Every day he saw light getting brighter. Soon it would blind out all shapes, all color. All his eyes would see was burning white."

Cari shifted from tethered foot to tethered foot. Watching us.

"Blinded by light," I said. "But then—"

"Hey guys," said Cari. "Do you mind if I sit down?"

She nodded at the wheeled wooden chair pushed into the well of the rolltop desk.

I looked at Zane. He looked at me.

"Look," she said, "I didn't get much sleep last night."

She glared at me. "Remember? You were there."

I scanned the desk for what might hide amid stacks of letters, paperclipped receipts, medical reports, and tax forms. A stack of utility bills from the era of America's first President George Bush lay in the shadows under the desk's cubby-holed face. Buried under that stack of paper was a long lump.

Under the bills I found a letter opener given to service station owners like our dead host. The blade was brass with dull dagger edges, though a powerful thrust might drive its six inches into soft tissue. Inscribed on one side of the handle was an oil company's slogan—"Good for your car wherever you are!"—a promise expanded with a second line: "So what we do is good for you!" The other side held the corporate logo and the date "1963"—the dawn of the Beatles and Lee Harvey Oswald.

My hand weighed the letter opener while Cari watched. "This wouldn't have been much use."

"You use what you get."

Zane put the letter opener in the box of sunglasses. I swiveled the chair out from the desk well, directed Cari to sit.

"Be good," I told her as she looked up at me.

"What else is on the ballot?"

Zane led me to the other side of the room where a giant colored map of America's landlocked forty-eight states filled the wall. Cities and towns—especially near this New Jersey home—were spiked by blue thumbtacks. Red thumbtacks spiked places like San Francisco, Seattle, Chicago, a pink stretch of Arizona where I guessed the Grand Canyon waited, and a tan corner of Montana that Zane said was Glacier National Park.

"More red than blue," said Zane.

"Bet you blue is *been there,* red is *wanna go.* But he was going blind."

"More every day," said Zane. "Like pushing down on the Cadillac's accelerator."

"He could never go to the places he'd never been. Never see them."

"He saw them every day." Zane nodded to the map. "Up there."

Zane shrugged. "There's always more road than time."

Creak! Metal and wood, floor and chair.

We whirled: Cari bent over the desk, tethered hands cupping her face as we heard: *"Ha-choo!"*

She saw us, said: "Excuse me."

I jerked her chair so fast inertia flipped her tethered feet off the hardwood floor.

"Wee!" she said. "Thanks for the ride, but after someone sneezes, you're supposed to say *'God bless you'* or—"

"Stand up!"

The empty chair rolled across the floor.

I grabbed her cuffed hands—still locked, the belt line still tight. My foot pushed the tether between her ankles (*still tied*) and she stumbled forward, would have fallen into me but my rigid palm on her thorax kept her away from my gun. I stuck my fingers in the pockets of her dead man's shirt, felt soft swelling—nothing in there.

Cari drilled me with her green eyes. "You're supposed to ask first."

I ran my fingers along the front of her waistband, felt her belly flex.

Zane told her: "We heard the chair creak."

"When you moved." I scanned the desk, the paper piles: nothing looked changed.

"When I sneezed," she said behind my back. "Or okay, maybe before. It's an old chair. Old things creak—you ought to know that, Zane."

"But they creak for a reason."

"Shoot me. Maybe I fidgeted. Maybe I flinched before the sneeze actually blew—it's an involuntary neural reaction, the only thing like it is—"

"We're done here," I said, directing her to shuffle out of the room, following behind her with Zane, no wiser *then* than I was before she sneezed.

We had that one day to live together in a real home. We did laundry. Ate tuna fish sandwiches for lunch. Took turns napping and standing guard. Zane sat in every chair. Stood in every room. Hailey admired our host's lack of a computer: *"What good would have plugging in done him?"* she said, nodding to the garage door beyond which Russell and Eric banged metal and a dead man knelt with his forehead on an oil case.

Even when it wasn't my job, I vibrated close to Cari.

Our family ate dinner at the kitchen table. We had knives with our metal forks and spoons. Plates that could break. Glasses that *were* glass, not nonlethal plastic. Eric cooked us defrosted chicken thighs, white rice Russell insisted on eating with ketchup, canned corn, and a cherry pie from the freezer. A dozen storm candles flickered in the dark kitchen and washed the six of us at the table with a soft white glow.

"You can see there's light in here from outside," said Cari as she lowered the fork in her cuffed and tethered hands. "People out there will know someone's here."

"People assume that things are how they're supposed to be," I said. "Stand on your hometown street at night. Look at houses or apartment windows with lights on. You realize you don't have a clue what's happening in there."

"Houses are full of dead people," said Russell. "Even when the lights are on."

"Not fair," said Hailey. "But there are houses full of people nobody notices."

"Old people," said Eric.

Cari said: "Teenagers."

We looked at her in surprise. She wasn't that young any more.

She blushed. "I know: teenagers are loudly everywhere, but that's because they're always looking for a way to not feel so lost. And some kids are frantically trying to make ordinary life something . . . something . . ."

Zane said: "Something special."

Cari concentrated on chewing rice so words didn't fall out of her mouth.

Russell smiled at her: "So, turns out you do think about stuff like that."

"Why wouldn't I?" said Cari. "I'm normal."

The five of us tightened.

Russell leaned over the table toward Cari, ignored my glare to back off, to let her be, to let us eat at least one dinner in peace.

"So," he told our witness, "since you're *normal* and an expert on what's going on in other people's houses . . . What goes on in the houses of people like us? People who aren't so young and aren't so old."

Cari's emerald gaze hit everybody: "People like us don't get to live in houses."

Metal forks and real knives clinked on our dinner plates.

Leftover chicken thighs smelled cold.

Later, the midnight hour when Hailey said: "All I need to be is lucky."

All six of us, dressed for the road, stood staring at the phone on the rolltop desk.

"Worked before," said Eric.

"But now Kyle Russo's had five days to clean up," I said. "Cover up."

Russell said: "Maybe he's figured that any move equals added exposure, that the safer risk is to let things ride, let nature take its course and let Blondie here and her bands of gunners do his work for him. After all, we're still just a bunch of maniacs."

"Mad dogs," corrected Eric.

"Yeah," said Russell. "We kinda helped him out with that one."

Hailey picked up the phone. Dialed a number gleaned from the brown matrix cards for Nurse Death as Russell ran to stand sentry at the dark living room's window.

Her call connected. She listened to the computer voice pronounce her options. Hailey pushed one button. Listened to another list. Pushed another button. Listened.

Zane whispered: "I hate having to wait while a machine tells me what I can do."

Hailey pushed another button—or rather, a button required her to push it.

"Call trace or caller ID won't have kicked in yet," said Eric.

Cari watched us.

Hailey punched in the ten-digit number of Nurse Death's cell phone.

Eric said: "Now we're hot. If we're hot."

The room heard me say: "I've never felt cool."

Hailey said: "Push *zero* to speak to a human being. How appropriate."

Our hearts beat out time we dared not waste.

"Yes, hi, I'm calling from my father's house out of town," said Hailey, knowing that her "in town" was not Bombay or Belfast or wherever this American cell phone company had outsourced its Accounts Processing factory. "I need to give you his address so you can send a duplicate bill here and I can pay on time."

Hailey read off our dead man's address that would confirm the factory's caller ID. "So that's two bills to send. Let's double-check both addresses."

Zane steadied a yellow pad for her to write while she held the phone.

"Okay," said Hailey, "like they say in the army—*tanks*."

She hung up, told us: "The way she laughed, she's either a great actress or she doesn't know about any trace/trap."

"We're still gone," I said. "Machines are in charge, not her. They could have reported this location seventy seconds ago."

"Or not," said Hailey, as we hurried to the garage. "But just like I got trained, Nurse Death or *whoever* bought her mission cell phone in a company name to protect her identity—and now we've got that address."

"Berlow Services, Inc.," said Zane. "In Wheaton, Maryland."

"Suburb of Washington," I said as we left the study. "Near the Beltway."

Russell ran from the front windows to join us. He snapped off lights as he came.

Cari argued: "So the nurse who you—the nurse you say killed the doctor, so what if she's got a cell phone registered to a company? Could be a dozen reasons."

"Only one that counts," I said, opening the door from the house to the garage. "And it says we've been going the right way."

Zane said: "Now we'll know when we get there."

"Lucky you," said Russell, nudging Cari into the garage: "You're on our bus."

All the lights glowed in that cavern. We closed the door to the house behind us. Stared at the dead man slumped over the oil case.

"I forgot his name," said Hailey.

"I don't want to know his name," said Russell.

"No," said Zane. "We need to remember."

"Harry Martin," I said. "His name was Harry Martin."

"*Tanks*," Eric told the body.

Cari said: "He's starting to smell."

Our stolen BMW sat jacked onto racks five feet above the cement floor. Its hood gaped open, its wheels were stacked in the corner, and its two front doors—with absent windows—leaned on the BMW's removed front seat. Stolen license plates from that stolen car were nailed on the wall amidst other crucified metal tags.

"Leave blanks for the cops to fill in," I said. "But show them the easiest answer."

Nowhere in the house would cops find ownership papers to the BMW awaiting its repairs. Nor would they find Harry Martin's driver's license, which nestled in Zane's wallet. That driver's license photo resembled Zane only because its image showed a man with white hair: looking old can be a sufficiently confirmed identity. Zane wore the same windbreaker as the old man in the driver's license photo. That jacket hid a full shoulder holster once held by the now-stored weapons' vest. And finally, Harry Martin's house held no papers proving he'd ever owned a 1959 Cadillac.

The Caddy glistened in the garage lights. Long and white. Shiny and bright. Swooping fins with red taillights. Four perfect black tires and a full gas tank. Our GODS and booty from the road filled the trunk.

Three people filled the backseat built for four: Zane sat beside the driver's side rear door, then next to him came witness Cari, feet still tethered, hands belted and cuffed in her lap. He told her: *"I'll be the one to get you."* She probably knew that he was messing with her mind, forcing her to fight concentrating on him in order to be aware of danger from all of us *if.* She said nothing. Eric rode by the curbside rear door.

We didn't need to vote: I drove. Hailey sat beside me with Harry Martin's maps on her lap. On the roof above the windshield and the rearview mirror, she taped the white matrix card black lettered: Kyle Russo.

"In case we start to ramble," she said.

Uh-oh, I thought: Are you starting to lose it, too?

At the wall by the dead man, Russell flipped switches to kill the overhead lights, leaving only the Caddy's dome light to glow in the darkness. Russell climbed in the front seat and slammed the door shut with a clunk that dropped us and the white beast into total blackness.

Where we sat for one long, deep breath.

Russell said: "Put on your sunglasses."

Cari's voice came from the backseat. "It's pitch dark in here, night out there!"

"So?" said Russell. "This time, we're going to start out cool."

We heard Eric obey, clip onto his regular glasses the pair of sunglasses we'd picked for him from the shoebox.

Cari inhaled to protest Zane groping to fit her with eye-doctor oversize glasses, but she rethought that and heeded the four magic words.

Hailey shifted beside me and didn't need to say she was ready.

"We're cool," said Zane from the backseat.

Cyber-wraparounds slid over my eyes.

The key turned my fingers. The Caddy rumbled to life.

And I said: "Hit it."

Russell thumbed the remote garage door opener at the windshield.

Clanking and groaning, a plane of blackness rose from in front of our growling Caddy's silver grill. Cold suburban night flowed into the garage with shimmers of streetlights and rainbow ghosts of neighbors' TVs and twinkling stars.

Russell said: "Now this is a road trip."

41

CARI ESCAPED IN the morning mist of Day Six.

We took off our sunglasses after blasting out of the garage, followed the dead man's maps, found a state road with no roadblocks of state trooper cruisers and *steel boyz* in civilian coats they never zipped. We stayed off the inter-state with its traffic control eyes. Gassed up at a mom and pop store too deep into yesterday to have surveillance cameras. Followed the road into a wilderness called the Pine Barrens.

Night fog swirled in our headlights. The highway ran straight as a bullet. We saw no other cars. Nobody said much. Nobody dozed in the great white beast.

The *out there* we raced through faded from black to gray. Fog floated amid scruffy pine and oak and black cherry trees crowding the highway. As we drove in that time zone between night and day, Zane said: "I need to . . . stop."

"Again?" said Russell.

"Too much coffee." Zane sighed. Confessed: "Too many miles."

"That's okay," said Hailey. "I've got to, too."

The white Caddy muscled off the highway, onto a bumpy side road. Gravel crunched under our tires. We stopped. Dust settled outside our windows.

My shoulders burned, my spine felt compressed, my right foot ached. I groaned as I stepped from the car. The others climbed out to stretch. Zane helped cuffed and tethered Cari slide from the backseat, put her dead man's white sneakers on the gravel road.

Quiet covered everything like the pale fog hiding the treetops. Cool air felt good to inhale. Smelled of pine and wet bark.

"Can't see more than thirty, forty feet off into the woods," said Russell.

"Don't worry," said Zane. "Out here, we're alone."

He told me: "I'll be right back."

"I'm going with you," said Hailey.

Cari said: "As long as she's going . . . I have to go, too. My guess is, this is the last best place you guys will let me do it."

"I'll come," I said.

Zane's poker face didn't change as he watched me shrug.

"Russell," I said, "key's in the ignition."

"Eric and I are cool," said Russell. "But get it done and let's get out of here."

We faced a forest jumbled on scrubby marshland.

Hailey said: "Which way?"

"Doesn't matter," I said. "It's all trees until you hit a road."

We left the gravel for packed wet earth, cushions of dead brown leaves and jarring rocks. Every footfall freed odors of mud and snapped branches. Tendrils of white mist snaked around our ankles. We could barely see through the bars of trees and floating gray walls you couldn't touch. The fog thickened as it rose from damp earth until the tops of twenty-foot green pine or winter-naked trees disappeared in currents of pale. Somewhere above that sea of clouds had to be the sky and a rising sun.

Invisible fluttering wings rushed overhead.

I led the others on what looked like an easy path—with her feet tethered, Cari had a difficult journey over rough ground or through trees. We'd zigzagged sixty steps beyond our last sight of the white Caddy when urgency tightened Zane's voice:

"Any time now."

"Have to find the perfect—*there!*"

The forest widened to a glen the size of a tennis court. Lightning had split an oak so it lay like a propped Y. Each fork of the Y-ed tree made a ledge on which to sit.

"That's ours," said Hailey.

Zane fidgeted as he and I watched her lead the tethered woman to the Y-ed tree.

Cari inched around to the far side of the split tree's farthest fork. Haley stood behind her and to her right in the gap of the Y. Their backs were to us.

Both women glared at us over their shoulders.

"Look away! Do your own thing!" ordered Hailey.

Zane and I turned to face a forest of quiet trees and drifting fog. I heard his zipper descend as—*why not*—I lowered mine. We heard the sound of Hailey and Cari dropping their slacks, sitting on the tree forks.

Liquid trickled onto the forest floor.

"*Ahh,*" sighed Zane. I joined him as he said: "When you got to, you got to."

Behind us, Hailey knew that Cari'd finished that business quickly, was taking her time standing up from bent-over-sitting-on-the-tree-branch as Hailey herself filled the morning with a long stream of sound. Finally finished, Hailey bent down like Cari had to—obviously—fix her clothing. She stood—came face-to-face with a whirling blur:

Cari—*Hands free! Feet free!*—right palm on the tree as she vaulted over it with a 180-degree turn that spun her to face Hailey. Cari used the torque of her vault to pivot on her left foot, spin another circle that closed the gap between her and the astonished Black woman, a spin that whipped Cari's right leg through a high crescent kick and slammed her over-size dead man's sneaker smack into Hailey's face.

The kick snapped Hailey around in her own half circle, would have dropped her even if she hadn't stumbled over the tree limb.

Something deep in Hailey refused to just *fall.* Call it guts. Call it street smarts. Call it the caliber of her soul. As she crashed toward the brutal earth, Hailey ripped the pistol from her waistband, tossed it toward us as she screamed.

Zane and I jerked around fumbling our hands to fix ourselves and fill them with something more functional than what we held in that *scream moment.*

Saw Cari crouched in the Y of the downed tree. Saw *free hands.* Saw her glare at Hailey who'd denied her a gun. Saw Cari whirl and charge away *feet free* into the trees.

Go! Don't shoot her, can't shoot her, *run!*

I knocked saplings out of my way. Leapt over logs. Slipped on a boulder—didn't stop as I charged through the forest, heard Zane racing behind me to my right, caught glimpses of Cari's blue shirt dodging through the trees and currents of fog, heard her pant and snap branches and crack through brush.

Leaves slapped my eyes. Thorns slashed my forehead. I bounced off a tree. Ran. My stomach heaved gasps of *wet forest* into my burning lungs. *Cari's in great shape!* Don't think. Don't stop. *Run.* Get her: got to *get her.*

Hunters and prey raced through trees and fog. Our vision bounced, saw her searching for a glimmer of *go that way* amid the fogged forest world rushing at her; saw us chasing her, glimpsing her, sometimes seeing her completely.

The dead man let us catch her.

She leapt over a dry streambed but Harry Martin's too-big shoes made her misjudge her landing. A stone caught the floppy toe of her sneaker, sprawled her into a pile of deadfall, and when she shoved herself up, scrambled for footing in the wet muck, a shoe went one way, her left ankle the other. Cari cried out as we burst through trees thirty feet behind her. She ran through a stand of poplars.

We saw her limp as she fought her way through another hundred feet of clinging trees on that sprained ankle. Burst out of brush and staggered onto a graveled road. Fell onto its rocks and dirt. Pushed herself up. Stumbled limping steps following the graveled road toward where it disappeared in the mist. Didn't quit. Wouldn't quit.

Until I snapped her image into my pistol sights, yelled: "Done!"

She heard my feet crunch gravel behind her. Dragged to a stop.

"Don't fucking make me shoot!" I yelled.

Brush crashed behind me.

My buddy Zane burst onto the road. Whipped the pistol from his shoulder holster, yelled: "Don't do it!"

Cari spread her gravel-scraped hands out from her waist. She'd left the handcuffs and rope belt back at the pissing tree where she'd picked those locks with the paperclip she stole off the dead man's desk and hid behind her upper lip through whatever she said or ate. Bent over to pull up her pants, she'd untied the tether between her ankles. Now she held nothing, wanted us to know that before she risked turning around to face us.

She saw me standing in the middle of the gravel road, two-handed combat grip on the pistol staring straight at her with its black bore.

She saw Zane, who'd worked his way across the road and up the barrow pit so he stood ten feet ahead of me and off to my heart side, pointing his pistol.

We made a triangle on a graveled road in the forest of a misty morning.

Suddenly, an epiphany seized me.

"Don't you do it!" yelled Zane.

He means Cari, I thought; yelled: "Cari! You're done running! This is over!"

"Nobody do nothing!" yelled Zane.

"Now is not the day to die!" I said. "Now is when to be a spy!"

Cari said: "What?"

Zane said: "What?"

Don't let your gun shake like that! I wanted to yell as his aim wandered. He had to be as tired as I was, throat dry, chest heaving, heart slamming his ribs. Us catching our breath had to be easy compared to Cari with her scraped hands, twisted ankle, and wild eyes facing two pistols hungry to blow her lead kisses.

Cari watched me combat-shuffle toward her, my pistol zeroed on her heart.

"Who are you?" I yelled to her. "What do you do?"

Zane's gun wavered between Cari and me: "Victor! You're here. It's now. Don't zone out, man! And stop, stop there, you have to stop!"

I stood fifteen feet from Cari in the middle of the gravel road. Zane stood by the trees, gun floating like the mist surrounding us. Again I yelled to her: "Who are you?"

Cari glared at me: "What are you talking about? You know who I am."

" 'Xactly!"

"Forget all those lies!" I yelled. "Forget your cover and your other cover, your mission and your real mission, whether you were launched to catch us or kill us. Forget *national security* and *need to know* and *don't get the bosses blamed* and *failing the fullness of your career,* forget all that and look at this new light!"

"Vic," said Zane, his gun more ambivalent: "Easy . . ."

"You know who you are?" I said to Cari, softly so ears hiding in the fog couldn't hear.

She blinked; shrugged.

That meant that even if she was humoring Mister Got a Gun, we had a chance.

"You're a spy," I told her. "And that means you're our salvation."

"What?" said Cari and Zane, together.

"A spy has to find out what's real."

She shook her head. "But you can't know whether or not I'm one of your hypothetical renegades!"

"I'll take that chance," I said. "This is getting too heavy." Lowered my gun.

Zane's pistol pointed toward heaven.

"You're a spy," I told Cari. "And you're out here in the fog. With us. And yeah, you got sent here to do us—whatever, however, I fucking don't care. Doesn't matter now. Not for this moment of clarity. And yeah, we're crazy, you're not, so what.

"Out here with us is *why,* plus enough *what's* to add up to *why not.* Why are we all here? Why did Dr. F die? If we killed him, what about Nurse Death? If we didn't get the gun that shot her *from her,* where did it come from? If she had it, why? *Rectal exams?* I don't think so, she was working a temporary mental hospital gig. Why is her cell phone set up as a classic Op cover job? And who is Kyle Russo?"

"He's a name written on an index card taped above the windshield of the white car you stole from a dead man."

"Exactly," I said for Zane's benefit, hoping he was getting it, too. "But why?"

"Because you can. Sometimes that's the whole reason for doing what you do."

"You are so cool!" I whispered.

Cari blushed. Her eyes finally let go of the gun in my hand. "What are you talking about?"

"The heart of your Op, of any spy Op, is knowing. Merely catching or killing us leaves you as ignorant as before. Here, now, you've got a chance to be who you are and do what you're supposed to do."

"What?"

"Be a spy. With us. On us."

"You . . . you're offering me a chance to join your pack of mad dogs?"

"You don't qualify. You're not crazy. But you're already our witness. Fold that into being more than dragged along until whatever's going on is over."

"Or be 'over' myself, dead here on this road." She didn't blink.

"We can shoot you anytime. Choose something better, smarter, more true. Be our witness. Be who you are. Be a spy. Find out what you don't know."

"Then?"

"When it's then, do what you do. Report. Finish satisfied."

"If I help you, odds are I won't be able to walk away."

"Nobody walks away," I told her. "So what are you going to do?"

Zane said: "He's right. Do it. If nothing else, you need to be here to make it the best it can be. Because we'll keep going, and you'll end up no better than us."

"You'd . . . trust me to . . . do *whatever* with you?"

"Hell no," I said. "We trust you to be the spy you are."

Cari said: "What if—"

"What if what if what if *what if!*" I yelled. "Fucking *find out*. Or walk."

My gun flicked toward the road waiting behind her back.

"Shit," she said.

Voice booming behind us! Hailey, calling out: "Sorry I'm late."

We all turned to see her standing at the edge of the forest and road, arms hanging down, a dazed look on her sweat-slick, thorn-scratched ebony face.

Hailey seemed to float like the fog onto the gravel road, glide toward us as inexorably as the dawn, stepping onto the gravel road, coming closer, closer.

"Sorry, Vic," she said. "Sorry, Zane."

"'S okay," I said as she stepped past me and walked straight to Cari—

—slammed the bore of her automatic against the white woman's forehead.

Freeze: all I could do, all we all did was freeze.

"Sorry," said Hailey and all Cari could see was the whites of her eyes. "Beat me once: *sorry,* shit happens. Beat me twice: makes me a *sorry* loser."

Hailey thumbed the pistol's hammer to full cocked with a *snick!*

Smiled as Cari trembled, the gun pressed against her forehead.

"Third time's the charm," said Hailey as her gun's black barrel bored a perfect third eye on Cari's skull. "Three strikes and I'm out—right? *O-u-t* out."

No quick karate move, no simple twist of fate would snap Cari to safety before Hailey's finger could squeeze the trigger/slam a bullet through Cari's perfect brain.

"So the *sane* move," said Hailey, "the *smart* move, the *good* move, the *rational* move, the *fucking spy move* . . . is one sweet squeeze of my finger. Preemptive strike. Problem . . . solved. Every future 'losing' battle with you would be averted. I'm dying anyway, but best to die free and make everything worth it."

Can't. Move. Can't. Talk. Can't. Think.

"Daaa!" The gun barrel thrust so hard into Cari's skull that she staggered as Hailey yelled: *"But I'm not smart rational sane!"*

And she whirled to her right—*Bam!* blasted first one, then all ten rounds in her gun—*Bam! Bam! Bam!*—one right after another, slugs zinging into the trees and fog, brass casings ejecting and clinking into the gravel, until the pistol slide blew back locked open and in the roar of gunfire echoes through the startled trees, in the gunsmoke swirling around her into the fog, she stood there, said: "Out of bullets."

I took the gun from Hailey's limp hand, told her: "We have more."

Beep! Beep! Beep! The sound of a car horn cut through the fog: Eric sounding recall after hearing war he could only hope was won by the right soldiers as Russell charged into the woods to *rock it* against anyone wrong in his gun sight.

Hailey didn't resist as I took her arm. Zane and I holstered our weapons, I stuck her empty Sig Sauer in my belt, realized: *Same kind of gun I used for my second suicide.*

"Well," said Cari as the horn beeped, "at least we know the way back to our car."

42

CARI DROVE.

"You sure about this?" she asked when I opened the driver's door for her.

"I'm beat and our crew ain't much better," I said.

"Tell her if she fucks us," said Russell, "I'll shoot off her kneecap."

"Tell her yourself," I said from the front seat between Cari and Zane.

"Hey Blondie," said Russell. "If you—"

"Got it." She roared our white Caddy to life, drove out of the Pine Barrens and merged onto the New Jersey Turnpike.

We were in the ride. We let voices and music from the invisible *radioland* make our moments. We listened for news reporting something that we needed to hear. Found zip. We never changed a station playing a good song. Our four lanes of fellow travelers zoomed south as fast as they dared. We traveled inside the law.

"Why fuck with life more than you need to," I said.

"'Xactly."

Russell adjusted his sunglasses. "Sometimes life needs you to fuck with it."

"Could I have something besides those optometrist blinders?" Cari asked. "The sun's coming up on me."

Zane passed her a pair of Bonnie Parker *gangster girl* shades.

Cari slipped them on. Asked me: "Are your hands shaking?"

"Not now," I answered. Truthfully locking every muscle tight.

"And Zane," she said, glancing past me: "You look . . . unusually calm."

He said: "I guess."

Cari faced our windshield, but I saw her sunglasses record the rearview mirror where Hailey rode with her head on Eric's shoulder, his eyes open, hers closed as her lips muttered soundlessly. Russell slumped beside her, the road vibrating his skull while he matched Hailey's private mutters with face-shifting, mouth-working soundless songs.

Cari said: "You guys need to hold it together."

Russell said: "Maybe we've held it *too* together."

"Sure," I said, my hands definitely not shaking. "That's been our problem."

The radio played the Beach Boys' "Don't Worry, Baby."

"Maybe that was Brian Wilson's problem," said Russell as that rock poet soared high notes in the radio song about being consoled and counseled by his lover. Russell had blared the song "Brian Wilson" about that Beach Boy's crackup through Ward C to taunt Dr. F just before the big *oh-oh*. "Maybe if Brian hadn't fought being crazy, he wouldn't have gone down."

"He was in pain!" I said. "He was doing what he thought would work."

Russell shrugged. "But what about the songs?"

A huge computer lettered sign over the highway glowed with official edicts:

TERRORIST ALERT   REPORT SUSPICIOUS ACTIVITY

"Do you think that's for us?" said Zane.

Nobody answered as we whizzed under the sign.

Miles of interstate highway, then the Caddy slowed.

"The Delaware Toll Bridge," said Cari. "Coming up fast."

With toll keepers. For drivers to pay. Pass notes to. Shout to.

Zane gave a five-dollar bill to Cari.

Forty, thirty, twenty miles an hour, the Caddy slid into a line of cars rolling toward a tollbooth where a woman in a uniform worked taking what she was given.

"State trooper!" I said. "Parked just the other side of the toll booths!"

"Don't see him!" said Zane and for a moment I feared I'd suddenly lost it, then Zane said: "Got him—No! Got two!"

Our white Caddy suddenly felt trapped in a rolling steel stream funneling down toward the wall of tollbooths.

"They're leaning on their cruisers talking to each other," I said.

"That's all they're doing," said Hailey. "Maybe that's all."

"Don't think about them and they won't notice you!" called out Eric.

We stared at our scientific genius.

"Is that true?" I asked.

Eric shrugged.

Six cars away, five, four, the Caddy rolled toward contact with the woman toll-taker. She had a badge on her white shirt. Was she hiding a gun?

Russell shifted in the backseat. His left hand slid behind the apparently sleeping Hailey. Russell could shoot almost as well with his left hand as his right.

The Caddy stopped at the tollbooth. The woman collector took the five-dollar bill from Cari. As she made change, the collector with a silver badge on her white shirt said: "Nice old car."

"Thanks," said Cari. "It comes with a nice old husband."

Two women shared a laugh and off we drove.

The state troopers seemed to join in on that joke, laughed with each other.

We never saw them give us a special look.

Russell and I checked on our mirrors.

"Didn't see her push any buttons, make notes, stop collecting tolls," said Russell.

"They take pictures," said Eric.

"Yeah," I said, "but even if the cameras caught our faces, by the time analysts or computers review them, we're gone."

"So all they'll know will be our incredibly discreet vehicle," said Russell. "Where we were when and which way we were going. Nothing to worry about."

"'Xactly."

"The trooper cars are still parked back there," I said.

"The only toll left is Baltimore's tunnel," said Cari. "Then it's free road."

"You did good," I told her.

"What did you expect," she said, not a question, not a glance at me.

And not a thing wrong with the way she paid the Baltimore toll. We dropped into a tunnel under the Chesapeake Bay, a sunless, moonless shaft of yellow brick walls smudged gray by toxic car exhaust. Air pressure squeezed my eardrums as we dove beneath seawater following the red eye taillights bouncing in our windshield while we fled the yellow eye headlights riding in our mirrors.

Then we swooped out to blue sky, the expressway curving like a seagull toward clouds. Baltimore receded, its glistening urban towers cupping the inner harbor where no freighters sailed away loaded with U.S. steel. The FBI Santa in the gym of my second suicide swore that even with its glitzy inner harbor, Baltimore was still a fine town for heroin.

"Thirty minutes to D.C.," announced our driver Cari.

Highway hummed under our tires.

Signs for the approaching Beltway zoomed past.

"Which way?" asked Cari.

Hailey opened a map, said: "Wheaton is . . . Take the Beltway West."

Cari nosed the Caddy into the right lane as the interstate began to split in a Y.

"Which exit?" she asked.

No one answered as the Caddy curved onto the massive Beltway.

Cari stole a glance at us. "Do you guys have a real plan?"

"Real," I said. "There's a concept."

"Shit." Cari merged our white Caddy into zooming traffic on the expressway girdling the capital of the most powerful nation on earth. "Can I make a suggestion?"

We took her idea and the second exit, joined suburban traffic that streamed past a thirty-foot-tall alabaster statue of Jesus. We turned onto a street that led past somber brick high-rise apartment buildings where a bus stop sheltered three men who looked Pakistani and were dressed for blue-collar labor. We passed a parking lot where men from every country south of Texas swarmed a contractor's idling pickup.

Zane said: "Stop in front of that convenience store, I'll find someone to ask."

Our white Caddy parked in front of a store that sold eggs, milk, disposable diapers, soda pop, condoms, and lottery tickets. The restaurant on one side of the store advertised Guatamalan cuisine, the restaurant on the other boasted Mexican fare, and next to that café, the windows of a "dollar store" had signs in English and Spanish. Across the street was a Chinese food carryout shed that also sold fried chicken and Italian subs through a bulletproof window. Kitty-corner from us was a delivery/carryout pizza shack. The pink stucco building on the intersection's fourth corner was a Maryland state liquor store.

"I thought the edge of D.C. would be . . . I don't know," said Zane. "Not like this."

"Times change," I said. "Places, too."

Zane left our white Caddy, crossed the street toward the liquor store.

Walked right past the shouting Black woman wearing lime green shorts and a white sweatshirt stenciled with the gold glitter letters RE SKI S. Her right hand gestured with an opaque plastic glass and her rant came through our open window.

". . . an' this is an *illegal meeting!* And there's nothin' in this here cup 'cept dietary cola!" Her eyes trapped mine. "Here a' comes a rip!"

Watching her meant not covering Zane. I let sunshine and shadow smells of the street stream into me until he jogged back to our car.

Told us: "I found a Vietnamese barbershop. Been awhile since I spoke *Saigon,* but the old man in charge was an officer for us way back when. He told me where to go."

Zane directed the white Caddy down a road lined with

trees, over a bridge in a park, past a gas station. We glimpsed painted houses with manicured lawns and back decks. A blond mom who traced her roots to George Washington's officer corps strapped her daughter into a minivan babyseat while an Ethiopian nanny watched.

"One world on top of another," said Russell as we turned onto a narrower street.

"Only one?" I asked.

"There's a police station coming up 'bout a quarter mile on the right," said Zane.

Hailey shuffled her maps. "You sure we're going the right way?"

Cari slowed the Caddy, said: "We can ask her."

"Her" was a flashily dressed, white sixtyish woman strolling on the sidewalk the same direction we drove— whirling around to stalk the other way, waving her arms and shaking her curled hair, bobbing down like a robin after worms and snapping back straight again to stir her hand in the air, all the while working her pink lipstick mouth.

"No wonder they can't find us," said Russell as we drove past the pink lipsticked woman directing the traffic in her own frenzy. "There's a crazy on every corner."

One block past the cop shop with its parked cruisers, we took a right at a bus station where global citizens waited in the crisp afternoon air, their hands close to their suitcases and bulky black trash bags, their eyes watching the white Caddy of yesterday's wealth motor past. We drove past a "metaphysical meditation chapel" housed in a former insurance agency, past a barber shop where an elderly Italian man in a blue smock waited in his doorway, past a comic book store with windows filled by cardboard posters of Superman and the latest pointy-breasted, market-born Hero Babe. We parked at a meter on a block of stores built for our twenty-first century.

"Eric," I said, "go with Zane. You know what we need."

"I'll come, too," said Hailey. The smart move was for her to stay close to Eric.

Zane grabbed coins from our cup to feed the meter and vanished into a store.

"Don't like this," said Russell from the back seat. "Parked in the open, split up."

"Me in the driver's seat," said Cari next to where I sat.

"Me right behind you." Russell shrugged. "I'm getting used to *us*."

"It's not a good idea to be out here," I said, "but it's the best chance we've got."

Tick-tock, my watch would have said if it had been built the same year as our Caddy. But Mister Tick-Tock was dead. Life was no longer work then recovery, hard then soft. My watch's second hand swept its circle with a monomanical *tick tick tick.*

We sat sweating in the cold white Caddy on that spring afternoon. Cars drove past. A city bus. Late lunchers ate at a franchised Mexican café. The steel-beamed skeleton of a building rose from the next block. A hardhat wizard walked an I-beam above the last long fall. I sat in our dead man's dream machine.

Tick. Tick. Tick.

Hailey strode out of the store holding a white plastic bag. Eric carried two bigger bags. Zane walked with empty hands, ready hands.

"God bless us everyone," said Hailey when we were all in the car, doors slammed, Cari keying the engine. "We live in a time when you can buy three disposable cell phones, charged and ready to go for cash on the counter."

The white Caddy slid into traffic.

Zane told our driver. "Great idea."

"Thanks," said Cari.

That had to be a smile of professional pride she couldn't hide.

Eric used white tape and a black pen to label the phones Alpha, Bravo, Charlie.

"Got car 'n' wall socket chargers," he said as he programmed each phone with the instantaneous dial/connect numbers of the other two.

"How long until we're there?" asked Hailey.

"Twenty minutes," said Zane.

Wrong: sixteen minutes later, we pulled into the parking

lot of a mattress store on Georgia Avenue, a decades old, low-slung suburban commercial strip.

"We can't quite see it from here," I said. "They can't quite see us from there."

Russell sighed. "Still wish we could drive right up and rock 'n' roll."

"Sure," said Hailey, "but this is where Nurse Death got her mail and we're spies, not commandos."

"Yeah, yeah, yeah."

Tick. Tick. Tick.

I said: "If we don't make it back . . ."

"We'll come after you," answered Russell.

Cell phone Alpha filled my hand. I punched the number programmed for Bravo, and eleven *ticks* later, the phone in Russell's hand rang. I slipped my transmitting phone in the right chest pocket of my leather jacket. One of the flash/bang grenades and ammo magazines rode in the jacket pocket above my heart, while barely covered by its unzipped leather, the holstered Glock .45 coiled on my right hip.

Zane and I slid out of the white car to walk up that road.

Russell took our place in the front seat. Rode shotgun like he was born there.

My voice said: "Let's go."

43

"DAMN IT!" I said as Zane and I stood between a parked van and a family SUV facing the address Hailey'd tricked from the cell phone billing department.

Russell's muffled voice crackled from the chest pocket of my jacket: *"What?"*

"Op silence!" I told the voice from a man who wasn't there. Not that such spy protocol seemed necessary. Not now.

Traffic whizzed past behind us on busy commercial/commuter Georgia Avenue.

Four flat storefronts faced us from across their parking lot. Second store from the left had the address Hailey'd scored painted on its glass front wall, plus the words:

Mail 4 U!

Zane said: "It's a postal drop. 'Berlow Industries, Suite 413' is really box 413. We got nothing."

"Maybe nothing is more than it seems," I said. "Cover me."

Bells tinkled as I pushed open the glass door and stepped inside Mail 4 U!

In front of me was the "business center" counter. Back from the counter stretched a room that held two desks where the store's staff sat. Past those desks was a long table with spooled brown wrapping paper, tape dispensers, a vase of scissors and styluses and marker pens. A second table held two fax machines, a computer. Five sizes of cardboard shipping boxes hung on a wall beside samples of gift-wrapping paper. Other displays sold labels, mailing tubes in three sizes, padded envelopes.

To my left rose a wall of mailboxes, all with combination locks, all facing the glass wall to the street, and all centered by their own square glass window. My casual stroll and scan found box 413: its peephole showed me empty.

Back at the business counter, I stared at the two employees.

A balding Black man sat behind the desk deepest into the business center. A photo of men on a factory floor hung on the wall behind his squeaky chair, photos of a wife and three kids stood on his desk. He looked tired. Wore a maroon sweater.

The woman with her red shoes propped on the desk near the counter blabbered into her cell phone. She could have been in college except she wasn't. Low-cut white jeans were painted on her thick thighs. Her green blouse strained to contain the flesh roll hanging over her waistband. She wore vivid mascara and lip-slick. Absolutely every hint of other color had died in her wispy jaw-cut peroxided hair.

I coughed. Coughed again, louder.

She told the cell phone: "So I was *like,* n'un-unh, and then he was all *like*—"

"Excuse me!" I said.

The man in the maroon sweater glanced up from an open file to see Cell Phone Girl hold a forefinger up to me as she said: "That is so not, *like,* the thing, 'cause I'm *like . . .* "

Maroon Sweater closed his eyes, then the file on his desk, brought it with him as he walked to where I stood at the counter. As he passed Cell Phone Girl, he put the file on her desk: "Trish, go ahead and refile the active applications."

"*Like,* what?" said Trish, her eyes on Mr. Maroon Sweater—then into the cell phone, she said: "No, not you. Don't worry, it's *like,* just some work thing . . . *Do so!*"

Maroon Sweater pointed to a short green file cabinet. "Please put them in there."

"Sure!" Trish's quick smile vanished into the phone: "*Like,* no way!"

He shook thoughts of homicide from his head as he joined me at the counter. "Sorry. The boss's daughter. But she's coming along."

"So I see."

"How can we help you?"

"I've been thinking about getting a mailbox."

"We can do that." He quoted me rates by the month, by the quarter, by the year.

None of the corners held surveillance lenses, nor did I see any "innocent" objects along the wall that might hide a video camera.

"I'm concerned about image," I told him. "What kind of people rent here?"

"We get all kinds."

He handed me an application form.

"Thanks." I put the application in my jacket pocket beside the flash/bang grenade and the spare ammo mags. "When are you open?"

"We unlock at six, lock up at eleven. Somebody's always working the counter. We used to provide unmonitored access to the boxes for 24-7 service, but we got vandalism."

"Too bad. You been doing this long?"

"Some days it feels like I'm not even here. Some days the two years I've been parking out back feel like forever." He nodded to the photo on the wall behind his desk. "I was production manager for a jacket manufacturer. Had fifty-seven people under me, most of them good. First, computers programmed either *yes* or *no* to half the questions I used to create answers for, then, the owners moved the factory to the free trade zone in Mexico."

Trish told her cell phone: *"Like,* that is just so *forget-about-it."*

He said: "At least I'm still a manager."

"There is that."

"Funny thing is, now it's happening to the folks in Mexico who got those jobs. The jacket plant is moving to China." The quiet smile that stretched his Black skin came from more than *funny.* "At least I didn't waste my time trying to learn Spanish."

I gave him a laugh. Nodded to leave, then *like* I'd had an afterthought, said: "If I was looking to rent a couple rooms or so for an office . . ."

My gesture swept across his ceiling. "Your boss got any extra space here?"

He shook his head. "There is no upstairs in this place."

"Afraid of that," I said. "See you."

And walked out through the door in the glass wall.

44

"WE'RE CRASHED," SAID Zane as we leaned against the back of a van in the parking lot outside Mail 4 U! That van blocked Maroon Sweater from seeing us through his wall of window. Trish wouldn't have seen us if we were pressed naked against that glass.

The voice in my jacket pocket said: "What's happening?"

What's happening.

Sunshine warms our faces in the cool spring air. Steel presses our backs as we lean on a plumber's van. Smells of asphalt and car exhaust and nerves swirl around us. With every beat of my heart, another Georgia Avenue car *whooshes* past our blank faces staring out at that great American artery.

Across that road's three lanes going north, across the one-step-wide concrete divider, across the three lanes going south waits a flat two-story mall, a rigid C-shaped gray concrete sprawl of wall-sharing shops. The All Things Jewish store. Ye Olde Magic Shoppe. The Used and New Uniforms store where red-lipped mannequins pose as nurses. The Viet Mine restaurant with dirty red curtains pulled shut over the windows behind a displayed square of newspaper. Red dragons emblazon the next shop's window, along with the name of a gung fu style I've never heard of. A Chinese grocery store so crammed with merchandise the window wants to burst. A store with opaque swirled windows crossed by a banner that reads ADULT VIDEOS DVDS MAGS; above that fogged glass door hangs a blue neon sign reading COYOTES.

What's happening.

Whoosh.

What if our Op is over. What if we got nothing to do, nowhere to go.

Whoosh.

We get caught. We get five coffins. And Cari . . .

Whoosh.

I slumped on the side of the road.

Whoosh.

"Victor? *Vic!* Don't zone out on—"

Whoosh sunshine swirling *bright light* . . . cool.

"Zane, what if it wasn't just Nurse Death's box?" I nodded to the uniforms store. "That's probably how she found this place, but here is perfect as a drop for an Op. The subway is a fifteen-minute walk south, the Beltway's a five-minute drive. This mail drop isn't convenient to her house or to her cover job at Walter Reed hospital. This is a Cool Zone: out of casually passing-by eyes of watchers, with easy and quick access to anywhere. Combination lock, nobody needs a key. There could be other outlaw spooks like her who use that box, come here. If we catch one of them, he'll lead us to Kyle Russo."

"You're really reaching here, man."

"That's the only way to get anything." I shrugged. "Besides, what have we got to lose?"

"There is that."

"So we go for it," I said, angling my head back toward Mail 4 U! as I pulled the cell phone from my jacket pocket. "They haven't seen you in there. Not that that matters if you get Trish."

45

"I'M ALL BROWN!" said Russell thirty minutes later as the six of us stood beside the white Caddy hulking in the back row of the nearby subway stop's huge parking lot.

"That's how you're supposed to look." Hailey suppressed a grin. "Brown shirt, brown pants, and that trendy brown baseball cap."

"It's not a baseball cap!" said Russell. "If I were wearing a ball cap, at least I'd look like I was a college goofus instead of just a brown dork."

Russell gave a handful of coins, crumpled dollar bills, and the receipt from the New and Used uniform store to Zane. Zane added change from his own purchase at Mail 4U! to Russell's cash, passed it to Eric, who was one of the Outside Crew. If shit hit the fan, cash might help an Outsider run.

Zane sorted the dozen copper pennies out of Eric's cupped hand. . . .

Threw the pennies helter-skelter across the subway's deserted cement parking lot.

Cari said: "What are you doing?"

"You know how it works," Zane told her. "If you find a penny, its good luck. Minority fundamentalists believe that if the penny is face down, you shouldn't take it because that's bad luck. I'm not sure I believe that."

"But you believe the other?" said Cari.

"I believe in luck. And call it confidence or heightened

awareness of possibilities or whatever, if you *think* you're lucky, you've got a better chance of *being* lucky."

Cari blinked. "But why throw away pennies?"

"I've been lucky." Zane shrugged. "Seems right to pass it on."

"You've been locked in a loony bin," said Cari, "your family is dead, your only friends are stone whackos, you've never been able to be in love, and you call that lucky?"

"Just because I'm a virgin doesn't mean I've never been in love."

"Oh shit, Zane, I'm sorry! They gave us your files, so— That was a cheap shot."

"Hey," he told her, "I'm lucky just to be here for you to hurt."

Traffic whizzed by on Georgia Avenue.

Cari shook her blond head. "No wonder they locked you up."

Zane smiled: "And now I'm a penny you've picked up."

I said: "We're ready."

"If it doesn't work . . ." I trailed off.

"We'll come running." Hailey jingled the keys to the white Caddy.

Five minutes later, Zane, Cari and I came striding, not running, toward the "adult" video/magazine store with the blue neon COYOTES sign in the two-story concrete strip mall on Georgia Avenue's river. I jerked open COYOTES' clouded glass door and freed an angry electronic buzzer.

Off to our left, tall shelves crammed with colored video boxes ran in ranks toward the wall covered by other boxes with lurid photos of human beings in circus poses. At the rear of the store, a moldy green curtain covered a doorway between shelves of DVD boxes. Cassettes filled the wall to our right behind the cash register counter. A color TV hung from the ceiling. In the TV, a shellacked blond naked woman with breasts swollen like concrete balloons ripped off the white shirt of a muscle punk who had a snake tattoo *s*-ing its way up his spine. The door clunked shut. The buzzer stopped screaming. We sank into TV blare and sensations of hard carpet, pine disinfectant, carcinogenic smog.

The pale creep perched behind the elevated cash register clinked a Zippo to light a cigarette. His head and his face both showed a three-day stubble.

Cari spotted one customer, a man in a suit and tie transfixed by the wall under the BONDAGE section sign. She stepped behind him and puckered her lips: blew a soft wind that mussed his hair.

Suit-and-tie whirled, saw *real woman,* his eyes going wide . . .

As she waved her credentials: "I've got handcuffs."

The customer cupped his hand over his face, stumbled past us to the front door, blasted the buzzer, vanished into where he dared to be seen.

"It's time for your dues and don'ts," I told the cashier. Smoke from the cigarette in his hand curled toward the ceiling. I waved the credential folder from Cari's youngest gunman and the cashier wand-muted the TV. "We're with your United Way."

"Federal division." Zane flashed credentials from the man he'd garbage canned.

The credentials' insignias said FBI, and they were true, even if the men who'd carried them plus their credentials from two other federal agencies had been liars.

Liars like us, but the cashier bought us with a blink of his hollow eyes, a purchase helped along by the glimpse I gave him of the cop gun holstered on my belt.

"Already gave," said the cashier. "Mostly locals, but we got points."

"Not with our team," said Zane. "We're a whole new league. You get to play."

The cashier sucked fire all the way down the white tube in his fingers. "Or?"

"Or we call in our other teams," I said. "IRS. Kiddie porn task force. Money laundry masters. Missing Persons hounds with computers that age and match photos. The Racket Boys who lost most of their budget to us and are hungry for an easy lunch."

"Mostly, though," said Cari, her eyes nailing him, "we'll make it personal."

"Right now," I said. "We don't know you. And you don't want to know us."

"I just work the place."

"We don't care," said Zane. "You're who we got."

The cashier stubbed out his cigarette on the counter. "What are we talking about?"

"What's upstairs?" I said.

"Storeroom. Old desk, couple chairs. Boxes of shit. The bathroom."

"Sounds swell," I said.

Zane said: "Now it's ours. For as long as we want it."

"And," said Cari. "Nobody knows we're up there. Not your loser customers. Not your boss or the owner on paper or the real owners or the mall manager. We got a big crew. You forget us all forever. Nobody knows we're here, not even you."

"What if I gotta go the can?"

Zane said: "Raise your hand."

"Fuckin' cops," he said. "You're all alike."

"What are your store hours?" I said.

"They're me. I get here long 'bout eleven for the lunch crowd. Close little after the late night snack crew. If I get the hungers, I trade tit-for-tat with the pizza delivery place or with the noodle shop slopes from couple doors up. I ain't feeding you, too."

"We bring in breakfast," I said, "so we need a set of keys and the alarm codes."

"Keys cost."

I dropped two twenty-dollar bills on the counter.

The bills went in his pocket, a ring of keys went in mine. Cari wrote the cashier's recitation of alarm code punch numbers on the back of a rental receipt.

"One more thing," I said.

"It's always one more thing with guys like you."

"Blue neon makes a nice sign," I said, "but why COY-OTES?"

"*C*ut *O*ff *Y*our *O*ld *T*ightass *E*xistence *S*tore."

I said: "You spelled *tight-ass* wrong."

His Zippo clicked fire to a white coffin nail. "It figures you know that."

We let the toxic cloud he exhaled blow our sails toward the back curtain.

"Refreshing to meet an honest man," I said when we stood in the upstairs office of the porno store. "It's exactly as shitty up here as he said it was."

"But you were right," said Zane as we pushed aside piles of cardboard boxes, spun two metal folding chairs away from the scarred metal desk and put them next to the windows. "Even dirty as it is, this glass gives us a clear view."

Zane stood in the window and trained the compact binoculars from the weapons vest across Georgia Avenue, over whooshing-past cars and down at Mail 4 U!

"I can almost read Trish's lips while she's talking on her cell phone," he said.

"Me, too," I said, my eyes hanging around Cari. "Right now, she's saying *'like.'*"

Zane shook his head. "So many people out here in the real world talk about themselves as if they were *'like'* characters in some movie."

"Everybody needs some handle on life," I said.

"What's ours?" asked Zane.

Suddenly an electronically amplified woman's voice vibrated the floor beneath our feet: *"Wow! Like, I never dreamed that two hunky guys would be my new neighbors! Come in."*

Our upstairs trio blinked.

Zane said: "He will turn off the TV."

Cari sighed. "Cover is cover. That loud, the downstairs creeps can't hear us."

"I was just going to take a shower. Want to join me?"

I held the cell phone close to my mouth as I punched the number programmed for Beta. Russell answered, and I said: "In position. Go."

"Oh yeah."

Five minutes later, a brown uniformed deliveryman walked down Georgia Avenue. The deliveryman carried a five-foot-long cardboard tube over his right shoulder. White tape randomly circled the brown cardboard tube—logically and rationally for more purposes than just to give the tube distinctive stripes.

"An oversized cardboard tube is the perfect spy tool," I said as we watched Russell walk toward Mail 4 U! "Carry it on your shoulder and you've got a reason for being anywhere, for going anywhere. Hell, bend your knees when you walk to show that the tube is heavy, and guards will even open the doors for you."

"Don't count on Trish getting off her ass," said Zane, binoculars trained across the store. "Do you think she'll recognize that I just bought the tube and label there?"

"Not a chance," I said.

"Mmm. Now it's my turn."

"In and out," said Zane, narrating the scenes he watched through binoculars. "Come on, Russell! What are you doing? Trish stashed the tube perfectly, tagged and propped against the wall right where we can see it, put a pink slip in the mailbox. . . . What are you—No! Don't talk with the manager!"

"Uh-huh."

Four minutes later, Russell walked out of Mail 4 U! Stood in front of the glass windows, his face toward Georgia Avenue and our second-story post across the street as he made a big deal about checking his watch. Walking away.

Two minutes after that, from the white Caddy with Hailey and Eric, he called my cell phone. I punched it on.

"Oh baby uh-huh do that to me."

"Vic?" said Russell in the cell phone. "Who do I hear?"

"Never mind! What were you doing? You were supposed to go in and out!"

"Yeah baby."

"Ah . . . Okay, but I killed two birds with one brown. I told the manager I had a pick-up at some motel near a subway stop on Georgia Ave', but I forgot to write down which one. He told me where motels are two miles down the road back in D.C. And it's not like the manager will ever see me again. If he does . . . Nobody remembers deliverymen."

"That's so good."

"Okay," I told Russell. "Recon them, find the one that will hide the Caddy the best. Get a couple—no, get three rooms, register us as the Harry Martin family reunion. Have Eric figure out shift rotations so . . . *um* . . ."

"So Blondie is never only with only one of us," said Russell. *"Oh yeah! Uh-huh! I've never done it like this!"*

Russell cell phoned: "Hey, Vic, whatever you're doing, I can't wait for my turn."

46

WE SAT ON metal folding chairs beside the porno store's upstairs window and put binoculars on whoever walked out of the afternoon and into Mail 4 U!

"What time is it?" said Zane, his eyes on our stakeout.

I glanced at my watch: "Four forty-two."

"Rush hour." Cari looked out and down at the stream of cars passing by. "Lucky people, going home."

"We'll get there," I told her.

"What if nobody picks up your tube?" she said.

"Hell," said Zane. "What if somebody *does* pick it up? Taxis don't cruise around here. Our chase car is at a motel twenty minutes away. We spot the pick-up, most we'll get is a visual of the guy, maybe a license plate. Unless he takes a bus or hikes to the subway, we won't be able to follow him or snatch him."

"We got what we got," I said.

Cari swung out of her black cloth blazer, draped it across the back of her folding chair. She wore Hailey's cashmere pullover. That too-tight red sweater stretched over Cari's no-bra breasts and I didn't think about Nurse Death's five eyes or inflated flesh featured in the TV playing under our shoes. Cari had Nurse Death's unloaded Walther PPK tucked into her belt, cosmetic armament for her fake role as a federal agent.

She combed her fingers through short blond hair, stretched—could have used the stretch as prelude to an attack, but didn't. The stench of ammonia drifted from the bathroom. She looked at me: I gave her a comforting smile.

Zane swung the binoculars up to watch the mail drop store.

Four minutes later said: "Customer. Went to his mailbox, found nothing, left."

"I never know whether to be glad or sad when my mailbox is empty," said Cari.

I said: "He could have been a scout."

Zane joked a Marlon Brando boxing movie line: *"I coulda been a contender."*

Cari watched Zane and I share a smile. Said: "What's it like to be crazy?"

"Same as it is for you," said Zane. "Everybody's different. Yet also the same."

"It takes guts to be nuts," I said.

"But that's the question here," said Cari: "Who's crazy and who's not."

"No," I said. "That either-or question ignores reality. Life is a whole lot of a whole lot, not just one thing or another. Crazy and brilliant exist at the same time in the same person, along with a whole lot more. A painting or a novel or a movie, a really great movie, can be funny and scary, sexy and suspenseful, all at the same time, everything swirling together, as long as its heart is true."

Cari nailed us: "What's the true heart of all this?"

"It ain't about staying alive," said Zane. "Busting out of the CIA's secret insane asylum rocketed us into a free-fire zone. We all knew that from the get-go."

"We had to do this or we wouldn't be us," I said. "We all gave our lives over to being spies, to finding out what was true and doing something about that. But we didn't do this just to find out what was true and fix it. We also had to do this to *be* true, to be us. Every spy lives in a world spun from lies. You can survive living in lies, but if the heart of you isn't true, then you're nothing."

Cari said: "But you're still crazy."

"Being crazy is living in a dream," I said. "But maybe *out here* is the dream and crazy is what's real. What matters is what you can make work."

"Plus what makes you happy," said Zane.

"Happy?" said Cari. "Babbling on street corners? Locked up in a padded cell?"

I told Zane: "She knows about Condor."

"You call that happy?" said Cari, neither confirming nor denying what I'd said.

"One man's happy is another man's Hell," I said. "And you'd be surprised what people get used to. But where we were, I call that trying."

"Trying is where everybody starts." Zane shrugged. "Since we busted out, since I made it through the subway meltdown—"

"What subway meltdown?" interrupted Cari.

"Never mind, he got by with a little help from his friends."

"Sure, obvious things made me crazy." Zane's eyes probed beyond the glass. "My parents' car wreck. Jumping out of an airplane to get hung up in war tree and watch a man I treasured die because of my great idea. Baking like I was in the Hell the nuns promised me. The dig-my-own-grave mindfuck. Tons of bombs blasting my nerves. Getting so fried with fear and pain that my hair turned white. Being smeared with heroin, packed out of the jungle like a monkey. All that whacked me, but hey: everybody gets a load."

A truck honked outside on Georgia Avenue.

"What *kept me* crazy was believing in my bones that I had to carry that load forever. I fought with everything I had to hold on to the weight that was crushing me. Carry that weight, no matter what, and never, never cry. Or else."

Cari said: "Or else what?"

"If you let go of your weight, you got nothing." Zane stared out porno's window. "Some people need to get down to nothing.

"Me, I melted down in the subway where Vic and Russell and strangers changed the moment and kept me from going batshit. Going batshit is another way of holding on to your weight. But them being there stopped me from going batshit. So I had to let go, and when I could breathe again, I was still hanging on to a moving train. My crying and letting go didn't destroy the universe. So while I was in the same place . . . it wasn't the same me.

"Dr. F getting whacked led me to zero," said Zane. The window reflected his sad smile. "Kind of rough on him, but Dr. F was my best ever penny."

Zane took a quick look at Mail 4 U! through the binoculars. Put them down on the window ledge and asked Cari: "What about you?"

"I'm not crazy."

"Are you glad or sad your crazy mailbox is empty?"

"Irrelevant," said Cari. "Instead of me nailing my mission, my mission has nailed me. Doesn't matter if I'm crazy or not, I screwed up and so I am screwed."

"I don't know about screwed," said Zane, "but you didn't screw up. You've been dealing with what's real, not what was expected. I'd say that makes you a star."

She stared at him.

"But do you know what's important right now?" asked Zane.

Cari shook her head.

"Crazy or not, we need to eat."

And I saw my chance: "There's that Vietnamese restaurant a few doors down."

"Saigon's everywhere out here. Makes sense for me to get dinner." Zane passed me the binoculars and asked Cari: "Can I bring you anything in particular?"

"Make it hot, make it a lot."

As the door downstairs buzzed Zane's exit, Cari said: "Was he always like this?"

"Yes. No."

She took his chair. We stared out the smudged glass window. Alone.

"So . . ." My gesture took in the cluttered second floor of our pornography palace, the traffic rushing in the street below, sunset's bleeding sky. "How you doing?"

"Well . . . *Way back when,* I never pictured being in a place like this."

"Who did?" I said. "Americans usually mean high school when they talk about *back when.* For the rest of the world, *back when* is usually either when they had food or when they didn't. What was way *back when* for you?"

"Yesterday. Forget about high school." She shook her head. "High school is America's cradle. We always believe we can rebirth ourselves into a new person—smarter, prettier, richer, more powerful. In the rest of the world, people struggle to be better and safer in who they already are. That's why way *back when* for us springs from our adolescent daze. We keep thinking we still got time to grow up and be somebody else."

"Who do you want to grow up to be?" I said.

"Alive." She lowered the binoculars. Kept her gaze out the window. "All there."

"And *here* isn't how you pictured *there.*"

"Got that right," she said. "Back then, all I wanted was out. To go somewhere special. Do something more than ordinary life. Do what nobody thought I could."

She laughed. "So guess what? Now I risk my ass to protect 'ordinary life.' And what do I get for 'special'? Trapped above a porno store with a couple of maniacs."

Cari put the binoculars on the window ledge.

"The real joke is that ordinary life finally makes sense." She gave me a wry smile. "But hey, I'm just a girl with no bullets in her gun."

"Where did you grow up?"

"Next do you want my horoscope sign? Wasn't the stars that got me here."

"Suburbia? The city? Small town? A farm?"

"*Ah:* persistence. Dull the resistant edge of your captive by bonding with her over details of her life."

Risk everything: "If you want to walk away . . . go."

Her green eyes didn't blink. Neither did I.

"Nah," she said. "I'd miss dinner."

Our eyes went across the street to the glowing lights of Mail 4 U!

"Iowa," she said.

My heart slammed against my ribs. "Are you married?"

"You know better than that."

"Is there . . . Do you have somebody?"

"You can always have somebody." Her blond head shook. "There's nobody."

"Me, either."

"That's no news flash."

"That's what we miss in this spy life," I said. "The chance to find anybody who's more than somebody."

"You always figure there's time," she said. "Even knowing what you and I know about *time*. In eleven seconds, I can kill a man—and that's hand-to-hand. Give me bullets for my gun, and forget about point blank: if I see him, I own him."

"We're all a blink away from the last bullet," I said. "Look where I am."

"Don't think I don't think about that. We all do. But when we hear about . . . crashes like you, we say it was just your time."

"Time changes."

"And grinds up people in the gears."

"I'm still here."

"Yeah," she said. "But I tried to nail you. I tried real hard."

"Better luck next time."

She blinked.

"Do you like poetry?"

"I never think about it."

"Then you're lucky. You've got a lot to learn, and . . . and . . ."

What, what happened?

"Victor! Vic!" Cari's leaning right in front of me and I'm still sitting in the hard chair, the window's turning dark now but she's leaning close to me, off her chair . . .

"Vic! You . . . zoned out."

"But I'm back. I always come back."

"So far. How long have you guys been off your meds?"

"Russell would say not long enough. Don't worry. We'll make it."

"Even Eric and Hailey?"

"Together they add up to a whole."

"How are you spelling that?" said Cari.

"See? You do know poetry!"

She glanced out the window: "An unmarked cop car just parked out front."

We crouched below the window ledge and stared out to the parking lot below.

A balding man in a cheap gray suit closed the driver's door of a Crown Victoria with two radio antennae on its trunk. He looked from side to side as if to be sure that he was alone. The cop in the cheap gray suit marched toward COYOTES' door and out of our angle of vision.

The angry electronic buzz told us the door had opened.

"I'm not getting trapped up here!" I said, filling my right hand with the Glock .45.

"What about Zane?" said Cari.

My left hand shot up: *Quiet!*

We scurried across the bare floor like mice in a cat's house, eased down narrow wooden stairs that somehow granted our wishes and didn't creak. Just past the bottom of the stairs, all that separated us from the sales room of the porno video store was the doorway filled by a moldy green curtain.

Smells like wet wool, I thought as I crouched beside that green curtain to peer through the gap between its edge and the door jam. Cari crouched behind me—I'd never let her be there if I hadn't trusted her. She could see over my head, shared my curtain's-gap narrow vertical view of the world.

We saw the cop shove a video cassette across the counter to the cadaverous clerk, say: "Might be more stuff I can find here that you need to let me check. But don't worry, I'll keep it all off the books."

The clerk said: "You cops are always too good to me."

Zane opened the door and activated the buzzer.

The cop turned to face the sound of a *man walking through the front door*—and as he did, his suit jacket rebelliously flipped open to flash the badge on his belt, busting who he was for any self-righteous, letter-writing, phone-call-making citizen. As he registered the sight of *white-haired stranger/hard eyes,* the cop's right hand instinctively brushed to his side and he growled: "What the hell you got in those bags?"

Zane blinked. Said: "Food. Vietnamese."

"You bring food . . . in here?"

Can't tip who we really are to either the cop or the clerk! Zane told himself, said: "Don't you get hungry?"

"Yeah, but I know when and where I'm supposed to eat."

Zane winked at the cop: "Guys like us eat where we want?"

Got that right, thought the clerk. *Fuckin' cops take it off the top.*

Nastiness wrinkled the cop's brow and he told the white-haired freak: "You mean something by that?"

Behind the curtain, Cari pushed me aside—

Stormed into the store.

I barely dodged getting seen by the cop or the clerk. Or Zane. My hand held the .45 beside my face in High Ready stance as I hugged the wall beyond the curtain.

"Oh man," said Cari, talking her way into the video store racks as the clerk, the cop, and Zane turned to watch her come. "The bathroom here is disgusting."

Fuck you, thought the clerk. *You got it for free.*

He caught the female Federal Agent's don't-fuck-with-me glance she threw him as she joined the other two badges and told the white-haired one: "We don't need any help."

Yeah, thought the clerk, *like you Feds could handle any real shit without backup.* But the clerk knew when to obey *the four magic words.*

"Hell!" said the local cop. "You got a woman with you!"

"What's the matter," said Cari. "Don't you think I can get it done?"

The cop flushed or blushed, depending on point of view. "What I think—"

Zane talked right over him: "Think we've got no trouble here."

Cari stole the reply from the cop and told Zane: "None we can't handle."

"Can't is a pretty big word," said Zane.

The cop said: "Hey! Ain't you talking to me?"

"Who else we got?" said Zane.

Behind the curtain, the gun barrel pressed my cheek.

Cari said: "We gotta be talking to you. It's not like we're

crazy or anything. Not like something's made us fall off into the deep end."

"Like somebody who just shows up when you least expect it," said Zane.

"You gotta be ready," said Cari.

"But somehow, you never are," said Zane.

Veteran of a thousand interviews, the cop knew these two citizens who'd walked in and caught him were trying to say something without coming right out and admitting it. His badge had them spooked, which was good, but he had to get them where he wanted them. The cop swallowed. "Sometimes unexpected stuff works out like, off the books."

"Yeah," said Cari, "like that. Nothing to write about."

"Hey!" said the cop. *Show these mere fuckin' freaky citizens who was boss.* "You people wanna get written up?"

"Nah," said Cari. "Though it might be a pretty good story."

That's right, thought Cadaverous Clerk, *cover your asses, cops.*

Zane smiled at the cop. "'Hope we ain't keeping you from going."

The cop heard that as a *confession* masking a *plea.*

The clerk heard that as a *putdown* masking a *kiss off.*

The cop thrust his forefinger at the freaky duo of citizens whose plea indicated they were smart enough to forget he'd ever been here. One last time, he warned them: "You be careful."

Wow! thought the clerk as the door buzzed and the local cop stalked outside. *A benediction! One tough guy cop blessing another. Just like on that old TV show* Hill Street Blues*!*

Zane told the clerk: "He's really not such a bad guy."

"Oh yeah," said the clerk who knew that cops always stick up for each other. "He's a sweetheart. Just like you."

"No." Zane's skull shaped his smile. "He's nowhere near as crazy as me."

"Back to the salt mines," said Cari.

As they walked toward where I waited behind the curtain, I holstered my gun.

We floated upstairs with the scented clouds of steamed Asian food.

"Close," said Zane.

"Very," said Cari.

Zane angled his head toward the porno store floor where they'd not gotten busted, told Cari: "You've got some nice moves."

"You don't do so bad yourself," she said, "for a crazy old guy."

I said: "And I'm just glad you both know what you're doing!"

"Yeah," said Cari.

"Yeah," said Zane.

"That's good news for all of us," I said, pulling the tops off cups of steaming tea.

They looked at me and opened carryout plates of Hanoi barbecued pork skewers over long, thick, limp, and somehow sweet white noodles.

Russell phoned and got the all clear to come in. He spotted our empty food containers. "We ate seafood at a wild place from a 1940s movie between the motel and the metro. Caddy's parked under the carport. Can't see it from the street, can't scope it from a 'copter. I rode the subway here."

"Alone?" I said.

"Solo and cool." He pointed at Zane, at Cari. "You two ride the subway home. Eric's scheduled tonight's last shift for Vic and me. I drew you a map, bought you fare cards."

"Just the two of them?" I repeated.

"Only way to keep the Caddy under cover. If Hailey'd come with me to chaperone their way back, Eric would be alone with the babble of TV commercials from other motel rooms. She didn't want to order him to grab onto the bed and do nothing else until we got back to help him cope. He's, ah, gravitating to uncontrollable absolutes."

Cari glared at me.

"Besides," said Russell, picking up the binoculars and scanning the glow of Mail 4 U!, "we gotta trust Blondie out there with just one of us sooner or later. All Zane needs to do is get her on the train home."

Zane said: "I think we can handle that."

47

A TRAIN RUMBLED through the blue night.

In the porno movie blaring from the TV in the store below Russell and me.

Outside, taillights of passing cars streaked the night red.

"Surveillance sucks," said Russell.

The Mail 4 U! manager had been relieved by A Distinguished Older Gentlemen who wore a tie while he sat behind the counter waiting for customers in the yellow glow of that store. Our binoculars showed him reading a book but I couldn't make out the title.

A woman's voice came through the floor: *"Where are you going?"*

"I'm going nowhere," said the man riding a train in the movie under our shoes.

"What makes a woman fall for a man?" I asked Russell.

"If I could answer that, I'd be the master spy."

"We can't do this here—can we?" said the movie woman.

Russell said: "Women think that what makes us fall for them is . . ."

He jerked his thumb toward the floor.

"What are you wearing under your dress?"

Russell said: "Man, if only it were as simple as it is downstairs!"

"Oh yes!"

Russell pleaded: "Please God, stay with the sound of the train! Or the fucking!"

God answered his prayer.

Said *No*.

The rumble of a train through a blue night. Groans and sighs. *"Baby!'s"* and *"Yes!'s"* All those acceptable movie sounds were wiped away by heartless computer-faked jazz, the kind of elevator noise a soulless person might think would flicker candles.

"There is a cosmic law," said Russell. "Don't whore the music."

"Women," I said, paused to find the perfect phrasing.

"Forget about it," said Russell, jumping my pause. "Don't talk to me about love."

"Who said anything about—"

But he was on his feet. I scooted my chair so I could see the glowing Mail 4 U! across the night traffic of Georgia Avenue and still watch Russell pace.

"Women," he said. "What I went through—what I *really* went through, what we found out in New York . . . You'd have thought my Op would have given me Zane's problem—the big one, not the heat freaks or the nightmares. I got lucky there, but . . .

"What's been gnawing me—*I hate that fucking music!*" Russell glared at the floor. Paced over it but the sound still came through its thin wood.

"What I did, Okay: *extreme,* but I was there out of love, right? Love of country. Love of freedom. Justice. That girl strung up in the bathroom stall . . . What pushed me into whacko was I did that out of love. I couldn't save her so I had to love her enough to . . ."

Russell stomped on the floor.

"Stay with me!" I said.

"Where the fuck else can I go! We are fucking here. We are fucking doing it. Because we love to do it. Because we love not getting it done to us. Because we love the sheer bold rockin' of this Op. Because . . ."

He stomped on the floor again.

"Women!" I said as porno music swelled. "Love!"

Russell loomed in my face. My arm flowed up to ward him off, my weight sank in preparation to rocket him back. I tried to sense him and not lose sight of the glow across the street where an old man sat reading and still alone.

"What drove me crazy was the bridge of love." Russell whispered above the *faking it* music. "What if you always had to walk from love to death?"

His words sprayed me. "What if love always means killing?"

"Would be a problem," I whispered.

"Wait one."

And he stormed out of the room. Left me on watch.

Okay, gonna be Okay. Russell's had breakthrough, must still have calming drugs in his bloodstream. Even if his crazy is more than just What He Did in the War . . .

Across the street: *Old man, still sitting there, reading, nobody else with him, cars flowing by on Georgia, coming up on closing time, gonna be Okay!*

Floor vibrating with the rumble of a train. A scream—train whistle? two actors?

Bam!

Glass shatters, tinkles . . . quiet.

Feet pounding up the rear stairs. My gun fills my hand.

Russell strides into the room.

Saying: "Where was—oh yeah, the love-death-murder thing. What I figured out in New Jersey is how all that was crazy *dumb,* not just crazy."

"Russell . . . You shot the TV."

"Only once."

"The clerk . . . ?"

"He's got a broom and no customers. I told him to fill out a reimbursement form."

"What if he calls somebody?"

Russell turned from the window. With eyes of fire, he said: "Would you?"

All was quiet in the night above the porno palace. We stared out the window.

Russell sighed. "Surveillance sucks."

48

MIDNIGHT. THE STRAIGHT-UP *tick* between a yesterday and a tomorrow.

Walking in the lime green second-floor hallway of our motel that was a grenade toss across the Maryland border into Washington, D.C.

Russell. Me. Corridor walls of closed doors.

"What I love about surveillance scenes in movies is that

something always happens," he said as carpet ate our footsteps. "The hero always sees what's going on."

"What good is a hero who doesn't know what's happening?" I said as caffeine from a cold Coke in my hand jangled my exhausted nerves.

Russell stared at me: "But you gotta have a soft spot in your heart for the hero who doesn't know what's happening."

"I suppose," I said.

"Yeah," he told me. "You suppose."

He stopped us at door 2J. The DO NOT DISTURB sign hanging from its gold knob had identical friends hanging on the next two doors. "You're in here with me. Next door is Zane and Eric, and up against the wall there are Hailey and Blondie."

"Her name is Cari."

"Whatever. As shaky as Eric is, Zane might be sleeping solo. Eric is probably curled up at the foot of Hailey's bed. Works for me. Puts two of us on Blondie."

A door opened and Hailey peered into the hall. She pressed her finger to her lips, flashed us the hand signal for all-clear. Vanished back inside her room and shut the door.

"You really want to be sentry?" Russell unlocked our room, handed me the key.

"Somebody has to."

"Damn. Lucky me. Four whole hours of sleep."

"Wake Hailey and Eric at five, drive them up to post, come back and crash. Before you go, wake Zane so he'll be on duty while the rest of us are sleeping."

Russell gave me a nod and a strangely sad smile.

The door clicked shut to a room where one of two beds waited for me. Made the DO NOT DISTURB sign dangling from its doorknob sway.

The ice machine *clunked* at the far end of the hall.

As tired as I was, I knew better than to sit down. Walking the corridor toward the windows at the far end, my finger tap sent the DO NOT DISTURB signs swinging. When I got to the dead end wall and the top of the stairs going down, I looked back: the signs now hung still. So much for me passing by.

Windows in the walls showed me the night. Out one side were high-rises that had grown up around this motel built back when being a twenty-minute drive from the White House meant you were out of town, not just in the extended city. Out the other window was a vacant lot sloping up to tracks for both the subway and real trains. Beyond them were office buildings dotted with cleaning crew or worka-holic lights. Lonely yellow eyes slid over the streets. After the birth of the twenty-first century, an extortionist sniper team dropped an innocent citizen five blocks from here, the desk clerk had told Russell. But cops caught those stranger killers, so we only had to worry about snipers who knew our faces.

I swigged the cold Coke and glimpsed my watch: four minutes past midnight. If I'd picked up the right pennies, in less than four hours I could crawl into a bed and fall asleep alive.

Coke shook in the bottle I held. Couldn't blame the caf-feine. Or the cool night.

How shaky were the others? Tomorrow is our seventh day off our meds. Not counting our NYC contraband highs, Zane calculated we'd only last seven days.

Watch me walk back down that motel's pale emerald hall. *Like* I was in a movie.

The first DO NOT DISTURB sign swayed with the wind of my arrival.

Cari was in there. With Hailey. And maybe . . . My ear suctioned to the wood of that old door. Yes, a man's snoring shook that wood, the strongest sound: Eric, but with his fit-fulness came feminine sighs that let me hope for their sweet dreams.

The second DO NOT DISTURB sign trembled before I got there. My ear didn't need to kiss 2L's old wood to catch muffled sounds beyond it. *Zane.* Who for years in Maine fought nightmares. That was the alone battle in there now, squeaking the bed, sending sounds out to the hall that could have been *"No! No!"* or *"Oh! Oh!"* All I could do was walk on. Hope he'd make it through his Saturday night horrors.

The third DO NOT DISTURB sign. Too late. Russell was already in there.

Walk on. Get to the other end of the hall. Stand sentry to the windows of the night and the closed doors. Hands shaking. But I knew where I was and what was going on, and that let me pretend it was all like a movie.

Any minute now, the lights will come on.

49

THE STUBBLED CLERK behind COYOTES' cash register waited until the door buzz died and I was inside his domain from the morning sunshine, then said: "What's that?"

"Coffee." I nodded at the white paper cup I'd taken from a gray paper tray of four such covered cups and set on the counter. Hanging from the ceiling behind me was a TV with a giant black tape X across its hole-blasted screen. "The boutique kind with steamed milk that sells for as much as a handful of bullets."

"Could've gotten me a mocha." The rich coffee aroma made him sniff.

"Could've, would've, should've," I said and walked toward the stairs' curtain.

He said nothing until I got there, then rasped: "Tell me about it."

Instead, I climbed the stairs to Hailey and Eric.

"Thanks," said Hailey. She nodded toward the window. "It's a slow Sunday morning. The Black manager showed up at 6. Trish stumbled in at 9:22, and that looked late. Nobody's touched the tube."

Eric sat holding his cup of coffee. Watching us.

"It's okay, man," I told him. "Drink it as you want."

He nodded. Twitched a smile. Sipped the hot steamed milk and coffee.

"How'd you sleep?" I asked. "I know you went to Hailey and Cari's room. Zane probably appreciated a room to himself, especially with his nightmares."

Eric's face twisted in thought. He opened his mouth to speak.

Hailey cut him off: "Eric, get the donuts off the desk, see if Vic wants one."

Eric walked the five steps away to obey.

As Hailey told me: "The chain donut shop on the corner was the only thing open when Russell drove us here. Thanks for finding better coffee. Where are the others?"

Eric handed me a sack of donuts. I took a chocolate one. "We cleared out of the room so the maids would think we were at the family reunion. Our crew is at a laundromat. They can do some wash, hang out in plain sight and be practically invisible."

"Hey, Eric," said Hailey. "Why don't you go use the bathroom. Wash up."

Without a word, he left us for the small closet near the rear stairs.

She'd moved him out of earshot, so I said: "How's he doing?"

"Holding on—barely. All the noise out here in the world is tearing him apart. Too many orders, too many options, too many voices besides ours and his own heart. Holding on to who he is keeps getting harder for him."

"He's never going to be free," I said. "You know that."

Hailey dropped her eyes. "I hoped that out here, before I died, maybe I could have helped him get stronger so that someday . . ."

"These are his best somedays. With you."

Hailey's eyes misted. "All of you know he's brilliant, but that's just what he can do. Who he is comes from his heart. From his essential nature. Our essential nature gets us every time. And his is about love. Pure love. Self-sacrificing, unflinching love."

"So he served his country as a spy."

"Yeah. And his essential nature led him to his perfect torturer and perfect private Hell. So much for self-awareness. So much for cosmic justice."

"How are you doing?" I said, pretending my coffee cup was shaking because I liked to see the tan liquid swirl.

"I'm dying faster every day. I'd hoped that I'd be with you this whole run. That at least I could see it through. But since we don't seem to be getting anywhere—"

"Hey!" I insisted. "We're here. We made it this far."

She showed me the lying smile a mother gives a child to soften the inevitable. "I'm shaky, but I'll hold on."

I glanced across the street. The tube sat where it was.

When I looked away from the window, Hailey's eyes were on me.

"How are you?" she asked.

"We're doing okay," I said. "And with Cari—"

"Forget about her." Hailey shook her head. "She's not for you."

Heartfelt shock colored my tone. "What are you talking about?"

Hailey shook a smile onto her face.

"Life sure dropped on your sorry ass," she said. "Plopped a dead man on the floor of your safe asylum. Put a hurt on your crazy. Not fair. Not right. *Again.* You knew the murder score totaled bad for us innocents. Letting that happen is like making it happen. So you squeezed the trigger for all this.

"You know why you grabbed Cari? Because she's you. Cool, tough, ruthless, a Hotshot. She walked into your life crackling with fire. She was the *you* that got lost in Malaysia. The killer-edge you. The secret needs-somebody-to-love you. All rolled into one more-than-a-woman—and the hurtin' from losing Derya meant you poured even more power into Cari.

"In one Stone Pony heartbeat, you bullshitted yourself that she was walking cosmic justice. Your redemption babe. Either she'd whack you into dead, or she'd pull us off the bull's-eye—plus love you. Either way, you figured hooking up with her would take you off the hook."

"But guess what, killer: she ain't that angel. For you, she's just a gun with no bullets and blond hair."

A toilet flushed in the bathroom.

What I wanted to say was how she was wrong.

What came out of my mouth was: "You know what happened to our last shrink."

"I'm already on the cemetery train."

Water turned off in the bathroom sink.

"You can come out now, Eric," called Hailey.

She protected him from having to say much of anything until Russell walked in, sent them both out to be picked up by Zane and Cari in the Cadillac.

"We'll pull a double shift," Russell told me. "Every time we cruise that white beast, we draw eyes."

"What are the others going to do all day?"

"Don't ask me." Russell stared out the window. "Surveillance sucks."

Lunch. Cheeseburgers and greasy fries from a fast-food pit stop two blocks away. The cadaver clerk gnawed a pepperoni and fresh tomatoes pizza. Long day's sunlight. Bloody sunset. Rush hour. A city bus belched black exhaust. Ginger pork skewers on flat white noodles. Two dozen door buzzes for men who hid their faces. A hundred scans of the Black manager working. A thousand views of Trish, *like,* jabbering in her cell phone. Twenty-seven customers in Mail 4 U!, thirteen of them using mailboxes. No one touched the white tape-wrapped cardboard tube behind the counter.

"Surveillance sucks," said Russell as my trembling watch ticked the palindrome of 10:01 and windows showed us another night of novels for the old man across the road.

"Spying is about seeing."

"Spying is about believing that there's something *to* see. You still got the faith?"

"The mail tube's still there."

"What if nobody comes to pick it up? What if we're looking at a dead drop used only by a dead woman? What if nobody but us cares about that tube?"

"What do you think I've been wracking my brains about all day long when I wasn't dealing with you pacing or bitching or the bad food or the stinking toilet or—"

"Don't get all *good soldier* on me! Do go all *tradecraft Op realities* and—"

Man's voice yelling through the floor: "*Yo!* Upstairs guys! I'm coming."

Russell looked at me: "Do you think he wants to volunteer?"

"I think he needs to use the bathroom. Again."

But Russell drifted to the opposite wall. I positioned myself to watch the stairs or outside the window with a flick of
my eyes. My leather jacket draped over the desk chair and
my gun rode holstered on my belt for the world to see.

The clerk joined us. Pale, still with a three-day blackish
stubble on his cheeks and skull. Bloodshot eyes. His sweatshirt fronted a French drawing of Le Fantastic Four, his
jeans came from a Dumpster. He wore red chuck sneakers
and a scowl.

"So where is it?" he said.

"Where's what?" said Russell.

"I'm not talking to you, Mr. Bang Bang. What about it,
Coffee Man? A deal's a deal. Where is it?"

"I don't know what you're talking about," I said, looked
across the street, saw no one but the old man in Mail 4 U!
"You haven't been busted."

"But I been broken. You seen it. You heard it. And promises
was made, but nobody's delivered, so I come to get the form."

"What form?"

"The reimbursement form. This is America. This is a legitimate business. You break it, you buy it. You broke it. Mr.
Bang Bang there swore I'd get me a reimbursement form,
but he ain't delivered on the deal, so I'm here to collect."

"Pay back?" My rage pulled Russell off the wall. "You
want pay back? You think you're owed? That your government . . . For a fucking TV!"

"With remote control," he said.

"Remote? Like in *remote possibilities*—that what you
mean? And you want a form. To compensate you for your
loss due to national security necessities, *gee,* that'll solve
everything. Well, let's see if I've got the form for compensa-
tion and redemption."

He crossed his toothpick arms. "That's all I'm talking
about."

I slapped my pants pockets: "Nothing there!"

I thrust my hand into one of my leather jacket's chest
pockets. "Nothing there!"

My hand dove into the second chest pocket, closed on a folded piece of paper.

"Wait a minute!" I pulled the folded piece of paper out to the light of this filthy room above a thousand faked film fantasies. "What do we got here?"

With great flourish, I unfolded the paper, saw a logo stamped across its top:

Mail 4 U!—Box Rental Application

My leer swept up to the clerk: "Looks like a standardized form!"

With a grand gesture I held up the form. "But damn!"

And I met the clerk's scowl with chagrinned worry. "It looks like I might have grabbed the wrong form from the office."

I knew he watched me shoot my gaze back to that printed sheet of paper with its instructive lines, unfilled out blanks, and unchecked boxes. "Yup, that's what . . ."

Then I saw what was right in front of my eyes.

Whispering from my mouth came: "My mistake."

Russell said: "What? Vi—*Buddy,* you okay?"

My eyes lifted off the form to find the clerk: "Thank you."

"Huh?" said the clerk.

Russell stared at me like I was crazy.

"We'll get the form to you in the mail."

"Why don't you bring it?" he said. "The mail ain't what it used to be."

"Because we won't be here tomorrow. Our day off."

"Day off? Figures. Government guys."

"That's us." I nodded to Russell. "My partner will take you downstairs. Get the address where you want the form sent. Give you an advance to carry you home tonight."

"Cash?" The clerk flicked his gaze from me to Russell and back. "Will, ah, will that advance show up in any of the paperwork that, you know . . ."

"We'll cover it in our personal expense reports," I assured him.

"Well okay then. I hear you." The clerk turned and went down the stairs.

Russell acted like I'd taken leave of my senses, but followed him.

As I punched a programmed number into my cell phone.

Five rings—*what's taking so*—Zane, breathless, answered: "Yeah!"

"What are you doing? Never mind," I told him. "Gear up. We're hot."

50

MIDNIGHT. OUR SEVENTH straight-up *tick* since we charged into the real world.

Zane and I lay pressed flat commando style on the slope up to a parking lot from the drainage ditch bordering the elevated Metro track. We huddled in the shadows between watch light poles on the train bed behind us. A bare bulb glowed on the back of a brick building. That light faded before it reached the weeds along the ditch. Through the gaps in the row of buildings came the glow of Georgia Avenue.

Back when we started, Zane had figured that without our meds, we'd crash and burn after seven days. Even with the grace our bootleg drugs had bought us, the way I was shaking told me he wasn't far from right.

Ride it out, I told myself as I lay there in the cold night. We can ride it out, ride through it. Oh, hell, manage it. Make being crazy work for us.

"Thirty-two minutes between subway trains," Zane told me. "We got twenty-one minutes before a train clatters past and somebody looking out the window might see us."

Zane wore a black stocking cap over his white hair, a purchase made at the same twenty-four-hour supermarket that had provided our unfortunate selection of gloves.

White cloth gardening gloves. Big, thick fingered, floppy even on Zane's hand that he wiggled in front of my eyes. "These make me look like Mickey Mouse."

"He's a tricky rodent," I whispered.

"Trick me."

"Hailey said they were all the store had. In this real world, you get what you get."

"If I have to get to my gun and get off a shot, we got trouble."

Two dark figures raced along the edge of the building toward us.

Russell and Eric dove into the ditch.

"Okay," whispered Russell. "No alarm circuit box we could see. And like you said, no cameras. They could have an infrared light beam system or motion sensor, but that would mean skipping over the obvious for the elaborate."

"Who'd do that," muttered Zane.

"This'll work!" I told him.

"Think Watergate," I told everybody. "Those burglars, when they hit the office of the psychiatrist to smear that dissident, they made it look like a routine break-in robbery."

"What happened to those guys again?" said Zane.

"They got movie deals," I said.

"They weren't breaking into an all glass, lit up office on one of the busiest streets in a city that's always working."

"So we got more drama," I said. "We're better pros."

We carried triple-strength thirty-gallon black plastic trash bags.

"Eric, after we walk around front, Russell will give you the signal and you'll pick the locks." Even with the amateur tools he'd fashioned, we knew Eric would succeed: an order was an order was inevitable. We worried about the time he'd need, the exposure that gave us, but every Op has its risks. "When we get inside, I know which file cabinet to check. Russell, you trash and grab whatever, pull open the desk drawers, turn over—"

"Rock 'n' roll, I know how to trash a place."

"Zane, you're lookout. Claim the curb like you're waiting for a ride."

Our two cell phones were conferenced into Hailey's as she sat behind the steering wheel of the white Caddy idling in the parking lot of the supermarket eight blocks down Georgia Avenue. Cari rode shotgun. If we got caught, if we went down, at least our witness might be free to scream our story.

Three white-gloved thumbs stuck straight up.

And I said: "Go!"

White-gloved rats scurried along the brick wall of the building. I peered around the edge of its brick wall. Saw no one walking along Georgia Avenue's wall of malls that even during the day saw few pedestrians. No stream of cars passing by on either side of the avenue's median. No lights of occupation in the strip mall across the road, negligible neon glowing from Viet Mine's sign. COYOTES' blue glow was turned off.

We whirled around the corner, Zane peeling off to claim the curb, Eric and I side by side as we scanned the glass wall front of Mail 4 U! and Russell . . .

Russell jogged away from us like he was following Zane.

"What the hell are you—?"

Before I could finish my hissed question, Russell whirled to face us—and the store. He wore his black leather trench coat. His white-gloved hands turned its collar up. Eric quivered beside me, waiting for Russell's signal to start picking the door lock.

A deep breath moved Russell. I heard him mutter: "Watergaters got no balls."

Whoosh! Russell charged straight toward the store's glass front, his arms pumping, his long coat flapping around his pounding legs . . . closer . . . closer . . .

Russell launched himself into the air, spinning as he flew so his back rushed toward glass pane. His white-gloved hands flew up to cover his eyes-closed face.

Pwshee! Russell exploded backward through the glass wall. Crashed flat on his back in front of the business counter as unexploded chunks of the window tumbled to the hard tile, shattered, and covered him with a shroud of diamond beads.

"Holy fuck!" yelled Zane from the curb.

Running, glass crackling under my feet, looking down—

Russell, black shoes, black jeans, black leather trench coat buttoned up to his neck, his white-gloved hands splayed out at his sides in a judo breakfall.

"Russell! Russell, can you—"

"Oh man," he moaned, slowly moving his limbs, his torso, opening his eyes. "It's a lot easier in the movies."

"Real life hurts. Are you functional?"

"About like always."

I helped him to his feet.

"*In* in a heartbeat," he said. "Less exposure time. 'Sides, cops wouldn't buy that real burglars know how to pick locks. That's Hollywood."

"Just trash the place!"

"Oh. Okay."

As I vaulted the business counter, my gaze swept back toward the crater exploded to the night in the glass wall beside the door—

Where Eric was obediently picking the lock.

"Eric! Forget that order! We're already in! Help Russell."

The green file cabinet. The manager had either made Trish replace the file or finally done it himself. I stuck what I wanted in my trash bag and threw other files into the air with a celestial gesture: *Let there be a blizzard of paper.* Russell crammed a portable TV from Trish's desk into his trash bag, tossed in her stuffed cloth fantasy figures that in a previous decade had been bartered like ingots of gold by millions of sane Americans. I rummaged through the manager's desk, laid his family pictures down so their glassed frames "amazingly" wouldn't break. Tossed random junk out of the middle drawer of his desk, put a penny face up in the drawer, and deeper in its recesses, left five folded twenty-dollar bills. The amazing karmic luck he'd tumble to after the inconvenience of this crime was, *obviously,* that burglars missed personal money he'd forgotten he had.

"We got it!" I yelled. "Let's go!"

And we ran out of burgled Mail 4 U!, Zane charging on our heels as we dashed back to the shadows and the path along midnight railroad tracks.

The white Caddy carried the six of us through the night. Red lights flashed to green. Taillights in front of us disappeared into suburban darkness. Headlights coming toward us on Georgia Avenue winked past our car. Hailey drove, Cari beside her with Zane riding shotgun. I rode the hump in the backseat. From my left, Eric held the flashlight on the stapled sheets of paper I'd found in the stolen file:

Mail 4 U!—Box Rental Application

Filled out fully and completely for the Berlow corporation. Including the blank where a bold print instruction read:

Federal law requires all boxes or convenience addresses rented or leased for the purposes of receiving public and/or privately delivered mail, packages, etc., be leased to persons or entities by/from a verifiable land address.

Verifiable land address.

"Seven-oh-nine Eastern Avenue," read Russell. "Suite 402. Washington, D.C."

Eric worked a map on his lap while I held the flashlight.

"Close," he said. "Mile south, less than a mile east. On the border with Maryland."

Zane said: "What else is in that file?"

"A photocopy of the check used to pay for a year's rent dated . . . five weeks ago."

"Cashier's check," I said. "Drawn on a bank from . . . Parkton, Maryland."

Cari said: "That's a two-traffic-lights town near the ocean and the Eastern Shore. Half a day's drive from D.C."

"Cashier's checks only show the bank, not whose money it is," I said.

"Not much intel take to show for committing felony burglary," said Cari.

"We'll see." I checked the map, gave Hailey directions to the verifiable land address for Nurse Death's Berlow corporate connection.

Our white car slid through the city night.

"This looks familiar," said Cari.

"Should," I said as homes flowed past us on the wide two-lane street. "You've been stationed out of Langley headquarters in Virginia, but everything inside the Beltway—whether or not it's Maryland or Virginia—is one city. Langley being farther out is only the geography of deniability from the White House."

"That's not it," she said. "Here, turn left here!"

Eric swiveled in his seat as I grabbed his arm and told Hailey: "Do it."

The white Caddy swung a tight turn, headed toward a well-lit juncture of five roads alongside a cement overpass for train tracks.

"The subway stop," whispered Cari.

"Mail 4 U! is walking distance from another stop," I said. "Good Op planning logically would put—"

"Go that way," said Cari.

And Hailey did, found Eastern Avenue a block away and turned left to head the same direction we'd been going before Cari's first command.

"Getting close," said Zane from the shotgun seat. "Maybe two blocks."

"Park there," said Cari.

Hailey slid the Caddy into an open space behind a soccer mom's SUV.

And I asked Cari: "Are you taking over now?"

"I think it's too late for that," she said. "But can I boss one quick Recon?"

"Go for it." I grinned but she couldn't see me from the front seat.

"Double date," she said.

Eric screwed out the dome lightbulb, then Hailey opened her door.

Zane climbed out of the front seat with Cari.

Russell and I got out, he slid behind the Caddy's steering wheel. Two women and Zane met me at the Caddy's grill. I slid my left arm around Cari's waist.

Zane said: "Ah . . ."

"It's okay," said Cari and I shot a *See!* look at Hailey, who shook her head. "This way you'll be on us from behind, cover and control, just like in the *how-to* books."

Zane draped his left arm around Hailey's shoulders, leaving her hands free, leaving his gun hand free. My embrace of Cari kept my gun hand free, encumbered her draw, but since her pistol had no bullets, nobody cared. In the *how-to* book, I could maneuver her; throw her out of harm's way. I held her close, cupped the curve of her ribs in the palm of my hand, felt the press of her back against my inner arm.

We walked like two loving couples on their way home, one couple in front of the other like horses paired to pull a stagecoach. The air was still. Quiet. Cool. Our shadows slid over sidewalks where there was not a smear of dog shit or spatter of blood.

This was the wistful hour. Streetlights lit the moment. All over town, bartenders were saying good night to patrons who'd met someone they hoped would still be special in the morning or who'd met no one and hoped that wouldn't matter in the morning. Diners burned their lights for insomniacs or taxi drivers. TVs in the houses and squat apartment buildings we passed were dark even without a big X of black tape on their screens. An invisible hound barked twice, but he was insincere.

We walked this border of many places, clearly into what you couldn't call yesterday but not so deep into tomorrow it could be that today. This street was neither postcard city nor cliché suburban, had a subway stop nearby and single-dwelling homes with covered front porches, wide lawns. Maryland was on our left, D.C. on our right. Up ahead of us waited a two-block-long neighborhood Main Street, with an ice cream parlor and a video rental store, vintage clothing shops, a tailor and an optometrist and a yoga school. We smelled weeds in a vacant lot. The scents of cement, of cold road and metal cars slid past us as our walk counted down addresses on Eastern Avenue.

"It'll be across the street on our left," I whispered.

There it was, a giant gray concrete box of a building, five stories tall, filling a corner and a vast span of two perpendicular sidewalks.

"Fuck!" whispered Cari as we drew closer to that building. I held her warmth close, her lilac shampoo perfuming my every inhale. "Fuck, fuck, *fuck!*

"Cross the street." Cari led us to the side street running

past the target building, to the sidewalk opposite those doors.

"Fuck me," she whispered as we walked up the side street.

I refused to think about that. Kept my eyes on the target building as we walked past it, past its this-side entrance, past a chain-link/locked gate parking lot where four cars and two unmarked vans waited. Past the next building, a squat three-story yellow brick affair with a sign for a law firm and a medical insurance company, past the last store on that side street, a huge retail outlet called Awake where long-faced teak statues from Tahiti shared window space with stone Buddhas and two kimonos.

"We are so fucked." She led us back to the white Caddy. "Get us out of here."

Russell drove, Hailey and Eric rode up front.

"That's one of our places," said Cari from the backseat between Zane and me. "An accommodation address, an off-the-books set of offices."

"Who's 'our'?" said Zane, though we all knew the heart of the answer.

"I'm not Office of Security, or even Operations. I'm in a street crew, part of the Special Activities Division, the Agency's paramilitary guys who—"

"Aren't they using Special Forces anymore?" asked Zane, who'd been one.

"Sure, but now the Agency has its own military capabilities. Me, a few other women, never get dropped into Afghanistan ahead of the Black Ops military units, but in a western city, we rock. We work with the Army's Deltas. We're the modern Hotshots. Three-person hawk teams, cyberwar units, chem-bio gunners, solo's—"

"Wait a minute," said Russell. "The acronym is SAD? You're a 'SAD' chick?"

"I'm a Hotshot," she said. "Doesn't matter what bureaucratic label I've got. The organization chart is a blur since 9/11. With our overseas wars, peacekeeping operations, antiterrorism Red Light crashes, UN blue helmet details, joint Black Ops with allies, budget battles and turf wars over the new Homeland Security Department, every federal shop scrambling to get its own counterterrorism unit so they can still be a player . . . It's all so fluid and multilevel classified, I doubt anybody knows who everybody is or what they're doing."

Zane said: "But you know that building back there."

"It's ours," she said. "SAD. We rent a few offices on the fifth floor. A field base where we can run an Op away from prying eyes but not far from CIA headquarters. Do our bureaucratic stuff without showing up on any office site listings. I've only been in it once. There are different covers: a therapist office and a 'consultant' suite to account for foot traffic if any civilian asks questions, but nobody out here does. They live in their own world, think Washington never crosses the border.

"So this means," she said, "your Nurse Death . . . *Cross-cover.* I should have realized when you showed me the address, but . . .

"Her corporate shell's verifiable land address is on the Eastern Avenue—D.C. side of the building. The *cross-cover* is that the SAD site uses the Adele Avenue—Maryland address on the same building's side street entrance. It would be a huge coincidence for them to both be there and not be connected."

"*Cross-cover* is one of the mistakes they teach you to avoid," said Hailey.

"Then either somebody didn't pay attention in spy school," said Russell, "or somebody didn't care."

"Except," Cari said, "that makes no sense. Say this whole mess is one of your *can-only-be-two* scenarios, some kind of . . . renegade Op, some spy group hiding in our group of spies. Why send Nurse Death to kill your shrink in Maine? This is Washington. You don't kill your problems, you promote them. Give them a high-profile job that will drag them into failure. Zero their budget. Smear them in a scandal.

"Okay, say you do whack somebody, say some creep from your team who's gone double but you can't legally prove it and can't double him back against the opposition. You sanction him where you're in full control. A federal garbage truck hits a car on the G.W. parkway. A mugging in the Post Office parking lot. A heart attack when nobody else is home. A suicide on your guy's sailboat in Chesapeake Bay and you cremate the body before the locals do an autopsy."

"Maybe hitting a target inside a secret Nowhere, Maine, mental hospital was somebody's idea of control," I said. "And now we're definitely not talking some bad boy group like al Qaeda or the cartels or North Korea or Cuba or anybody but us."

"But who us?" Cari shook her head as we drove through the deserted D.C. streets. "Your Dr. Friedman was on his way from superstar to big shot. Even if the Agency went in for an illegal stateside wet job—which they don't, that's too . . . politically naive and dangerous. The guys who run our government aren't stupid."

"That's a relief!" said Russell.

"Even if this was a way-off-the-shelf Op like Iran-Contra," said Cari, "you couldn't get enough bureaucrats to sanction a hit on someone like Dr. Friedman because you couldn't convince them that their asses would be covered. And there's no reason to kill a superstar like him."

"That we know of," said Hailey.

"He's a shrink, for God's sake," said Cari. "The only people he'd worry are . . ."

"Crazies like us," I said. "So we keep looking guiltier."

Eric said: "What difference does that make now?"

"He's right," said Zane as we drove down Sixteenth Street, aimlessly headed straight toward the three-miles-away White House where none of us had ever been, where Dr. F would now never shine. "Doesn't matter. We are where we are, and that keeps looking more and more like we got wrapped up in a sanctioned Op."

"Sanctioned by who?" argued Cari.

"If 9/11 has proven anything," I said, "it's that the left hand of our secret warriors doesn't always know what the right hand is doing. And sometimes they fight."

"I still can't buy your renegade Op crap," said Cari. "Doesn't happen."

"Has," I said.

"Times are different now," she said.

"Oh."

We topped a rise and the lights of downtown D.C. twinkled in our windshield. Twenty blocks away glowed the white marble institution where the President slept.

"Nothing's changed," I said. "We can't run forever and we can't go in—we're whacko escapees wanted for murder of our shrink, plus now kidnapping and assault."

"Burglary," said Russell, "with trashing."

"No fingerprints," said Eric. "Wore gloves."

"We need more intel to sell our story to somebody who'll care," I said.

Cari said: "What are you talking about?"

51

THE NEXT DAY. Tuesday. Day Eight of our renegade op. High noon.

Russell's black trench coat flapped as he walked three paces behind me on the sidewalk of the main road past the SAD gray blockhouse. When he'd reconned that mostly innocent building at 9:15 A.M., he carried a mailing tube, wore his deliveryman uniform. But he changed clothes for our noon hit.

Said: "I am not dying in brown."

We marched toward the front door.

On the far side of the building, Eric paced toward the side door. His glasses and pudgy shuffle pegged him as a nerd. The gizmo he made from a battery-powered jigsaw hung strapped under his nerd jacket that also held Nurse Death's Walther PPK. Loaded.

Ten feet behind Eric strolled what looked like a father and daughter. The daughter had just-dyed brown hair. The eagle-like father wore a black knit cap.

Eric and I were Clockers, our watches synchronizing our pace and thus the pace of those behind us walking Drag, their eyes covering our backs and scanning the street.

My hand pulled open the front door to let the trench-coated man behind me swing inside the building with *hands empty* as at that exact same *tick,* a nerd opened the side door for a father and daughter to swoop inside, *"Dad"* sweeping the entryway corridors with his gaze, *"Daughter"* zeroing the stairwell.

Inside looked like Russell's recon photos developed at the one-hour.

Russell and I entered our stairwell, slowly climbed. *Don't arrive out of breath.* Smelled like concrete cinder blocks and carpet cleaner, ghosts of sneaked cigarettes.

Fourth floor. I swung open the stairwell exit: Office corridors . . . *clear.*

Eric's team surfed around the corner on radio waves from an easy music station torturing unseen officer workers. Somewhere a phone rang. Stopped.

Our teams met at a solid brown office door on a sunlit corridor of office doors.

But this door bore the number 402 and the corridor's only government-issue lock.

A Campbell 21/25 high-security lock, Eric's guess confirmed by recon pictures. Doors on offices one flight up held identical locks. The Campbell 21/25 is one grade down in quality from the Q Clearance locks on Weapons of Mass Destruction.

Dyed-brown haired Cari slid a hardware store Plexiglas shimmy out of her left sleeve. A loaded Glock from her old crew rode her right hip.

Eric swung his motel room engineered gizmo out from his jacket.

Zane held his pistol pointed at-the-ready toward the white ceiling.

I drew the tranquilizer dart gun from the weapons vest. Whispered into the cell phone: "Set!" to Hailey who grudgingly agreed to function as Double-E (Evac/Evade) because Cari had to be on the hit: *"What good is your witness, your spy, if she can't see?"* From the white Caddy idling beside a nearby church, Hailey transmitted: "Clear."

Life can come down to one door. A brown slab to *no going back.*

This brown slab. This door. With its lock that said we're up against our stronger selves, the sentinels in the shadows who'd created us. We were up against Uncle Sam.

And he had it all. Night vision goggles. Satellites streaming video surveillance from outer space. Infrared scanners to "see" through walls. Caves of computers calculating faster than a speeding bullet. Stealth warplanes with smart bombs for surgical air strikes. Body armor and flamethrowers. A billion dollars in secret bank accounts. SAD shadow warriors and Trouble Boys and Hotshots carrying silenced machine-guns. Black helicopters. The atomic fucking bomb.

All on the other side of that door.

We had a few stolen weapons, a dead man's white Caddy, a lot of crazy.

My left hand circled the safety spring handle on one of the vest's flash/bang grenades. Eric pulled the pin so I wouldn't need to put down the tranquilizer gun. He optimistically tucked the pin in my shirt pocket so we could disarm the grenade *when*.

We all looked at Russell.

Standing tall. Sunglasses on. Black leather trench coat belted shut. Arms stretched down along his sides. His right hand held Cari's pistol fitted with its silencer: that weapon looked like an ebony samurai sword.

Pride flashed in me that this was a good day to not commit suicide.

Snick went the cocking hammer on Russell's gun.

Eric penetrated the lock hole with the gizmo's resmithed hacksaw blade.

Cari slid the shimmy into the door crack, wiggled the dead bolt.

Eric's saw vibrated the lock. Her shimmy tricked the steel dead bolt into the void he made of the tumblers. Eric pulled out his gizmo—turned the doorknob. Pushed.

Cari spun away from the door, drawing her gun to face one hallway corner.

The door swung inward as Eric zeroed the other hallway corner with his Walther.

Russell leapt into the office, his silenced gun scanning like the ultimate third eye.

Zane, in behind Russell on the right, pistol swinging to cover that flank.

Me, on Penetrater Russell's left with my tranquilizer gun as Preferred Shooter.

Ticks froze.

Until Russell whispered: "Oh, fuck."

"What?" hissed Cari from the hall.

"All in!" I whispered.

Eric stumbled against a doorjamb, but made it in ahead of Cari, her gun swinging a safe arc to not put any of us in her line of fire as her eyes widened with what she saw.

What we all saw.

An empty office. Bare white walls. Bare ivory tile floor. Bare ceiling except for standard fluorescent light fixtures. A storage closet standing open and empty.

"Close the door," I said.

Zane did and its latch click echoed through this bare room.

No prisoners. No interrogations. No evidence. No tracks.

"Gotta be the right place!" Russell's pistol sought a reality beyond what he saw.

" 'Xactly."

Ever cautious, Eric replaced the pin in my flash/bang grenade.

The telephone filled my left hand. "Stand by."

Hailey transmitted the okay that let us know she was still out there, still safe.

Zane shone a flashlight over the empty closet walls. Jerked open the only other door and flinched from the blinding white glare of sparkling toilet fixtures.

Cari ran her finger over the windowsill. "No dust."

"Smell that?" I said and everyone sniffed. "Pine ammonia. Look at the walls: absolutely clean white. I bet there isn't a fingerprint or DNA drop in this place."

"Give me somebody to shoot!" Russell whirled from blank wall to blank wall.

"Can't," I said. "*Here* isn't *there* anymore."

"Um," said Zane as sunshine streamed in to us through the landlord's blinds over the windows: "Does it occur to anybody else that the only thing in here now is us?"

"Fuck!" Russell zeroed his pistol at the shut exit door.

"Shhh," I said. "Shhh."

Closed my eyes. Heard the rushing void of this empty room. Heard no radio through the thick door. No clatter of a city street beyond these bare walls. No ring of bells from the nearby schoolyard. No laughter of children as they dashed back to class. No whirl of dust particles dancing in golden shafts of sunlight breaking through the windows and sliding past the blinds.

My eyes opened.

Spotted Magic Marker red letters on the ivory tile floor.

Three letters. One word.

run

52

"THIS IS A terrible idea," said Russell that night as we trudged through the forest.

"It's my last one," I said, my shoe slipping on damp dead leaves.

"That's what I'm afraid of," said Russell. "Guy like this, times like these, he's bound to have tech security, bodyguards, countersurveillance coverage, home heat."

"He might not live here anymore," said Hailey. "He might not be home."

"And, Victor," said Zane, "even if he is here, you barely know him."

Eric said nothing as we muscled our way through the dark woods.

"One of us should have stayed with the car," said Cari.

"No," I said. "We're a package deal."

We marched through a night of trees.

Washington, D.C., is full of forests. The biggest one cres-

cents through the city centered by a vein road called Rock
Creek Parkway for commuters to zip from swell northwest
neighborhoods to money castles of steel and glass along K
Street and stone government bureaucracies stretching up
Pennsylvania Avenue to the white icing Capitol dome.
Though the swath of forest separating Rock Creek Parkway
from houses and apartment buildings is sometimes barely
five blocks wide, the park meanders for miles and is treasured turf to joggers, horse trail riders, bold lovers, bicy-
clists, deer, coyotes, and more than one murder.

The forest we marched through barely deserved that name.
Call it a glen or a glade or a swath of wild trees along a ravine
preserved because its aesthetic worth outweighed the cost of
zoning exemptions. In point of fact, those woods were not in
Washington, D.C., but rather were across the Maryland border in the ritzy suburb of Bethesda, and then not even in
Bethesda itself, but in a Korean War era subdivision surrounded by a low stone wall. The subdivision had a name
straight out of a Victorian British novel and four unguarded
gates leading to its chessboard blocks of grand houses.

Our white Caddy drove through the main stone gate at 8:35
that night. I rode shotgun, directed driver Zane past glowing
dwellings in which many a dad and mom had just gotten
home from the big office to eat warmed-up dinner at the mirror polished dining room table and wait for Sarah and Ben to
clumpity-clump downstairs all giggly in snug pajamas with
that warm toddler smell and give the seldom-seen parent a
kiss 'n' hug around the neck *night-night* before they ran back
upstairs past MommyDaddy's scuffed briefcase full of Important Work that surely could Fix the Whole Wide World.

"Would help if you had an address," said Zane.

"Not really," I said. "Getting here was almost like one last
field test. It's an outback place. A cabin. Like a
groundskeeper's place, servants quarters, it's not much."

"Out here, *'not much'* rings in at a million dollars," said
Hailey. "How does he afford that on the checks he's gotten
from Uncle?"

"Rented it for years," I said, remembering a discussion

from my congratulatory NOC agent graduation evening of red wine and cheese with a handful of Agency priests and bishops. "When his landlord on the main lot put the whole package up for sale, he got loans and bought it, reversed the economic structure so that now he rents out the big place to afford to live in the cabin.

"These woods are the only ones in this development," I said as we cruised past a wall of shadowy trees on our heart side. "He has to be in there."

We left the Caddy glowing with purity under a streetlight near the swim club, watched the lit windows in the nearby big houses stay empty, and walked into the woods.

A cold damp forest smell swallowed us. We could see a corpse length in most directions courtesy of the urban glow trapped by a curving sky. The skins of visible trees glowed a shade of pale grayer than the pallor of our faces. Rocks stubbed our feet and deadfall snapped under our shoes. Spring was officially here, but that night kept such news a secret. Bare trees pressed toward us like a crowd at a rock concert or pallbearers at a funeral. Branches scraped cheeks, foreheads near blinking eyes, clothes. An owl hooted. Who knew if he'd spotted us or was working his own covert agenda. Our plan to move in a straight line choked in thick brush and interlaced trees too stubborn to step aside. We followed a ravine through the tangle.

"Look!" Russell pointed off to his right.

Through a score of sentinel trees, I saw a log cabin under a tall watchlight, with a vast apron of grass running from it to a three-story white house.

"Is that it?" said Zane.

"Gotta be," I said.

Zane whispered: "If you're wrong . . ."

"Wrong or right," said Russell, "it ain't good."

We made sure none of us had twisted an ankle, gotten lost. Spread out in a skirmish line, crept to the edge of the forest. Waited twenty minutes.

"Lights on," said Zane. "Shades down, can't see who's inside."

"No sign of anybody out here in the big cold dark but us

crazies," said Russell. "Course, we'd never see a Marine Corps sniper. And there could be an Office of Security cover car or van parked beyond the big house, in the street."

"Where we could have driven," said Zane.

"You know better than that," Cari told him. "We made it this far."

"Almost fifty yards of open grass between here and there," said Russell.

"'Xactly."

"Eric?" I said.

"Could be motion sensors. A web of infrared beams dropped all around the cabin. Horizon radar. On-site alarm. Instant relay to a react center."

"Or a barking dog," said Hailey.

"Fuck it," said Russell. "We going or are we gone?"

"Walk it like you own it," I said.

And led them out of the trees.

We spread out in a single line, a wave of six people walking across a night glade from the woods to a well-lit cabin. Walking slow. Standing tall.

No bullets shredded our chests. No machine guns rattled the night. No popped flares lit the sky. No spotlights hit our faces. No snarling German shepherds charged.

We made it to the front porch.

Cari knocked on the door. I stood to her left. The others fanned out in a tight line behind us. Again, Cari knocked.

The cabin door swung open and there he stood—his right hand out of sight beyond the doorjamb. The lamps behind him and the watchlight above us glistened the silver of his thinning hair as his lean face locked on Cari.

Blink, his smile dying as he truly saw me.

Same heartbeat, I blurted: *"Please no!* No gun, no alarm if that's what your right hand is on, please no. Give us, give me a chance."

His focus zoomed out to the quartet waiting on his lawn; zoomed back to Cari as he said: *"Agent Rudd?"*

"Yes, sir."

I said: "Please, whatever you're thinking, Sir, *don't.* I'm going to move."

My right hand eased out from behind my leg. Showed him what I held.

"Tranquilizer gun," I said. "Over-under barrels, two darts. Cari—Agent Rudd—says the neurotoxin takes ten seconds to put you down. Not unconscious, but you'll be good for not much for at least half an hour and we may not have that much time."

"Really," he said.

Kept his right hand inside the cabin where I couldn't see it.

Cari said: "Sir, on my belt. One weapon, I'm armed. I'm not here as a hostage or a prisoner. I'm operational. These people represent no threat."

"Really."

I said: "Director Lang—"

"Deputy Director," he answered. "And that's a classified title. What's your—"

"Sir," I said, "you can work me in a minute. Right now you need to know you're safe but we're serious. If we'd come here for wet work, I wouldn't be holding a tranquilizer gun and by now, you'd be past feeling whatever's hidden in your right hand."

"Ahh."

"One step at a time, right? But we've got to move. And how is up to you."

"How about we all go back in time?" he said.

"We're ready if you're able."

And his smile came back. "Maybe we should think of something else."

"You should invite us in."

"The place is a mess," he said. "And small, for the . . . six of you."

"We don't mind."

"So I've been told."

And I had to smile. Wipe it off.

"We showed you our trust," I said. "Because it's just a tranquilizer gun. Because nobody squeezed any trigger when you opened the door. Now it's your turn. Fair's fair."

Lang frowned. "Fair? Like in a negotiation? Do you think I asked for this?"

"What you ask for doesn't always come. What's in your hand? A weapon? An alarm signal? A ham sandwich?"

"That's what you're *asking?*"

"We're both doing more than *asking.*" My stare broadcast I wasn't ceding him control.

Lang shrugged. "I'm holding a 1911 Colt .45 automatic. Beautiful weapon with a bullet for each of you."

Behind me, Russell said: "Never happen."

Lang's gaze filled with the whacko samurai in the black leather trench coat.

"That I believe," said Lang. "You're . . . Sorry, I don't remember all your names.

"But," he said, "now . . . I'm going to slowly turn to my right—keeping my body in the open doorway. I'll lay my pistol on that table. Walk to the far wall where there's only the kitchen sink. Count to ten, then turn around with my hands empty.

"All of you," he said, "may come in. You can shoot me in the back or not, but if you do, forget the tranquilizer darts: have the balls to use a real bullet."

That's what he said. That's what he did.

When he turned around, he saw us all standing there in his house. Door closed.

"So," said Lang, watching Zane pick up the .45. "Agent Rudd, good to meet you. First, are you all right?"

"Yes, sir, I—"

"Do you know where you are? I suppose it's more important where you've been since your team was neutralized—reports say your men are fine, by the way, though we are worried about you. It's like you got teleported to Sweden."

His blue eyes kept their warm hold on her, yet also watched as the rest of us fanned out in this living room/dining room/open kitchen of a solid-log-walled cabin.

"Stockholm syndrome," I told Cari. "He's worried you've lost your will and rationality, gone over to your captors."

Eric added: " 'S a kind of crazy."

"No way, man," argued Russell as he opened the door to Lang's bedroom, let his eyes search it. "Stockholm is its own place."

"Go ahead and snoop," Lang told the samurai peering into his bedroom.

"Hey," said Zane, "we're all spies. We don't want you to hit us with a surprise—and Deputy Director Lang, don't so *casually* drift toward your computer workstation."

Lang stopped where he was. Gave us all a smile. "Call me John."

"Okay, *John* . . . " said Zane, motioning the senior spy in the room closer to me. Zane gestured to our technical expert, pointed to Lang's computer: "Eric, check it out.

"And hey, *John*," said Zane: "Do you always answer your door holding a .45?"

"These days," said Lang, "what do you want me to hold?"

"Where's your security?" said Zane.

"You mean beyond my pure heart and a classic Colt?"

"You know what we need to know."

Lang shook his head. "From what I've read in the action reports over the last week, I don't think anybody knows what you want to know."

Zane wouldn't let him wiggle away: "Why no coverage outside? No guards?"

"I'm an ex-brick agent. A street dog. Back-up boys or minders covering me feel like wolves on my heels. Make my hairs stand on end. I insist that I be left free *most* of the time. Besides, every Trouble Boy the Agency can beg, borrow, or steal is running up and down the Eastern Seaboard. Looking for you. How ironic that all I had to do was stay home."

Eric let first his eyes, then his fingers caress the computer system on a table, asked: "Video monitoring? Technical countermeasures? Alarms?"

"Window and door alarms wired in to the Office of Security and the local badges. Motion sensor for this room when I activate it. Panic button on the wall by the bed, one on the wall there by my leather chair."

Knowing him, I said: "What ones wouldn't we find?"

"Very good, Victor." He eyes kept weighing and courting Cari. "You might not find the button mounted under the computer desk—I accidentally kneed it once and two minutes later. . . . Let's see if we can avoid another riot blitz."

"Let's," I said. "What else?"

"You'd find the pendant button if I had it on, which I don't, it's on the bed table."

"You know," I told him, "we'll find everything else."

He smiled. "Good luck."

The man who'd talent-spotted me for the Agency, the executive who here, in his modest home, had hosted the informal graduation ceremony that secrecy allowed when I became a deep cover spy, the bishop of the church of intelligence who fire-axed partitions and ran my debriefing on the day of my second suicide, the man who Cari said had been "bumped up, some sort of cardinal in the new Homeland Security maze," that gray-haired, slight but strong man named John Lang stood in the living room of his cabin and raised his hands to be body searched.

Smooth, I thought. Don't wait for us to ask or tell you what to do. Volunteer. Work on winning our trust. Seduce us with your cooperation. Until.

He caught the knowing shake of my head. Knew I knew. Knew I knew he knew.

We're trapped on the circle of knowing, I thought as Zane ran his hands over the spy who was about his same age. Trapped chasing each other round that circle *until.*

I'd met Lang at a *bagua* martial arts seminar not far from this cabin. Like tai chi or aikido, *bagua* is an internal art, only its practitioners specialize in circles, in turning and twisting and walking around an opponent, deflecting attacks until the circled foe gets dizzy or out-of-rhythm/balance— and at that *until,* the *bagua* expert blasts his foe with a myriad of shattering techniques.

We've got to get off this circle.

"He's clean," said Zane.

"How are all of you feeling?" said Lang.

Trying sympathy. Empathy. Bonding.

"Still crazy?" he said.

Trying provocation. Challenge. Destabilization.

"We're still not stupid," I said.

"No one's ever thought you were stupid," said Lang. "That's why all this . . . wildness and killing doctors and nurses proves what everyone knows: you are . . . medically challenged."

Russell said: "Man, you Washington warriors love to spin words."

Zane said: "He'll spin us if we give him a chance."

"My guess is you're all already dizzy," said Lang. "Even if you weren't crazy, coming down off all your medications must be quite a crash."

"As long as we're together, we're together enough," I told him. Forced my hands to stop trembling and knew he saw my effort.

"Whatever you say," said Lang. "You've got the guns."

"No," I said, lifting the Colt .45 out of Zane's belt before he could say anything, turning and holding it out to Lang butt-first. "We've all got 'em."

The intense blue eyes of the old spy blinked. He stared at the offered pistol. Made absolutely no motion.

"Go on," I said. "Take it."

Out of the corner of my eye, I saw a subtle change come over Russell as he stood in the bedroom door, knew he'd filled his hand.

"Take it," I told Lang again.

So he did. Let it swing down to his side, barrel pointed to the floor.

"But if you use it," I said, "have the balls not to shoot me in the back."

Walking to the kitchen sink gave him my spine. Let me get a drink of water with a glass from the drainboard. Hid my shaking hands.

Behind me, Cari said: "Sir, you and I . . . They're not our opposition."

"Really," he said. "All evidence to the contrary."

"Not all evidence," I said, staring out his kitchen window to the night. "What have you got in your hand?"

"A great bluff? A madman's move? You tell me."

"What would you believe?"

"That's always the problem. I believe I'm standing in my living room with five self-professed, violence prone, fugitive maniacs who outgun me and one supposedly outstanding agent who . . . well, who's also here. What do you want me to believe?"

Russell said: "Give it up. This is going nowhere."

Outside the kitchen window, the night moved. But I saw nothing.

I said: "Ask."

Genuine curiosity rang in Lang's answer: "Ask what?"

"Whatever," I said, turning from the sink to face him and the faces of my fellow fugitives, of Cari. "What do you want to know?"

We saw wheels spinning in his eyes.

Lang finally said: "Why did you come here?"

Right to the heart of where he was and where this might go.

"You've got enough chairs," I said. "Sit on the couch and we'll tell you."

Oh what an opera we performed! A saga of sound and fury and whacko, scenes like jump cuts of a Marx Brothers' movie: *Interior. Night. Cabin.* Yellow glow, audience of one trapped on the couch. We played our parts and we were great, because besides being a manipulator, every spy is an actor.

Russell sang "Lying on the Floor Just Like Doctor Friedman Did" but got cut off as Zane raced behind Hailey to demonstrate how Nurse Death nailed her whack job only to have Hailey scream: "Watch out for my blood!" I said: "I know, Mr. Lang, since we busted the crime scene, forensics won't back us up, but at the time, it was a good idea to take him with us, though, I'm kind of sorry for taping him to the fence." Russell said: "And I'm sorry for freezing up and not dropping Nurse Death alive." Zane waved that off: "Forget about that, it was bathrooms." I interjected: "Bathrooms and love," then Zane continued: "If we're going to start getting sorry, I've got the burned-up police car."

Lang said: "The burned-up—"

"Mirror," blurted Eric. "Broke mirror. Bad luck. Sorry."

"Wasn't your fault," said Hailey. She told Lang: "Eric's triggered by any comprehensive order. Won't stop, can't stop obeying no matter what, like—*Eric:* explain the thing you made at the memorial shivah."

Eric rocketed to his feet: "Leonardo da Vinci created the—"

"Sit down and stop, Eric," I said and he did. "If Hailey hadn't been careful with what she told him to do, I couldn't have ordered him to stop even if this cabin was burning down around us. It would have been like that shrink woman he grabbed onto."

The CIA Deputy Director (covert) frowned: "A shrunken woman?"

"She doesn't matter," said Russell, "but your blonde there—"

"Who?" said Lang.

"Me," said Cari. "I dyed my hair as a disguise."

"The point is," said Russell, "I was going to get laid, but she fucking stopped it."

Lang said: "The two of you—"

Simultaneously, Russell shouted: *"No way!"* and Cari yelled: *"Not him!"*

"But we got a great car out of it!" I interrupted to quash Russell's anger. "Even if that guy was dead, it got us all the way to the hit this noon on the SAD building."

"Why was a building sad?" asked Lang.

"No sir," said Cari. "Our SAD. Up by the Takoma Park metro."

"What *'hit'*? You killed—"

"Nobody," I quickly said.

"Well," said Zane. "Nurse Death bought it, but that was a combat mishap."

"And then," I said, "the empty office told us to *run*."

We ran out of breath.

My watch took a sweep of ticks before out of Lang escaped: "Wow."

And he said: "So this is all of you being all together?"

We all gave him a shrug.

"Okay," he said. "Now you're here. Now—"

"You got anything to drink?" said Russell.

"No booze!" I yelled.

"Don't worry," said Lang. "I don't want any of you drunk. In the fridge, there might be some Cokes."

Russell flowed into the kitchen, jerked open the door, said: "Wild! Beer."

"No," I said.

He gave a bottle to Zane, took one for himself, opened one for me.

Rudeness is the last thing we need, I thought as I took a sip of cold golden brew. I raised the bottle in salute to our host. "Thanks."

Cari said: "Director Lang, they've got something. Stumbled onto something."

"But," he said, "aren't they still . . . crazy?"

Zane said: "Yes. And *oh look:* we're still sitting right here in the room."

"No offense," said Lang. "I was just trying to get an analysis of intelligence."

Zane took a swig of his cold beer.

Lang put his eyes on Cari. "And you're sure you . . . have bullets in your gun?"

"Here." I handed him the tranquilizer gun. Took off the weapons vest with its ammo pouches, stun gun, three looped-on flash/bang grenades, and dropped it on Lang's lap. "Add all that to your .45 and you've got more bang than any one of us."

"But don't forget," said Russell, the beer held in his left hand, his right hand empty and calm. "Quality tops quantity."

"My philosophy, too," said Lang. "So . . . You showed up here to surrender?"

"Not hardly," said Russell.

"Not ever," said Zane.

"We came here so some of us could get safe," said Hailey.

"We came here to help you help us help you," I said.

"We came here to nail that whacker Kyle Russo," said Russell.

Lang blinked: "Who?"

All six of us started to answer, but Lang took command: "Stop!"

He pointed his index finger at me like he didn't care that if it had been a gun, Russell would have given him a third eye.

"Victor, you and you alone talk. Debrief. No dramatics. No adventures—I'm still lost up around Asbury Park. Give me this 'something' you've convinced Agent Rudd is real. And what or who is Kyle Russo?"

Twenty minutes later, after I'd gone from the assassin's technique to the check that paid for the dead-drop that led us to the SAD building, I was done. Cari told me: "Good job, Victor. Good briefing."

But Lang said: "You've got *not much* of *who knows what.*"

"Well," said Zane, "it's something."

"Everything depends on how you add it up," said the spymaster. "And all this *not much* is what you want me to bring in with you to the Agency?"

"Actually," said Russell, "until we know *what's-what,* no way are we going in."

Lang exploded. "So what are you going to do? What do you want me to do? You must have a plan! Did you think you'd come here and I'd take over your . . . crusade or investigation or *mad dog* run or whatever, and then you'd all end up all right?"

"Well . . ." said Hailey.

"What do you want me to do? Run Kyle Russo and the addresses of empty offices and public mailbox stores through my computer over there?"

"You could do that?" I said.

Zane said: "Don't forget about that cashier's check from the small town bank."

"Tomorrow," said Lang, "I can send a team there. It's about a three-hour drive, near the Atlantic shore. When the bank opens, they can get the records. Cashier's checks may seem anonymous, but the issuing banks keep records of where the money came from for the checks, who bought it. No way of avoiding it."

"If you scramble a team," I said, "then . . . there'll be people we don't know."

"More people," said Russell, "less control for us."

"But first . . ." I nodded to his computer. "You're wired into the Agency?"

"For practical purposes," said Lang, "with my access codes, I am the Agency."

Zane said: "Eric?"

"Customized computer. Probably NSA."

"A cast-off," said Lang. "Five generations old for them."

"Got a special modem. Power pack. Satellite connection. Probably antihacking protocols way past commercial fire-walls. Could tele-conference, camera unplugged."

"If they can see you," said Lang, "they can see you. I prefer privacy. As for the rest, all I know is that it works."

"So give it a shot," said Russell. "With Eric eyeballing, what do we got to lose?"

Lang sat at the computer. Following Zane's command to *"Watch what he does there so he can't alert help,"* Eric scooted next to Lang's chair, Hailey's hand on his shoulder. Eric entered commands into the computer until a "window" appeared in the lower-left-hand corner of the monitor. To me, it looked like flashing cyberspeak. To Eric it decoded the operations of the computer whose keyboard he relinquished to Lang. Zane stood behind the CIA master spy, while Russell leaned against a wall where he could see the crowd at the computer and the locked front door.

I stood next to Cari. Feeling the beer relax me, I whispered to her: *"Thanks."*

"For what?" she whispered back.

Lang said: "Can I start?"

Zane said: "Go."

Colored light flashed from the computer monitor as one screen of security warnings gave way to the next. Required code words got typed in by Lang.

I whispered to Cari: *"I could never have gotten him to believe us without your help. You were terrific."*

"All I did was be a spy. Report."

Lang said: "Okay, I'm at the full-indices search. This is top access. Not just Agency systems, everywhere from NSA to the Pentagon to the White House."

"My ass is on the line, too," Cari told me.

"I couldn't ask for better company."

In the search mode, Lang typed in Kyle Russo, Nurse Death's real name, the SAD building, and other "hard data" we'd logged on our index card matrices. Hit Enter.

Cari turned and found me softly smiling at her. She shook her head. Closed her eyes. Opened them, said: *"Victor, I don't, it's not, you're not—"*

"What the hell is going on?" said Zane.

All of us stared at the computer screen except Russell, who from the far wall flowed to combat ready.

"Access Denied" filled the computer screen. Colors and images flashed behind those blazing white letters. Lines of code streamed through Eric's peek-a-boo window.

"Crazy!" yelled Lang. "It can't deny me access! I'm on the fucking National Security Council! An Agency double-D! And fully black cleared!"

Eric blurted: "The system's backtracking! Machine trying to turn camera on!"

Bam! Bam! Bam!

The computer hard drive box on the floor slammed into the desk with crackling sparks. The high security modem whirled off the desk to the floor. The monitor screen cracked and shattered and glass splinters rained down on the keyboard and the hastily jerked-back hands of D.D. (covert) John Lang.

Russell whirled from blasting the computer to scan the cabin door and windows.

Left Zane to press the bore of his own pistol against Lang's head as that man rose and backed away from the crackling corpse of his machine.

"Did you do this?" yelled Zane, his free hand again taking the .45 from Lang.

"Do fucking *what?* You watched me the whole time! So did Eric! It was that maniac in black who shot—"

"It'll be me who shoots you *if,*" said Zane. "Eric?"

Our engineer shook his head: "He did standard stuff. Hit a trapdoor."

"So it wasn't him?" said Zane.

"His queries hit snatch-to-blast program. Anybody who

logged in some component of data we searched would have been locked out. Backtracked."

Zane lifted his gun bore off Lang's silver-haired skull.

"Whatever's going on in your guys' heads," said that spymaster, "take a few more seconds to think before you react."

"You're still alive," said Zane.

"What you watch, watches you." Russell kept his eyes on the door. "Even if the camera was unplugged, who knows what got turned on—to us."

"Eric," I said, "how much time?"

"Human factor. Soon as he hit the trapdoor, even if his box's signature wasn't known, trace-trap the link. He says his known response team hit in two minutes. Figure, co-opting them or triggering bad boys is more difficult . . . Three minutes minimum. Max . . . Who knows."

Lang stared at us: "What did you people do?"

"Not us, man." Russell pointed to the computer corpse. "You hit the tripwire."

"'Xactly."

"Now you're one of us," I said. "And we've got less than three minutes."

Lang said: "But I'm . . . An Agency executive. Hell, a White House star!"

"So was Dr. Friedman," said Cari. "Or he would have been, *if*."

Those words from a probably sane colleague made Lang blink.

"We gotta go," I said. "Hard. Fast. Now."

Eric added: "No gear of his. No electronics. No cell phones."

"Can I grab a coat?" said Lang, *getting it*.

And he did, pulling a worn navy peacoat out of his closet, letting Eric and Zane pat it down. The two of them burdened Lang like a pack mule with the coat, the weapons vest, the tranquilizer gun. We took his dented Land Rover because the thirty seconds we used to grab his keys, race out to the street and cram ourselves into it bought us at least fifteen minutes we didn't need to spend crashing through the woods

to get back to our Caddy. We dumped his trackable Land
Rover in the shadows of the pool shed, he dumped his bur-
dens of coat and weapons vest and guns in the trunk of the
Caddy. I keyed the white beast to life as Eric jumped in beside me, Hailey taking shotgun next to him. Our backseat
was door-to-door meat: Zane, Cari, Lang, Russell.

We roared off into the night, blasted through the neighborhood's gate and onto the main road, turned left because
that way looked the darkest.

Russell hummed: *"Bum bum-pa-bum, bum ba bum-bum-
bum . . ."*

"We're not 'The Magnificent Seven'!" said Lang, recognizing that movie theme. "We're seven spies on the run from
some phantom taped to the roof of this stolen car."

Russell said: "Yeah, we need our own theme song."

"No," said Lang, "we need a plan. What have you got left
that you haven't—"

"The bank!" I yelled. "They'll have the records of the
cashier's check to set up Nurse Death's Op! It's only three
hours away! You could badge them and—"

"Great idea. Except Eric didn't let me grab my ID."

Eric said: "Could have been microwired."

"What about his clothes and body?" said Zane.

Cari said: "You guys! No!"

"Now, let's all be professional," said Russell. "Double-
D . . . strip."

"Right here? Crammed in like a sardine with all of you?
Buck naked in traffic in a white vintage Cadillac? Don't you
think that might draw attention?"

"Only need shoes," said Eric. "Probably."

"Check them, don't chuck them," said Cari, who'd com-
plained about first dead Harry Martin's sneakers being too
big, then the spare pair from Hailey being too small.

Crammed into the backseat, Lang couldn't reach his feet.
Zane took off the D.D. (covert)'s lounge-around-the-house
black Chinese *gung fu* shoes, passed them up to Eric.

"Doubt it," said Eric, passing the shoes back to be put on
Lang.

"I'm Seventh-Floor shadow exec," said Lang, "not a street

dog on an Op where tracking me might be worth the bud-
getary expense and effort."

The rearview mirror showed me arms and bodies turning
and shifting to get comfortable with a chorus of groans,
apologies and anger.

"This won't work," said Lang. "We can barely breathe
back here, and you want us to drive three hours to some town
on the Eastern Shore, wait until the bank opens at what, nine
A.M.? Packed in here like this, we're a magnet for police-
men's eyes, a bright white classic violation of no seat belts
and overcrowding. We're a traffic stop waiting to happen,
and when that does . . . Did you say you already got away
with burning up one police car?"

The turn signal blinked as my answer.

"Where are you going?" asked Lang.

"Car shopping," I answered.

"To go where?" said Hailey.

"The bank. The more we get, the better to nail Kyle Russo
and skate clean."

"Director Lang doesn't have his credentials," said Cari.
"Mine and those of my guys are probably hot. If we flash
them and the bank officer checks . . ."

"Don't worry," I said, cruising past homes where lights
snapped off for the night. "We'll think of something."

Thirty minutes later, in the parking lot of a strip mall
where the nail salon, bicycle shop, and health club were
closed, our Caddy sat parked beside a four-door maroon
Volvo with Maryland plates and a bumper sticker for kids'
soccer. The parking lot glowed with lights from the quick-
stop market where Hailey bought the last four plastic-
wrapped things posing as sandwiches and convinced the
bored cashier who never took his earphones off to let her
make fresh coffee in their machine, fill white Styrofoam
cups while we took turns using the dimly lit rest rooms. Our
group huddled for a picnic on the hood of the stolen Volvo.

"I can't believe this," said Lang. "I mean, okay, the over-
ride wipeouts in my computer happened. I know they did. I
saw them with my own eyes. But . . . still . . ."

"You should have seen Dr. F," said Russell, chewing his

sandwich, that like mine, tasted somewhere between cardboard and ketchup.

"I did," said Lang. "I got pulled into the loop for the hunt of you guys. Saw all the crime scene photos. Him on that fence."

He shook his silver-haired head. His exhale was visible in the cool night air.

"CIA boss Helms, Kissinger on the NSC, and Nixon, they hid that the Agency was propelling the Chile coup from all the Deputy Directors, Congress, the press. But that was back then!"

"So were we," said Zane.

"But nowadays, *me,* in the huge spy wars we got slammed with after 9/11, my job is to know what all the clowns in our circus are up to! You think that's easy? Hell, long before it came out in the press, I had to do my own 'spying' to find out that the National Security Agency was breaking all sorts of post-Watergate, *Big Brother* privacy laws to snoop on anybody and everybody. Petty bureaucrats and blind believers on the White House National Security Council accuse me of being a spider walking on all their webs. If I hadn't figured out how to get the Vice President and Secretary of Defense to like me, I'd be in bureaucratic solitary confinement, stuck in an isolated executive suite over in Langley. Instead, I set up the Ops compartmentalization program so it all links to me! And now. Who could hijack my system? Terrorists from al Qaeda or ghosts from Saddam's Iraq or the Taliban? Cartels of some kind? The Russians—one of their *mafiyas* or whatever faction runs Moscow these days. Iran, no way, North Korea, maybe, but China doesn't want a flap with us, so . . . who?"

"What if it's an inside job?" said Cari.

"Inside us *is* us!" insisted Lang. "This isn't the movies. There's no grand secret internal conspiracy of evil. Hell, I'm a boss inside the mother organization legally designed to be a grand secret conspiracy targeting evil, and even with the best hearts and minds in America, we can barely keep track of ourselves!"

"Exactly," said Zane, "so a renegade Op—"

"What 'renegade'?" said Lang. "In the real world, in the rational world, there's always some agenda. What agenda requires a renegade group when the gigantic octopus spy beast of our country already has fear and ambition on its side?"

Hailey said: "Why kill Dr. Friedman?"

Lang shook his head. "Why any of this? It doesn't make rational sense."

"Don't ask us about rational sense," said Russell. "We're mad dogs."

"Taking me where?" Lang waved off his own question. "I know. The bank."

"Even stopping for gas," said Cari, "I figure it's only about four hours."

"I'm tired of road tripping," said Russell. "Let's get to a stone certain gig."

"Almost there," I said, hoping that wasn't a lie.

"Sure," said Russell, knowing that lie or not, what I said didn't mean good news.

"We got the cell phones to keep in touch," said Zane. "Getting separated shouldn't be a problem."

"So no tight caravan?" asked Lang.

"Probably best to be spread out," I answered. "Trying to stay tight will attract attention. If one group hits trouble, the other will get the call and be able to catch up or double back, surprise the opposition."

"Who goes with who?" said Russell.

"I'll take Cari in the Caddy," I answered instantaneously. Thought, then: "We should split the sane fugitives up, a witness with credibility in each car."

"Eric and I need to stay together," said Hailey. "We'll ride with you."

"Director Lang," said Zane. "You get to ride with the boys. And you get shotgun. Russell, you popped it, you drive it."

"Wild!"

"What about you?" Lang asked the white-haired whacko.

"I'll be behind you all the way."

"I bet you will," said Lang. "It's cold and I'm old: Can I get my coat?"

He nodded toward the Caddy's trunk.

"Sure," I said. Tossed him the keys. Watched him walk away from us.

Russell casually stepped to the far side of the stolen Volvo. His eyes rode Lang, and no matter what direction we faced, the silver-haired man held all of our attention. He disappeared behind the huge, rising white trunk lid of the Caddy.

"Now is when," whispered Zane. "This is his first chance to counterattack."

Lang was twenty-one counting-down beats away from *taking too long* when the Caddy trunk boomed closed. He wore his navy peacoat, unbuttoned and hanging open to show his empty belt as he walked toward us with the Colt .45 in his hand—held by its barrel. He walked straight to Zane.

"Hold onto this," Lang told Zane as that white-haired warrior took the pistol from a silver-haired spy. "We'll all feel better, and if I need it, I know where you are."

The spymaster walked through our huddle, circled the Volvo past Russell, opened the front passenger door and climbed in. Shut the door.

I said: "Let's roll."

53

NIGHT RIDING TOWARD the dawn of Day Nine.

"Whatever happens now," said Hailey in the white Caddy's backseat with Eric as we hummed over a dark highway, "all this will be over. When we show up at that bank, we walk onto Lang's runway. We're out of control tomorrow."

"If we get tomorrow," I told her.

"Tired," whispered Eric. "Heartache."

"I know, Baby," said Hailey. "I know."

She'd never called him *Baby* or any endearment before. We'd reached some end.

Or some beginning.

My hands trembled on the steering wheel. The gauge needle reading three-fourths full felt like a lie. Our rush felt like we were running on fumes. The car smelled like sweat, cold coffee, old Styrofoam, gun steel, mud clumps fallen off filthy shoes. Cari rode shotgun. I narrowed my eyes at the yellow dotted blackness beyond our windshield, told myself I could smell her lilac shampoo. But it was just my imagination.

"We'll be okay," I said, my glance at Cari telling everyone I was talking to her. "And a lot of that is because of you, all you've done, how great you are to—"

"Victor, don't." Cari's eyes rode the road. "I tried to bag you. Barely missed."

Tires hummed, but I wouldn't give up. All she had to do was see what was meant to be. Eventually. Inevitably. But I backed off, made a cliché joke that wasn't: "Well, there's always a chance you could get it right now."

"Always. Never." Cari shook her head. "Those are two of your favorite words. But they mean the same thing. You need a bigger vocabulary about certainty and time."

"*Now* is *won* spelled backward," I said.

"What the hell does that mean?"

"Don't ask me," I said. "I'm crazy."

"Cari," said Hailey, "what happens if we get something from the bank?"

"I figured that out when we were driving across the city," answered the sane person in our car. "By now, there's a burn on Lang. But also now, there's two of us besides—with—you maniacs. Seven voices are a lot to not listen to. And Lang . . .

"What I saw driving through town was the Capitol dome. Glowing in the dark. My guess is that's where we'll push this to the next level and get out of the gunsights. Lang spent time there as a liaison between the Hill and the Agency, knows people."

"Oh great," I said. "Congress is crawling with people I trust."

"Turn on TV camera lights and they'll crawl over broken glass to get there," said Cari. "Lot of them are fickle butterflies chasing bright lights. But there are worker bees inside that white dome. Soldier ants who get things done. More heart and guts than you think. If nothing else, on Capitol Hill we can pull people with clout onto the bull's-eye that made your doctor dead. The more people Kyle Russo needs to control and the more powerful they are, the harder it is for him to operate—and make us pay for it."

Memory whispered through Eric: "You can't kill everybody."

The road rumbled. Perhaps ten minutes in front of us rolled another stolen car with two madmen and one silverhaired spymaster.

"We've got time to kill," Zane told Cari when he cell phoned her from somewhere ahead on the dark highway. Red taillights of cars not containing him and the others made occasional dots in our windshield. "We're taking exit thirty-two toward Parkton. Follow, but hang back, let us find a place to coop until dawn and the bank opens."

We were on the exit ramp when he called again.

"Go through town," Zane said. "Take a road on the right marked with a WILDLIFE SANCTUARY sign. Follow it to WATERFRONT ACCESS PARKING. You should be here in fifteen."

"Imagine living in a place like this," said Cari as we cruised down a Main Street three blocks long with stores that had clung to that pavement since the Beatles. No more than a hundred homes stood behind those fronts. "You're not at the beach. You're not on a farm. You're not in the city. Your town doesn't have a real center, a heartbeat to keep it going, make it different. Everything you see around you fades every day. Strangers drive past you on Main Street on their way to the rest of the world. What do you do?"

"You turn on the TV and live in the same nowhere that a billion other people do," I said. "Or make your own reality. Or get out. But I'm more worried about dying here than living here."

"There's the bank," said Hailey.

We cruised past a tan brick box with glass windows, a trimmed lawn, a parking lot where an electronic lettered sign flashed the time: "2:37."

"Dillinger would love that bank," I said. "Smoked windows, easy getaway."

We followed the road through trees until it dead-ended in a paved parking lot where, at the far end, sat the stolen Volvo. Beyond that parked car, the darkness shrouded horizon rolled with blue-black water. The front passenger door of the Volvo opened and John Lang stepped out, wrapping himself in his navy peacoat as he replied to our guys inside the Volvo, closed the door and jogged over to direct me to park the Caddy on the other side of a lamp pole's cone of white light.

Cari lowered her window as I killed the engine.

Lang leaned in: "Feels good to stretch."

And he opened the door for Cari.

As she climbed out, so did I.

Hailey led Eric out of the backseat to stand by Lang. I walked toward the white beast's swooping tail fin so I could join them on the other side of our car. Smelled the cold water, spring trees at night, garbage from a Dumpster, firecracker smoke.

Cari asked Lang: "How's Zane?"

"Hold up a sec, then you tell me." Standing beside Cari, Lang called out: "Vic: Zane thinks that since here we'll need an official presence, I should take charge."

"Go ahead," I said. Cari stared at the Volvo and the way she did that made me want to look away, look out at the dark rolling water. "You be the boss."

As I circled around the white Caddy, Lang said: "Eric, Vic says I'm in charge, so you follow all my orders. Hold on to Hailey so she can't run or shoot or take command."

What? I whirled, saw:

Hailey wrapped in a bear hug by Eric.

Zap-crackle! Cari spasms, crashing to the broken asphalt as—

Zing! Oww—burning fire sting—my left cheek, reach up pull out . . . a dart.

Lang stood pointing a monstrous long black finger pointed at me.

Gun! Charge him draw—The Glock cleared my holster and my right arm swung up and the Glock flew from my suddenly limp fingers as my legs turned to rubber and my charge wobbled side to side and time/space stretched like Silly Putty and Lang is six feet away as my left hand swings up to grab/strike/deflect—

I flopped over my own momentum, flipped through the night—*black clouds stars swirling spinning dizzy*—slammed on my back, head bouncing on stones to *white light.*

Back, 'm back. Eyes can see. Roll in my sockets. Jaw slack, mouth open. Drool on check. Wipe . . . My hands, arms, legs, *me:* glued to parking lot asphalt.

Zap-crackle! Noise nearby.

Lang's voice says: "Two zaps ought to do Cari, don't you think, Eric? Don't answer. The pleas in your voice annoy me. Keep tight hold on Hailey, even now that I've got her gun. Like Vic said, she is not the boss. I am."

My legs are not connected to life. My arms belong to someone else.

Shoes walked away on asphalt pavement. My eyes rolled.

Cari lay stretched out near me. She trembled like a soundless epileptic.

Volvo door opens. *Zap-crackle!*

Something dragged across pavement. The shape of hunched-over Lang. Gravity thumped a weight near me on the broken surface of the night. Shoes walk away.

Volvo door opens. *Zap-crackle!*

Something else dragging across pavement. *"Shit!"* says Lang. My head moved. Lang dumped Russell a yard from my open palm. Russell smelled smoky from the flash/bang grenade Lang popped in the parked Volvo. Lang used getting his coat from the Caddy to loot the weapons' vest, grab one of the grenades, the tranquilizer gun, a stun gun with which he "zap-crackled" the flash/banged Russell and Zane, and then Cari. Now Lang had given them all a second zap.

Suddenly he looms over me. Silver hair glistening in the cone of light.

Kneeling—sitting, he's sitting on my loins—*breathe, hard to breathe, can't*—

John Lang's face. Handsome, lean, late-fifties face. Framed by the dark cloak collar of a navy peacoat. He's staring down at my slack jaw look. His weight flows off me. On to his knees and hands. Peering down at me. Face to face.

Closer. His face coming closer—*can't move, can't*—Is he going to kiss me?

Vampire. Closer, like he's—

But he turned his face to the side. His eyes swept with his skull off to my left as the side of his face lowered closer, closer . . .

His ear suctioned to my forehead.

54

AND I KNEW.

The press of Lang's ear suctioned to my forehead crushed my skull on stones.

"I can't hear the voices in your head," Lang told me as he rose to his hands and knees and peered down at paralyzed me like a jaguar over his prey. "Are yours a chorus or a lecturer? Do they speak in sentences and paragraphs? Shout out words? Or are they more like . . . a vast knowing that shimmers in you?"

"Laglle-lyypht!" Drool trickled down my cheek.

By the white Caddy, trapped in Eric's grip, Hailey yelled: "What do you want?"

Lang stood, turned toward her. "What do any of us want?"

Eric sobbed. Held her tighter. Obeyed the command of our boss.

Finger, my left little finger twitched.

Lang told Hailey: "You want to kill me. Now *shh,* or Eric will feel fire."

"Afftha-afco."

"Something to add, Vic?" Lang checked his watch.

"About twenty-five more minutes before you're functional, but that doesn't mean you just have to lay there and be useless. Hey, make a contribution."

"Eez . . . '*e*."

"'*Crazy?*' Is that what you're trying to say?" He shrugged. "That's as good a word as any. Though once you name a thing, you limit your understanding of it. Of course, understanding is overrated. Let go of *why*. Embrace . . . *wow*."

Call Dr. F's murder and all it triggered a mad dogs' mess.

Not an internal, off-the-shelf, renegade conspiracy subverting America.

Not an external, evildoers' attack on America.

All this was mad dogs being manipulated and mauled by one of their own.

Lang stepped over me.

Foot, my right foot twitched.

He left my field of vision. My skull rolled on the asphalt. Zane lay crumpled near the heap of Russell. Electricity expert Eric once told Group Therapy that a stun gun could neutralize a normal person for twenty minutes. Zane and Russell had been flash/banged, then zapped with a stun gun. Twice. They were down for a long count.

The tranquilizer gun's neurotoxin glued me to the pavement. I could move my eyes, turn my head, feel twitches in one finger and one foot.

A Caddy door opened. Closed. I rolled my head that direction.

Found Lang smiling as he used the ignition key to open the Caddy's trunk.

"Victor," he told me as he rummaged in the trunk, "this is your fault."

No! Not true!

Jaw, my jaw moved like I wanted but I couldn't control my tongue.

"You were my find." Lang tossed his navy peacoat onto the parking lot asphalt. "I'd been a Trouble Boy in Asia, too. So I kept an eye on you as I moved up in the Agency, at the Counter-Terrorism Center, to that jumble called Homeland Security."

He lifted the weapons vest out of the trunk: "In 1917, German submarines terrorized the East Coast. The scandal of our unpreparedness prompted the federal government to reorganize what the politicians and press called *'a clumsy mess of secret service agencies.'* One thing we've always known how to do is draw absurd charts.

"The point is," he said sliding into the weapons vest, "if the more things change, the more they remain the same, then why be realistic?"

Lang clicked shut the snaps on the weapons vest. Grinned. "How do I look?"

Arm, left arm pulsing. My lips tingled, but let out: " *'ee. Mmm . . . eee.*"

"*'Me'?* Don't be so self-involved." Lang replaced the stun gun in its vest pouch. He Velcroed the tranquilizer gun in its straps near two looped-on flash/bang grenades. "If we talk about just you, you'll miss the big picture.

"But it's not a big picture. When your eyes open, you realize it's tides of movies. Swirls of *is* and *was* and *might be.* If you hear the trillion whispers, you can surf on them. Learn how to shape the waves. The surfer no longer rides, the surfer rules."

In the dark night of that parking lot, a silver-haired man in a weapons vest leaned from side to side, black *gung fu* shoes gripping the asphalt as he surfed a tsunami, his arms waving not for balance but to stroke the experience.

Like the *bagua* adept he was, Lang swooped through a circle, spinning and twisting from surfer to dragon and back again to all of them as a man in a weapon's vest.

"You fell into a hole in Maine," he told me. "I got elevated to the inner circle of the National Security Council in the White House where my hands can do . . . oh so much."

Foot, can't move either foot.

Out of my mouth came: "See you. They'll see you 'razy."

Lang smiled. "No, our wise men judge the world by what they see in their mirrors."

My tongue licked my lips: "Dr. Friedman."

"Couldn't derail the idea to bring a shrink into our midst. Tried to for months. Precedent: during Watergate, national security executives secreted a shrink on the NSC staff because they feared Nixon was nuts and walking around the White House where it's easy to squeeze triggers—even on Weapons of Mass Destruction. Dr. Friedman's CIA file called him a 'spotter.' He might have spotted me."

Lang walked into the cone of light.

Said: "I couldn't risk that. Getting locked up. I wasn't going to let Dr. Friedman make me into one of you. Hey, I'm a lucky man. I like who I am."

My arms tingled. *Flex them.*

"Friedman was going to temporary duty in Maine before meeting me," said Lang. "I knew I had to kill him where there'd be a safe, logical explanation for his murder. New York is a classic killing ground, but he was coming straight to his new job. I had to stop him from showing up where I was. Plus, the five of you were perfect to frame. I found someone to deal with him, a military nurse who was a junkie. Persuadable out of patriotism plus fear of jail and her own permanent termination. Trainable by a vet who thought he was working for SAD.

"In a world where people accept only what someone says they 'have a need to know,' a visionary voice assumes awesome power."

Something rubbed the pavement with a harsh sound.

I craned my neck, forced my shoulders off the asphalt to see—

Cari, trying to stand, her right hand pawing her empty holster.

Velcro ripped open as Lang strode to her. Said: "Relax."

Lang shot a tranquilizer dart into Cari's leg.

"Agent Rudd," he said as he pulled the dart out of her limp body and set it on the pile he'd made of our gear, "just lay there and listen like a good spy."

He restrapped the tranquilizer gun on the vest beside the grenades, drew the stun gun from its pouch, gave Zane and Russell each a third zap.

I struggled up on my elbows. Legs attached to my numb body stretched dead before me. I saw Eric hugging Hailey

tight as they stood near the white Caddy, tears running down
their cheeks.

"Your fault, Vic," said Lang. "Even if the lower echelons
would have called Friedman a murder, nothing too bad
would have happened to you obvious suspects."

"Says you."

"Yes," said Lang. "As your creator, says me.

"And this!" He waved his arm. "I loved your escape! I was
rooting for you to vanish, I really was. But did you heed my
warning? Did you run? No. That was stupid."

"Stubb'rn."

"Words words words!" he said. "What silly things they
are. We need to work.

"Besides, Vic," said the man who'd molded me into the
mad dog I was, "I'm finally giving you what you want. You
rebelling and breaking out of the Castle is your third suicide.
Only this time, you get to succeed."

There it was: dead-on truth. All I had to do was lay there and
I'd get what I'd sought for so long—freedom from the pain of
responsibility. All I had to do was forget about everyone else
Lang had trapped in this dark night. All I had to not think about
were the global millions who this maniac spymaster of the
world's only empire could caress with his cold crazy hands.

"We never get to pick our time," I'd told Derya. *"We only
get to pick what we do."*

And as Lang held my only living friends and me in his
trap of that parking lot night, he said: "Do you know what
we have here?"

His gesture swept over everything: The cone of light where
he stood and where I sprawled on my elbows. The pile of pistols and gear beside the shocked-out heaps of Zane and Russell. Cari slumped to even greater numbness from the
neurotoxin than me. Hailey trapped in Eric's embrace beside
the white Cadillac.

"What we have here," said Lang, "is an answer to evolve.
All we need to do is take what we've got and spin it to a productive truth.

"Frenzy foils forensics," he said. "Five escaped maniacs.

One innocent hostage, a brave CIA agent, kidnapped, killed in the line of duty. Our connections, the Maine asylum reports marking you as the pack's leader. Stolen cars, you stormed my house. Shot it up. Snatched me out here. Why? Who knows, you're all crazy."

Stall: "They'll check y'r hard-drive. Look for oth' tracks."

"Good!" said Lang. "Role-play me to be sure we've got it right. But don't worry. The only reason for gumshoes to check my machine is to match the bullets to guns you mad dogs fired. Plus, I bet Russell destroyed my computer drives. I built those trapdoors, and when I triggered them by doing the routine any intruder would have used, those systems got wiped. The SAD building—no one knows you were there. Those matrices, your index cards somebody might shuffle into a pattern that shows I'm Kyle Russo. I'm thinking . . . Why not a fire?"

See it! Vision! A chance. The five of us hanging from the crane. A pillar of smoke above a mall. A wreck on a dark night highway. A ghost movie projected on an apartment ceiling. But the new movie had a ticket price figured in blood. No matter how the minor plot details spun out, I'd have to pay the price. And so would my only friends on earth.

Then and there, I realized the bottom line of being alive:

Sometimes all any of us can do is choose which crazy wins.

Lang said: "Let me spin you and the real world . . . an explosion.

"A frantic gun battle as Agent Rudd and I break free. She's the hero. Grabs a gun, blasts away. I get one, too—not mine, that's too easy. I've kept my prints off all but the barrels on your pistols, though it's long odds that that matters. Especially if there's some kind of explosion and fire.

"Wait!" Lang's eyes blazed. "Afterward, I do the spy thing and valiantly clean the scene up while I'm waiting for rescue! Clean it up to cover this mess all under wraps, no reporters, no congressional snooping! And that brilliant, responsible effort on top of all the other evidence, that makes this a pure, credible, desirable truth!

"Our only big question is," he said with a frown, "who dies first?"

Numb from the waist down, my arms too poisoned to do more than prop me on my elbows, I said: "You do."

Ever so slowly, his face turned from whispers of a future to see me staring up at him from the asphalt parking lot of now. And he said: "Really."

Drawing a deep breath meant breaking steel bands circling my chest, but I did it and as loudly as I could said: "Essential nature."

A frown scarred his image. "Is this your illusion? That it's my essential nature and therefore . . . *what?*"

But the fight to regain my breath robbed me of the power to reply.

"Or are you asking *when?*" said Lang. "*When* did I realize my essential nature? I was always . . . unique. Ironically, the sniper shot of my self-awareness happened after our last meeting. Are you still trying to succeed with suicide?"

Words spit from lips: "Essential nature!"

"That's what I'm telling you! My awakening came in the Situation Room in the basement of the White House the night after 9/11 while smoke and dust swirled around New York, across the river at the Pentagon, in that Pennsylvania field. The best minds in our marblized politics were huddled around the Sit Room table and every one of them wanted to know *why.*

"Out of me burst: *'Why not?'*

"Believe me, I had to dissemble that careless wisdom to stay in the room!"

For the third time, I forced out: "Essential nature!"

"Of what?" Lang yelled. "Of visionaries like us? Of a spy? The essential nature of a spy is to deceive and manipulate, to lie and die."

Chest burning, heaving. Heart pounding 'gainst crushing ribs. Roaring in my skull. White—Don't zone out! *Can't say it!* Got to say it. *Can't do it!* No better choice.

My eyes went from Lang to the white Cadillac where Eric held Hailey locked in his embrace. That couples' eyes found mine as my soul tore to free the words: "Not him!"

Lang said: " *'Not him'* means *not me? 'Essential nature'?*"

Hailey's face glowed in something like a smile: "Eric! Obey the boss's order! Make it worth it! Hold me so we'll be together forever!"

Her command rode within the horrors Eric had no choice but to obey, rode within them and swelled them into a vision shaped by the essential nature of his loving heart.

Lang whirled toward Eric and Hailey, his own essential nature sensing danger. He ripped the tranquilizer gun from its straps—empty. But he was a man keen on close-quarter combat and he charged the intertwined couple standing beside the white beast. He swung the tranquilizer gun—smashed it into Hailey's blocking arm as Eric bear-hugged her waist. Lang's backswing slammed the short club below her face-blocking arms, hit her breasts above Eric's encircling grip and she cried out—

Grabbed Lang and pulled him close.

Lang flowed with his attacker. Three intertwined bodies slammed into the Caddy. Eric twisted with all his pudgy might and they spun around on the side of the car. Lang's back slammed against metal. The force of that collision flung the tranquilizer gun from his grip. Hailey held him close with one hand—sank her other hand like a claw over his mouth so that all he could articulate were gurgled screams and grunts. Eric obeyed orders and held her tight with one hand, used his other to pound the boss.

The boss who mashed against the windows of the Caddy doors. The boss who fought to stay on his feet as Eric pistoned his legs to crush their huddle against the car.

They slid along the front door, to the back door.

The silver-haired spymaster slammed the stun gun prongs into Eric.

A jolt of electricity shot through Eric—no: *another* bolt of electricity crackled through this man who'd endured a hundred worse shocks. This bolt zapped through his back to his chest—and then conducted through him as a diffused charge shocking the two people Eric pinned to the metal car.

Eric trembled, dazed. Hailey slumped, her hands falling to her sides. She might have fallen, but Eric held her tight. Holding her meant holding the shocked Lang, whose sheer insane will kept him upright as their intertwined trio slid to the rear of the car.

Hailey's hand brushed the gas tank cap an instant after consciousness returned to her eyes. Brushed it as Lang regained strength.

"Eric!" she cried.

With a twist of her wrist, a jerk of her arm, she thrust what she held between their three faces for all of them to see: the cap to the Caddy's gas tank.

Eric yelled: "Hold me forever!"

Was he repeating? Was he asking? Was he telling? I never knew.

As Hailey yelled back: "Yes!"

And Eric reached into the bundle of flesh pinned against the rear of the Caddy, found the pins on the two flash/bang grenades in the vest Lang wore.

Pulled them free.

I saw two grenade safety handles spin out of the trio— threw my back to the pavement, my hands flopping over my face with its already singed-off eyebrows.

Two flash/bang grenades burst as one bright white spark-throwing flame beside the Caddy's fume-spewing open gas tank.

The white beast roared a tremendous explosion and an orange fireball lit the night. Over the prone forms of four spies on the blacktop blew the big heat.

55

THE CLEANUP OF the accidental explosion of a Federal waste disposal truck parked beside an old car near the waterfront of the wildlife preserve near Parkton, Maryland, was almost complete by 11:15 that next morning, Day Nine of our crusade. Husky workers in lumpy coveralls waved a carload of five teenagers away from the entrance to the parking lot, telling them: "It stinks down there. Couple of our guys even threw up."

The Alpha girl in the group told her friends: "I can smell it. Smells kind of like gasoline and burned rubber and . . . *eew!* Burned hair and stuff!"

The teenagers drove back to their boring hometown where no one ever had to sentence his friends to die. They counted themselves lucky for not getting caught skipping school and to keep their cover intact, told no adults about what they hadn't seen.

By 11:15, the charred skeleton of a 1959 white Cadillac had been winched into the cargo box of a huge truck, swallowed by that darkness as if it had never been.

Other things had been bagged and hauled away in unmarked panel vans.

By 11:15, the local banker had satisfied FBI credentialed men who were officially investigating a ring of cashier's check thieves. His information complemented ours and added up to an Op Finding initially scoffed at in the darkness of First Response that, by 11:15, became both credible and true.

Which meant by that 11:15, SAD gunners—who'd surrounded Zane, Russell, and I when they showed up—relaxed and left us alone.

We three maniacs stood at the shoreline.

By 11:15, the sky was blue. The waters of the ocean inlet in front of us had calmed to easy ripples. Birds glided overhead. Each of our inhales bore less and less of the stench of explosion and fire death.

Russell said: "Was what they both wanted, Vic."

Zane said: "You didn't get them anything they hadn't signed on for."

"Yeah," I said.

"Not like before," said Russell.

"Never is."

The water rippled.

"But both times," Russell told me, "you played the best gig you had."

Finally, I believed that. Said: "Guess I am a hard man to kill. Guess that's okay."

"'Xactly. And we're damn lucky to still be here."

The water rippled.

Russell held out his hand. We watched it tremble. He shrugged. "Anybody want the meds they offered us?"

"Nah," I said. "*Saying no* got me this far. With a lot of help from my friends."

"Breakthroughs," said Zane. "All of us."

"All of us who made it," said Russell, staring at the fire-smeared pavement.

"We all made it," I said. "Welcome to the other side."

"Too bad your GODS were in the Caddy," Zane told me. "The picture of Derya. The snow globe."

I shrugged. "Maybe not."

"*'Not'* is *not* more coffee," said Russell. "My heart will pound out of my ribs."

"And I'll have to pee . . . again," said Zane.

"I don't want to drive," I said. "Not for a while."

Russell said: "Do you believe them? About us not having to go back to the Castle after the next couple days of debriefs—if we don't want to."

My shrug came easy. "Well, we busted out once. Lucky we're still crazy."

The three of us laughed.

A seagull screed overhead.

"Of course, they could always medicate us with a lead pill," said Russell.

"The ultimate in mental health treatment." I shook my bullet-free skull. "They need us. They won a great spin. They saved the world from a homicidal maniac running amok in the White House. We're the proof of their success, even if we're a secret."

Russell shuffled, shrugged. "I might go back."

Zane and I stared at him.

"Not to stay," he said. "But . . . I'm not sure the real world is ready for my encore."

Couldn't help myself, I tousled his hair like he was my kid brother.

And he grinned.

Cari split off from Agency bishops and joined us. "We're going now."

"Okay," I said. "Where?"

"Ahh . . ." She looked at Zane.

He looked at me.

Russell stared at the rippling water.

"Vic," said Zane, "I'm not with you anymore."

"We're together," said Cari. She took Zane's hand in hers.

"What?"

Russell stared at the rippling water.

"It's been a long trip," she said. "For everybody."

Remember looks. Words. Sounds. Closed motel room doors.

"Who knew about this?" I whispered.

Russell said: "Everybody but you."

I shot them my harshest bullet. "He's old enough to be your father!"

"We have something else in mind," she said.

Something inside me fell. Something inside me let go. I said: "Well, fuck me."

Zane answered: "No. But now . . . I could. Can."

And his grin soared my heart.

"Wild!" said Russell. They knocked fists like two dudes in the 'hood, and Russell said: "Later."

" 'Xactly."

Walking away, Cari held Zane's hand with the strength of a woman who'd settled for no less than special and he held her with the patience of a man who knew how to wait.

Water lapped the shore by my feet.

"I told you that you didn't get women," said Russell.

"Look who's talking," I muttered.

Waves rippled in front of us.

"So," he finally said. "Do you know what you want to do?"

Waves rippled in front of us. The sky was blue overhead. Behind us was a black smear of smoke on the asphalt, glistening diamonds of shattered glass. Waves rippled.

And I said: "Yeah."

Thank You Very Much

Sources, inspirations, givers, beacons, touchstones: Robert Baer, Tim Bernett, John Burdett, Natalia Aponte Burns, Barbara Carr, Lou Campbell, Eileen Chapman, Tom Doherty, Johnny Fago, Leora Freedman, Bonnie Goldstein, Harry Gossett, Rachel Grady, Chris Harvie, Jeff Herrod, Irina, Joe Lansdale, Terry Little, lonely planet publications, Karl Mailer, Serif Mardin, Marlon Mark, Susan Collins Marks, Matrix, Lou Mizell, Dan Moldea, *The New York Times*, Mona Okada, Jay Peterzell, Mike Pilgrim, John Pomfret, Presque Isle (Maine) Public Library, Linda Quinton, Bob Reiss, Cari Rudd, Derya Samadi, Bruce Sayre, Ricki Seidman, Yvonne Seng, Nat Sobel, Jeff Stein, The Stone Pony, Simon Tassano, Richard Thompson, James Wagonner, *The Washington Post*, John Weisman, Bill Wood.